ASHES

THE BLEEDING HEARTS SERIES BOOK 3

DYLAN PAGE

Edited by Angie Ojeda Hazen
Contact: https://www.facebook.com/LunarRoseEditingServices

PA & Author Services by Bibiane Lybaek and Ashton Reid with Affinity Author Services
Contact: https://linktr.ee/AffinityAuthorServices

Cover Design by Jodie-Leigh Plowman @ JODIELOCKS Designs
Contact: https://www.facebook.com/groups/JodielocksDesign

Formatting Services by Savannah Richey @ Peachy Keen Author Services
Contact: https://www.facebook.com/PeachyKeenas

To the boys I grew up with.
Our childhood years together were some of the happiest of my life.
You will always be my brothers. Thank you.

You are allowed to be both a masterpiece and a work in progress simultaneously.

— UNKNOWN

Trigger Warning

Chapter one

Vail: Eleven Years Old

"THAT'S THE STUPIDEST DARE YET…"

"You're just saying that cuz you don't want to do it."

"No, I just thought you'd be more creative, is all."

"Look, Bishop." Lee shook his head, laughing as he watched our friend squirm. "Either you stand up, quietly do the Macarena until your next turn, or I can make you chug some of Casey's mother's special hot sauce. You're lucky I'm giving you a choice." He fixed Shaw with a wide, white grin, and said, "What's it going to be?"

Lee, Casey, and I all stared Shaw down, waiting to see which dare he was going to go with. Secretly, I was hoping he would do the Macarena. Despite the fact that he had been my friend the longest out of anyone in our group of four, Shaw Bishop had always been the most closed off. He rarely spoke, and I couldn't remember the last time I'd seen him smile, but he was loyal as hell, and living in this shithole

1

neighborhood, a loyal friend was *not* something you threw away.

Apparently, Lee's mind was also on my wavelength. He probably wanted Shaw to remove the stick from his ass and just be a damn kid for once, instead of acting like a fucking brooding teenager. He watched our friend scowl back at us with a huge, shit-eating grin on his face while he played with one of his thick black, shoulder-length dreads. Out of all of us, I'd say Lee was the most easy-going and probably had the most conventional home life. He had never suffered physical abuse from either of his parents or family members, nor did they suffer from any sort of addiction. They were just dirt-poor. His parents worked endless hours to support him and his grandparents, whose medical needs were the main reason behind the influx of bills. But since he moved here three years ago, he'd been stuck with the three of us.

I couldn't help but notice Casey's expression, though. Of course, I hardly ever missed a thing she did.

She was curled up on her sleeping bag on the floor, wearing an old David Bowie t-shirt that once belonged to her mother, and a pair of grey sweats that had multiple patches sewn into them, also courtesy of her mom. Like the rest of us, she'd been participating in every dare thrown her way. She'd already been forced to sing the national anthem, and I got to say, the poor girl definitely couldn't carry a tune to save her life. Her next dare was to knock on the neighbor's door (who rented the main floor of the duplex over the basement suite she and her mom lived in) and tell them that she picks her nose. The last one was pretty brutal, though. Shaw forced her to deep sniff one of Lee's boots. One thing I loved about Casey, was that she never backed down from a challenge. She completed all three dares without hesitation while making sure we all witnessed her eye-rolling and heard the curses she muttered under her breath.

But now, she just seemed upset. Her big doe-like dark brown eyes, which looked nearly black depending on the light, especially against her porcelain skin, were locked onto Shaw, and her hands were tightly clasped around the stuffed lamb in her lap as she watched him. I couldn't help the spark of jealousy I felt towards him at that moment. Of the three of us, it was always Casey that he was the most gentle with, the one he allowed to touch him or hold him. I mean, I got it; they both had abusive, prick dads, and I guess it's just how they bonded. But every time we all got together for a sleep-over, he was the one that got to sleep next to her, claiming she helped with his anxiety when she was close. Just once, one of these Saturday nights, I'd like to be the one that laid next to her. I knew I wasn't alone here.

I glanced over at Lee, who was still watching Shaw with a bright smile on his face. But I wasn't fooled. I'd seen how he acted around Casey, too. Any excuse to carry her around (he was without a doubt the biggest out of all of us), or to tickle her and mess around with her, he took it. I knew Lee Knight was just *dying* for a chance to take Shaw's spot one of these nights.

But...

I sighed and ran a hand through my dark, bronze coloured hair, further tousling it as I waited patiently for Shaw to man up and just dance for us already. I refused to be an asshole to him. I was his friend. If something as simple as being close to Casey kept his demons away, then so be it. If I were older and had a chance, I would have beaten his dad down for the bullshit he had done to Shaw and his mom. The stuff Shaw had seen... no six-year-old should ever have to go through. Even though he was now living with his aunt and uncle, he still suffered from nightmares. So I remained quiet and stretched out as I lounged back in the easy chair I always claimed when we played, and waited.

3

"Fine..." Shaw hissed between his clenched teeth and went to stand, his floppy, blonde hair falling over his face.

"Jesus, dude, it's just dancing," Lee laughed loudly, and I smiled, unable to resist how infectious it was.

Shaw flipped him off, his dark blue eyes hidden but visibly narrowed behind his hair, pausing for a few seconds as if he was about to throw himself into a tiger cage, and then he started to dance. Lee and I both bent over, laughing hysterically, while Casey simply shook her head and raised her eyes to the ceiling, as though wondering why she hung out with us.

"Everything alright in here?"

We all looked up just as Liza Cooper appeared in the archway of the sitting room where we always spent our sleepovers in, wearing a dressing gown over her flannel pajamas. She had dark hair like her daughter, but with greying strands in it. The only other similarity was probably their pale complexion. She had layered up, despite it only being the first week of September; nights were already growing colder.

"We're good, Mom," Casey smirked. "Just trying to see who will chicken out first."

Ms. Cooper chuckled. "Okay then. But I've just locked up for the night, so no leaving the basement... and *no* drinking the toilet water this time!" Her eyes flashed to Lee, who grinned wickedly at her. Last weekend, he'd dared Casey to drink a shot of water from the porcelain bowl, but had been stopped at the last second when her mother walked in on us all in the bathroom.

"Don't worry, Ms. Cooper." Lee held his hands up. "We learned our lesson from last time. Germs. Diseases. Got it."

Casey's mom just laughed and shook her head. "You kids are nuts. Well, I'm off to bed. Turn on the space heater if you get cold, okay? And I'm making waffles in the morning, so no late-night binging!"

"We won't," we all said together.

Another reason we loved our weekly Saturday night sleep-over at Casey's house was that her mom was probably one of the best cooks and the nicest person I'd ever met. She puts my mom to shame. Even though she and Casey lived alone in that shitty basement suite, she'd made the place really comfortable. The sitting room had a thick, shag rug on the floor, with cushy, mismatched furniture she got from Goodwill, but she made covers for everything out of bold coloured, soft materials and placed pillows and blankets everywhere. I hadn't even noticed the stained ceiling or cracks in the walls. Honestly? I'd say this place is better than the shithole bungalow I lived in.

"Alright. Night!" Ms. Cooper spared her daughter a kiss on the head this time. Last week, when she had pulled Casey in for a big goodnight hug and kiss, we'd all teased her relentlessly for it, and she begged her mother not to perform any more public displays of affection towards her in front of the three of us again.

We were left alone once more, and the game continued with Shaw selecting me for the next dare, all while dancing like an idiot on the spot to zero music.

"What's my dare?" I asked, straightening up a bit. There was no way I was going to be the first to chicken out. I never had, and I never would.

"Talk in third person for the rest of the game. Every time you fail, all three of us get to punch you as hard as we can."

I laughed loudly, "Vail likes this challenge. Accepted."

I heard Casey giggle and instantly felt smug, knowing I was the reason for it.

Keeping my gaze on her, I couldn't help but think of how pretty she was, especially when she smiled. Her lips curved upwards, and dimples appeared in her cheeks. She was so freaking cute. At this moment, I'd decided I was going to take advantage of this game and put myself ahead of the other two guys. They were going to hate my guts for a little bit because of it, but it would be worth it.

"Casey…" I said, keeping my gaze fixed on her.

She immediately became stern and met my stare dead-on like the champ she was. "St. James," she said seriously, addressing me by my last name.

"Dare you… to kiss Vail on the lips." It would have sounded so much cooler if I hadn't referred to myself in the third person. But I didn't waver as I held my face in an expressionless mask, something I'd been perfecting this past year. I found that it unnerved people when I did it, and I liked the feeling of power it gave me over them.

The room went deadly silent. Even Shaw had stopped dancing. He and Lee both stared back and forth between us, their expressions completely shocked and disbelieving. But I focused on her, curious to see what she would do.

Casey's dark brows furrowed as her eyes narrowed. "Really, Vail? You think I'm scared of catching your cooties? You forget, I was in the pond with you when you peed. I don't give a crap."

"Then, if you aren't chicken, come over here and give Vail a nice, sweet kiss." In my peripheral, I noticed how Shaw was practically vibrating in anger. His fists were clenched, and his eyes were more shadowed beneath his messy, blonde hair. Lee, meanwhile, had lost all sense of humour as he watched us, his face surprisingly void of any emotion. Huh, I didn't think that was possible. He usually wore a confident smirk, like I wore my void, cold mask.

Casey hesitated. She actually hesitated.

This was the same girl who would pal around with us on our bikes as we rode through the streets of Harley, the low-end, scariest, shittiest place in Ashland, without fear. This was girl who I'd seen single-handedly beat the crap out of Hunter Tremblay, and hadn't batted an eye when he managed to bloody her lip or when he pulled a clump of her long, dark hair out of her head. She was going to drink toilet water last week, for Christ's sake! But at the prospect of kissing me, she'd gotten all nervous.

I watched as she chewed on her full bottom lip, and I couldn't help but grin at her. I didn't realize this dare would make her so uncomfortable. But I was a greedy little bastard (at least, that was what my dad had always said), and I wanted that kiss. So I puckered my lips at her and made a kissy sound before clucking like a chicken, which I knew would only enrage her, making her only more determined not to back down. Casey hated it when I teased her, and like me, she had never lost at a game of chicken.

Sure enough, she lurched to her feet, her face set and determined, and I felt a wave of anticipation wash over me. I knew the other two guys were watching as she slowly stepped over to where I had been lazily lounging, like a king, in the navy armchair next to the space heater. I didn't move, except to tilt my head back to look up at her, a small, smug smile on my lips as I waited. She paused again and slowly reached out to cup my face, something that I hadn't been expecting her to do, but I decided I liked it. She crouched over me, and I could feel her fingers trembling a little against my cheek, but I didn't say a word. She halted an inch or two away, and we stared into each other's eyes... my grey-green gaze daring her to go through with it; her beautiful brown ones uncertain and a little anxious.

"Case, you don't have to..." Lee said suddenly.

"We don't have to count this dare-" Shaw said at the same time.

But just as they both spoke, she made up her mind, gently

7

pressing her mouth to mine, effectively silencing the other two.

Her lips were soft, much softer than I had thought they would have been, and I couldn't help but grin against her mouth. I slid a hand up her arm and hooked it at the nape of her neck, keeping her in place as I kissed her back. It lasted for only a few seconds before she pulled away, and I let her go. She didn't look at me again, nor did she say anything. She just walked back to her sleeping bag, sat on it, and looked up at Lee, "Ready for your dare?"

It was hours later, and I woke up with a start in the dead of night. The soft, orange glow from the space heater created large shadows from the furniture along the walls, and as I looked around, trying to figure out what woke me, I couldn't stop the shiver of fear that raced up and down my spine. After living in Harley my whole life, I'd become accustomed to hearing gunshots in the night, or the arguing and the occasional beatings from neighbors as couples would hash it out. But my senses had also grown hyperaware to notice when something was wrong. And I was not alone.

From across the circle of bodies, I noticed Shaw shift and lift his head a bit from where he had been curled up in his sleeping bag. Beside him, Casey was sleeping soundly, and I spotted that their hands were clasped. Not unusual. I have caught them holding hands so many times over the years; I had learned it's more of a comfort thing than boy-likes-girl. Shaw was releasing her hand to move a little more, his face pointed towards the archway leading into the hall. We both listened, waiting...

I heard the soft breathing of Lee and Casey as they continued sleeping. From one of the small windows at ground level to the grass outside, I heard the tapping of one of the dead bushes, hitting the glass again and again. But that was not what woke me. I know it. It was something else… something out of place.

Thump!

I tensed and sat up a little more in my sleeping bag, waiting…

Thump… thump… click-click…

That was coming from the front door. I was absolutely certain.

There was more scuffling, more scratching like someone was messing around with the handle, and I immediately knew someone was trying to pick the locks to get in. I'd been about to lurch to my feet to get Casey's mom, when she suddenly appeared, bat in hand, and raced into the sitting room.

"Come with me. C'mon kids, wake up!" she hissed softly, but I could hear the urgency in her voice. She's lived in Harley for years. She's no fool. She knew exactly what was happening and the dangers that came with it.

"Huh? Mom? What's going on…" Casey yawned as she came to and rubbed her eyes. Beside me, Lee stirred and sat up, looking confused.

"Shhh… quiet, now. I need you kids to come with me."

"What's wrong?" Casey's voice, even though she was whispering, somehow pitched a little in fear.

"It will be okay, but I need you kids to go to my bedroom and hide in the back of the closet." My eyes adjusted a little more to the dimness of the room, and I finally saw the cell phone she had cradled between her cheek and shoulder. She had gotten the police on the phone. I got to my feet, ready to take charge, and I held a hand out to Shaw, who took it and got to his feet.

Bang! Bang! Bang!

Whoever was at the door was now throwing their body against it, and it rattled in its frame.

Casey cried out as her mother moved towards it, bat raised, and shouted, "Whoever you are, I'm armed, and the police are on their way!"

Just as Casey was about to run after her mother, Lee scooped her up in his arms and carried her down the hall to the bedroom with Shaw and me following. We did as we were told and crawled over the stack of old shoes and slippers until we were all hidden in the back of the bedroom closet she shared with her mom. Casey was crying softly, but Lee held her tight, hugging her close. I could hear him as he murmured something in her ear, but he had been speaking so quietly that I couldn't make out the words. Knowing him, I would bet he's picking the perfect thing to say to comfort her. He had always been good at that. Optimistic, easygoing... like a teddy bear, Casey said once. Though he had cringed at her words, I could see him fighting back a smile of pleasure when she'd wrapped her arms around him, laughing as she teased him. She's the only one he'd allow to get away with calling him that. And right now, he was being that for her. Good.

Shaw sat on my other side, and the guy looked bored. *Bored*. His head was resting back against the wall, eyes glazed over a bit, and he looked like he had been about to fall asleep. Seriously, this kid is only eleven, and the idea of a home invasion by a potentially armed crackhead or criminal didn't phase him in the slightest.

As for me, while I was not the one to comfort the others, I was also not deadened to the seriousness of the situation. I felt around Ms. Cooper's closet until my fingers brushed against one of Casey's hockey sticks that was propped up in the corner. I grabbed it and positioned myself in front, ready to defend my friends in case shit got real.

Crash!

I heard Ms. Cooper's scream from the kitchen as the door broke in with an ear-splitting bang. I wasn't sure how we managed it, but none of us cried out. I listened hard, and I heard Casey's mom shouting, as well as the distant ring of the metal bat as she landed it on the bastard who had busted in here. Where the fuck were the cops?

There was a scuffle from the hall, then the heavy thud of someone being shoved against a wall. It was a sound I knew well... having heard it many times when my old man would use my mother as a punching bag. Which meant either Casey's mom got the best of the intruder, or...

I jumped to my feet and threw myself into the bedroom, ignoring the hissing protests from my friends. Gripping the hockey stick, I ran into the hall to see Ms. Cooper lying in a heap on the floor, looking dazed as she gingerly touched her forehead. Now I get a good look at the asshole who had broken in and attacked her. With just one look, I knew instantly that this guy was a serious drug addict. Judging by the condition of his body, I was a hundred percent positive that he was on the same shit my old man liked to use.

His body was withered and skinny. In the dim light, I could tell he'd lost most of his teeth even from here. His eyes were bugging out and coming off crazed, like he'd been trapped in some haunted nightmare and couldn't tell what was real and what was not. His pallor was sickly, his skin yellow-tinged, with blue, almost black, veins clearly visible along his arms. What was even more disgusting was that the sores that were pitted in the crook of his elbows and down his forearms, and other visible areas of his skin like his neck and parts of his sunken face, were leaking pus. He was literally falling apart from all his drug use. However, like all those addicts, he had this weird energy that someone in his state shouldn't be capable of. Even being struck by a metal bat (I can see blood oozing from his head, trickling down the side of his neck) hadn't slowed him down. It was like he wasn't even aware of it.

He hadn't noticed me yet. Instead, he stepped over Ms. Cooper's unmoving figure and moved into the family room where my friends and I had just been sleeping. I made my way down the hall and stopped at Liza's body. Bending down, I touched her shoulder, and she opened her eyes, her gaze unfocused. After a few seconds, she recognized me, her eyes widening in alarm, and made a slurred objection, "N-nnooo… Vail… hiiiiiide." She mumbled and tried to push me back down the hall, but her hand fell limply to the floor instead, her head thumping back against the floorboards.

In the family room, I heard the addict moving shit around, most likely looking for stuff to steal so he could sell it and buy more crack, meth, or worse. I'd take care of him in a minute. I reached for the bat that had been forgotten on the floor just as I heard a board creak softly behind me. I glanced over my shoulder, not surprised to see that it was Shaw who stood there, ready to back me up. In the doorway to the bedroom, Lee was there, one arm wrapped around Casey's stomach, and the other clasped over her mouth to keep her from screaming at the sight of her mother on the ground. She was fighting him, kicking as her legs hung in the air, struggling to free herself, but Lee was already massive. There was no chance she'd break loose. He'd keep her safe. I trusted him completely.

Shaw reached for the hockey stick, which I handed over, and then I picked up the discarded bat. Liza protested more. I knew she wanted us to keep hiding, but I couldn't let this go. The fucker broke in here, attacked her, and would steal anything he could find that held value. Ms. Cooper worked damned hard to support her and her daughter, and I couldn't just stand by. I'd seen addicts almost on a daily basis. They were so lost to their habit and the pull of drugs that they were willing to do *anything* to get their next fix. Only two weeks ago, there was a news story of a couple who had done some new street drug called 'Bones' together. The girlfriend ended up pulling a knife on her boyfriend, wholly disoriented in her unstable delusion, and gutted him. Police showed up after neighbors complained of overhearing a domestic dispute, two hours later, I might add, and found the girlfriend pulling the guy's intestines out of his stomach and playing with them. I felt my rage building to think that one of these unpredictable addicts was in here, threatening the only people in the world I cared about...

I peered over at Shaw one more time, our eyes locking. Even in the low light of the hall, I could make out his blue eyes. His gaze had nothing behind it, as was to be expected. Shaw was deadpan and cold, but my friend. He had my back. I nodded to him once, which he immediately returned, and we jumped to our feet and threw ourselves into the room with the intruder.

I didn't remember much... only that I had seen the sick fuck standing next to the television, holding Casey's framed class photo from this year in his grimy hands, and the next thing I knew, everything went black. I could barely breathe. I felt dizzy and shaky and had to blink several times in order to clear my vision. It was like stars were blocking my vision, flashing white lights.

"Hey, kid! Hey!" Someone's voice, one I wasn't familiar with, was yelling over my head. I could feel hands suddenly gripping my shoulders and squeezing hard. At once, my heart lurched in my chest, and I threw myself away. I didn't care who the fuck that was, they shouldn't be grabbing me. Don't squeeze me. Don't touch me.

His hands wrapped around my throat as I was slammed back

against the wall. I cough, spitting over his wrists, clawing at his grip in a hopeless attempt to free myself.

"Don't you ever touch me, you little shit!" he screamed into my face, but I didn't even look at the fucker. My eyes moved over to the still figure on the floor... Mom.

"D-don't... touch... h-h-" I choked, trying to tell him off as I gasped for air. If I had to watch this piece of crap hurt my mother one more time, I was going to kill him.

He laughed in my face. The disgusting scent of booze and sweat wafting over me, made me sick. "She may be your momma, boy. But she's my wife. And I can do whatever the fuck I want with her..." He reached over for the cigarette he'd discarded on the table, which was still burning, and picked it up, leaving behind a burn in the wood. "If I wanna hurt her, mark her..." He smiled, still holding me against the wall with one hand as he turned his attention to the woman who was now struggling to lift her head.

"V-Vail?" she moaned, and I wrenched at the hold on my throat, wanting so desperately to save her. But I couldn't. I fucking couldn't. I watched as he leaned down and pressed the bright, cherry end of his cigarette to her shoulder, and I saw red. She screamed for me, over and over, the breaking cries forever scarred in my mind.

"Vail... Vail..."

"Vail!"

I blinked.

I was sitting in the corner of Ms. Cooper's living room, almost hiding behind the lounger chair I had been sitting in hours earlier when we were playing chicken. There was a body on the floor being wrapped in bandages, and hooked up to syringes, as a stretcher was brought down into the basement to carry him out. That was when I realized I was covered in blood. My hands, arms, t-shirt, and the sweats I'd gone to bed in, were all covered in blood spatter. I was shaking, my face and fingers were numb, and I was wrenching at my hair like I was trying to rip it out of my skull. I gazed up at the faces of three police officers, who were all watching me with nervous apprehension. Off to the side, I saw Shaw sitting with a paramedic, who appeared to be checking him over, but besides a little spatter covering his shirt, he seemed fine—bored, even, if not a little uncomfortable with the medic who was trying to examine him. As I expected, every touch had Shaw wincing uncomfortably.

"Vail!"

The voice that had snapped me out of my spiral called again, one I would know anywhere. It was *her*. I peered around one of the officers to see her standing with Lee, who'd been holding her back.

"Casey?" I whispered hoarsely, feeling like I'd ripped my vocal cords. Had I been screaming?

At her name, she pulled away from Lee and ran to me, ignoring the pigs' protests about me being a danger, and threw herself into my lap, wrapping her arms tight around my neck. I felt a weight lift from my shoulders as I hugged her back tightly, burying my face into her dark hair, and squeezed my eyes shut as I released a long, shuddering breath.

"Are you okay?" I whispered to her.

"Are you kidding me?" she said, incredulously. "Am *I* okay? Are *you* okay?"

I couldn't quite speak yet, and honestly, I didn't know if I was. All I knew was that holding her made me feel like I wasn't alone, so I just held her tighter.

"... dad's not in the picture anymore-" Lee's voice floated into the room, and I looked over the top of Casey's head to see him standing before one of the cops, arms crossed, almost as tall as the pig he was talking to. I was glad it was him and not me. I couldn't speak to a police officer without having to battle an extreme urge to lay one on them. Fuckers had let me down one too many times. And seeing the glare in Shaw's eyes and knowing his history, I knew he was feeling the same way.

"Are there any other relatives she can stay with while her mother recovers?" Krispy Kreme asked my friend. Lee glanced my way, his dark brows pulling tight. Casey didn't have anyone but her mother and us. Keith was an abusive prick, and although they had left him two years ago, Liza wanted nothing to do with him. She couldn't go home with Shaw. His aunt and uncle, a minor improvement from his former life, were unstable as hell, constantly arguing and scraping by thanks to his aunt's gambling problem. As for me, well, my mom was barely getting by after everything we went through with my old man. Her nerves were shot, and though she tried to hide it, I knew she was a closet drinker. She was a shadow moving around our shitty, falling apart bungalow. A ghost. She couldn't even take care of me, let alone someone like Casey.

I nodded to Lee, both of us knowing what the best course of action would be, and hid my face in her hair again.

"She can stay with me and my parents," Lee said at last. Several seconds of silence followed before he added loudly and firmly, "She knows my family and has stayed with us before. I'll call them now."

"Fine," Krispy Kreme replied. He didn't actually give a shit where she stayed. Casey was a Harley Rat, just like me, Shaw, and Lee. We were all Harley Rats. No one in Ashland would give a shit about what happened to us. We'd be lucky if we lived long enough to see graduation, and even if we did, chances were we'd be delinquents, according to the mayor and his team of corrupt boys in blue.

Casey pulled back to look at me, her wide eyes strained with worry, but she didn't cry.

"Your mom…" I whispered to her.

She nodded and bowed her head. "She'll be in hospital for a few days, but they said she should be okay. Just a concussion…" She reached down and plucked at the bloody shirt I was wearing, making a face. "Let's get you cleaned up, alright?" She stood and headed down the hall, no doubt finding a wet cloth to wash away the blood covering my arms and face. I gingerly rose to my feet as the room started to clear. Lee had his phone out, messaging his parents to come to pick us up, and Shaw was giving a paramedic the cold shoulder after it was suggested that he go to the hospital. Shaw hated hospitals. There was no chance in hell he'd willingly go back to one. So he just turned his back and started gathering up our sleeping bags and backpacks, without saying a word.

I was about to follow Casey down the hall to the washroom where she was waiting for me, but then I caught sight of the broken picture frame on the floor. It was busted, the glass shattered, and the photo was poking out between the fractured pieces. I reached down and pulled it free, holding the picture in my hands. It was taken just a few weeks ago at the beginning of the school year. I remembered that her mom had forced her to wear a maroon, corduroy overall dress with a grey knit sweater underneath. Instead of her usual ponytail, Ms. Cooper had braided her hair the night before so that it fell in waves for Photo Day. She'd arrived at school red-faced and furious, but all I could recall was losing my train of thought at the sight of her, so much so that my mouth fell open.

"Either you guys stop staring at me like that, or I'll kick you in the balls so hard you'll be eating them," she hissed as she passed by us. I hadn't realized I wasn't the only one ogling her. Both Lee and Shaw had the exact same expression as I did on their faces. However, at her threat, we all snapped out of it. We knew Casey well, and when she dished out a threat, she meant every word. I'd been victim to a sack kicking from her, and it was no fucking joke. Didn't walk right for the rest of the day.

But in this picture, I could stare at her all I wanted. Her large, chocolate coloured eyes sparkled from the lights, and her lips were slightly parted in the smallest of smiles, something she promised her mother she'd do… smile showing her teeth.

"Vail! Get your ass down here and wash up! Mrs. Knight won't let you in her car if you're covered in blood, you douche-weed!" Her shout snapped me out of my trance. Without a second thought, I folded up the photo and shoved it into the pocket of my sweats.

"Coming, darling!" I called back, snickering when she responded with a revolted gagging sound. I stepped over the bloody carpet, not at all fazed by the squishy feeling beneath my feet as I headed her way. It was just another weekend in Harley.

Chapter two

Casey: Sixteen Years Old

"West-End trash…"

Nylah turned her head to glare in the direction of Amanda Kerr and the Barbie Squad, narrowing her eyes at them. I knew she was about to go off on the girls, but she couldn't afford a possible suspension. Not with it being the very start of basketball season of our senior year, so I quickly straightened up from where I was leaning against the lockers, and called over, "It's kind of funny when we get to hear you use your entire vocabulary in one sentence."

Amanda's bubblegum pink mouth dropped open, her pale blue eyes narrowing before she flung her overly dyed blonde hair over her shoulder and readied herself to come back at me. She stretched a leg out, shifted all her weight to one hip, a sign that something nasty was coming my way before she smiled and said, "Once a Harley Rat, always a Harley Rat. You're lower than the shit on my shoe. You're not even worth my next breath."

Her friends guffawed like a bunch of hyenas while their queen smirked at me. But *Nylah* was the real Queen of this school, and as hard as Amanda tried, she would never be able to take her place. And right now? Nylah was pissed and ready to go into full attack mode. I reached out, gently pulling her back by her shoulder, and shook my head at her.

"Basketball…" I whispered so only she could hear. She was practically vibrating beneath my hand. Her grey eyes were fixated on Amanda and her squad, but the weight of that one word was everything to her. She needed to keep her record clean if she wanted a full scholarship to McGill to play basketball while earning her science degree. I stepped ahead, placing myself before her, not afraid to get another week of detention if it should come to that. I've faced worse than the likes of Amanda Kerr and her Bitch Barbie's. I smiled at her sweetly, tilting my head to the side like I would as if I were talking to a toddler, and said, "I've been called worse by better… *from* Harley."

We didn't stick around to see her reaction. As much as I didn't mind getting into another fight, I knew Mom would be disappointed. So I had my say, hooked my arm through Nylah's, and turned us, heading down the hall away from the high-pitched shrieks, name-calling, and insults following us, as Amanda lost her shit.

"You should have just let me deal with her, " Nylah grumbled, allowing me to steer her away.

I almost wanted to laugh. As tough as she was, Nylah really was just a sweetheart through and through, which was part of the reason why she was so popular. She was smart as hell, nice to everyone, and beyond beautiful. She was of mixed heritage, with her dad originally from South Africa, while her mother's family was from Germany. Her skin was always tanned and flawless and glowy, which only made her grey eyes stand out even more, and she had a sprinkle of tiny freckles across her nose. Her chocolate-colored hair with its natural blonde highlights was super full and curly, and I watched it enviously as it bounced with each step she took. She was statuesque, tall and athletically built, made to play sports. Add to the fact that her dad was a detective with the Ashland police, only raised her cool-factor with the kids at our school on The Hill.

And of all people that she chose to befriend, she had chosen me.

I came here at ten years old, right at the beginning of November, fresh out of Harley with my mother and her new doctor boyfriend, Matthew Hart. Being from Harley immediately had taken points away in terms of my social standing. The fact that I had an attitude and was ready with a fist cocked to anyone who gave me a hard time? Well, let's just say I gained a reputation fast. Mom sobbed and begged me to be good, and even though I hated making her cry, old habits die hard. I was used to getting into physical altercations or running my mouth. It was how I'd survived since birth and had never gotten me into trouble up until this point. Now, I was expected to hold my tongue and to turn the other cheek when someone insulted me or if I sensed a threat. Despite the fact I ended up in detention every day those first two weeks in November, I felt like I should be getting a medal for not giving any of the other kids stitches for the shit they were pulling.

Used, wet gym socks somehow had made it inside my locker (the smell stuck around for almost a month after). A girl had cut off a chunk of my hair with her scissors in art, to which I responded by simply ripping out a sizable chunk of her own straight from the roots. The new bike Matthew had bought me as a welcome-to-your-new-home present was vandalized: the tires had been slashed, the seats torn up with the stuffing removed, and the words; 'Harley Rat', 'Trash', 'CB Whore', and 'Go home' carved into the paint. I'd heard that Amanda Kerr and her friends had been behind it, but there was no proof. Only speculation. Despite all the bullying I endured, the school did nothing and determined that *I* was the problem. There were phone calls from my mom and Matthew to the principal, meetings were arranged, and the parents of other kids were notified. In the end, I was told I had to change my ways if I wanted to be accepted at this school with their esteemed and highly prestigious students.

Only Nylah reached out to me.

She'd returned from a vacation in the middle of November, having missed the "welcome" I'd received, and walked right over to my empty table at lunch, then started firing questions my way. At first, I'd been suspicious as hell. No one was this nice on purpose. I ignored her, throwing out the fancy lunch Matthew's cook had made for me, and hurried off to class. But she just wouldn't leave me alone. Everywhere I went, she popped up, chattering away and being all friendly and shit. I tried to lose her, but she was relentless. Eventually, I grew tired of trying to ditch her, and my loneliness kicked in. I used to have three friends… three great friends. We were practically siblings. But after I moved here, they ended up cutting me out. None of them had called me back, answered my letters, or bothered to come to visit like they'd promised. When I tried to arrange to see them, I was ghosted. It was like I never existed. So fine. *Fuck 'em*, I'd thought, and accepted Nylah Bryant's hand in friendship.

And what a weird one, at that.

I'd never had girlfriends. After being around boys for my whole life, I felt like the girly stuff was a scary new prospect that I wasn't sure I was ready for. I'd been wearing my school uniform in the most disheveled of ways so that I was more comfortable than presentable. I wore my white button-up shirt untucked, tie loose, and I bought my navy cardigan several sizes too big so that it was swimming on me. Nylah, being the girly girl that she was, went to work on me the day I finally accepted the fact that she wasn't going anywhere. It took some time, but when puberty hit, I finally gave in to the girlish side of me that was apparently dying to come out. I dyed my dark hair a shade of lilac, relented on wearing clothes that actually fit my body, but still preferred to walk around in a pair of black combat boots.

Meanwhile, at my side, Nylah walked with grace in a pair of shiny black and white heeled oxfords. At five foot ten, she towered over my five foot five. She liked to tease me by resting her elbow on the top of my head like I was a piece of furniture.

Now, however, we sat in the atrium that overlooked the quad, our usual lounging corner vacant so we could sit and chat in a pair of cozy, gingerbread brown leather chairs. It was toasty warm inside and a perfect spot to get some sun on the first actual cold day of the Fall, lounging at the glass wall that looked over the courtyard. It was the last week of September, and we've had more sunny days than not. But today, there was actually ice on the windows that had formed beautiful crystal patterns around the edges, and for a few minutes, we sat in silence, enjoying the peace.

"A biker came by again," Nylah confessed, finally.

I glanced up at her, brows raised, "Where?"

"Outside my house last night."

"Are you sure it's not just one of your neighbors who got themselves a bike? You know, suffering from a mid-life crisis or something." She was convinced that MC guys have been following her around for the past month or so. The more she saw them, the more she started to panic, and I did my best to reassure her that these weird sightings were just coincidences. People rode bikes. None of this was unusual. However, it *was* strange how much they seemed to pop up wherever she went.

"In our neighborhood?" Nylah bit her bottom lip. Her usually calm demeanor was now anxious as she tapped the arm of the lounger over and over. "Come on, Case... *no one* where we live would be caught dead riding a chopper, especially this time of year with it getting cold again."

"It's been mild lately." I shrugged it off. The bikers who had been making these appearances liked to keep themselves hidden behind a bandana or, on occasion, beneath a full, black helmet... unusual for riders of a Harley Davidson. They appeared when she stayed after school to practice, was at an away game, or arrived at school early to work on projects for the social committee. "There is a large MC presence in Ashland. Always has been," I said to her, wondering if it was one of them. The most common one being the Celtic Beasts with their blue dragon jackets, who roamed through most areas of Ashland, more often than not, downtown. Occasionally, you'd see one wearing a Black Spade with flames around it, but they tended to stick to my old neighborhood or in one of the border towns.

"Not up here on The Hill," she insisted. I guess she had a point. The Hill was in the East-End of the city, a sanctuary for the extremely wealthy in Ashland.

"Crime has been getting pretty bad lately." I had begun playing with the silver buttons on my school cardigan, which was part of our uniform. It was true. The presence of a major crime organization was no news. Ashland's crime rates had shot up over the years. It should be no surprise that it's extended beyond downtown and the West-End to here. Everyone knew of a mysterious group called the Faceless, who apparently ran everything, including the MCs.

The news was filled with stories about drive-by shootings

at known gang hangouts, bikers showing up in the low-end, grunge neighborhoods and beating the shit out of some small drug dealer, dead bodies showing up in the city river or dump. Last week, they found a cop who had gone missing, rolled up in a rug, and tossed into a junkyard. He'd almost been crushed by one of the compactor machines. Two months ago, two young bikers with spades on the backs of their jackets were found on the edge of town, dead and strung up on telephone poles, their bikes in flames. It was always the same. Drug dealers or bikers. Some bodies were found in their rundown homes in Harley, others in the most random of places. Like a single biker who was found in the park, sitting on a bench after having shot himself. There were even car bombs downtown, close to Town Hall where the mayor and other city council members worked. Ashland was quickly becoming a shit show.

I peered over at my friend, who was still nervously drumming her fingers, her gaze far away as she stared out the window at the frost covering the courtyard.

"Ny-laaah," I sang her name, hoping to snap her out of whatever dark thoughts had distracted her. I didn't want my friend to be afraid. When she flicked her soft gaze my way, I'd already set my face so that my eyes were crossed with my tongue snaked out between my teeth, and my nostrils flared as big as I could. She burst into a fit of giggles. She loved the fact that I had a rubber face and could twist it about for her entertainment. I watched as she relaxed her shoulders, her natural smile now emerging, and added, "I'm sure it's nothing. Just the biker gangs getting more brazen and ballsy... sticking it to the man, right?" I winked at her, and she chuckled, shaking her head before her nerves seemed to get the better of her again. "What is it?" I asked.

She let out a long, drawn-out breath and stared down at her lap, avoiding my gaze. I leaned toward her, now really concerned. She was never one to shy away. This new behaviour now had *me* nervous as I reached out and touched her knee. Slowly, she raised her grey gaze to me and said softly, "But it's the same biker, Casey."

I bit my lip. Well, *this* was new information. Even though we both tried to wave away our worries, hearing now that it was the same bike each time sent alarm bells off in my mind.

"Same one," she whispered, her hands shaking a little. "I only saw his face once when I left practice early? He's huge, with long hair and a beard, with tattoos covering his body. I could make out three skulls that were covering his entire throat. He..." She trailed off and peered over her shoulder as though worried someone was listening in. But the other students kept their space, all too busy looking at their phones or else were wrapped up in their own conversations to pay us any attention. She looked back at me, her expression sober and worried. "It was like he was... I dunno, like he was *waiting* for me."

I felt a shiver race up and down my spine. This was something we couldn't explain. Why was this guy everywhere she seemed to be? Why would he be waiting outside a school? Was he a pedophile? I couldn't think of anything to say that was reassuring.

"It's the same bike, black with that weird pale ghost along the sides. It's so distinctive. And with the size of this guy... I mean, how many bikers have a bike with that graphic on the side, who are nearly seven feet tall?" She shrugged and tucked a thick curl behind her ear. "I know it sounds nuts. I mean, how narcissistic can I get, right? But, I swear, he was watching *me*. I came out, got into my car, and drove away. He followed until I got to the gated community and then kept on driving, taking the turn-off that leads back south out of town. The timing was just weird. But I swear, I'm not making

26

this shit up. I've seen that same guy and that bike more than once over the past two months."

I tried to think of something to say that could have possibly explained these weird coincidences and sightings, but honestly, I thought I was just nervous to say what was *really* on my mind and scare her even more.

Her dad was a freaking detective, for crying out loud! In a city riddled with crime and known for the major organization that was running it all. From what I knew about Mr. Bryant, he was one of the few good ones. Any time I was at their house, he was stressing over paperwork in his office, arguing over the phone with his superiors, or venting to his wife about the crookedness in the department. Now that I think about it, him being one of the few good cops meant he had a target on his back in the city. It had been just under six years since I left Harley, but I knew how these things worked. Any hint of a suspicious or worthy cop, and the guy disappeared.

"Have you told your parents?" I asked her.

She shook her head, still looking nervous as hell and anxious as she twisted her fingers together in her lap.

"I think you should."

"Why? And just add more stress to their lives? No, I can't do that to them." She shook her head and sighed, seeming to snap out of her moment of concern and doubt. "Dad already has so much on his mind. If this ended up being nothing, it would only waste his time and worry him needlessly."

"But what if it's *not* nothing?"

She smiled at me, her resolve strengthening, and I knew I was battling a lost cause by continuing to question her. Once her mind was made up, she was all in. "It's fine, Casey. Really. I'm sure it's nothing, and I'm just being... I don't know, egotistical?" she laughed, now back to her usual self and got to her feet. "C'mon, let's get some coffee before our next class."

I wanted to push her to talk to her parents, but I knew it was over. Nothing I said would make a difference, so all I added was, "If he shows up again, please say something, alright?"

She rolled her eyes, "Fine. If the mystery biker appears on my doorstep, I'll tell Dad."

"Promise?"

Nylah's carefree facade dropped a fraction at that. Nope. I wasn't having it. I got to my feet and fixed her with a hard stare. I didn't care if I was shorter than her. It didn't matter. She knew what I grew up with, and so when I went serious on her ass, she paid attention.

"Promise me, Nylah," I said to her, holding out my pinky. She'd started our pinky promises back when we were ten, and it's something we've never stopped. So when I held mine up before her face, she sighed in defeat and hooked hers with it and squeezed.

"Promise."

Seriously, where the hell was Mom and Matthew? I had known they'd be out late celebrating their anniversary, but it was nearly eleven. I texted Mom's cell again, then my stepfather's, and lounged on my bed, aimlessly scrolling through my various social media accounts as I waited to hear back. I had a message from Patrick Cook, asking me if I wanted to hook up again this weekend. I ignored that one.

Patrick was fun to mess around with at parties and stuff, but he wasn't my type. He was a big jock, played football and wrestled, and had the typical good looks of an all-around high school heartthrob with his dark hair and blue eyes. As much as I enjoyed a nice, drunken fuck with him, that was about all we clicked on. He liked to talk sports, high school and professional, fishing, and his dad's ranch out in the west, where he spent his summers.

Me? I spent my time doodling in my notebook, still wondering what the hell I wanted to do once high school was over, but kept coming up blank. Matthew was encouraging me to travel around for a year, but Mom was worried I'd fall behind if I did that. It had been a hot topic of debate in our house as of late.

I stared at my screen for a minute, deliberating something, and not for the first time. Finally, I opened all my social media apps and typed in, "Vail St. James," but nothing came up. I typed "Lee Knight" next. Nothing. Lastly, "Shaw Bishop," and nada. Nothing on *any* of them, the boys I once knew. It was like they didn't exist. I then wondered if life in Harley was so different that even teens there didn't use social media the way the ones on The Hill do? I knew things were different between the two zones of Ashland, but were they *that* diverse? Had I changed so much?

I tried one last time to look up the boys who had once been as close to me as my own mother, feeling almost like there was a sense of desperation just to see their faces again. How different were they? Had they changed or stayed the same? I wanted to find them and shout them down for abandoning me when I needed them most... isolated in a place that was so unfamiliar, with people who hated me, who were out to get me. I'd been pulled out of the only world I'd ever known and thrown into a pit of snakes at this school and was expected to just survive. I'd been holding onto their promise that they would stay in touch, that they'd visit me here, and call. But nothing. The moment I left, I ceased to exist for them. Had it all really meant nothing? Everything we'd been through?

Frustrated, I tossed my phone aside and lay back on my blankets, staring up at my ceiling. I didn't know what was taking Mom and Matthew so long, but I was starting to feel anxious and needed an outlet. I was tempted even to call Patrick for a late-night hook-up, when the doorbell rang.

What the hell...? I glanced over at my alarm clock, the bright red letters reading 11:22 pm. Who was coming around this late at night? In my old neighborhood, I'd be peeking out the windows, phone in hand, ready to call 9-1-1, but here, in a gated community in the most prestigious area of Ashland, I felt perfectly safe as I got up and went down-stairs in my sleep sweats and t-shirt. However, the moment I peeked out the peephole and saw two cops standing there, I felt like I'd been submerged in a vat of ice water.

I didn't remember deciding to slide back the lock and open the door. It was more like I was running on autopilot. My body was just running through the motions until the next thing I knew, I was sitting on my living room couch. The two cops were standing over me, as I listened to them explain how my mother and stepfather were both killed by a drunk driver on their way home this evening. They mentioned something about needing to bring me into the station. Some of Matthew's colleagues at the hospital identi-fied them both, and something else about whether or not I wanted to see them one last time, but I wasn't registering anything. There was a loud buzzing in my ears that seemed to be blocking everything out except for one thing...

Mom. My mother, whom I loved more than anyone in this world, was gone. Matthew, my stepdad, who treated me like his own daughter, was no more. I would never come home to see my mother pruning her white hellebore and filling the bird feeder with fresh seed. I wouldn't hear Matthew call out, "Hey there, pumpkin!" when he would come home from the hospital after a long day of work. Those were the first two thoughts that popped into my head, and I immediately felt so stupid for thinking them. I mean, I just finished hearing that my parents were both dead, and I'm thinking about Mom and her flowers and Matthew's childish nickname for me. What was my problem? I should be crying my eyes out right now and demanding to see them.

Instead, I found myself staring up at these two officers, feeling like I'd been turned into stone. My face and my fingertips grew numb, but I couldn't seem to digest what they were telling me. I could tell they were uncomfortable with my reaction, but at this moment, I could give a fuck what they thought. Instead, I just said, "I need a drink of water..." and I walked like a zombie, heading into the kitchen to pour a glass, which I downed in a second, and then poured another and another. My hands had started to shake, and I felt like I couldn't breathe. Why couldn't I fucking breathe? When I slammed the glass down on the marble countertop, it smashed, sending glass everywhere. Cursing, I bent down to clean it up, not thinking as I started to scoop up the shards. I heard the two cops come rushing in, but I ignored them as I tried to collect all the pieces.

"Wait, wait, you're going to cut-" One of them hurried over, but it'd been too late. I didn't even realize I had sliced my hand until the blood began to flow, sliding down my wrist to drip onto the floor.

"Oh Jesus, shit!" I quickly stood, throwing the pieces into the sink, and reached for the paper towel. "Mom hates dirty floors, let me just get this... I-I..." I froze. Mom... *oh God!*

Next thing I knew, I'd collapsed to the floor, one of the police officers was holding me in a comforting embrace, but I held back a sob as I struggled to maintain my control. *Mom...* she was gone. She wasn't going to care that there was blood on her white Italian tiled floors. She wouldn't know that I've broken a glass, not that she would have cared much

31

about that anyway. She would have been more concerned about seeing my bleeding hand than anything else. But she wasn't going to come in, clean it, and wrap it up for me. Neither was Matthew. I was alone.

Mom... Mom... My breathing hitched as I tried to wrap my head around this, but my stubborn side was trying to bear it all. I didn't want to cry in front of these officers. I'd never liked anyone to see me weak. Maybe that's leftover from growing up in Harley, where tears were seen as a weakness, and that was the last thing I wanted to be. So I screwed my face up, biting my lip as I fought to hold back the suffocating grief that was itching to break free. When I was alone, I would cry my heart out. But not now.

The other officer came over and pulled my hand toward himself, pressing a wad of paper towel into my palm to slow the flow of the bleeding. "We can get this checked out at the hospital. We'll take you when you're ready."

More thoughts came crashing into my head. Mom had no other family. And Matthew, he'd been from the states. His family was way down in New York, and he rarely spoke to them. I had no one else. No one. I was all alone. All alone... what the hell was I going to do? I remembered Mom constantly muttering about having to get her will and everything organized, but she'd get sidetracked and would put it off. What was going to happen to me? I felt sick to my stomach from chugging all that water. When I thought about her and Matthew, dead, it made it even worse. I could feel my grief in my throat, like I was choking on it.

"Do you have anyone you can stay with for the time being?"

Nylah. I nodded, sucking in quick, sharp little breaths as I shakily got to my feet. I'd pack a bag, send her a message. At the mention of her father's name, Phillip Bryant, the officers said they'd bring me to her house after.

By the time I'd packed my bag and locked the house up behind me, I went back to being numb again. I didn't know what I was going to do now. The only thing I wanted in the world was my mother's arms around me. It felt like a punch in the gut to realize that I would never have that feeling again.

Chapter three

Casey

"Why can't I stay here?"

"You legally cannot stay here-"

"I'll get emancipated! I won't go..."

"Then until you are eighteen, you will be put into foster care-"

"This is bullshit!" I yelled, jumping to my feet. "I'll be seventeen in November! Most kids my age are completely capable of living alone!"

"These are the laws according to our province, Miss Cooper." The social worker met my heated glare straight on. She had zero sympathy for my situation, and I could tell just by the hard way she looked at me. How she spoke as if she was tired of dealing with difficult teens, and also how she kept glancing at her watch as though she had more important places to be than sitting here with me discussing my life. "If you have living guardians that permit you to live alone, that would be different. But as you have no source of income

34

and are under the age of eighteen, Ontario Children's Services will not agree to you living independently. And your father-"

I burst into a fit of hysterical laughter at the mention of that man. "Please, my father? He may have donated his sperm to my mother, but that fucker is *not* my father!"

"He does have a record, several arrests for drunk driving, and multiple house calls for domestic disturbance, but no charges were made against him by your late mother," she confirmed, checking her notes.

"Yeah, cuz she was too scared to try to convict him! He'd be locked up for twenty-four hours and then released!"

"To which she could have filed a restraining order-"

"And what? What could she have done with that? Wave it in his face if he tried to break in? Please." I shook my head and started pacing back and forth before her. We were in Nylah's living room; her mom and dad had moved out into their backyard to give the social worker and me some privacy while she disappeared to her room. I really wished Mr. Bryant was here right now. He'd be able to talk some sense into this woman, I was sure of it.

"That is speculation, Miss Cooper. And as his record has been clean since he and your mother separated, has been working a steady job, and has expressed to us that he wishes to claim his custody rights, this is how it has to be. When you are seventeen, you may apply for emancipation if you still wish to." She peered at me over her square, black-framed glasses and smirked, "Or, since you're moving to Harley, most likely you'll end up knock-"

"That is *quite* enough of that!"

I spun around and felt a weight lift off my chest at the sight of Phillip Bryant. He was dressed in his casual clothes today, as he was off-duty, in jeans and a blue polo shirt. His dislike for this woman was evident in how his almost black eyes were narrowed as he ambled into the room.

"Hi Phil," she smirked at him, and I immediately wanted to scratch at this woman's face. One thing I knew for sure about Nylah's dad was that he *hated* being called Phil. Her addressing him like this, plus the way she talked to me, says so much about how miserable and mean this woman was. I decided that I officially hated her.

"Jackie." He gave her the smallest of nods before looking at me. "Why don't you go on upstairs and find Nylah, hon? Dinner will be ready in half an hour."

I knew he was dismissing me, but I wanted to know what he was going to say to this bitch. However, I respected Mr. Bryant too much to be a brat and refuse his request. I bowed my head and hurried out of the room, making sure my steps were silent and slow once I rounded the corner, hoping to eavesdrop just a little.

"Your job is to *help* these kids. You're supposed to have their best interest at heart, but you make yourself the enemy. Why?" He rumbled in his low, deep voice, "It's people like you that make these kids lose faith in the system."

"Please," she let out a nasal laugh. I could just picture her long, horse face all scrunched up as she did it. "We both know once that girl goes to Harley, she'll be pregnant before she hits eighteen, or, if she's even lucky enough to graduate, she'll be living off the government's teat for most of her life... just like the rest of them."

"The rest of *them*?" Mr. Bryant's voice, if possible, went even deeper, and I shivered in response. He. Was. *Pissed.* "And what the hell is that supposed to mean?"

"Oh, oh! Nothing like *that*, Phil." She laughed nervously now, even as quickly as she tried to backstep. This woman seemed to have already earned herself a spot on his shitlist. "You know how people from Harley are... they are a burden on this city. Nothing good comes out of that place. Nothing-"

"I'm from Harley, Ms. MacDonald. So what you're saying applies to me, too."

There was a minute of silence following this statement, and I was pretty sure both he and that social worker were as still as I was, waiting for the pin to drop.

"I'm going to give you a chance to go back and start again," he said to her. "Though God knows you don't deserve it. You've gotten away with a lot till now, and honestly, you should have been fired years ago, but I guess fucking your boss has its perks, eh?"

"I-I... I mean, how did you... how dare you-"

"So here's what's going to happen. Since I can't legally take Casey from her father, if she is willing, I want to be listed as her emergency contact. If that son of a bitch touches her or so much as *looks* at her the wrong way, she has every right to leave and come here. I'll fill out the fucking paperwork. If she even complains to you about him, I want documentation and a phone call within that minute. I know you and your fuck-buddy boss have some underlying scheme going on-"

"Casey!"

I spun around from where I was standing at the bottom of the curved stairwell to see Nylah lounging against the upstairs bannister, her brow furrowed as she stared down at me. "Shhhh!" I whispered, hurrying up the steps before her dad heard us.

"What are you doing there?" she asked, her brows pulled together as I made my way toward her. She'd gone into caring friend mode, and I could see the concern on her face. "You okay? Anything I can do?" She peered over the railing to where her dad and that bitch were still duking it out.

"I'm fine. Quick, let's go paint our nails or something." I

hurried past her, heading into her bedroom. We'd been sharing her bed for the past two weeks, but it had been so easy living together. I knew how Nylah liked her room organized, so I was mindful of how I cleaned up after myself or what space I took. I hopped up onto her large, white, canopied bed, only to have her crawl across to me as she laid her hand on my forehead. "What are you doing?" I laughed, pulling away.

"'Let's go paint our nails," she repeated, her brows raised incredulously before she burst into happy laughter. "My God! You've officially lost it. But I'm going to take full advantage of this."

"I'll compromise; you can paint them this one," I said, holding up a dark purple shade called 'wine'.

I saw how her sparkling, grey eyes flickered to a frosty pink colour, and I immediately swatted it away. "No, Ny! No!" I scolded her.

She rolled her eyes and stuck her tongue out at me. "Fine! Dark and broody it is, my dear!" She laughed and grabbed some kleenex from her bedside table. "Now no squirming this time, or you are gonna owe me a new comforter."

I left the graveyard, and my mind whirled from everything, shivering as the bite of fall in the breeze was cutting through me. I had to walk down the hill to make it to my bus, then transfer at The Station, which was a mini-mall center where there were a dozen fast food places and small but expensive shops selling clothes, jewelry, and antiques (the sort of stuff people who lived on The Hill liked to shop for). It encircled The Hill's main bus station, where I'd catch another back to Nylah's house. I could have accepted the ride she offered me, but I just wanted to be alone whenever I visited Mom and Matthew.

By next week, Mid-October, I'd be back in Harley with my father, and everything I'd been suppressing for six years was going need to quickly resurface if I was going to survive.

The social worker's words have been echoing in my mind the past week. I don't know what else Mr. Bryant said to her, but before Nylah could finish painting my nails, we heard her storm out, slamming the front door behind herself so hard the crystals on the chandelier hanging in the foyer clinked against each other. I desperately wanted to know how the conversation ended, but all that happened was that he came up to Nylah's room and found us on her bed, then told me basically everything I'd already overheard. I would have to go to my father's, but if I needed out, I was to call him, and he'd see what he could do.

I'm so glad he gave me that lifeline.

I saw my father at Matthew and Mom's funeral. He was a fucking embarrassment. He was drunk, slobbering, and wailing loudly, as she was lowered into the ground, going on and on about how she was the only woman he ever loved. Eventually, Nylah's dad stepped in and escorted him away so I could say goodbye to Mom and my *real* father in peace.

Matthew had been everything Keith Cooper was lacking. He was sweet to my mother, and when I met him, he was incredibly kind and accepting of me, despite the snotty ten-year-old attitude that I gave him at first. He was patient, and almost annoyingly kind. The fact that he was a doctor, the same doctor Mom saw after break-in, in fact, meant that he was smart with a steady, comfortable income and wanted Mom and me out of Harley as soon as possible. So on the first of November that year, twenty-three days before my eleventh birthday, he'd moved us out of there and into his home on The Hill.

After seeing how much he loved Mom, how he made her happy, and how gentle he was with her, I relented, and our relationship grew as well.

To hear Keith, bumbling drunk Keith, claim that *he* loved her after all he did... I wanted to puke. His stupid, drunken rages were always directed at Mom. She was his punching bag when he was in a violent mood. He had drunk any money he made away, forcing Mom to have to start hiding it after working small jobs on the sly while he worked as a taxi driver. After he got arrested for a DUI, Mom packed up our stuff while he had been locked up in the local jail for thirty days, and we moved into that old basement suite. She filed for divorce and mailed it to him when he was in lock up, and then she got a job at the local supermarket. We lived in that basement, just us two, until she met Matthew. But those years living alone with her were the best of my life while we had lived in Harley. And as much as I loved Nylah, the friendship I'd had with my three childhood friends had meant so much more to me than anything else I'd ever experienced.

And you might see them again...

I lounged on the second bus, gazing out the window as I got lost in my thoughts: Mom, Matthew, Keith Cooper, and the three boys.

What if they were gone? Dead? What if they weren't? Would they recognize me? Would I recognize them? And if we did, would we have anything to say to each other? We were different people now, for sure. Mostly though, I just wanted answers. Why had they shut me out? Was there a reason, or were they just being assholes?

If it was the second, I felt a sting in my heart. I thought our friendship had run deeper than that. I thought it had been something worth savouring. I had to remind myself that it obviously wasn't what I'd thought, or they wouldn't have ghosted me all these years.

I was so lost in my thoughts that I missed my stop and quickly had to signal the driver to pull over at the next one. It was only a couple of streets back, winding through the lavish gated community. Mr. Bryant didn't earn much money, but Nylah's mom, Laila, was a successful artist who sold her work across the country. Once she explained to me what it was exactly that she did, talking about different colours, brushes, something about lighting, and as much as I loved art, I couldn't help but zone out after she hadn't stopped for nearly ten minutes straight. I just nodded and smiled as she went on for another twenty minutes talking about some artist friends of hers in Europe that I hadn't heard of. I glanced at Nylah, who even though she was watching her mother speak, I could recognize the glazed sort of look in her grey eyes as she attempted to be respectful toward her mother. Clearly, she had mastered looking attentive while actually not paying attention at all.

I finally made it to their winding, stone driveway, leading me around a perfectly manicured yard to their house, which resembled a modern stone castle of sorts. It was unusual but beautiful, and it had fit in perfectly with all the trees which blanketed the property, giving them privacy from the road. I stopped about halfway up the drive. It'd been getting dark out, and the warm lights from the windows were casting a glow on the grass. Inside, I knew that Laila was nearly done making supper, something she insisted upon doing almost every night unless she had a new series she was working on. She was big on family time. Nylah's dad was probably going through his old record collection, looking for something to play in the background while we ate, and Nylah was getting the table set, of course. Every night. A routine.

I could feel my heart clench as I thought about how

similar it was for me at my house. Except Matthew was the one who enjoyed doing the cooking at night, while Mom set the table and I picked out music for a playlist to listen to. I would never have that again.

I sniffled, not realizing until that moment that I was silently crying as I stood there, staring up at a house with a happy family living inside. All safe. All loved. In a few days, I was going to be torn away from them and thrown into a pit of snakes all over again. Once kids at Harley Institute (really? Who names a high school that?) would hear I was from The Hill, it wouldn't matter that I was originally one of them; it would start me off on the wrong foot. It would just be a repeat of what I went through six years ago when I came here. Only, kids from Harley were a whole different ball game. I adapted to life here once Nylah befriended me. Would I be able to go back?

The cool, Autumn wind buffeted me, and I shivered. I couldn't stay out here all night. This was one of the last authentic family dinners I was going to enjoy until... until... fuck, who knows? I had no family left; Keith doesn't count. I was alone.

I pushed my emotions down, way, way down, wiped the tears from my cold cheeks, and marched up the rest of the way, my ears pricking once at the sound of a Harley Davidson disappearing into the distance.

Keith was too busy working on the day I was moving in with him, so Jackie McCuntface picked me up from the Bryants. I had a hockey bag full of clothes, and two boxes of personal items, which she refused to help me load into the trunk of her station wagon. Nylah stepped in, narrowing her eyes at the woman as she stomped by her. As if Nylah was anything threatening. She was more like a beautiful-looking kitten when she was angry. She bowed her head, her thick curls hiding her face from me as she carefully pushed one of my boxes way into the back to make room for my bag. When she straightened, I saw her quickly wipe a tear off her cheek as she quickly turned away to grab the other box.

I could feel a slight sting in my eyes, too. I was just better at hiding it. If I broke down in front of her, Nylah would become a puddle and would beg her dad to keep me here. But right now, Mr. and Mrs. Bryant were talking with Ms. McNeedsToRemoveTheStickFromHerAss discreetly off to the side, and judging by how her parents were both glaring at the bitch, it's a conversation I didn't want to be a part of. I lugged my bag of clothes and hoisted it onto the bumper before I started pushing it back, struggling against the weight. In an instant, Nylah's perfectly manicured hands appeared beside mine, and she helped me get it in. Done, I closed the trunk and turned to her, only to see her grey eyes glimmering with tears she tried holding back.

Shit... I'm gonna break...

"Casey," she whispered, her voice cracking a little.

"Shit, don't, Ny..." I lowered my head, feeling like I was going to choke. It felt like the universe had some sort of problem with me, and I didn't know how to fix it. Mom and Matthew's lawyer told me I'd be inheriting the value of their estate, but that wouldn't be until I was eighteen. They *had* taken out life insurance policies, but again, I was still under-age, so I wouldn't see that money for over a year. Their estate was to be sold, the money from the sale put into my inheritance which was held by Keith, who apparently would invest it for me, as Jackie claimed. Until then, and until I was old enough, I had to play by the government's rules. Which meant leaving the last good thing I had in my life. In a month, my whole world had been turned upside down.

Losing my mother, Matthew, my family home, and now my best friend.

She nodded furiously, wiping her eyes with the backs of her hands, and cleared her throat, "Right, I know. Toughen up, Nylah!" She laughed, but I could hear how forced it was.

Taking her hands in mine, I squeezed them as I looked up at her and gave her a small, shaky smile. "Thank you for incessantly pestering me all those years ago."

She laughed for real this time, shaking her head as she pulled me in for a tight hug. "You were just so damn cute, scowling at everyone, like an angry kitten."

Before I could argue against the picture she painted of me, she picked me up and swung me around like a rag doll, another habit that never died. When she set me on my feet, I could hear the low heels of Ms. McMyPerfumeIsn'tHiding-MyBOProblem as she walked around to the driver's side of her car before she snapped, "Ms. Cooper, let's get going! I want to beat traffic." Then, she climbed in, leaving me to say one last goodbye.

Mrs. Bryant pulled me away from her daughter, embracing me just as tightly. "You need anything, we are only a phone call away, alright?"

The concern in her voice choked me up, stealing my words away, so all I could do was nod in response. When she passed me off to her husband, he whispered, "If anything goes wrong, you have our number. You call me, alright? If I can't get there in time, I'll send a squad car to pick you up."

"It'll be okay, Mr. Bryant," I said to him, trying to sound confident about the situation. I didn't want them to worry. They'd done so much already. "Thank you for everything you guys have done for me."

"Think nothing of it, hon." He peeked over my head toward the car that was idling behind me, and narrowed his eyes ever so slightly before stepping back so that Nylah and I could have one last hug goodbye.

"You message me the moment you get in, alright?" she said, her voice anxious as we embraced.

"I will. But don't worry about me. I grew up there, remember? I'll be fine."

"Yeah, but-"

"Really, Ny, I'll be okay. You worry about yourself. I want to hear you're giving basketball your all and that you're kicking ass in all your classes. You need to get into McGill." I pulled back to fix her with a hard, stern stare, and she chuckled then hung her head, trying to hide the guilt on her face. "Hey!" I snapped. She met my gaze, and I smiled at her, holding back my grief. "You were meant for great things."

"So are you."

Even though I didn't believe her, I nodded anyway and pulled away, eager to get going. This was like slowly pulling a band-aid off your arm, prolonged and painful. I needed to just go. So I gave her hands one last squeeze, waved to her parents, who had moved back to their front door to give us some space, and climbed into the car. I watched out the window as we drove away until we rounded the corner in the drive, and the trees blocked her from my view. How long would it be until we were able to see each other again?

Chapter four

Casey

I WAS BACK.

Driving over the train tracks that separated the West-End from downtown Ashland, the stark difference in appearance and the *feel* of this place, I felt a flood of emotions running through me. Seeing the old brick structures, the trees that lined the sidewalks (which had gotten more prominent over the years), and some old shops I recognized, felt so nostalgic and strange. But there was something different. Maybe it was because I was no longer a child and had been away for so long, but everything seemed darker now. The people, the stores, the barred-up homes, and the alleys all carried a heavy weight to them. The neglect was evident as I took in the missing letters on storefront signs, boarded up windows, graffiti on almost every available free space, and the trash piled up everywhere…

Had it always been like that? Or was I blind as a kid? I figured I had an understanding growing up here. Maybe I'd seriously forgotten how bad it was with living on The Hill these past few years? Or had it just gotten worse? Perhaps Mom had shielded me from a lot more than I thought. Or the boys did. I quickly shook my thoughts of them away as we turned off one of the main streets and into a neighborhood of shabby apartment buildings and small bungalows.

I glanced over at Jackie, whose nose was wrinkled like she smelled something foul (her... it's her. That perfume she was wearing hides nothing), and curled her lip at the sight of a group of young men gathered on a corner as they laughed about something, their breath rising into the cold air in white clouds. I could guarantee this woman had never stepped foot into Harley unless she was forced to for work.

We slowed as we came upon a group of townhouses, and I peered up at them, unimpressed with their condition. They were ancient, probably one of the original structures of Ashland, give or take a few decades. Made of brick, with ornate stone-lined peaked roofs, and covered in dead vines, I'm sure they were once beautiful. But now, they were covered in graffiti (which, in all honesty, made them look marginally better as the artwork itself was great), the tall windows barred, and the high stone steps that were leading up to the front doors were crumbling. The original wooden doors, all painted black, were shielded by aged, bronze, barred screens.

We stopped at the one on the very end, which bordered a small green space, where the trees were overgrown. The concrete square flower beds were empty of soil, some littered with litter, a discarded traffic cone, or trash that the crows were fighting over. It didn't look like a place very many people would hang out, even in the summer.

Jackie parallel parked along the sidewalk and peered nervously around us. It was getting dark already, what with it being the middle of October, and from the way she was checking the area, I knew she was making sure no one was watching, waiting to jump us the moment we unlocked the car doors.

"Grab your things quickly, understand?" she hissed at me.

"Why?" I asked, feigning ignorance.

"Just do as I say!" she snapped. "I don't want to get robbed!"

"Why would you get robbed?" I changed my voice to sound as innocent as possible, and she turned to me, her perfume mixed with her B.O. now flooding my nostrils, and I tried not to gag.

"Don't be smart!"

"I find it funny that you are okay with leaving me here, when you're so obviously terrified and when you're supposed to be thinking of *my* welfare," I said to her, holding her stare.

"Please," she scoffed, "You're used to this place. I, however, have never lived here, and that makes me a target. Now get your stuff together, and let's get going!" She dug into her overly large carpet handbag and pulled out a ring with several keys on it. I jumped out and decided to grab my bag of clothes first, carefully climbing up the steep stairs as I lugged it behind me while she undid two locks on the screen, then two more on the front door, before walking in. I guess Keith gave her a set to use for today. I unceremoniously threw my bag in after and hurried back to the car, balanced both boxes on top of the other, and barely managed to lift them and bring them inside myself while Jackie went around turning on lights.

The house was narrow and old. The dark wood floors creaked and smelled like old lumber and alcohol (which was not a surprise to me, seeing as Keith was the owner of this place). Off to the right was a sitting room with a single, old brown eighties-looking couch arranged in front of a television and a coffee table. In the corner was an electric fire-place, which Jackie turned on, but that was it. No photos, no plants, no décor. Even the old, green patterned wallpaper was peeling. It made me think of my old home with Mom and Matthew and how we had family photos over the mantle, vases of fresh flowers (white hellebore were her favourite) from Mom's garden or the greenhouse, and some random pieces from Matthew's world travels, that were from when he was in his twenties.

The curtains were drawn over the bay windows that overlooked the street. In the back of the room, an archway showed off the tiny and outdated kitchen, which Jackie entered, turning on the overhead light, and walking straight to the fridge, and opened it. Even though I was standing behind her, I knew she wasn't impressed by the way her hand clenched around the door and the small shake of her head. The freezer didn't get a different reaction either, which was jammed packed with frozen meals.

She shut the door and turned to me, her nose wrinkling slightly. "Your father said that your room was upstairs. I suppose we might as well get this out of the way now…" She strode past me, pulling out a clipboard from her massive bag, and started scribbling notes down. I had no idea what she was doing, but I followed, grabbing my bag of clothes to haul up the creaking, wooden steps.

The upstairs was as narrow as the rest of the house and had a similar feeling of disrepair with the peeling yellow wallpaper and uneven floorboards. There was a storage room at the very top, then a tiny bathroom that had defi-nitely not seen an upgrade since the eighties with its yellow tub and sink, or was that just from age? My room was the last one, and it was pretty underwhelming when Jackie opened the door to reveal it.

It was small and cramped, and Keith had shoved a single

bed that just managed to fit along the far wall, with a single window at the foot of it, which looked out onto the street. A tall dresser was placed beside the head and by the window was a simple oak desk. The closet was just big enough for me to stand in. But I figured I could go to the dollar store and find storage baskets to fit my extra clothes in. The ceiling had yellow stains from a leak in the roof, and the walls were basically just drywall, the joint compound not even sanded down. In one corner, there was even a stack of boxes that Keith had labelled, "Storage," which only confirmed to me that this was a junk room before he found out I'd be coming here.

Jackie scribbled a few more notes down before she turned to me, "Your father said his shift ends at 4:00 am. So you'll see him tomorrow. He has registered for you to start Harley Institute on Monday and has ordered your books." She held up the keys she'd used to get into the house, and I took them. "He said to keep all the locks on except for the bolt and top and floor locks so he can get in later. Do you have any questions?"

I stared at her, not sure of what else to say. It was clear she didn't really care about her job. That much I figured out on day one. It was just a paycheque. Her question was just standard procedure. She didn't really care, and that was fine. I wanted her gone. I needed to be alone. So I just shook my head, and she breathed a sigh of relief.

"Okay, then. We'll be checking in from time to time. You have your mother's lawyer's number, I assume?"

I nodded. He had given me his card so that I could call with any questions about the inheritance I'd be receiving or the life insurance money. I didn't see myself wanting to contact him about any of that any time soon. I was still grieving. I'd much rather throw that money in Jackie's scrunched-up horse-face if it meant I'd get Mom and Matthew back.

"Very well. I need to get back to the office to file this." And without so much as a goodbye, she marched right past me and hurried down the steps. I followed, locking the doors behind her as instructed. It may have been a while since I've been back here, but I wasn't completely lost on the severity of things. Mom had constantly reminded me to keep our doors and windows locked. Break-ins were not uncommon, and if a door or window was left open, it was an open invitation to thieves. Behind the door, I could hear her peel off, no doubt speeding the hell out of here.

I shivered in the cool house, the electric fireplace not working fast enough to my liking, and decided to busy myself unpacking. I put all my clothes away, set up my books along the back of my desk, along with my laptop, put away my toiletries in the tiny bathroom down the hallway, and set up my more personal stuff on top of the dresser... like a photo of Matthew, Mom and me at Christmas last year, my childhood stuffed lamb, and my mother-of-pearl jewelry box.

I spent the rest of the evening exploring the rest of the house. Keith's room was on the main floor behind the stairs, and the basement was locked off. I heated up one of the TV dinner meals from the freezer and found my new textbooks in a clear sealed bag that had been thrown in the corner of the kitchen. In one day, I'd be attending a new high school.

My stomach suddenly felt like it was full of butterflies, and three names echoed again and again in my mind... *Lee... Shaw... Vail...*

It took forever to fall asleep last night, so by the time I did wake up, the sun was streaming through a crack in the curtain over my window. I moaned, rolling over to bury my head beneath my pillow, only... there was no bed there. I fell to the floor on my stomach with a hard smack, knocking the wind from my lungs. I coughed and gasped as I sat up, and from downstairs, the quick running of heavy footsteps raced down the hall, up the stairs until Keith had burst through my bedroom door in just his underwear, looking freaked the fuck out.

"Casey! What the fuck did you do? Jesus! What happened?" He ran to the window, throwing the tattered blue curtain aside to check the lock, thus revealing his hairy, practically naked body to the neighborhood. He spun around to face me, and I quickly held up a hand, shielding his crotch area from my view as I wheezed, slowly catching my breath again.

"Fell... out of... bed..." I gasped, and Keith visibly relaxed.

"Fucking Christ!" He sagged where he stood, his hand over his heart as he rolled his eyes to the ceiling like he was silently saying a prayer.

I got up, sitting on the edge of my bed; my lungs slightly recovered, but I kept my eyes averted. My birth father still didn't seem to understand that his near-nakedness was making me uncomfortable because he moved closer and placed a hand on my shoulder, ignoring how I tensed.

"You rest okay?" He sounded as awkward and uncomfortable as I felt.

"Yeah, yeah, I'm good. Just gonna shower and make sure I'm ready for school tomorrow." I peeked up at his face, avoiding to focus anywhere south of his neck carefully. He really looked nothing like me. He had a sunken, long face, with ruddy reddish-brown curls and pale, blue eyes. He had ruddy cheeks, evidence of his drinking. I tried to spot some sort of physical similarity between us, but there was nothing. Not our noses, chins, even our ears. It's like God literally made me a mini version of my mother, though we really only shared the same colouring. Clearly, my looks must have come somewhere down her line of the family.

When I met Keith's stare, I noticed how he flinched slightly, as no doubt he saw the resemblance with my mother, too.

"Okay, kid. You just do what you gotta do today. I'm gonna catch a few more hours of shut-eye. I get Sundays off, so I'll be around if you need anything, alright?"

"Yeah, sure. Thanks, Keith." I lowered my head, trying to ignore how weird it felt to be talking to him. Even at the funeral, he didn't look my way or say a word to me. He was too hammered to notice much around him, save for Mom's casket. Before then, the last I'd seen of him was when I was turning nine, and he showed up at my birthday party absolutely trashed and started a fight with my mom. I was so livid, and I had gone into defense mode, ready to try to beat the crap out of him for yelling at her, when Lee had scooped me up, throwing me over his shoulder like a potato sack as Vail and Shaw collected my gifts together, and we took off. We raced down two blocks to Lee's place, where we sat in his living room with his grandparents, who were bedridden, opening my gifts, chatting with the sweet, elderly couple, while his mom served us popcorn and called my mother to let her know we were safe.

Now this man, the one who had scared me out of my home and who Mom had run from, was half-naked, holding my shoulder and looking at me with what felt like false concern as if he was *trying* to act like the concerned parent, but there was no heart behind it, and it just made it more awkward.

Finally, after a few agonizing seconds, he seemed to catch on with how uncomfortable I was and lamely let me go, and he trudged out of the room, closing the door behind himself.

The rest of the day with him was hell. I stayed up in my

room for as long as I could, but eventually, I had to go down and at least try to make some sort of effort with Keith. He was lounging in his sweats and a long sleeve shirt, the electric fire going, and the TV was set to a CFL game. As to who was playing, I didn't pay attention. Nylah had gotten me into basketball, and football only reminded me of Patrick. But I made myself some tea and sat on the other end of the couch, and attempted conversation. However, as it turns out, Keith was too absorbed in his football game, and most of my questions were answered with a grunt, a 'hm,' or an 'uh-huh.' I'd have to try later when he was free to focus.

So I went up to my room and double-checked my bookbag, which was a leather satchel bag Matthew had bought me last year, to ensure I had all my texts, notebooks, and stationery supplies before I snapped the clasps shut. I'd already been texting back and forth with Nylah, letting her know everything was alright while I was checking in on her. I was thinking about that biker she'd mentioned and wished she would tell her father, but she swore she hadn't seen or heard anything since before I had stayed with her, so all was well.

When Mr. Bryant even texted to make sure I was okay, I was tempted to let him know about it, but knew that Nylah would lose her mind if I said anything. Since things had been quiet, I kept my mouth shut and assured him I was doing okay.

I tried to distract myself, to calm the building tension in my chest about tomorrow, but I was too worked up. I was nervous as hell. I needed to toughen up if I was going to survive. This was going to be different from the kids at the private school I attended. I was going to need to adjust quickly if I was going to survive my final year of high school.

My plan?

I needed to keep my head down. Don't draw attention to

myself. Don't get involved in anybody's shit, which means no snitching, and just concentrate on my studies. Survive. Endure. In a year, I'd be getting my parent's life insurance money, which would be more than what I knew what to do with. If I could just survive high school in one piece and graduate, I could live off that money for a few years as I decided what it was I wanted to do, if I hadn't figured it out by then. Once I was twenty-one, I'd receive the rest of my inheritance, and I could do whatever the hell I wanted, and I could leave Harley and Keith and all this bullshit behind me.

That night when I went to bed, I felt more confident with my game plan. I could do this. I just needed to hold my tongue, keep a low profile, and pray that no one noticed me.

Chapter five

Casey

WHEN I WALKED through the doors of Harley Institute on Monday morning, after getting through security, I felt a tension building in my chest when I surveyed around and saw that I didn't fit in here, and all the other students saw it, too. I figured the outfit I'd picked for today would be plain enough to blend in, but I still stuck out like a sore thumb. I was in a pair of high waist light blue jeans, a grey, long sleeve crop top, and my growing out lilac hair was pulled back into a high ponytail. Even my low-top white sneakers stood out. With the glares I received from the girls and the slow once-overs by the guys, I took one look at their more casual attire and realized my mistake. My jeans were designer... all of them were. They were the only ones I had, seeing as Mom had bought them for me. My idea of simple jewelry was a pair of pearl studs that had been given to me last Christmas by my mother but was now catching enough attention from the girls alone. And my black, leather satchel? Well, I could feel my cheeks redden as several kids pointed to the designer gold label. Attending the private Academy on The Hill, all the kids used bags like this, but here, I felt like this would be better used by someone working in an office than the backpacks and crossbody bags.

Lowering my head, I hurried to the Administration Office to sign in, eager to put as much distance between myself and my peers until I felt better prepared. The school itself was dingy, making it clear that the city barely placed any money towards the public schools here. The floor tiles were orange and white, the walls were a beige concrete, and the once red lockers were all drawn on, rusted in places, and scratched to shit. The hanging fluorescent lights had wire cages covering the bulbs, which I could only assume would protect them from being smashed. Was my elementary like this? I couldn't remember noticing this sort of stuff. Had I really become shallow and close-minded like the Hill kids?

"Miss Cooper," the receptionist called me over and handed me several forms. "Have each of your teachers sign these and return at the end of the day. We'll take your student ID photo now. You have to carry it around with you everywhere, as a teacher or member of security can ask for it at any time. Your locker number. Don't give out your combination to *anyone*, you understand me? We have a problem with thefts here, so I suggest that you don't keep any valuables in your locker... or on your persons, for that matter." Her eyes flicked up to the small pearl studs in my ears. "We have surprise locker searches every so often, and your cooperation is mandatory. This is a map of the school." She handed me a double-sided piece of paper with a layout of all three floors, plus the basement. "If you are sick, you need a parent to call in on your behalf. There is a list of extracurriculars posted on the notice board outside the office, if you are interested in joining any groups or sports teams..." Her eyes scanned me up and down, and I knew she was trying to figure out where I would fit in here. So was I. She shook her head and tapped the paper that had my schedule on it. "Rooms starting with one are on the main floor, and two's are on the second..."

"Let me guess... three's are on the third?"

She narrowed her eyes at me and muttered, "Yes. The gymnasium is in the basement, along with the weight and locker rooms. Any questions?"

"No, ma'am."

Her eyes narrowed even more as though she thought I was being sarcastic. I wasn't. At the Academy, we were expected to address adults in such a way. But I guess here, that meant something different. "Here is a list of drills we practice at the school and what to do. We will announce when we are practicing a fire, bomb, or shooting drill."

I turned to stone at her words, focusing hard as she prattled on, only pausing to take a breath once. A bomb drill? Holy crap... School shooting drills were not uncommon, and we practiced those even at my Academy, but for some reason, hearing about them here made the hairs on my neck stand up on end.

"I trust your father gave you the textbooks we mailed him?"

"Uh, yeah. He did. I got them." I quickly scanned the schedule. It was alternating days, which meant I'd have to be careful and really pay attention to the way they flipped from morning to afternoon day-to-day. I had English and Math 30, Phys. Ed, and stopped at the sight of Home Ec. as one of my options. "Um, Ms. Hoffman? I didn't sign up for Home Ec."

"Your options are limited, Miss Cooper, seeing as you are joining us in the middle of the semester," she sounded irritated by my question, as if I chose to inconvenience the school by having to register in the middle of October. "You'll have to take Art next semester." Her large, pale eyes rolled up my way, the way she held her face reminding me very much of my social worker. "Go on then and get sorted out. It's a big school, so you'll need the extra time to find your classes." And without another word, she turned away to answer the phone and waved at me with a flick of her wrist, which I took as a sign that I was excused. I backed up quickly, looking at the map to determine where my locker could be, but the numbers weren't specified. I'd just have to check the first set when I ambled out and count up from there until I found 326.

As soon as I stepped out of the office, I was immediately elbowed so hard that everything in my arms went sprawling to the floor of the busy hallway. I spotted a group of girls that stood close by, watching me with obvious mirth and wicked intent in their eyes.

Ignore them, Casey. Remember your plan. Just pick your stuff up and move on.

I looked away from them, gritting my teeth as I quickly moved to grab my things before they got trampled by the rest of the student body. When I had everything, I glanced again at the girls and noticed the one standing closest to me had the biggest smirk of all. Her hair had been dyed with purples and reds. I couldn't even tell what her natural colour was. She had also had heavy makeup on her face, and was dressed more fitted for a club than school. I blew a loose strand from my ponytail out of my face and hurried away, not wanting to get involved in too much drama on my first day. I eventually found my locker near the backdoors of the school, right next to a flight of stairs. Once I wrenched open the door, which was sticking, I'd been met with more hostility from passing girls. I couldn't quite understand what exactly their problem was, only that they shoved me when they passed or tried to slam my door shut, nearly trapping my fingers. I sighed heavily, closing my eyes for a moment before I continued on like nothing happened. I expected a little bit of hazing but not actual physical contact. At least, not this soon.

Don't react... don't react... they want to see you rise to their baiting. Don't give in to it... I told myself over and over again, trying to ignore how that little bubble of rage that was coming to life in my chest. I remembered how long it took me to learn how to suppress my instincts from Harley when I moved to The Hill. But now that I was back here, those old habits were stirring to life again. I just needed to contain it, so I didn't get myself killed.

It'd only been ten minutes, and I already felt like an outcast. Moving down the halls had only solidified that point when I was met with an assortment of less than welcoming looks. Most were curious, but others were downright terrifying, filled with hostility. The more intimidating expressions were coming from other girls, I noted. So I followed the school's printout map to try to find my first class, which was English, up on the second floor. Rushing up the steps and hurrying down the hall, I made it to class before the bell rang, and I picked a seat near the back, discreetly keeping my head down as the other students slowly filed in. I could feel everyone looking at me when they came into class, but I ignored them all as the seats filled up. Only when our teacher had come rushing in, straightening his dark-rimmed glasses and running a hand through his balding hair, did everyone quiet down and face forward. The bell rang, and he breathed out a panting breath (he clearly ran here to be on time) and grinned at the class. "Good morning, everyone! Happy Monday!"

Of course, he was met with grumbling and nonchalant

murmurs.

He grinned but shook his head. "Oh, don't you all sound like you're ready to continue our study of Othello!" I couldn't help but smile at his attempts to be enthusiastic. I'm also relieved because I studied Othello last year. At least I wouldn't fall behind in English. Just as I was feeling a wave of reassurance wash over me, he caught my eye and beamed. "Ah! A new student! I'm Mr. Kennard." He touched his glasses again as they slipped down his nose. "Please, come up here and introduce yourself to everyone!" He held a hand out beside him, gesturing to the empty space in front of the whiteboard. Any sort of growing affection for this man vanished on the spot, and I wanted to curl up in a hole and die. I minutely shook my head at him, my eyes widening. A few of the students snickered.

"Come on now, don't be shy. Everyone needs to get comfortable with public speaking. It's an important asset in life. Tell us your name and a little bit about yourself."

I withered slightly in my seat, but reluctantly got to my feet and shuffled to the front of the room. When I faced everyone, I'd twisted my fingers together, praying to God that none of them recognized me at all. "I'm Casey Cooper," I said softly. "I just moved to Harley recently to live with my dad…"

"What school did you attend before you came here, Casey?" Mr. Kennard asked with a smile on his face. I knew he'd been trying to be friendly, but honestly, the last thing that these kids needed to hear was that I had moved here from The Hill, known as Ashland's snob-central, to every other community in the city. Just like Harley was known as Ashland's Piss-Bucket.

"I-I went to a private school," I murmured.

From somewhere in the back of the room, I heard a wolf whistle, and two guys high-fived each other like idiots. I narrowed my eyes at them. My chest tightened when I noticed the one with dark brown hair and amber eyes, as he seemed familiar. He peered back at me and pursed his lips, blowing me a kiss, his silver lip piercings on either side of his bottom lip were glinting under the light of the fluorescents, standing out starkly against his tanned skin. His friend across the aisle was dirty blond with hazel eyes and a septum piercing. They have a hard edge to them, and honestly, I shivered at the way they checked me out so blatantly.

"And what do you like to do, Casey?" Mr. Kennard asked after he gave the boys a stern, warning glare.

"Um…" I shifted on my feet, lowering my eyes to the white floor. "I like to draw. I play basketball, but not competitively," I added with a quick side glance at Mr. Kennard, just as he opened his mouth, no doubt to encourage me to talk to the coach of this school about joining the team. I wasn't as good as Nylah, with her long, goddess-like legs. But I was scrappy from playing ball as a kid with the guys. I stuck to outdoor courts in the park, where she and I would spend an hour playing some days in the summer evenings when there hadn't been a party to go to. "And, uh… " I felt my face burn as old activities came to mind. Going to The Hill's Shopping Center with my friends, parties at some rich kid's mansion, boating with Mom and Matthew in the summer. The more I thought about it, the more I realized what a privileged life I'd been given when I left here, and I instantly shut down, registering that anything else I said would only alienate me from my peers even more.

I think Mr. Kennard finally saw how uncomfortable I was, because he nodded and flashed me another smile before handing me a very worn copy of Othello. "Well, welcome to Harley, Casey!"

No one in the class made any sort of greeting to me, except for those two dickwads who had high-fived each other, "I'll welcome her to Harley," the one I thought I'd recognized shouted, "How about you meet me after school in the back of my truck?"

"That's enough, Mr. Tremblay!" Mr. Kennard snapped at him.

Tremblay... Hunter Tremblay! I felt a shock in my system as a memory came crashing back to me.

I was eight, and the guys and I were playing baseball with some kids in our neighborhood that we knew from school. I'd been batting when Hunter and his small gang emerged on the other side of the field and began to taunt Lee, who had played before me and managed to make it to second base. I couldn't hear everything that was being tossed his way, but knowing Hunter and judging by the rigid way Lee held his features, it was nothing good. I'd stormed across the field to confront him, to tell him to fuck off and leave my friend alone, when one of his cronies, Mark DeLuca, reached out and grabbed one of Lee's dreads. I'd lost it then, and the next thing I knew, I was sitting on Hunter's chest, and pummeled away at every part of him I could reach. A few feet away, Mark held a hand to his head, blood dripping down his face and arm, and my bat discarded on the ground nearby. From behind, a set of hands pried me off of Hunter just as he grabbed a handful of my hair and ripped, but I didn't care. Now he would have to go around Harley knowing every boy in our class saw him get his ass beat by a girl. No one fucks with my friends. Especially Lee, Shaw, and Vail.

I avoided Hunter entirely as I moved back to my seat, which luckily, was a few rows away. Yet off to my right, I could still hear those two talking about me for the whole class to hear.

"She looks like she gives good head with those full, pouty lips-" the dark blond said, but I didn't recognize this creep at all.

"Mr. Fraser, that is quite enough-" Mr. Kennard tried to shut them up, but Hunter had cut him off.

"Hey Bryce, while she's sucking you off, I'll grab a handful of that purple hair to hold her in place while I fuck her from behind." In my peripheral vision, I saw Hunter craning around his friend to watch for my reaction. But I kept my face impassive and just opened my notebook to jot down the study notes Mr. Kennard had pre-written on the chalkboard for us to copy.

"Detention, Mr. Tremblay!" Our teacher practically shouted the words. His face was red as he glared at the boys. "After school every day this week." Hunter grumbled under his breath, but Mr. Kennard wasn't done, "Want to make that two?"

Finally, the class descended into silence and focused on the lecture on the Tragedy of Othello.

When the bell rang after English, I was already packing up my satchel with my books and up and out of my seat, having gotten Mr. Kennard to sign the form earlier when we were reviewing Act 1. I couldn't tell if Hunter recognized me from our childhood, but I wasn't going to stick around to find out. Even though I wanted to keep a low profile, as I wandered the halls, I kept glancing up at the boys who would pass me, briefly checking their faces for one of the particular three, but none seemed familiar to me.

The school day was split into four extra-long periods, with lunch breaking them up in the middle of the day. Next was P.E., then Home Ec. after lunch, and Math 30 at the end of the day. Phys. Ed took place in the school basement, and I headed down, finding the coach's office where three teachers had their desks set up. Seeing as I was new, my gym strip had to be ordered in, so I filled out a sheet with my size and was given an invoice to bring home to Keith.

My teacher, Mrs. Reeves, explained that P.E. was kind of old-fashioned here. Girls and boys were split into separate classes. There was the main gym, and beside it was the weight room. A glass wall separated us, so we could still see each other, yet not interact. I bit the inside of my cheek, holding back a laugh at the old-school concept, however, I was also feeling relieved at the same time. After wandering the halls this morning, and the sort of looks and catcalls I'd already gotten, I'd be lying if I said I wasn't at all nervous by the intense testosterone that was running through this school. The guys just seemed so much more... confident here. More sure of themselves. And the air around some screamed danger.

Mrs. Reeves, a pretty and much younger teacher than most of her colleagues, explained that we were in the middle of a gymnastics course, which would go on for another week after this one before we moved on to something else. My gym uniform would be delivered by the end of this week, so in the meantime, she told me I could use this period to study in her office. She left me there to teach her class, so I pulled out the small assignment from English on Othello, deciding to get it out of the way now so that if I was assigned any math homework tonight, I could focus on that instead, as math was the bane of my existence.

By the time the bell had rung for lunch, my anxiety, which had temporarily abated, came back full force. I could hear the thunder overhead of hundreds of footsteps from students who were gathering for their midday break. The thought of stepping into that cafeteria, being in the open for all eyes to see, made my palms clammy, and my heart hammered against my chest.

C'mon, Casey... you used to be tougher than this! It's just lunch. No one gives a shit about you. Don't be so narcissistic.

Packing up my bag, I ventured out, getting lost behind a

small crowd of girls that had just come out of the changing rooms, all of whom ignored me completely as they chattered away with each other, walking to lunch. I followed silently, hoping to use them as a shield in the cafeteria. Still, to my disappointment, they veered away down the eastern corridor, leaving me standing alone outside the double doors to where the loud chorus of voices reverberated through the steel that separated me from them.

I took a breath and pushed one of the doors open. Inside, the room had a long lineup of food selections that overlooked an arrangement of long tables. Most were filled, though a few others did have smaller groups and pairs of friends keeping to themselves. I could actually feel the shift in the room when I joined the lineup and grabbed a tray. I could hear whispers hissing around the room behind me as I checked over the food options. I immediately ruled out anything cooked directly from the kitchen. The smell coming from the warming pans was sour, and everything resembled weird coloured soup, despite the claims that it was meatballs, macaroni and cheese, and what I could only think was supposed to be some sort of fettuccine alfredo, but the noodles were swimming in a watery-looking white sauce. There were a bunch of foiled wrapped hot dogs, some pre-ordered sandwiches and bags of chips, cookies, apples, bananas, and a small selection of pop and drinks. I ended up grabbing a turkey sandwich, an apple, and a small carton of chocolate milk. I knew better than to eat a banana in public. In the past, I always made eye contact with the wrong person, and it got real awkward real fast.

I found a seat at the end of a long table, close to the far wall, where four other pairs of friends were eating together. I figured here in my little corner, I'd be ignored, and I could eat in peace.

Should have known better. From the moment I sat down

and pulled out my notebook to doodle on, a shadow from the other side of the table was casting a shadow over the page.

"So... you're the new princess of Harley?" a voice said, and when I peered up from where I'd been sitting alone in the cafeteria, I saw the same group of girls from this morning who had knocked me down as they stood right beside me. The girl at the front with the dyed red and purple hair had her arms crossed, and she was looking at me with pure disgust.

"Uh, hi." I tried to keep it civil and smiled at her as I held out my hand. "I'm Casey-"

"I know who you are," she practically spat at me and ignored my hand. "... you're the new girl... the one from The Hill, am I right? And you transferred from some preppy private school?"

I retracted my hand slowly and frowned slightly, feeling the animosity rolling off of her. I said nothing. How the hell did she figure out I was from The Hill? Around her bony frame, a slight movement caught my eye, and I quickly glanced over to see that Hunter, Bryce, and a group of terrifying-looking guys were watching this interaction go down. They had definitely mentioned to her about what happened in English.

"Well, watch your back, new girl," she sneered at me, and I held back a laugh, hardly believing that this was actually happening. "Miss Truffle slumming it in Harley. I give her... what do you think, ladies? A week before she moves back to where she came from, crying like the spoiled brat she is?" She let out a loud, shrill laugh that caught the attention of nearly everyone who was sitting within twenty feet of us. It was starting to feel a little like West Side Story. I was kind of worried she was about to start snapping her fingers in rhythm before challenging me to a rumble.

She leaned forward, palms on the table, and all traces of humour gone. "Any rich bitch who comes into my school and thinks she can look down on me needs a reality cheque." *And yet, you were the one looking down at me right now,* I thought to myself. "This school is ours," she gestured at the girls behind her. "And you don't belong here. If you do anything that pisses me off, I'll come after you. You insult me? You won't fucking get away with it, you understand? We'll make you disappear."

"Okayyyy," I said slowly, trying to follow. "How will I know if I'm doing something that you consider insulting or stepping on your toes?"

She smirked at me. "Don't worry, we'll always be around to remind you."

I glimpsed at the other girls. They were all pretty skinny, save for a few curvy ones in the back. Though it had been years since I last scrapped with someone, I had been hopeful that it would come back to me. However, taking on this group, especially on my own, would be the worst way to start my temporary life in Harley. I couldn't risk fucking it up, or else I wouldn't ever be able to leave here. "I'm sorry if I give the impression that I look down at you," I said, my eyes on the table. I felt a sense of anger awaken in my chest as I meekly apologized to this bitch. "I don't at all. I just want to go to class and graduate like the rest of you."

She cackled and shook her head. "Oh, honey." The way she said it made me want to slap her. "You *are* a long way from home, aren't you?"

"So… I guess you aren't part of the welcoming committee, hey?" I said before I could stop myself.

She raised an overly plucked brow at me. "Excuse me?"

"Nothing. Just, you don't exactly scream positive vibes." I shrugged, trying to appear relaxed, but I was definitely tense as hell. Nearly everyone in the cafeteria was watching us now.

She peeked over her shoulder at the other girls and laughed, "Are you serious? Who do you think you are?"

"Well, I *tried* to introduce myself, but you kind of cut me off. I'm Casey Cooper, Senior-"

She narrowed her dark blue eyes at me. "You've got some nerve starting this shit with me!"

I shook my head, now regretting my smart-mouth. "No, I haven't done anything. You're the one who approached me and started things off this way, so I just went along with it." I shrugged. "I don't have the energy to try to get someone like you to like me. If you don't want to bother making nice, then fine. I don't care."

Her friends teetered and whispered to each other.

I went on, "I have zero desire to..." I shook my head, trying to think of the right word, "... *usurp* your position in this school. I just want to go to class and be left alone."

She smiled at me, but it wasn't genuine in any way. It'd been malicious and twisted. She scanned me over one last time before she murmured, "Nice earrings." She walked away with her minions following after that.

I rolled my eyes, shook my head, and resumed my reading.

A huge shadow loomed over me before I could even get a paragraph in, and I slowly peered up into a familiar face. Fucking Hunter Tremblay. Seeing him standing now, I could make out how huge he'd become. He had always been taller and bigger than the other kids in our old neighborhood, but now his bulk had turned into muscle. He was dressed in a black long-sleeved shirt with a torn army jacket and relaxed, worn jeans. My eyes slid from him to the rest of his group, searching for another face I might have recognized, but they were all strangers. Even Mark DeLuca was absent.

"Casey," he said, his voice now deep and baritone. He smirked at me as his dark amber eyes moved up and down my body, "you've grown up."

I glared at him and sat up straighter. "Well, obviously, numbnuts. That's what typically happens as you age."

I thought he'd glower at me or come up with some sort of insult or sarcastic quip. Instead, he actually smiled as though he was enjoying this. "Still the same dirty mouth you had back then. Only..." he tilted his head to the side, "... now that I look at it, it's got me thinking other dirty thoughts..."

I rolled my eyes, knowing he was just trying to get a rise out of me, and returned my attention to my book. "Please. Like, I haven't heard that before. Go get some original material, and try again, maybe, never?"

Knockback the sass, Casey, I scolded myself. This sort of backtalk was just going to get me into trouble, but it was coming out of me like word vomit. My stubborn side won before I could stop and think.

Sure enough, one of his huge hands had come crashing down on the table in front of my tray, causing everything to rattle, and then hovered so close over me, it was suffocating. Especially when the smell of his body spray was overwhelming the space. I was so startled by the reaction that I looked up from my book, eyes wide as I watched him tilt his head to the side, a lock of his dark brown hair falling over his forehead, and he murmured, "You're a hot piece of ass, Case... who would have thought that a scrawny tomboy would become so fuckable?"

Honestly, the look he was giving me sent shivers up and down my spine. His dark eyes were empty, his expression humourless and intense.

"Can you back up a bit? I can see up your nose from this

angle," I blurted out but held my composure, praying he wouldn't see that he'd managed to intimidate the fuck out of me. We weren't kids anymore. Hunter had become a beast. If he wanted to hurt me now, he could. Easily.

His eyes tightened, and he did actually back away, but only a little. "Well, *princess*, you're going to have to align yourself to a crew sooner or later. No one survives Harley Institute as a loner."

I clenched my teeth at his words but kept my eyes on the page of my book.

"I suggest you decide quickly," he said, his tone soft and threatening all at once, and left back to his own table filled with huge, frightening-looking bastards. It didn't surprise me that Hunter ended up joining a group like that... a crew, as he said. A gang, most likely. I noticed that the "mean girl" who had been here right before Hunter, was draping herself over his shoulders, but he didn't seem to notice her. He simply murmured something to the other guys at the table until he finally had enough of her and shoved her back. She pouted, shooting me a nasty look as though it were my fault he rebuffed her, and went back to her skank squad.

Hah! I smirked to myself... *skank squad*. I was definitely going to keep that nickname. It was better than "Mean Girls." I shook my head and took a sip of my chocolate milk, and went back to my book.

Chapter six

Casey

"Fuck me, that ass!"

"Bet she rides like a fucking champion…"

"I'd give up masturbating forever just to see her naked for a minute."

These were the comments I heard as I walked past Hunter's table, and a few members of his group were still sitting at their table in the cafeteria. I flipped them off over my shoulder, ignoring them entirely as I headed to Home EC, which, luckily, was close to my locker.

The room is set up with several mini kitchens, an area with some very outdated sewing machines and various materials, and round workstations. As I step in, I'm immediately met with hostile glares from the other girls, and I can't help but feel disappointed. I guess it really was going to be like The Hill all over again.

I scanned the room as the girls hung out in their respective kitchens, all of them working in their little cliques. Our teacher hadn't arrived yet, so I took a minute to scan the other students, searching for someone that might hopefully extend an olive branch to me.

There was only one girl who hadn't looked up and glared daggers my way. In fact, she only glanced at me once with little to no interest, before returning to what she was doing. She was lounging on the kitchen counter in the back, a cook-book in her hands as she leaned against the wall, and there was no one else with her. Honestly, as I took her in, I could almost understand why.

She was dressed in black leather leggings, with a rocker t-shirt on... a band I didn't know, unfortunately, and a black leather jacket and wedge heel boots. She looked like she belonged on a motorcycle. But as I stared at her, I couldn't help but think how beautiful she was. Her hair was almost black at the roots, but the rest was dyed a cerulean blue. Her skin was pale, and her eyes were large and nearly matched her hair. She was tall and willowy, much like Nylah. She had an air of confidence around her that I couldn't help but instantly respect and admire. I walked over to her, ignoring the other girls, and headed to the back, deciding to take a chance and trust my instincts. As scary as she appeared, something about her told me she was a good person... maybe just misunderstood. It was stupid, I knew, but so far, she was the only one in this room who looks like she gives zero fucks about the new girl.

"Hey, mind if I join your kitchen group?" I asked her as I stopped by the edge of the counter. Slowly, her blue eyes slid up. For a moment, I felt like I'd made a horrible mistake talking to her, but I resisted the urge to step back. I smiled warmly at her and nodded my head to the side, indicating to the other girls, "The rest of the kitchens appear to be full."

The blue-haired girl leisurely took me in, studying me as her eyes scanned down and then up again. Her frightening expression changed then, and she came across as both amused *and* confused. She raised a dark brow to me, "So... you're the princess, hm?"

I closed my eyes for a moment, and I felt my shoulders sag. "Seriously? Is that really going to be my nickname here?" I thought only the leader of the Skank Squad and Hunter were calling me that. To hear her say it too, well, it pissed me off. I was the farthest thing from a princess.

She shrugged and chuckled, "There are worse names to be called."

She had a point. "I suppose that's true..." I grinned at her. "But I'm hoping the others will get more creative before the day is out." I glanced over at the rest of the girls who were watching me with pure loathing.

The blue-haired girl smirked, looking from them to me. "They're parasites. Sheep..." She shook her head and tossed the cookbook aside. "They'll probably try to make your life a living hell until they realize you aren't after the title of *Queen Bee*."

"And who currently owns that title?" I raised a brow in question.

She shrugged. "Depends on who you ask." She grinned, "If you talk to the student council and prep, they'll say Rebecca Thompson... top of the class, head of the Social Committee, and destined to leave Harley to do greater and better things." Her grin widened, "If you talk to the Jackals, they'll vouch for Celeste Wood," she grinned at me. "And I saw that she already *kindly* introduced herself to you at lunch."

So *that's* the name of that bitch. *Good to know*, I thought, as I filed her name away. "The Jackals?"

Just then, the bell rang, and an older plump woman with white hair came rushing in, clapping her hands, "Alright ladies! Get to your stations! I want to start the second half of the semester with something sweet! So pick a dessert dish and get going!" She hurried to the back where her desk sat and leaned over her old, worn computer to quickly type something.

I looked back to the blue-haired girl and held my hand out to her, "My name is Casey Cooper," I told her.

She smiled, her eyes twinkling, and she took my hand. I noticed that she had a tattoo on her inner wrist. It was black, but I didn't get a chance to see what it was. She released my hand, stood, and her jacket hid it from my view. "I'm Meredith Nadeau," she told me. "And you are welcome to help me bake some rocky road cookies."

I smirked, glad that at least *one* student in this school was giving me a chance. And rocky road cookies were my favourite. I tossed my books down, followed her to the cupboard where the pink aprons were hanging, and helped her gather ingredients from the pantry and fridge. Meredith opened the page to the recipe, and we stood side by side, prepping our dish.

"The *final* group..." she said suddenly, "... and whose opinion is the *only* one that matters, falls to Vendetta, and they don't have a Queen Bee. They're against stupid bullshit like that."

"Vendetta?"

She nodded. "Don't be fooled. The Jackals are a *gang*. Vendetta is a *crew*. Huge difference."

"What *is* the difference?"

She grinned at me. "Gang's get involved in illegal shit. They try to muscle their way into the school system, but it's Vendetta that works to keep it out. Think of them as body-guards. They look out for the best interest of the general populace and for Harley."

"They sound nice," I said absent-mindedly as I gathered some mixing bowls and whisks together.

She tossed her head back and burst out into laughter,

earning a hard look from our teacher. Meredith waggled her fingers at her before turning back to me. "Make no mistake, princess, Vendetta are tough as fuck. They've done plenty of crap to earn their place. They're the power stronghold in this school and in Harley. Plus, with their backing…" Her voice trailed off, and she bit her lip like she had said too much. Backing? Who could be backing a high school group? And why?

Oh hell, no, I want nothing to do with this shit, I think.

"The respect they have isn't just because of muscle… they're smart, and they're *careful*." She shakes her head and gives me a hard, warning look, "Whatever you do, don't cross them."

I raised my hands up before me. "Hey, I just want to graduate and then get the hell out of this city."

Meredith stared down at me, watching as I began mixing the dry ingredients. I kept my head bowed and continued what I'd been doing, wondering what her story was.

"Can I tell you something, princess?" she said after a minute, as I started to mix everything together.

"Um, sure?" I stop and look up at her, hearing the serious tone in her voice.

"If you want to survive in this school, you need to pick a side and fall in."

"What if I just want to keep my head down and stay out of all of it?" I asked as I started mixing the dry and wet ingredients together. "How do I know what side to pick?"

She shook her head. "Doesn't work that way. You're pretty, like a shiny new toy. There's already been talk about you being here."

I let out a long breath and stopped what I was doing, turning to her, "I grew up here in Harley."

Meredith's dark brows rose high on her forehead. I could tell she hadn't been expecting that. "No shit?"

"No shit." I went back to what I was doing.

"Huh... well shut me up!" she laughed, taking the dough from me and beginning to spoon out little scoops and spread them onto a pan just as the oven dinged that it was at temperature.

I watched as Meredith stuck the cookies into the oven and forced myself to turn away and start cleaning up, "So, there's the Jackals, Vendetta... anyone else I should know about?"

"Company, but they attend Harley Public... they're a bunch of criminal wannabes. They like to show up randomly and start fights and shit. Occasionally they get their hands on some firearms, shoot off some bullets, and get arrested. Dangerous and stupid. A lethal combination." Her eyes were shining a little as she told me this. I felt like she was enjoying telling me the ins and outs of Harley, catching me up to my past. "I guess you could say they are the big three... but of course, I'm sure you know about The Faceless, even from The Hill."

"The Faceless..." Yeah, I knew about them. Everyone in Ashland knew about them. Poor Mr. Bryant. Those fucking bastards kept him up most nights as he worked his ass off to try and get them locked behind bars, but the system was corrupt, with members from that organization planted in City Hall and the Police Force. "Yeah, I've heard of them, alright."

"Stay away from anyone wearing a Celtic Beasts cut," she said firmly, "they're tied into that crime group." I noticed how she was suddenly wary and even a little fearful at the mention of that MC.

"Are you a part of one of the high school groups?" I asked her.

She smiled. "Of course. Why do you think all of these girls steer clear of me?"

"Are they not involved in any of the main three?"

She shook her head. "These girls will sometimes show up at parties, used for quick fucks, but then they're kicked to the curb. They were deemed too pathetic to be brought in. They're called groupies."

"Is there no way I can just hide in the background?" I could feel a slight panic washing over me. "I mean, no offense, but I don't want to be a part of a gang. Can I not be a... a *normie?*" I scrunched up my nose, trying to think of a nickname for who I would rather be.

At this, Meredith actually threw her head back and laughed hard.

"What's so funny?" An annoying habit of mine was when I could hear someone genuinely laughing, I would automatically start laughing, too, even if I had no idea what had gotten them going. I started, and I internally cringed at myself. "What?" I asked.

Meredith wiped under her eyes and shook her head at me. "Oh, princess... you're too cute. They're going to fall all over you." She smirked just as our teacher flashed her another warning stare. "You aren't going to be brought in as a gang member, princess. Like I said, you look too much like an outsider, despite the fact you're from here. And no way would you end up as a groupie. No, if anything, you'll be made someone's girl."

"I'm not interested in dating," I said and moved over to one of the spare round tables as I waited for our cookies to bake. Meredith joined me, and we both pulled out our notebooks. "My life is a little too... *chaotic* right now to deal with all of this. I didn't come here to get involved with anyone or any drama. I just want to do my school work and survive senior year."

"Aren't we all?" she mused, twirling her pencil between her long, slender fingers. "Unfortunately, sometimes other things get in the way of our careful planning that we have no control over…" Her voice sounded sad all of a sudden, and I found myself only more intrigued by this girl. She lifted the corner of her mouth again. "Either way, this next week will be interesting for you. I'm sure you'll be approached by the groups. You just need to decide for yourself where you think you belong."

As much as I wanted to remain unknown here, unseen, it sounded like the choice wasn't up to me. If there were groups who were interested, they're going to make it known. My only hope was if I could bore them, turn them off, or make it clear I'm just another student who wanted to get through high school and not be a bother to anyone. If it came down to it, it sounded like Vendetta was the one to support. Of the three, they seemed to be less involved in the illegal crap I wanted to avoid. I wanted to ask Meredith who she was with, but I felt like we weren't there yet, socially. She clearly wanted me to decide for myself, and I appreciated that. She could very well nudge me into the direction of her own crowd, if she wanted. But I could tell she won't.

"Any advice?" I asked her, rewriting some of the notes I'd made in English.

"About life? Cuz I'm not the best person to come to," she said, sounding highly entertained but quickly sobered, getting all serious on me. "Know that Company won't be able to protect you, especially since they go to Public. They'll probably notice you at parties or school events, though. But steer clear of them. Like I said… they're dangerous and stupid." She instantly grew incredibly somber as she held my gaze, her blue eyes like stone sapphires. "The Jackals and Vendetta, however, whoever you pick between those two, you'll make an enemy of the other. The Jackals and the Beasts are tied. Vendetta… Well, they have their own supporters. They're just more discreet about it."

I wondered what she possibly meant by *supporters*? I doubt it was the Faceless, as the Beasts were tied with them, which meant so were the Jackals. Who else was around that could be working with Vendetta? I couldn't think of another group that had any sort of strength to challenge the other three.

"So, either gang or crew?" I raised a brow at her, deducing for myself that she must be part of Vendetta.

She grinned and nodded.

I pursed my lips, thinking over everything she said. "Thank you for filling me in." I didn't know what else to say. I didn't like that I apparently had to pick a side to survive here. Maybe I could be a silent supporter of one or the other? Honestly, the thought of joining Hunter and his goons made my stomach roll. And if they were a legit gang, like running drugs and shit, then I was staying the hell out of that business. But if I chose to support Vendetta, silently backing them like other students, maybe everyone else would leave me in peace? I just needed to figure out who was a part of it.

I glanced at Meredith, who had abandoned her notes and, to my surprise, had brought out some yarn and some spool and a half-finished project and went to work. Our teacher, who I found out was named Mrs. Adamson, because of my schedule, didn't come over and bother us at all, and stuck to the other girls, which only fueled my assumption that Meredith was a member, or at least, dating a member.

The timer went off, and she jumped up, put on some oven mitts, and pulled the cookies out while I found the cooling racks. I appreciated her honesty, and though some of her words were a little harsh, I couldn't understand the meaning behind them. I may be originally from Harley, but I got out for a time. I wasn't here when things started going seriously downhill. She knew I didn't want to be here. She also didn't seem put off that I lived in the northwest, and despite the nickname, she at least had the graciousness to forewarn me.

We split up our cookies between us and wrapped them in saran wrap. When she saw me pick up my black leather book bag, she smirked and shook her head. I knew what she was thinking… that I'm a typical private school girl, innocent and pure and with no idea of what was in store for me, despite the fact I explained I was from here. I've clearly forgotten a lot of shit.

"Keep your eyes open, princess," she said to me, seriously. "You seem nice, and it's not your fault you've been away so long that you've no idea how things are done here now."

I was surprisingly not offended by her bluntness. "Thank you for talking to me."

She smiled. "Make no mistake, honey… I may seem nice, but I'm as rough around the edges as the rest of them." The bell rang for the next period at that moment. She gave me a wink and a heads up, munching away on one of her cookies.

The last class of the day is Math 30, up on the third floor of the school. I hauled ass up the stairs, but the bell had already rung by the time I sprinted through the door.

My teacher, Mr. Fortin, scowled at me. "I don't like tardiness," he said curtly. "Take a seat, Miss Cooper," he said, either having already heard I'm the new kid or deduced so because I'm the last one into the room.

I glimpsed around and saw that there were only a few empty seats left, so I picked one lined up with the doorway near the back and hurried over. Unfortunately, all the girls in the room narrowed their eyes and turned away. I guess I won't be invited to any sleepovers anytime soon. Quickly getting out my text and notebook, I listened as Mr. Fortin started talking about Trigonometric Functions & Graphs. I kept my head bowed over the review sheet as another pair of footsteps entered the room.

Mr. Fortin sighed hard in frustration but didn't call out this student as he did me. Instead, he grumbled, and I heard the squeak of the marker as he wrote on the whiteboard. I kept my head down over my notebook, copying the notes he was making as the tardy student passed, taking the empty desk behind me. Moments later, there was a shuffling beneath my chair that has me jumping in alarm. Peeking down, I saw two legs extended out on the floor on either side of my seat, coming from behind me. Whoever the guy was, he apparently had never heard about boundaries and personal space. I scowled when his dirty shoe touched my bag, so I kicked his foot. Two kids on my right gasped when I did it, and I glanced at him. They were watching in horror as though what I'd just done was an act worthy of treason. I rolled my eyes and went back to copying down Mr. Fortin's lesson.

The guy behind me shoved my bag again, and I gritted my teeth and muttered, "Douche-Goof…"

I heard him chuckle and realized he heard me, but I didn't give a shit. He kicked my heel this time, and I swung my leg back and managed to clip his leg. He let out a grunt, and I smirked. Good. Now he could frig off and leave me alone so I could concentrate on the class. Just when I thought he was going to leave me alone, I felt his foot kick my bag so that it slid forward, and unable to stop myself, I let out an exasperated grumble.

"Miss Cooper? Is there something you wish to share with the rest of the class?"

The guy behind me finally stopped, most likely because the teacher's eyes were locked on us.

"No, Sir."

"Are you sure? I understand you are new here, and I don't know what kind of respect, or lack thereof, students from your *Academy* show their teachers, but at Harley Institute, I ask for no disruptions! Is that understood, Miss Cooper?"

"Yes, Sir." I was seething in my seat. I could hear some bitches across the room snigger, but I ignored them.

"Casey?" The guy behind me murmured, and I froze. *How the hell does he know my name?* But I was so pissed at him for getting me into trouble that I ignored him and hunched over my notes. I didn't need another strike with this a-hole teacher.

I felt a hand suddenly touching my shoulder, and I realized that this annoying prick behind me was trying to turn me around. I wrenched away, flipping him off over my shoulder and muttering just loud enough for him to hear, "Touch me again, and I'll cut off your fingers and sell them on the dark web so some psycho in Russia will use your prints to leave behind at a crime scene."

Whoever was behind me, he was utterly unfazed by my threat because he chuckled, a deeper, baritone sort of chuckle, yet didn't touch me again. I heard him move around for another few seconds, then the *beep-beep* of his cell phone as he typed something out. The guy was so annoying he didn't even mute his phone! Who did that? I decided that tomorrow, I was picking out a new seat.

The class was dead quiet, but I could sense the guy behind me moving a little closer instead of away. It was like I could *feel* him leaning over his desk to close the space between us, and for a horrible minute, I was thinking he was about to cut off my hair, or burn it, or something. I didn't want to draw attention from this douche-wad teacher, so I bowed over my notes, leaning farther away from him. I even slid my chair and desk forward ever so slightly to get a little extra space. The sound of my chair scraping across the tile was loud and sharp, and Mr. Fortin glared over his shoulder, searching for the culprit. When he couldn't pinpoint exactly where it had come from, he went back to writing down the lesson plan.

When he did, my chair slid back, and I realized this guy was pulling me close again! What in the ever-loving hell?! I'd been about to whip around to finally confront him, when the sound of running footsteps from the hall heading towards our door caught everyone's attention. I took the opportunity to give the jerkwad behind me a death glare and tell him off, but instead, my voice lodged in my throat.

I was gazing into a pair of black eyes, a face so handsome and familiar that I instantly recognized him. He was older now. All the childhood fullness of his face was gone and replaced with a sharp cut of his jaw. His black dreads were shoulder-length, his cheekbones high, and his skin a beautiful warm brown. His bottom lip was slightly fuller than his more defined top one, and his dark eyes were slightly upturned.

"Lee…" I whispered, feeling like I just got punched in the gut. Before I could say anything else, the door to the classroom burst open with a crash.

"Excuse me, you are *not* a part of this class this period!" Mr. Fortin's face had gone beat-red, but even I could hear the adjustment of his tone. How was it he didn't raise his voice, yet still was able to speak so sternly? He was afraid of this newcomer, and I stared back to the front, my mouth dropping as I stared at the man who had charged in here like the hounds of hell were chasing him.

Vail St. James.

I knew it was him immediately. He stood at the doorway, one hand holding the door open, the other leaning on the frame. He was panting as though he'd just ran here from the other side of the school and then some. His bronze-coloured hair was messily strewn about his head, looking effortlessly styled. His face had grown more square, with dark stubble covering his jaw, and the look in his bright hazel eyes as they locked right onto me sent a flurry of butterflies fluttering around in the pit of my stomach. But that feeling went away at the look of rage on his face. He was furious.

"Casey?" he snapped, his tone dripping with disbelief.

Hearing him say my name, his voice now so much deeper than when I last heard it, rolled over me like a shock to my system. In seconds, I was now in the presence of two people I'd cared about more than anyone in the world. All the old memories came flooding back to me, the bike rides, the ball games, the swims in the local pond, our sleepovers... all of it hit me at once, and for a moment, I felt like I was going to fall out of my chair. Two of the boys I'd once wanted, once had, were here.

"Mr. St. James-" Mr. Fortin snapped, but before he could finish, Vail marched down the aisle, scooped me up in his arms like I weighed no more than a kid, turned, and strode out of the room.

"Really now! That's eno... Mr. Knight! Where do you think you're-" Mr. Fortin's objections were cut off as we left the room and the door slammed shut behind us. I craned my neck around to peer over Vail's shoulder to see Lee following us close behind, my things tucked under his one arm, and his own bag hitched on one shoulder.

"Guys, I... stop! Put me down! What the hell-" I squirmed in his arms, but Vail didn't falter in the slightest. If anything, he hoisted me up, so I was pressed against his chest, our faces much too close. But he didn't look at me. He walked with purpose, knowing exactly where he was taking me, and with Lee shadowing us closely, I almost felt scared. I held onto Vail's black long sleeve shirt as he carried me down all the way to the main floor near the back of the school and into an empty classroom at the end of a quiet hallway. Were there even classes back here? It seemed so remote.

"You tell him?"

"I just said to meet us here," Lee replied, closing the door behind us as we entered and stood by it as if keeping watch. Neither turned on the overheads, so the only light in the room came from the four small, narrow prison-style windows on the far wall. Vail set me down, so I sat on the vacant teacher's desk, and stepped back, giving me a chance to look around.

It was obvious now why they brought me here. This classroom had clearly been turned into a junk room. Broken desks, chairs, and bookshelves were gathering dust in the back, with buckets of what I assumed were paint or cleaner products stacked in a corner. This desk was dusty and worn, the surface scratched to hell, with lewd cartoonish drawings etched all over. Nervously, I gazed at the two boys I had both wished and dreaded to see again.

Lee was still standing by the door, his arms crossed, and now I could see exactly how huge he'd become. He must have been close to six foot five or six, and his arms were thick with muscle. I felt like he could crack my head by simply placing it into his elbow and flexing. Though he was watching the door, his eyes would flicker across the room back to me often, like he was checking to make sure I didn't suddenly vanish on the spot or something.

And *Vail...*

A girl never forgets her first kiss, and he had been mine, the sneaky bastard. But I sort of fell in love with him when he did it. It was so… *Vail*. And then he crushed my heart and cut me out, and the other two followed suit. Seeing him now was absolutely soul-crushing, and my heart twisted painfully.

I remembered how much I needed them, how many times I called, messaged, and left voicemail after voicemail, begging them to call me back and how they never did. My brain slowly started to catch up to everything, the shock of seeing them again now wearing off. I felt that bubble of resentment I'd been holding onto all these years, now rising in my chest. Narrowing my eyes at the two boys and crossing my arms over my chest, I arched a brow at them. "You know, instead of carrying me all the way down here, the easiest thing would have been just to call me back six years ago," I snapped.

Lee's lip twitched like he was fighting a smile, while Vail's eyes tightened for just a moment, like he was in pain before his mask slipped back into place. He reached out for me, but I held up a hand, warning him to stay back.

"Careful, bruh, she threatened to sell my fingers on the dark web." Lee ran a hand over his face, and that smile he'd been fighting vanished completely, his composure back now.

"Did she now?" Vail didn't take his eyes off me, and like Hunter, his eyes moved up and down, taking me in, but it didn't creep me out like when Hunter did it. After all, I was doing the exact same thing. He was not as big as Lee; then again, no one is. But at around six foot two, he was still intimidating. It'd been obvious he worked out a little, and I felt the hard planes of his muscles beneath his shirt as he carried me.

Yep, no doubt about it. These two boys grew the fuck up, and *damn*. I was in trouble. Both were gorgeous in their own way, both standing with that confidence I'd always loved. That same familiarity was there, but it was different now. We were different. We were older, and God only knew how much we'd all changed. But a small part of my heart was aching for them, wishing that we could just go back to the way it was. I broke that hope a second later when I reminded myself that they had dropped me at the first opportune moment.

But why did they bring me here? Why were they not saying anything? And why was Vail now looking so pissed off? I'd been here less than a full day, and somehow I'd managed to offend him. Being back here in their presence was hitting me like a sledgehammer, but I held it together on the outside to look cool and collected, while inside, I was screaming. More seconds ticked by in awkward silence, and a little voice at the back of my head kept whispering, *Where's Shaw?*

"What the hell do you guys want?" I said finally, hoping I seemed braver than I felt. "Was there a reason you had to bring me to some storage room in the middle of class? And my legs aren't broken. I can walk, you know." I narrowed my eyes at Vail, whose face remained impassive. Damn it! He'd seriously perfected that mask, so I turned to Lee instead. "And *you*," I crossed one leg over the other. "Thanks for getting me into trouble on my first day. Math is already a nightmare for me. Throw in an ass-hat like Mr. Fortin, and I can kiss any hopes of sweet-talking myself into a passing grade goodbye."

Again, the corners of Lee's mouth twitched. Son of a... he was actually entertained by this!

"You two suddenly gone mute?" I looked back and forth between them, but when they remained silent, I decided I had enough and jumped down from the desk. "Fine. We're done here-"

Two sharp raps on the door, followed by two kicks, stopped me in my tracks. Lee immediately opened the door, like that had been some signal he'd been waiting for, and a third person entered, head down, hoodie pulled up, almost entirely hiding their face in shadow. But I knew instantly who it was.

"Why I give a fuck who "Princess" is, I don't-" he was muttering, his voice, which was once childlike and whispery, was now deep and raspy, as if he'd been screaming for hours on end. Shaw lifted his head, the light from the windows revealing his features to me, and my heart stilled.

Shaw was the smallest of the three, though, I wouldn't say six feet was short by any means. He was leaner than the other two, swimming in a black hoodie and jeans. His blond, floppy hair was very much the same, only a bit longer as it fell over his dark blue eyes. His skin was pale, his cheekbones high, and his face was masculine, features reminding me of a Viking. And his beautiful, pouty lips I'd always admired parted a bit as he stopped dead in his tracks at the sight of me.

"Casey..." he breathed, his voice catching in his throat as he whispered my name. He staggered for a moment, looking like he might fall over, but instead, he ran at me with surprising speed that had me crying out in surprise and retreating, only to be blocked by the damn desk.

The room erupted as Shaw grabbed me, and I found myself flying backward while both Lee and Vail began shouting and came at us. I could see their faces around Shaw's arm, and they appeared terrified, which only added to my own shock and fear.

"Sh-Shaw?" I cried, trying to pull away. *What the hell was he doing?*

But as quickly as it started, it all stopped. Lee and Vail froze, observing us, while Shaw crushed me to himself, his arms wrapped around me so tight that it almost forced the air out of my lungs. He buried his face into the crown of my head, his lungs expanding like he was breathing me in. He was hugging me. Shaw, who never liked to be touched by anybody, was holding me flush against his body and had turned me so that he was pressing me into a wall as if trying to shield me from everything else. He and I held hands as kids, yeah, however it had been only twice since I'd known him where he had allowed me to actually hug him. The first time was when I announced I was leaving, and the other was when I had left.

His breathing had begun to quicken, and the next thing I knew, his whole body seemed to shudder, and he sagged into me as though he was physically drained.

"Shaw? You ok, man?" Lee called over to us. Why did he sound so nervous? I tried to peer around Shaw again to see the others, but he had me completely immobile in his arms. For someone lacking in muscle like the other two, he was surprisingly strong. He didn't let me move an inch.

"Let her go," Vail snapped. His attitude was seriously getting on my nerves.

"No," Shaw's raspy voice broke again when he finally responded.

"You might hurt her-"

He practically snarled in response, "You promised!"

"I know I did, but we don't know anything yet."

I stood there, shaking in his arms, confused beyond belief, semi-terrified, and so overwhelmed that I had to fight back the tears. I reached up and lightly tapped his shoulder, his body twitching slightly at my light touch, and whispered, "Shaw?"

He pulled back just enough so he could look down at me. I could see how haunted he was just by staring into his deep blue eyes. He had dark shadows around them, and I knew then that he still suffered from the nightmares of his child-hood. *Fuck... goddamn it, Shaw.*

"Why did you shut me out?" I whispered to him.

Shaw's eyes tightened slightly at my words, and he vehe-mently shook his head, his hoodie still pulled up over his floppy blond hair.

"Why are you back here, Casey?" Vail asked suddenly, and I wanted nothing more than to march over to him and slap him across his face. The way he hurled those words out like he was genuinely disappointed to see me stabbed me right in my heart.

I gently reached down and retracted Shaw's hands from my body. At first, he refused to let go, but begrudgingly did at my gentle prodding. He stepped aside yet lingered close, much closer than the other two, watching me from beneath his dark hood. I faced Lee and Vail, reminding myself to hold my composure. I wasn't going to break down now, not with the way my old friends were glowering at me.

"I don't owe you any sort of explanation whatsoever. To *any* of you." I straightened and held Vail's glare. "If it helps, I'll ignore you, and you can go back to ignoring me. I just want to get through my final year in one piece."

"You shouldn't have come back, Casey," Vail said to me. "It's too fucking dangerous here."

"Yeah, so I've heard. Jackals and Vendetta, right? Gotta pick a side or some shit?" I scoffed and crossed my arms. "I'm not getting involved with any of that crap."

"It's not like you'd have a choice," Lee said, and I looked at him, brows raised.

"There's always a choice. I choose to keep my head down, graduate, and then I'll be gone." I glared back at their asshole leader. "Just like you wanted."

Vail rolled his eyes, his entire demeanor cold and distant as he moved away to sit on one of the old, abandoned desks. "Like Lee said, there's no choice, darling."

"Don't call me that," I told him, hating how it sounded coming from his mouth as he sneered at me. "Now, I answered your question, so are you going to return the favour?"

"Depends on what you're going to ask... *darling*."

I withered a little inside but chose to move ahead like I hadn't heard it, "Why did you guys shut me out?"

Silence followed, and I could feel the tension rising in the room, especially from Shaw, who stayed behind me. I looked around at them all, but the only one who would meet my eyes was Vail. So I held it in and fought back the tears, but I could feel myself on the brink of cracking.

"Why? I needed you guys. I thought we were best friends? But the moment I left, it was like none of it mattered. Did it?"

Behind me, I could sense Shaw moving closer, and I saw how Vail's hazel eyes flickered up over my shoulder to minutely shake his head, as though warning him off me. *What, am I diseased or something?*

"You know what?" I said after a minute of silence. "Fuck all of it. I guess that's what it was. Nothing. I don't know why you dragged my ass down here like this if you weren't going to talk-"

"Why are you back in Harley, Casey?" Vail asked again.

"I *told* you already… I had no choice."

"That's not an answer."

"And you didn't answer my question. So I guess we're at an impasse." I held my hands out at my sides before letting them fall, my frustration now getting the better of me. Punching something would feel really good right about now. "So here's the deal. I'm going back to class, and we'll walk by each other in the halls as if we don't know each other. Just like you want." I walked to the door, but stopped to grab my bag and the books Lee had discarded on the floor, casting a warning look at him. "You kick my shit again, and I really *will* take your fingers." I opened the door and slammed it shut behind me, but not before I heard him chuckle.

Chapter seven

Casey

WHEN I LEFT VAIL, Lee, and Shaw behind, there was almost no point in me returning to math class with it being so close to the end of the day, but I needed Mr. Fortin to sign that form so I could hand it in to the office. My emotions were all over the place after seeing them again, and I was reeling. I felt dizzy, disoriented. The blast from the past and the emotions that came with it were heavy on my heart.

You got this, Casey. Don't let anyone see you weak. Hold it together 'till you get home...

I braced myself as I paused outside the classroom, sensing that this teacher was *not* going to be happy to see me back in class after being carried out by two guys. Sure enough, the moment I walked in, he was ready, and after his withered old face reddened in anger, he told me off for disrupting his class, for the disrespect I'd shown him, and how I wasn't going to get away being an entitled brat here just because I was from The Hill.

By the time he finished, the bell had rung, and I could hear the other kids snickering as they gathered their stuff and stalked past me, one or two managing to clip my shoulder as they passed by. Left alone with him, Mr. Fortin continued to bitch me out for another minute before I awkwardly asked him to sign my form. I swear to God, this guy's face went so red, I half expected to see smoke coming out of his nostrils and ears. I was about to ask if he was okay when he snatched my form from me and read it over carefully, as if I had some ulterior motive planned. Like, what did he think I was getting him to sign? Rights to his RRSP or savings or something?

But once he noticed the other signatures from my other teachers, he grumbled something unintelligible under his breath, snatched a pen, and scribbled his name down, flicking the end so hard that it ripped the page the tiniest bit. Thrusting it back at me, he hissed, "Don't be late or interrupt my class again, Miss Cooper. Do you understand me?"

"Yes, sir." I nodded and took the form, rushing out of there as fast as I could.

I made my way back down to my locker in record time. Apparently, when the bell rang at the end of the day here, kids were eager to get the hell out. And why shouldn't they? This place felt like a prison. By the time I made it to the back hallway where my locker was, it was practically deserted, save for a few stragglers.

I fumbled with my lock, trying to remember the combination, when the sound of approaching footsteps informed me that I was no longer alone. I checked over my shoulder quickly and found myself surrounded by Celeste Wood and her Skank Squad.

"What?" I asked wearily, not in the mood. I lifted my hands up and let them drop to my sides, where they smacked against my thighs. "What have I done? I haven't seen you since lunch…surely I haven't managed to piss you off already?"

Celeste merely smirked at me and nodded. At once, several girls lunged, and I was smashed back into my locker. They stretched out my arms, holding them so that I couldn't push them away. Slowly, Celeste stepped forward. "I really do like those earrings…" she said. When she reached up to take them, I reacted. I braced back against the locker and kicked, getting her in the gut. No fucking way was this bitch taking these earrings from me. They were a gift from my mom. In hindsight, I obviously shouldn't have worn them to this school, but I hadn't even thought about it. I'd woken up and gotten dressed, forgetting that I had them in already. It wasn't until Celeste pointed them out at lunch that I realized my error and wished I hadn't worn them. But no, I wasn't going to get that chance.

"You fucking cunt!" Celeste screeched and slapped me hard across the face. It stung, but her hit was pretty weak. She gave me two more before she whipped her hands to my ears and yanked hard. I cried out, thinking she'd torn my lobes, but as luck would have it, the backs simply popped off and clattered to the floor, allowing the pearls to easily slide loose, which she pocketed.

The girls who had been restraining my arms shoved me down to the floor, adding a few good kicks to my side. I cringed and coiled up against my locker, trying to shield myself. But they were cowards, only landing a few before they scurried off, not wanting to get caught by security. As I laid there, hunched over, I couldn't help but think that the guards of this school were seriously inept. Several times I'd been confronted today, and none of these bastards were anywhere in sight.

I breathed in and out several times, wincing as I clutched my side. I didn't think they were broken, but they ached…

bruised probably. I pushed up off the ground, my eyes squeezed shut as I moved, and leaned against my locker, pressing my forehead to the cool metal. I wouldn't cry... not now... and sure as hell not in this place. I felt my earlobes, making sure they were still intact and sighed in relief when I found they were. If I didn't cry at my mother's funeral, I sure as hell wouldn't be crying over a pair of earrings. I opened my locker and grabbed my coat, ready to get the hell out of there. The hall was nearly empty; the few remaining students that had stood by and watched me get cornered were now peering at me curiously as I went on like nothing happened.

My nerves were shot by this point, so when I gathered my things and turned around, I nearly jumped out of my skin when I saw Vail standing nearby, leaning against the wall opposite, watching me with his arms crossed. His face was unreadable, dark, and he seemed like he was fighting back the urge to also have a go at me. I ignored the part of my brain that was admiring every part of his body and his gorgeous face and reminded myself of the abandonment, the exile, and now, the hostility.

"What?" I hissed at him.

"Want to call in a favour?" he mocked, the corner of his mouth lifting slightly.

I faced him, closing my eyes for just a moment, and licked my lips, tasting a bit of blood on my tongue. Huh, I must have cut it somehow in the scuffle. But when I looked at him again, his expression had changed, from his usual dark and calculating to one that now somehow managed to become even more frightening. Holy shit... this was *not* the Vail I once knew. This was someone else entirely.

Seeing this side of him threw me off, and I stumbled back, uncertain. But I managed to collect myself as I cleared my throat and met his steely glare. "I don't need any favours," I said firmly, not understanding what he meant by that.

"Sometimes, bad things just happen... and you can let it destroy you, or you can suck it up and move the fuck on." I slammed my locker shut and fixed him with a dark look of my own. "They were *just* earrings..." I said to him, and I turned and left, forcing myself not to look back.

When I got home, Keith was passed out drunk on the couch. I snuck past him up the stairs and hurried into my room, where I shut myself in. Only then did I release a long, weary sigh and collapse on my bed, completely spent. Today had been exhausting both emotionally and physically. Running around that school all day, feeling tense as hell as I braced for pushes and shoves, along with the blast from the past, had seriously done a number on me. I pulled my phone out of my bag and texted Nylah, checking in to see how practice went. She had been my only lifeline since I got here and my only real comfort. But also, I wanted to know if she'd seen that biker around. I was still freaked out to hear she thought it was the same guy. Something about it just sent shivers up my spine, and I found myself randomly thinking of her throughout the day, hoping she was being safe.

Downstairs, I could hear the television blaring while Keith snored away, and decided to keep myself busy until he left for his shift cabbing fares around the city of Ashland. So I sat at my desk, pulled out some homework, and tried to focus, yet I couldn't distract my mind no matter what I did. My eyes glazed over as they drifted to the side to stare out the window at the grey, darkening landscape. With the end of October approaching, daylight didn't last long anymore, and I often woke up in darkness and came home in it. It seemed to suit my current mood, at least.

I thought about what Meredith had told me... about the

gangs and how it was expected that I would need to pick a side. She made it seem like I wasn't going to get out of it, but I still fully intended on blending into the background. Hopefully, whatever attention I'd inadvertently caught would pass over time. If not, I'd make it known that I was a supporter of Vendetta. Hopefully, aligning with them, whoever they were, would be enough to survive till graduation.

Celeste was a whole other problem altogether. She didn't care that I hadn't picked a side yet. Her grudge against me seemed more based on the fact that I'd come from The Hill than anything else. Most likely, she felt intimidated and was striking first before I could step on her toes. It made the most sense. She had probably lived in rough areas her whole life, and this was how she kept her power on top. I had no intention of "taking her place" especially since that place seemed to be at Hunter's side, but I *was* determined to get my earrings back. Fucking bitch.

Then... there were the boys.

What the hell was I going to do?

Why was Vail so angry? Why was Lee so... silent? And Shaw... my God. My heart ached at the way he trembled when he held me, the way his voice broke, everything. Seeing the three of them again had affected me more than I thought it would. I didn't know what I was hoping for, but it hadn't been this reaction. The hostility, the confusion, and clear aversion... well, except Shaw. Lee was flirty at first, but he changed completely, going cold when he realized it was me. There were brief moments where his facade broke, but he quickly regained his composure and stood with Vail, who had been furious to see me again.

I was just going to have to ignore them. It made my heart hurt at the thought, but that was what they wanted or agreed to, at least, on their part. Why? I didn't know and most likely would never know. So I had to concentrate on myself and think about how the hell I was going to survive until graduation.

Head down, get my earrings back, and act like those three didn't exist.

The next day, I was a little more careful with what I picked to wear for school. Going to the Academy meant uniforms, so I never had to think about selecting an outfit unless I was going out with friends. But as I rummaged through my stuff, I realized how out of place I actually was. Mom had bought me all designer stuff, high-end, and even the plainest clothes screamed a high price tag. The simplest thing I could find was a pair of dark blue skinny jeans, a black, loosely fitted top that I tucked into the front, and dark heel wedges. I left my lilac hair down in its usual waves but wore no jewelry today. I wasn't making that mistake twice.

Despite what I told Vail by my locker yesterday, it *did* hurt that the earrings gifted to me from my mother were taken by a bitch like Celeste Wood. But I wouldn't allow my pain to show. It would only give the kids at this school something to feed off of. If they didn't know who I was and why I was suddenly a part of the student body, then they would have less ammo to throw my way.

I kept my makeup simple since I already had pink pouty lips and long, dark lashes, which I'd been told gave me a dreamy resting look, so I just put on some lip balm and liner with a touch of mascara. I had really hoped my choice of dress today would have helped me blend in better.

How wrong I was.

Not only did Celeste and her Skank Squad corner me again right at lunch, but this time they stole my small leather backpack. Luckily, my wallet was in my locker, as well as my phone, but all of my loose money and my student ID were in there, along with any pencils, pens, and my notebooks. To add insult to injury, the bitch was wearing my mom's pearl earrings today. The girls left me sitting on my ass on the hallway floor, and I wiped a tiny smear of blood off my lip with my wrist. Luckily, that seemed to be the only injury I obtained from their attack. Other students skirted around me as I picked up my textbooks and threw them into my locker. I grabbed Othello and my wallet, and trudged off to the cafeteria, keeping my head down as I bought the same lunch I had yesterday and sat in the corner again, minding my business.

But I could hear Celeste sitting with Hunter and his crew, laughing loudly and tucking her hair behind her ears as she showed off her new bling. I silently seethed, but I didn't let it show on my face. I bent over my book, tucking a wavy strand of hair out of my face, and quietly ate my food.

While I ate, I kept scoping out the cafeteria, taking in as much as I could. Any information would be key to my survival here. The general school population was made up of jocks, nerds, band geeks, and all those in-between. I'd also noticed there were groups of girls that seemed to be groupies, who wandered between the tables of harder-looking kids who must be part of smaller crews and gangs, throwing themselves at the guys, hoping for attention of some sort. Some of the girls got it, a guy wrapping an arm around their waists, and they would pull her in. They would giggle and might even sit on their laps or get a kiss, but then she would be sent on her way. They weren't members. The girls who were, were then treated differently... with more respect, at least. Meredith was one of them.

I saw her sitting with a group of scary-looking guys, and she was one of the few girls. But when she spoke to them, they listened. She didn't have to flirt or offer herself for their esteem or protection. I could only assume that these were members of Vendetta, as I had kind of put together she was one of them. She glanced my way, catching me in my observation, smiled, and gave me a friendly wave which I returned before I went back to reading my book.

"Hey there, princess." I peered up to see a brown-haired, scary-looking bastard standing beside my table. When I caught his eye, though, his expression changed, and he gave me a small smile. At least when he did that, it helped eliminate the coldness I initially felt coming off of him. But, God damn, I hated that nickname.

"My name is Casey," I said and held out my hand. He took it, the corner of his mouth rising even more at my polite but probably odd gesture. I couldn't help it. It was instilled in me to introduce myself this way, thanks to the Academy. But I think this guy liked it.

"Casey." He released my hand and leaned against the edge of the table. He'd just come from that group of jocks, the ones who wear the school's black and red letterman jackets, with the wolves on the backs. "I'm Peter," he informed me. "Senior."

"Likewise," I told him, wondering what kind of bullshit he could possibly send my way. So far, the only one who had been remotely friendly toward me was Meredith. The odds were stacked against me.

"So you're on the cusp of escaping this place like me, eh?"

"Can't come soon enough." I crinkled my nose as I thought about how much longer we had to go. June just seemed so far away.

He laughed a little, but it seemed genuine. Maybe he wasn't putting on an act? "You'll get out of here soon enough," he told me. "So I hear that Celeste Wood has taken it upon herself to welcome you to Harley."

He said it like a statement, not a question. I withered a

little, hating that this appeared to be the talk of the school. "She has." *Just shrug it off. Shrug it off...* "I'm honoured, actually. The fact she even bothers exerting any sort of effort on me is shocking. Didn't think I'd be so worth her time, but what can you do?"

Peter's brown eyes seemed to dance a little at my statement, and he laughed again. "She's a typical jealous, spoiled, conniving little bitch," he told me, "and she's threatened... plain and simple."

"Well, I've figured that out for myself."

"I could help you out, you know..." he informed me, lowering his voice.

"What do you mean?" Instantly, I tensed up.

"I can offer you protection."

I stared up at him, praying that he wasn't implying what I thought he was. "Meaning...?"

"I'll make sure no one fucks with you. And she won't if..." His voice trailed off, and I caught the suggestive undertone.

I held back the urge to gag. *Was he seriously going to say what I thought he was?*

"Everything comes at a price, princess," he said at last, biting down on his bottom lip, and I felt myself die a little inside. At his mention of a price, I instantly wanted to curl in on myself. It seemed that was the only way girls could pay for anything around here.

"I see..." I said slowly while I took a long sip of my chocolate milk. "Well, thanks, but no thanks. Not interested, and I can promise you that I never will be."

"Well, you should think about it. Seems like Hunter has his eye on you." He glared over to where the Jackals were gathered, and sure enough, Hunter's amber eyes were on Peter and me in a freaky scowl that made me shiver. "He's not worth your time. Neither is Company." I noted that he hadn't mentioned Vendetta.

Honestly, what could I say? I didn't know enough about these groups to be having an opinion. If I could have it my way, I'd rather just be left alone by everyone. Day two, and I'd already been approached by two groups, possibly three if I counted Meredith as part of one. Then there was the 'favour' comment from Vail yesterday. However, I'm going to assume that was some bullshit, smartass remark he was making in response to seeing me get my ass kicked by a bunch of girls. If he was part of one of these gangs, which one would he fall under? I hadn't seen him at any of the tables at lunch.

"Thanks for the heads up," I told Peter, a hint of sarcasm in my tone, but he missed it completely.

"No problem, Princess." He gave me a flirty wink and headed off to where the rest of the jocks were sitting. They all leaned in close to him when he returned and spoke softly amongst themselves.

I looked around and noticed that our conversation hadn't gone unnoticed. Hunter, Bryce, Celeste, and other guys watched me with narrowed eyes from the Jackals' table. *Great, what did I do now?* And at Meredith's table, I saw a few of the guys sitting there had also been watching, too. My appetite vanished, and I gathered up the rest of my food and tossed it, leaving the cafeteria as quickly as I possibly could.

"How are you doing, Chickadee?" Meredith sang a song under her breath as she skipped into Home Ec. and found me already browsing through the recipe book for something to make today.

"I'm fine," I furrowed my brow at her, wondering why she was so chipper.

"Just fine?" Her eyes flicked to my empty lobes and made a tsk-tsk sound. "Not what I heard. Glad they aren't ripped."

For the love of...

"Is there anyone in this school *not* talking about me?" I grumbled between my teeth.

"Gossip has been slow since those girls disappeared," she said, her voice tightening.

"*What?*" I asked, my eyes going wide and mouth dropping. "Girls have disappeared?"

Meredith nodded, appearing as troubled as I felt. "It happens a lot here, especially lately..." Her voice trailed off for a second before she turned and picked up a frilly pink apron from the hook on the wall and tied it on, contrasting sharply against her leather tights and a dark, graphic tee and blue hair. "Anyways, with that bitch-cunt after you, it's been spreading like TMZ."

"Super," I mumbled, my mind still whirling with the way she seemed so accepting of the girls' disappearance, thinking that me being bullied trumped that news made me sick. The kids here were as bad as the Academy. I guess no matter where you went, gossip was still gossip.

Meredith poked my side, catching my attention, and offered a small, mischievous smile. "Stop pouting. No one here really likes Celeste, anyways. At least, the people who matter don't. She's used, old news, but she clings on hard..." Her smile disappeared. "She's a Jackal Whore. She's not even a real member of their club. She thinks she has respect because she's Hunter's go-to fuck, but that's all she is. The moment he decides she's done, that's it for her."

For a moment, I felt kind of bad for Celeste. She was being used until deemed worthless and would eventually be spat out like old gum. It painted a dreary picture.

"You need to pick a group to side with, Chicky-Poo. It's the best way to keep safe here," Meredith reached over and stopped me from turning the page. "I'm craving brownies, and they're Haldon's favourite." She turned away to grab supplies before I could even ask who that was. But I shrugged and went along with her choice. I enjoyed brownies, anyway.

"I'll be a silent supporter, but I really don't want to get involved in... whatever the fuck it is that they do," I said without thinking. *Shit, Casey... you're talking to someone who is most likely a member of one of these crews.* But Meredith just laughed and shook her head, not looking the slightest bit insulted.

"Don't worry, you wouldn't be invited to become a member." She chuckled as she brought over a bag of flour, baking soda, and sugar. I followed with some eggs and butter.

"Well, I don't want to be a groupie, or whatever, either," I muttered as I gripped a mixing bowl. "If I have to pick a side, I will."

"I know, Cutie-Patootie. You *just want to be left alone...*" She was quoting me from yesterday. "But tough luck, Buttercup," she went on, managing to fit two new nicknames. "You don't get a choice in Harley. The best you can do is take the better of the shitty options presented to you and hold the fuck on for dear life."

"Is that what you did?" I asked before I could stop myself. When her smile dropped and she looked down at me, I felt my face go red with embarrassment. "I'm so sorry, I didn't mean it like-"

"It's alright." She lowered her head, giving me a small smile, but it didn't reach her eyes. If anything, she seemed sad. "I think most of us here have gone through something, and we had to find refuge somewhere. I found mine with my crew." She bit on her thumbnail. Her words only confirmed my suspicions of where her allegiance laid. "They've saved my ass countless times..." When she faced me again, she added, "If you're alone, your chances of disappearing like those other girls increases. Find a group, stick to them. Safety in numbers."

I didn't want to pry, so I didn't bother asking what she meant by that. It felt too personal, and if she wanted to talk about it, I figured she would have kept talking, but she didn't. So I dropped it, and we focused on our task at hand.

By the end of class, we'd made some fresh brownies, separated them, and I walked off to my final class, which just happened to be English with the two asshole Jackals I disliked so much. I walked into class, keeping my head down, and took my seat.

"Hey, Princess." Hunter made a flicking motion with his tongue, and I openly gagged.

"What's the matter, bitch? Too good to roll around with East End filth, hey?" Bryce practically spat at me. I noticed that one boy, the one with a beautiful tanned complexion and long black hair that fell nearly halfway down his back, was watching our interaction closely, his black eyes full of disgust when his intense gaze slid over to the guys.

"No, I'm just not interested in desperate assholes..." I murmured as Mr. Kennard came strolling into the room.

"What the fuck did you just say?" Bryce hissed at me and I could feel the hairs on my arms rise. *Goddamn word vomit...* I got carried away again and let it slip, and now, my big mouth was going to get me into trouble again. But before I could say anything, the bell rang to signal the beginning of class, and a discussion had started about the progression of Othello. However, the entire time, Hunter and Bryce were glaring at me, and I knew that I'd need to make a quick escape out of here as soon as the bell rang. I was tense in my seat the entire period, hovering on the edge of my chair. In my peripheral, I saw the long, dark-haired boy was still watching, looking back and forth between me and the two assholes. But I didn't look over. I remained focused on my notes and kept my fists clenched on my lap.

Finally, when the bell rang, I leapt out of my chair and booked it.

I got lost in the crowded hallways as students hurried out, desperate to leave school behind for another day. I glanced back over my shoulder to see Hunter and Bryce in hot pursuit, but I was small, and I could easily let myself get lost in the swarm of people. I scurried to my locker and grabbed my bag and coat, and slammed it shut, ready to run down the hall to freedom. But as I passed the stairwell, a hand shot out and roughly ripped me away from the crowd. I inhaled a huge breath, about to yell for help, but a huge, meaty hand slapped over my mouth, and I was hauled up the stairs like I'd been as light as a feather. The sense of fear was prickling all over my skin when I saw Bryce amongst the four guys who were herding me back up the stairs. Students made a wide berth for us and avoided eye contact. I kicked and shouted against the hand, muffling my scream, but it was of no use. I was pulled into a small alcove halfway up to the second floor and held there as the guys surrounded me, hiding me from the view of any passing students. I was terrified and shaking. I had no doubts that the one holding me was Hunter.

"That smart mouth of yours is already getting you into trouble, Princess," Hunter murmured in my ear. I shuddered and tried to shake my head, but he laughed lightly. "I can think of better ways to put those luscious lips of yours to use…"

I struggled again, but he lifted me up off the ground, crushing me against the wall of the brick alcove.

"I've always loved your snarky attitude." His voice was

husky, and his eyes stared straight into mine in a way that frightened me.

"Super," I said to him. "Now, do you mind backing up a step? You're invading my bubble. I have boundary issues."

He ignored me and instead, leaned in closer and muttered, "Didn't use to."

"Let. Go. Of. Me," I hissed at him.

"What are you going to do, little Cooper? Going to kick my ass? This isn't primary school," he chuckled. With his free hand, he reached up and tucked a lock of my hair behind my ear. "It's not so easy now." I shrank away from him, but I really had nowhere to go. His buddies had all turned, facing away, their bodies shielding us from anyone who might be loitering behind to talk with their friends before heading home.

"*Not* interested-"

"You're not giving me a chance, Princess. You're still stuck in elementary when all we did was fight. I'm over fighting with you…" His hazel eyes roved down over my body, and I recognized the gleam in them.

"I want *nothing* to do with you, and whatever the fuck it is, your group of fucktards are up to. I just want to get through this year in one piece."

He pressed his lips tightly together, and the hand on my waist clenched a bit. "My *fucktards* are my fucking family. We look out for each other."

"And what about the petty crimes? Or is it worse than that? What kind of shit have you gotten involved in, Hunter?"

"We do what we have to do to survive here, Casey," he growled.

I glared at him, trying to understand what he was thinking. It'd been just for the briefest of moments that I saw it… a flash of pain. I thought about what I had said… petty crimes and what other shit he could have gotten into… his group being his family, and his comment about survival. For a moment, I felt a tug at my heart. I leaned forward just a little bit, and his eyes widened slightly, surprised by the move. But I forced myself to soften a bit for him.

"What about Mark?" I asked him gently.

There it was. I saw the way he broke just a bit at the mention of Mark DeLuca, the boy he'd run around with when we were kids. I hadn't seen him anywhere in this school, and certainly nowhere near Hunter. The look on his face only confirmed my suspicion. Mark was gone. "I'm sorry," I whispered.

The corners of his eyes twitched ever so slightly. His nostrils flared, but then, his grip on me loosened just a bit, and he nodded stiffly. I slowly stepped to the side, glad that he let me, but before I could walk away, he grasped my hand again. The look he gave me was unsettling, the cocky smirk he always had on his face was gone, and I realized I was seeing the *real* Hunter that he had been buried underneath all his bullshit.

"I've liked you for a long time," he said, holding my hand tightly. He tugged gently, urging me closer. I ended up standing right back where I had been, Hunter standing much too close, pressing an arm to the wall over my head. "I've wanted you for a long time, but you were always with those three. You always picked them." I saw a flicker of animosity in his eyes. "They never let anyone near you. And I wanted you so badly. Seeing you now," he exhaled shakily, "it's worse."

"Hunter-" I said in warning, shaking when his other hand released my wrist and began to slide up my side, skimming over the curve of my breast. I slapped his hand away, but the action only seemed to make him more determined to try and change my mind.

He gripped the small of my waist and pressed his hips to

mine. "I want you." He leaned in and ran his tongue up the side of my neck. I squealed and tried to pull away, but it only made him more grabby and aggressive.

"Stop it, let go!" I tried to push back against his chest, but he didn't budge.

"I've always wanted you, Casey." He licked his bottom lip. "I knew you'd grow into a-"

When he slid his hand down my stomach to grope me over my jeans, I reacted. I swung my leg and managed to kick him in his shin.

"Fucking hell!" He slapped me hard across the cheek, and my head snapped sideways. Before I could do much else, he reached out then and snatched my upper arm, hard. I cried out and tried to yank it out of his grip, but he held on tight.

"What are you doing?" I shouted at him. "Let me go!" Despite the slap he'd given me, I still had it in me to fight back. I twisted away, attempting to flee the alcove, but his hands, which were still wrapped around my arm, tightened, wrenching my skin in his hold, and I yelped out in pain. His friends closed in, sealing off any sign of an exit, and I knew I was close to pissing myself when they all turned and leered at me. "No! No, please... d-don't! Let me go!"

Bryce lunged then and grabbed my legs while Hunter lifted me up by my arms. They both managed to hold on while I did my best to kick and flail, hoping to get them to lose their hold. I even shouted and tossed my head back, hoping to reverse head-butt Hunter, but nothing I did helped. Laughing, they carried me up the last of the stairs to the second floor's main hallway and hauled me across the hall to where a door was ajar to a classroom. Through the skinny window of the door, I could see that the lights were out, and my stomach rolled when I realized they were going to lock me in there with them. I struggled more, trying to pull free from his grip, but my fight was nothing to this prick. His friends joined in his laughter as they followed, all eager to get going.

"Stop!" I cried, "Please, stop! Let me go!" I twisted in such a way that Bryce lost his grip, and my feet clattered to the floor. I flailed as hard as I could, and Hunter's hold loosened.

"Shut up!" he hissed and tried to move in for a better grasp so he could force me into that room with him and his buddies. My hands reached out and seized the edge of the doorframe, and I clung on for dear life. I could feel my grip slipping, so I made one last effort to save myself... I screamed.

Hunter ripped me away from the doorframe and slammed a sweaty palm over my mouth, cursing loudly in my ear as he dragged me into the dark, vacant room, his friends filing in after. I was easily hauled over to the empty teacher's desk, Bryce moving ahead to sweep the papers, pencils, and pens to the floor to make space, and my heart nearly stopped. I'm going to get gang-raped...

I managed to open my mouth just enough that I could bite into Hunter's palm. My teeth clamped down so hard that I tasted blood, and he yelled out, trying to pull his hand away, but I held on.

"Fuck! Get her off, get her off!" he shouted, releasing me as I'd hoped.

The moment he did, I took off, sprinting towards the door, ducking under arms and weaving around the others who were caught off-guard. I was at the door, ready to tear down the hallway, but an arm gripped me around my middle and hauled me back. I kicked my legs and clawed at his arm with my nails, and I heard Bryce's voice cussing me out, but he didn't let go. He used his body to hold me against the wall, one hand pinned both of my own over my head, and he glared into my face, panting heavily from the struggle.

I could still taste Hunter's blood in my mouth, some of it

dribbling down my chin, as I spit it into Bryce's face, nailing him right beneath his left eye. The bastard barely flinched but reached up with his spare hand and wiped it away. From behind him, Hunter was seething, holding his hand tight as he continued to curse me. I was about to scream again, but Bryce brought up his spit-covered, bloody hand and pressed it over my mouth, silencing me before I could call for help one last time. I tried to break free from his hold, to push him away, but his body was like a stone as it pressed against me, and I was horrified when I felt him grow hard as I struggled. The fucker was getting off on this!

But the more I struggled, the more tired I became, and when I saw one of their cronies move to shut the door, I felt a wave of hopelessness wash over me. This was seriously going to happen.

The door was several inches from shutting when an enormous figure barreled into it, smashing it right back into the asswipe, closing it, sending him flying—next thing I knew, Lee stepped into the room with Vail and Shaw right behind him. Vail reached over and flicked the lights on, illuminating the space and revealing the members of the Jackals to them.

Lee's eyes took in the five figures before him, and despite being outnumbered, he smiled... a slow, creeping smile that made him look terrifying, nothing like the Lee I remembered. To my surprise, despite having more members on their side, two guys backed up close to Hunter, looking nervous. Bryce, however, didn't move a muscle at the sight of Lee, and remained where he was, pressing me into the wall. It wasn't until Shaw stepped around his friend that I felt his body jolt slightly. Shaw was hidden beneath his bulky sweater, which was what made Bryce so uneasy.

Shaw's deep blue, shadowed eyes lock onto me, taking in the sight of my hands pinned above my head, my mouth covered by Bryce's blood and spit smeared hand, and how his body is pressed up against mine, and takes a step forward, stopping only when Lee swings an arm out to halt him in his tracks. However, at his movement, Bryce flew into action, swinging around and bringing me with him so that my back was pressed to his front, like a shield, while he moved back to Hunter and the others. He pulled his hand from my mouth and held my throat instead, his arm wrapped over my stomach to keep me in place, and hissed in my ear. "You make a sound, and I'll strangle you. You try to run, and I'll strangle you. You try to fight back? I'll fucking break your neck."

I could feel the smear of blood on my chin, and I looked to the three standing on the other side of the room. Shaw was still watching Bryce and me while Lee was scoping out the others, though his gaze kept flickering to me every few seconds. I thought of how his sheer size was intimidating enough without his menacing glower.

Vail stepped forward then, but his eyes were focused entirely on Hunter, and from here, I could sense the loathing radiating from him as he centered himself before the other two.

"What the fuck are you doing, Tremblay?" he said slowly, his voice so calm that it came off more chilling than if he'd shouted.

Hunter straightened and held out his hand for the guys to see. "Little bitch bit me. Just teaching her a lesson is all."

Vail smirked at the sight of my bite mark. "Let a little girl beat you up again, hey?"

When he said little girl, I couldn't help but scowl at him, despite my predicament. *Little girl, he said. Fuck you, Vail!* But I held it together when Bryce's hold around my throat tightened ever so slightly, reminding me of his warning.

"Look, we're having a private conversation. You guys

could leave and mind your own fucking business," Hunter seethed at him.

Vail's gaze scanned the others, briefly noting how Bryce was restricting me, before facing off with his old adversary again. "A conversation, you say? Doesn't look like it."

"Doesn't matter what it looks like. It doesn't concern you."

"See, that's where I disagree." He took a step forward, and to my surprise, all of the Jackals stepped back. Out of the three, they were the most scared of *Vail*? Really? I glanced at the others in disbelief, and sure enough, they gave the impression they were nervous as fuck. Even Hunter was fidgeting where he stood, his weight shifting back and forth, and his eyes were moving quickly to the door and back as though trying to discern if he could make a break for it and make it past Lee and Shaw. "I think it's pretty fucking clear that Casey wants to leave. Isn't that right, darling?" His hands clenched at his sides, and his voice dropped, a dark edge lacing each word, causing another wave of uncertainty to run through the Jackals. Even Bryce's grip on my throat loosens a bit, his hand sliding down to seize my shoulder instead.

"Yeah, I'd appreciate it if I could leave," I shouted, making sure that every damn person in this room heard me.

Silence followed this, and I swore to God, I was practically choking on the testosterone in this room. Vail looked at Bryce and nodded his head. "You heard her. Let go. *Now!*"

The bastard hesitated for a second, but released me with a slight push. I stumbled forward and was immediately pulled into Lee's thick arms. He spun me away from the others and walked me out of the room, leaving Shaw and Vail behind, outnumbered.

"What about-"

"They'll be fine," he murmured in his deep baritone. He guided me down the hall to the nearest washroom, which just so happened to be for guys, and pulled me in. Next thing I knew, he'd lifted me off the ground and set me on the counter, then grabbed several paper towels, wet them in the sink, and turned to me. He held them up, his black brows raised as though asking for permission, and I nodded. Carefully, he took my chin between his fingers to hold me in place, and gently wiped away the blood and spit.

"How did you guys know?" I asked him softly, feeling an ache in my throat from screaming.

"Midnight," he rumbled, slightly turning my head to the side to inspect the red mark on my face from Hunter's slap.

"Midnight?"

"He's in your English class. Saw them follow you out..."

I recalled the guy with the long black hair and how he was observing our interaction. "His name is Midnight?" I asked.

"He's Metis. It's his preferred name. But he was born Haldon Cadot."

Haldon... Meredith mentioned him in Home Ec.

"He's... a friend?"

"He's part of our crew, yes."

Crew... which meant Lee and the other two must be part of Vendetta. Which meant if they were, and Haldon was, then I was right about Meredith, too. I waited quietly, as he cleaned up my face; his touches were slow and gentle. Lee always had a comforting way about him that made me feel safe. He had been like my giant teddy bear. But now, he was ferocious and had a frightening edge to him that I hadn't seen before. At the same time, I wasn't as nervous about Lee as I was about Shaw or Vail.

He finished, tossed the paper towel into the overflowing trash, and pulled his phone out to send a text before pocketing it again. When he faced me, he rested his hands on either side of my thighs on the counter and lowered his head so we were eye to eye. "They do anything else to you?" he asked. I could hear the threatening undertone, and I knew that blood would spill if I said they had.

"They didn't get a chance to get that far," I whispered, my voice breaking from the sting in my throat. Those assholes should be fucking thankful that it hadn't. I could see it on Lee's face. He would turn right around and head back into that classroom. "So much for me keeping a low profile, hey?" I laughed lightly and coughed at the sting in my throat, my attempt at making a little joke at the situation falling flat.

"In Harley, it doesn't matter what *you* want. That's not how it works here," he said to me, his dark eyes moving over my face repeatedly, almost like he was noting the changes in my features now that I was older, committing them to memory. "Here, it's about making the best of a shitty situation and holding on until an opportunity presents itself that you can escape. The world doesn't give a shit about what we want, and neither does anyone else. They'd sooner watch us burn than help pull us from the ashes of this shithole."

"Who will?"

"*Everyone* else." He lowered his head and sighed heavily, as though he had the weight of the world on his shoulders. "Why the fuck did you come back here, Casey?"

Because it was Lee, because he'd always been so good, so sweet, I told him. "Mom died." The words were heavy on my tongue, and I felt a weight sitting on my chest when I said them.

He stilled, and I saw how the muscles in his arms flexed again and again, like he'd been trying to hold his composure, but was failing. "What happened?" he asked me, his voice breaking a little.

"Car accident. She and my stepdad were both killed."

He nodded, still not looking at me as he was digesting this information. "And now?"

"I have to live with my dad."

"Fuck!" he snapped and straightened. I could see how his eyes shone, almost like he'd been holding back tears, and for a moment, neither of us spoke until he reached out and wrapped his huge, muscled arms around me. He embraced me into his hard, warm chest, and I melted into him. Lee always did give the best hugs. "I'm so sorry, babe," he whispered over my head. I held on to him, pressing my cheek over his heart, the steady thump-thump of it comforting. I could feel myself breaking a little when I realized how much I needed this comfort, to be held and consoled. Nylah had been there countless times for me, but to have someone like Lee holding me was entirely different. I felt like I *could* show my vulnerability to him and allow him to take care of me. So I allowed him to comfort me, clinging to him while he rocked us slightly side to side.

The door to the bathroom burst open, and I could hear Shaw and Vail arguing over something. Lee didn't let me go, so I couldn't see what was happening.

"-should have let me cut his lips off!" Shaw was snarling.

A scuffle followed this and Vail's heavy panting, "It didn't need to go that far. Just calm the fuck down and think about it-"

"No! That dirty motherfucker had his hands on her, his mouth! I want to fucking gut him!" Shaw spat, and I shivered, believing he meant every word of it.

"Not now. The others didn't know where we were, and we had no idea what they were packing. If we are going to throw the first punch, I want to make damned sure we have our guys around to back us up."

Their little tussle ended abruptly, silence following, until Shaw rasped, "What the fuck is going on here?"

Lee pulled back slightly, and I could see the other two standing there near the door, watching us curiously. Lee glanced down at me, and I shook my head ever so slightly at him, begging him with my eyes not to say anything about Mom. With the way Vail had been all Captain Asshole on me, I wasn't exactly feeling comfortable opening up about something so personal and devastating to him.

"Just comforting her. Fucking pricks didn't get far enough, but look." He turned my face, angling it upwards and to the side, so they could see my reddened cheek and what I can only assume was bruising that had been forming on my throat from Bryce.

Shaw immediately lost his shit again, and Vail had to physically restrain him. But even with their size difference and Vail being the bigger man, I could see the struggle. Shaw was much stronger than he looked, and he managed to shove his friend off twice. Vail finally pulled Shaw in, hugging his friend tight, and whispered in his ear so that only he could hear. Shaw immediately clammed up at the touch, and I could see his face twist as though he were in pain from being confined, but as I continued watching slowly, very slowly, he relaxed and finally nodded his head, giving in.

"Thank you-" I started to say.

Vail shook his head. "That was a freebie, darling," he said, cutting off my gratitude. "Stay out of trouble cuz we might not be around next time."

I narrowed my eyes at him and jumped down from the counter. "Well, I didn't *ask* for your help. You offered it on your own."

"So you screaming wasn't a call for help, then?"

Why was it every time I was around Vail, I just wanted to slap the shit out of him? "You call helping a girl not be gang-raped a freebie?" All three of them winced at my words, and I shook my head in disgust. "If you had stood by, knowing what was happening when you were in a position to help but didn't, then you are a piece of shit, too." I sidestepped around him and pushed open the door, first warily checking the hallway for Hunter or any of his crew. Still, seeing it empty, I hurried down the stairs. Behind me, I heard footsteps following, yet no one called my name. I spun around, my heart hammering in my chest, but I instantly relaxed when I saw it was just Lee.

"What do you want?" I asked, my anger ebbing away when I noticed it was him.

"Making sure you get home okay."

I shook my head. "I'll be fine."

"I'm sure you will. But I'll be watching just in case."

I "Don't bother, Lee."

"This isn't a debate, Case," he said, all humour gone. "I'm coming with you, and that's it."

Chapter eight

Lee: Ten Years Old

"Do you need another blanket, honey?" My mom emerged from the hallway of our apartment, carrying at least two extra quilts and the comforter from her and dad's bed. Casey, Shaw, Vail, and I were all squashed together on the living room floor, right in front of the TV. After we left Casey's house, Mom had brought us straight home and put together a space on the floor for us to sleep on. It was late, probably the early hours of the morning, and yet Ma was moving around, making sure *we* were safe and comfortable. But I knew she had spent long hours working at the dry cleaners during the day, then came home, switched off with my old man so he could go to work at the airport while she took care of Gran and Gramps. She was exhausted. Yet here she was, doting on Casey like she was her own daughter, making sure she was okay, comfortable, and served us all some hot tea.

Casey was lying on the floor between Shaw and me, with

Vail stretched out along our heads. That guy had seriously lost it back at her house. He was definitely a skinny kid, yet he took that guy down and kept him there with his fists for a solid two minutes before the police showed up. No one could snap him out of whatever realm of crazy he'd fallen into… no one, except Casey. All she did was call his name, just like the rest of us, and he seemed to snap out of his fog.

She had that effect on him.

She had that effect on *all* of us.

She snuggled down under her blankets after my mom hugged her goodnight, whispering words of encouragement. "Your mama is a strong lady. They said she'd be all right and on her feet in a couple of days. So don't you fret about it and get some rest, honey," she whispered to my friend before taking her empty cup and tucking her in.

Despite the chaos and shitty way the night had played out, having this girl lying beside me was enough to make me smile again. I was always jealous of Shaw every sleepover, being the one to hold her hand while they slept. Now, I got a chance to snuggle close and knew what it felt like to have her beside me. We all settled down. Ma went around turning off all the lights, and double-checking the locks, then disappeared down the hall to the room she, Dad, and I shared.

The four of us laid there in the dark, the only light coming from the nightlight in the hall, which cast a comfortable glow, illuminating just enough that I could make out the shapes of my friends. Behind me, Vail collapsed in a heap and was asleep in seconds. I didn't know how he could sleep so peacefully after what he did. I'm pretty sure he managed to beat that guy within an inch of his life. He was damn lucky it was a break-in, and he was a minor. Yet, he remained utterly stoic once Casey had calmed him down, acting as if nothing had happened. We all had been questioned and sent home with Ma while Ms. Cooper was transported to Ashland

General. On Casey's other side, Shaw settled down, but I knew he was aware of every creak and unfamiliar sound. Occasionally, he would lift his head, studying the dark shadows of the room carefully, before he laid his head back on his pillow. It took him a little longer than the other two, but eventually, he passed out, too.

I, however, laid awake, thinking about what I'd just seen. I knew Shaw was fucked to hell, but Vail? He always seemed so in control, so disciplined. Tonight, he wasn't. He lost it when he attacked that guy, and what I saw was messing with my head. I worried for him. I saw someone who was actually hurting inside despite acting like a pompous ass half the time. I reached up, finding his leg, and gave it a little pat.

Don't you worry, bro. I got you. Just like you always have my back, I'll have yours. I thought, smiling to myself. I didn't know what I would have done without these three.

I remembered my first day in second grade when I arrived at Harley Elementary. All the fucking kids in my class came at me, pushing me down into the mud, throwing rocks and shit, calling me names I knew would make my old man go quiet and seethe in his easy chair in the corner of the sitting area.

And then...

It all changed.

Rocks came raining down on my attackers, giving them a taste of what it felt like to be on the receiving end, and I looked up to see a girl with long, wavy dark hair, dark eyes, and pale skin cursing and shouting at the others. The sight of her as she had defended me, coming to my rescue without another thought, I remembered that feeling in my chest when the others scattered, and she walked right up to me and held out a hand to help me up. The way she smiled at me, the dimples revealing themselves in her cheeks, the shift from fury to sweetness so quick it threw me for a moment. But I gratefully took her hand and got to my feet.

"You're Lee, right?" she asked me, tilting her head back to see my face, and grinned.

"Uh, yeah..."

"I'm Casey Cooper. This is Vail and Shaw." She gestured over her shoulder.

It was then that I realized she wasn't alone. Two boys, one bronze-haired, the other pale blond, were with her, shouting obscenities at the other kids who had ran off.

"Don't listen to those idiots," she glared after my attackers, who had run to a safe distance on the other side of the playground, gathering beneath the metal jungle gym. "They're mouth-breathers."

I laughed at her choice of name-calling and looked over myself, taking in the cuts and scrapes I'd gotten from their assault. My palms were skinned from when I fell, and I was gonna be hurting for sure. I held back my tears at the sight of the blood on my hands. I didn't want these guys to think I was a baby. But when they spotted the red droplets, all three flanked me as they accompanied me to the washroom so I could clean up. Even though it had been the boys' room, Casey came in, climbing up on the counter and swinging her legs, waiting patiently as I washed myself off, while the other two had chosen to take a leak in the stalls.

"Thank you guys for helping. You didn't have to..." I mumbled, still nervous and unsure. Were they expecting repayment in some way? I didn't have any money to give them. My parents were so poor I was wearing clothes that were falling apart and, in some cases, too small. My shoes had holes in them, and most days, I didn't have lunch.

The girl, Casey, raised a brow at me, looking confused, "Of course we did. Why would we just stand by and watch? You did nothing wrong."

From one of the stalls, the toilet flushed, and the one called Vail stepped out, zipping up his pants, not at all put off that there was a girl in here with us. "Those guys are going to end up in a dumpster someday," he said casually.

"Vail!" Casey scorned as he washed his hands. "Don't say things like that!"

He just shrugged. "It's true. That's what my dad..." He stopped, biting his lip for a moment, before he playfully flicked the water in her direction, making her squeal. I smiled at the sound while he dried off his hands, and Shaw emerged, head down and silent.

"Anyways, I know those guys were mean to you, but not all the kids here are like that," she said to me.

"Naw, most are pretty cool. But Hunter and his goof-troop are dumb shits-"

"Vail!" Casey scolded him again, but he only grinned in response to her chastising tone.

He crossed his arms over his chest and leaned back a bit. "Do you like tetherball?"

"Sure," I said, not wanting to admit that I had no idea what he was talking about.

"Let's go play, then. I challenge you first." He led the way out, with Shaw following silently behind him. Casey reached over and took my hand and walked ahead, tugging me along behind her. A smile curled up on my lips at her confident walk as she led us across the courtyard to a free spot where a ball connected to a long chain was hanging off the top of a pole. Vail ran ahead, claiming it before another kid could, and Shaw trudged along, hands in his pockets and shoulders slumped. That kid needed to relax a little. He seemed... high strung.

Casey released my hand and ran ahead, laughing as she peered over her shoulder at me. The sun hit her face, the lighter strands of brown in her hair shining, and I fell in love at that moment. Before I could run after her, I caught sight of Shaw over her shoulder, sprinting back in my direction, his focus solely on me, and he looked pissed.

Whoa, whoa... what was his problem? I froze where I stood and lifted my scratched-up hands, hoping he'd stop and explain what he was so pissed about. It was then that Casey glanced back as her friend raced past her, and her smile disappeared.

"Lee, duck!" she screamed.

I immediately threw myself down, the sound of the air swishing hard overhead, as though something had just missed me by centimeters. Shaw leapt over my body, and I could hear him tackle someone, the sounds of rocks scraping across the pavement, of metal clanging on the ground loud in my ears. I peeked over my shoulder to see Shaw had taken down a guy nearly twice his size, and a metal bat was lying on the ground beside him. Shaw grabbed the kid's head and smashed it back into the pavement again and again, over and over until the kid stopped moving altogether. In the background, I heard other kids screaming, footsteps running, and next thing I knew, Casey was helping me off the ground again, while Vail tried to pull Shaw off my would-be attacker.

"You fucking try that shit again, DeLuca, and I'll take your fucking eyes!" Shaw screamed just as several teachers came running over.

"Mr. Bishop, language!" One shouts over the massive crowd that had gathered. "You know better than to... than to... oh my god. Oh. My. God! Someone call Principal Weiser! Get the school nurse! Where is Shaw? Where is he?"

But Shaw was gone, as was Vail. Casey was tugging on my hand, pulling me through the crowd just as the teacher began making demands of the students. "Did Shaw do this? Who saw? Anyone? Did anyone see Shaw do this?"

But no one stepped forward with information. No one volunteered as a witness, and it was minutes later that Casey guided me into a trailer behind the school where cleaning supplies are kept, and we found the other two. Shaw had his shaking hands under the running water in the corner, with Vail murmuring to him.

"Shaw! Are you hurt bad?" Casey ran over to inspect his hands, but when he raised his head, his deep blue eyes met my gaze and *held it. He said not a word but gave me a small nod, which told me everything.*

That day, I found my extended family.

I rolled over where I was lying, facing Casey's back, and smiled. Slowly, I reached out, my fingers barely skimming over her back, until I found a lock of her long, dark hair. I wound it around two of my fingers, stroking the soft strands with my thumb. I could hear her breathing softly beside me in her sleep, and sure enough, when I craned my neck over her shoulder, I could see her and Shaw had their hands clasped. Lucky bastard. But again, he needed her. Just like Vail did when he lost his shit. Just like I did when I needed to remember that I *was* worthy. That there were people who cared about me, and that this whole world wasn't fucked. There were good people, like my friends. We cared. And if it weren't for us, shitheads like Mark DeLuca, Hunter Tremblay, and their gang of "mouth-breathers," as Casey once called them, would be terrorizing everyone at our school. We kept them at bay. We were the only ones brave enough to stand up to them.

I knew that I was viewed as the muscle in our group, even at ten. I was a foot taller than everyone else and twice as wide. I was made for fighting, though I didn't like it. I felt like I didn't belong here in Harley since my family was dealt a shit card in life, or maybe we were being punished for something? I hated it here. I hated fighting. I hated the divide and the injustice. I felt like I was weak for not clicking with this life.

But I *was* strong.

My three friends made me strong.

Together, we were the best versions of ourselves. We looked out for each other and everyone else. We were a team, and we believed in each other.

Beside me, Casey sighed and rolled over, facing me. Next

thing I knew, she snuggled into my chest, one arm falling over my side. I felt breathless as I adjusted to the shadows of the room and could make out her pretty face. In her sleep, I noticed how the corner of her mouth lifted when I wrapped my arms around her and held her back. I thought about Vail and how that lucky manipulating bugger got to kiss her tonight.

She nestled in some more and relaxed, falling back into a comfortable sleep. Behind her, Shaw was breathing slow, steady breaths, and I knew he was okay. Gazing down at her face, I knew I would never take advantage of her like this, so instead of getting the kiss I wanted, I lightly pressed my lips to her forehead, brushing her hair with my fingers, and fell asleep, holding my girl in my arms, and my two brothers close by. We were together, safe, and strong.

Chapter nine

Casey

I LEARNED a lot during my first week. Rule one, never carry anything of value on yourself. Rule two, never linger alone at your locker. It was the perfect spot to be jumped by someone looking for you. On my third day, Hunter reappeared, muttering threats over my shoulder about finishing what he started with me. I ignored him and moved away. From then on, when I arrived at school, I prepacked a vintage Air Force bag that I'd found at the nearby thrift store with all the books I'd need until lunch, so I wouldn't have to keep going back to my locker after each class.

Another lesson I learned was that this school had multiple drills: for fire, shooters, bombs, and other potential lockdowns. And most of the time, it wasn't just a drill; it was for an actual threat. On Thursday during Math, the alarm went off, three shrill blasts, and without pause, all the kids piled up into the corner of the classroom while Mr. Fortin closed and locked the door. I followed suit, wondering what the hell was happening when I heard a helicopter outside and realized the police were here. I had been terrified at that moment, shaking as I sat crouched on the ground.

But shortly after, I felt an arm wrap around my shoulders, and I peeked up to see Lee sitting on my other side, and he was pulling me close. I didn't know where he had come from, as I had initially been squashed between two other kids who I had never spoken to. But I was so grateful at that moment I had forgotten I'd been keeping my guard up around these guys all week. Once Lee escorted me home, which was basically him walking five feet behind me the entire way and then watching as I hurried up my steps to my front door, he hadn't said a word since.

And now here he was, with his arm around my shoulders, reassuring me. There was nothing underhanded about the move. I could feel it. He was just being... *Lee*.

So I huddled into his side, trying to keep myself calm and collected as I listened to the sounds of sirens outside and lots of shouting. When I heard actual gunfire going off, I covered my ears and shut my eyes. It'd been ages since I heard gunshots, and the sound echoed in my mind with memories I wish I couldn't remember. The other students were as cool as cucumbers, sitting patiently and all looking relatively relaxed as all of this was going on. I glimpsed up at Lee and noticed that, despite the fact he was lounging with one leg bent, the other resting alongside my left one, his jaw was tense, and his eyes never left the door to the classroom which was still locked shut.

I got the feeling that he was keeping watch in his own way, and I wondered for a minute what he would do if someone did try to get in here.

There was some more shouting outside, and I cringed away, his hand tightening on my upper arm as he held me.

He reminded me of a cat, ready to strike should the moment call for it.

I felt his fingers in my hair, stroking the long strands, occasionally looping them around his hand with a playful tug before he resumed combing through it again. This old action comforted me more than anything. As kids, Lee had always been the one to play with my hair, braid it, something I taught him how to do the first year we met, or just to stroke repeatedly. I slowly peered up at him, and his eyes came to me. We were so close I could feel his breath on my temple, watching as he licked his bottom lip in a way that sent a little thrill through me. God, I'd always loved his mouth. Always wondered what it would have been like to touch them, to kiss him...

But then, as quickly as it all started, it was over. The alarms shut off, the lights came back on, and Mr. Fortin unlocked the door and went back to standing before the board to resume the lesson. All the kids rose and sat back in their desks as if we were just taking a midday break and not hiding in case a shooter was trying to storm the school. Lee let me go and went straight back to his seat, his silence unsettling me. It was so unlike him. When I settled back at my desk, which was in front of his, I whispered, "Thank you."

There was only silence behind me. For a brief moment, I wanted to confront him and ask him why? What had I done to deserve the cold shoulder from them all? But then again, I'd told them I wanted to be left alone. So I hunched over my notebook and scribbled down the notes from the board. In my peripheral vision, I could see a helicopter flying by the window at my side. I glanced over, momentarily worried that the shooter was back, when I caught sight of my reflection. I stared back at myself, but it was the hand reaching out behind me that caught me off guard. It took me a second to realize that Lee was reaching out, as if he wanted to touch my hair but was stopping just short of actually making contact. The look on his face, the tight pained expression, made my heart wrench.

They *were* leaving me alone, as I'd requested. But I could see how much he wanted to reach out and play with my hair like he used to, weaving the strands between his fingers when we sat side by side.

At least, I knew Shaw and Lee missed me.

Vail was another story altogether.

If I saw him in the halls, he ignored me, not even looking my way. I was less than nothing to him, and it stung.

We later found out that several members of Company had come onto school grounds, apparently seeking out specific guys that were a part of the Jackals. Fists had been thrown, guns were drawn, and in the end, one of the Harley Public guys was shot in the leg by a cop, and two others were arrested. The rest scattered, and the guys who were part of the Jackals that had been involved were brought in for questioning.

By the time it was the end of my first week, I was exhausted. Not only was I trying to attend my classes and catch up on the curriculum, but I was constantly on guard when I was at school. I always looked over my shoulder, watched out for Celeste and her crowd, and hurried off in the other direction when Hunter or any of the Jackal members were in the vicinity. On top of it all, every lunch hour when I sat in my usual spot alone, I could see the members of Vendetta, figuring out it was them because Meredith and Midnight, or Haldon or whatever his name was, were always sitting with them. But on occasion, I'd see Shaw, Lee, or Vail sit with them at lunch, talking softly with their heads close together. This only confirmed my earlier suspicion when Lee had mentioned being a part of a crew. They were members. And from what I could see, they were always treated with the utmost respect. When they joined Vendetta for lunch, the space was cleared for them, and the rest seemed to hang on to every word they said, which usually came from Vail.

I was also keeping in contact with Nylah, messaging her back and forth, but it wasn't the same as seeing each other in person. I desperately wanted to grab a taxi and spend the weekend at her house, but I also knew she had a lot going on with school and sports. She kept reassuring me that she hadn't seen that stalker biker at all, but I didn't believe her. Whenever I asked, she would change the subject after a quick, *nope*. Mr. Bryant also messaged, checking in to make sure everything was okay, and though Keith and I were *not* bonding, I didn't want to cause problems. He was dealing with a lot of stuff with his job when I left. I could see the strain on his face at supper when Laila talked about her art, or asked Nylah and me about our days. So I told him I was fine, that things were going well, and left it at that.

But it was a lie.

When I woke up that first Saturday morning after my first week of school, Keith just arrived home from a night shift, and he was beyond enraged. I guess some late Friday night partiers stiffed him on their fare. I had no idea, of course, since I had been just sleeping in my little twin bed when he burst in in a rage, the door smashing open with a bang.

"Wh-what? What is it?" I sat up, rubbing my eyes, my heart pounding from the sudden crash that awakened me from my sleep.

He simply walked in and started in on me, shouting about how I ruined his life. How he now had to work himself silly to support me, that the first child support cheque he received from the Government was barely enough for a week's worth of groceries, and that I was a drain on his life… as if any of it was my fault. Living with him now, I saw the angry, bitter, drunk that Mom had briefly told me about when I was four- teen and had asked about him. She'd been honest about it but didn't want to elaborate. I could feel a rage building inside me as Keith paced my room, shouting and blaming me for everything wrong in his life. I refused to cry.

Instead, I stared up at his ruddy red face that matched his hair, glad when I saw nothing of myself there. That would make it harder to distance myself from him. I listened as he rambled on about nonsense, blaming me for shit that was far from my fault, and I struggled to keep a passive expression on my face. There was no point in arguing with an angry fool. It would be like picking a fight with a pissed-off chicken. Nothing would change. He'd still be an angry chicken by the time I finished arguing my point.

"... your bitch of a mother, fucking me over, leaving me for that rich prick..."

No, he fucking didn't.

Goodbye composure. Bringing up Mom and Matthew? Nuh-uh! He could insult me all he wanted but to go after them when they weren't even alive to defend themselves? To throw insults their way for wanting nothing to do with him because he was a leech? When *he* got to live while they were buried? No fucking way.

I threw my covers back and jumped to my feet, wearing my pink piggy pajama bottoms and a light grey tank, and I glared at him. "Do you think I *want* to be here? Do you think I asked for *any* of this?" I shouted. "I lost everything! Every- thing! It sucks that I disrupted your pathetic little life, but *you're* supposed to be my father! For once, why don't you fucking act like it?"

With a snap, his hand came flying out and struck me across the face. My head whipped to the side, my hair hiding me from him like a purple curtain. I froze. Mom and

Matthew never struck me. Not that I ever gave them a reason to, but still… I'd never been hit so many times as I have this first week back in Harley.

"You little fuck!" Keith hissed at me. "You talk to me like that again, and I'll really give you something to bitch about!" He stormed across the room and slammed the door shut behind himself as he disappeared downstairs. Hopefully, to sleep off his anger.

Stunned, I stood there, lightly touching my cheek. I could feel the tears brimming my eyes, but no, I *wouldn't* cry… because if I started, I wouldn't be able to stop.

On Monday, the mark on my cheek from Keith was bruised, but I did my best to cover it up with makeup. It was still noticeable, but you had to look really hard. I avoided Keith all weekend, though Sunday was difficult as it was his day off, so I hid out in my room and worked on my schoolwork, hoping to keep my grades at the top level. Nylah would be so proud of me. We'd texted back and forth a bit over the weekend, but I knew she was busy with basketball and all her extracurriculars, so I tried not to distract her and kept my messages to a minimum.

I slipped on a fitted zip-up grey hoodie with patches of red roses sewn onto the back and slipped into my white sneakers. Pulling up my hood to hide my face, I headed off to school, hoping this week would be better than the last.

My first class was Math 30, so I hurried to my seat, pulled out my books, and kept my head down and my hood up. Most of the students ignored me, thankfully. There might have been a whisper or two, but then everyone went back to talking about their weekends with each other. I sat back in my chair just as Lee walked into the room, and his gaze met mine. I saw how his eyes flickered to my cheek, and for a moment, he looked pissed as hell, and it scared the crap out of me. Quickly, I lowered my head and bent over my books, pretending to re-read the chapter of our homework assignment.

"What happened?"

I stiffened as my hood was plucked away, exposing me completely. Behind me, Lee had taken his seat but was leaning in so close, I could feel his breath on my ear.

"What do you mean?"

"What happened to your face?" His voice was deadly.

I shrugged. "This is from that bitch Celeste and her skank squad…" I kept my eyes down on my books, refusing to turn around to face him.

"Don't lie to me." His voice deepened, and I felt the hairs on my arms rising, even beneath my sweater.

"I-"

"I can tell how old a bruise is, even hidden under makeup. That one is new. So who did it?"

"Maybe I'm just super clumsy, and I walked into a door?" I said, nonchalantly. "Or I tripped while playing basketball… hell, I'm so damn clumsy, it's amazing I'm not covered in marks."

"Stop lying, Casey."

Crap… even after all these years, he could see through me. Why did that make my stomach jump, my heart pumping just a little faster, at the thought of Lee being so intuitive to me?

"I had a run-in with a relative."

"Your old man?"

"Yes. But if you think this is bad, you should see *him*." I looked up just as Mr. Fortin walked in, looking irritated as he always did.

"You're a terrible liar, babe."

At the nickname, I felt my cheeks flush, and I lowered my head again, choosing to remain silent. But he left me alone, at least. When the bell rang, I was on my feet and rushing out of class. I didn't need to be vulnerable to any of these guys right now, and Lee's sweet protectiveness, his hidden affections, that stupid nickname, they were all getting to me.

The day was pretty quiet, but when I stepped into the cafeteria at lunch, that's when shit hit the fan. I grabbed a tray with my usual favourites, but when I turned to head to my table, a hand came crashing down onto my tray, knocking all of my food to the floor. The lunchroom went eerily quiet, and I watched as a stiletto crushed my sandwich.

"Well, *that* was a waste," I said, amusement lacing my words. I couldn't let the other students see me as weak, so I used humor as a defense. When the heel stepped onto my chocolate milk box, and it burst, and the owner of the shoe yelped, I couldn't help but laugh. I stared into Celeste Wood's eyes. "What did you think was going to happen?" I asked her.

"Listen, you little whore," she hissed at me and kicked my milk carton away, rather than risk slipping by stepping on it. "I don't know what you've done to get all the guys in this school drooling over you, but *I'm* the Jackals number *one* girl. Got it?"

I burst out laughing again at her words, wondering if she was going to break out into song next. I felt like I was in a cheesy episode of Degrassi. When I faced her again, smiling wide, I saw the confusion on her face. "Seriously? *That's* what this is all about?" I shook my head at her. "Come *on*, Celeste… don't be so petty and insecure. As if I give two shits about any of the guys in this school." The lie had fallen from my lips so easily. I could sense Vail, Shaw, and Lee watching this altercation with interest. They were sitting with Vendetta today, their presence standing out the moment I walked in here. "And the Jackals? You can keep them, bitch." I

walked around her, deciding just to leave the cafeteria altogether, but her long, manicured hand snatched at my arm,
keeping me in place.

"You fucking stuck-up cunt!" she snarled at me between
her teeth. "I'm the fucking queen of this school-" she prattled
on, but my eyes moved to my pearl earrings that she'd been
proudly wearing since she stole them from me. I tuned her
out, barely taking in the threats and insults she hurled my
way. When her hand raised in an obvious intent to hit me, I
reached out, seized the earrings from her lobes, and ripped.

Celeste let out a high-pitched shriek and released me, her
hands springing up to her ears in horror. I saw the blood
trailing down the side of her neck, and I knew I had done
some damage.

"These are mine," I sneered at her, raising my voice.
"Touch anything of mine again, and I'll *really* fuck you up.
You'll walk away with scars, bitch." Right now, I couldn't
stand this chick and her constant attacks. It was the last thing
I needed in my life. If she had just left me alone, then her ears
wouldn't be fucked. She earned her injury. I turned and
stalked out of the lunchroom, leaving her wailing loudly with
her friends gathered around, consoling her. None made a
move to follow me, and it all became crystal clear. The sheep
would only follow the shepherd's command, and right now?
Their leader was down.

I knew everyone was watching, but honestly, I couldn't
give a rat's ass. I shoved open the lunchroom doors, raising
my hand behind me, and I flashed everyone the Italian bird
without looking back. Since arriving at this school, I'd been
bullied, insulted, and almost gang-raped. I had been told
that I needed to fall in line with whichever gang officially
claimed me, and I didn't have a choice in the matter. No
fucking way was I going to align with Hunter and the Jackals. I'd initially decided to then support Vendetta, but Vail

had pushed me away... again! Well, I'm done. Fuck everyone.

"Seriously, Celeste is such a fucking idiot!" Meredith was practically cackling when I met her in Home Ec. after lunch. I grinned as I cracked some eggs into the mixing bowl and started whisking them. "I mean, when the chocolate milk burst all over her shiny shoes? Oh man, I was hoping she'd slip and fall in it!" She wiped her eyes, beaming at me as she watched me start our brownie mixture. "Did you really tear her ears?"

I shrugged, "No idea. There was some blood, so I guess so."

Meredith was positively gleaming. "Bitch deserved it. " She hip bumped me, and I grinned at her.

"I don't think I'll ever want to wear these earrings again, but it's more of the principle. She's been after me since I arrived, and there's nothing to back her bullshit. I'm done with it."

"Damn straight, Kitten!" She laughed again. "Show us your claws! I swear to God, you gave every guy in that room a boner!"

I burst out laughing just as Mrs. Adamson glared our way, having heard Meredith's choice of words.

"Sorry, ma'am." Meredith waved at the older lady and shook her head as she got the dry ingredients mixed together. "Anyways, you should have seen Hunter afterwards..."

I cringed a little at the mention of Hunter. Last week was still very fresh in my mind, and I felt a chill rush through me at his name. "What about him?" I mumbled.

"He basically told Celeste that if she touches you again,

she's done. That she was never an actual member of their club and was just a groupie, so she's replaceable. The girl threw a hissy fit. No female at this school wants to be a groupie. That's basically a kind term for *whore*. They're meaningless to members."

"You are a member," I said.

"I am, indeed!" Her jovial mood continued.

"Are you dating that one guy in Vendetta? Midnight or whatever?"

"Haldon Cadot?" She winked, ignoring the fact that I basically called her out for being a crew member. "Midnight is a nickname only members use for him. We've been together for a little over three years now. We live in an apartment not too far from here with a roommate."

"Someone else in your club?"

She shook her head. "Naw, he's a few years older than us. We basically rent a room from him, but he's a really nice guy. Super trustworthy. Not shady in the least." She smiled at me. "Those are important qualities in a person in Harley."

I knew that. It was why Vail, Shaw, Lee, and I stuck together as kids. We had absolute trust in each other. Well, we used to.

"Have the guys approached you yet?" she asked suddenly, and for a moment, I thought I'd spoken my thoughts out loud.

"What?" I asked, quickly looking up at her in alarm.

"Vail… has he spoken to you?"

"Why would he?" I turned away to slowly start mixing the dry and wet ingredients together, hiding my face from her.

"Just with the way he's been acting lately, I'd say you seem to have piqued his interest…"

I snorted in disbelief. "Yeah, okay. And the sky is red."

"I'm serious, Casey. Has he come to you?"

"I have zero desire to become a groupie," I said flat out

and faced her. "Vail hates me. He wants nothing to do with me, and that's just fine. I want nothing to do with him, either." Even as I spoke the words, my heart twisted in my chest. *You liar!*

Meredith simply laughed again. "Oh honey, I know that. You aren't the type at all. Celeste might not see it, but the guys know you aren't... *a lady of loose morals.*" She snickered.

I scowled at her and leaned back against the counter, crossing my arms. "I don't want to be a member of a... club..." *Gang,* I think in my mind. "That's why I said I'd be a supporter."

She shook her head. "A crew, honey. We're a crew."

"Same difference."

"We aren't the bad guys in this school, Casey," she said, going all serious on me, but I listened, as she'd been the only one to tell me anything about this place and how to survive here. "The real bad guys are outside of these walls, and they're trying to break in. That's why the Jackals are so fucking dangerous."

"What are you talking about?"

She reached for the mixture and poured it into a greased pan. I observed as she carefully spread the batter out so that it was nice and even before she talked again. "Why do you think Vendetta and the Jackals are at odds?"

"Old rivalry?" I answered, thinking about all the times we fought with Hunter and his boys as kids.

She shook her head and smiled. "Give us more credit than that,"

"Sorry. Okay. So it's nothing to do with old rivalries?"

"No, there's a bigger picture here. I know enough that I want to help, but it's the higher-up members of our crew who keep things tight to the chest. It's for safety. Protection. The more everyone knows, the more danger we're all in."

She said this so matter-of-factly that I laughed for a

second, before her wide eyes flicked up to me, her expression deadpan and solemn. "You're-you're serious?" I said incredulously.

"As a heart attack." She stuck the pan in the oven and headed over to one of the round work tables where we'd left our bags and took a seat. She pulled out the same knitting project from the first day I met her and got to work on it, and I soon realized she was making a blanket. I sat across from her, waiting to hear more. "If an olive branch is extended, take it," she said finally, and counted her stitches carefully.

"Like, an offer to join a crew?"

"An offer for protection," she said after she finished and kept going.

"I am not selling pussy for protection," I said blatantly, and she giggled.

"No, I can't picture you doing that. And I highly doubt Vail would use you that way."

I narrowed my eyes at her, confused. "What has Vail said about me?"

Meredith's blue gaze flicked my way, suddenly looking uncomfortable. Great. I could only imagine what he said.

"Nevermind, Mer. It's okay. I won't put you in the middle of our bullshit."

"Bullshit?" She seemed puzzled.

"Yeah, but really, it's fine," I sighed and lounged back in my seat, feeling tired and defeated. "I *was* picking Vendetta's side, but it's been made clear I wasn't wanted," I muttered.

She shrugged. "Ignore him. He's just being an ass. Guess that's the price he pays for being the leader." *Huh? The leader? So Vail was the head of Vendetta?* "From what I can tell, you haven't been written off by the crew. Stay close to me. If you don't have anyone looking out for you, well... you're gonna get grabbed."

"Already have," I muttered, thinking of Hunter and Bryce.

"What was that?" she asked quickly, looking suddenly afraid.

"Nothing," I shook my head and pulled out my spare notebook, one I enjoyed doodling in and scribbled a quick sketch of a dragon's face, bent over, a small tear sliding off the end of its long nose. Around it, I added in several white hellebores as if they were falling around it, dancing in the wind.

Mom... I was thinking of the one word as I shade the petals of one of the flowers—her favourite.

The oven dinged, and Meredith put down her knitting to check on our brownies.

"Again, ladies?" Mrs. Adamson came over and shook her head to see that we'd baked the same thing as last week.

"What can I say? They're scrum-diddly-umptious!" Meredith beamed at her and set them on the cooling rack.

Though she continued to shake her curly white hair, I could see the smile twitching on the corners of our teacher's mouth before she walked away.

"If I did that, she'd probably have grabbed that spatula and smacked me upside the head with it," I told her when she joined me back at the table.

Meredith puckered her lips and blew a kiss in my direction. "Can't all be as adorable as me." I rolled my eyes and bent over my dragon sketch again, my mind drifting as I thought about what she'd told me, about Hunter's gang versus Vail's, wondering what the hell they both wanted from me? "May I ask you for a favour, Casey?" Meredith said softly, breaking the silence.

At the seriousness in her tone, I immediately dropped my pencil and stared at her. Meredith's smile was gone, and though she was lounging back in her chair. Her arms were crossed defensively over her chest, and she was biting her lip, looking nervous.

"What's up?"

She glanced at the other girls in the room, but they were busy in their own little worlds to listen in. She let out a long, heavy sigh between her lips and looked up at me with apprehension. "I have some... *crew* business to take care of tomorrow night. Unfortunately, Haldon is coming, too, and my roommate is working a night shift. Haldon's grandmother needs to go to bed early on weekdays..." Her voice trailed off as I listened. I'd never seen Meredith look so nervous. I wasn't sure where she was going with this conversation.

"Okay?" I said, hoping she'd continue.

"Look, I'm just going to say it. I need a babysitter."

Oh! I gaped at her as her words echoed in my head. A babysitter. "You have a baby?"

"I have a *toddler*," she corrected me. "Her name is Amelie. She's two and a half. Haldon's grandmother watches her during the day while we're at school, but by the time we get home, she's pretty much done in. It's a lot, especially for a seventy-two-year-old lady. Normally Haldon and I aren't paired for certain... *tasks*... but in this case, pretty much all members are involved."

I processed everything she just said. She and Haldon have a two-and-a-half-year-old daughter. A child who was just several months younger than their relationship. But honestly, I'd seen the way they were with each other at school. They seemed happy. They were making it work. The fact that they were even trying to finish high school despite their circumstances was pretty admirable.

"What time do you need me to stop by?" I asked.

Meredith's expression perked up, "What?"

"What time should I be at your place? How late?"

"Um, from six to maybe one in the morning? Two at the latest?" She pursed her lips as she told me the late hour.

"No problem," I answered her easily, and I could see she'd been surprised by my reaction. "I used to babysit all the time in my old neighborhood. Not to brag, but I'm pretty good with kids. And I have my CPR training all up to date, too." I mentally said thank *you* to Nylah for dragging me along with her for that one.

"You-you're okay with it?" Her voice was soft, and for once, Meredith actually sounded vulnerable, and it shot straight to my heart.

"Yeah, no worries. Gotta be hard finding a sitter last minute, hey?"

"It can be, yes," she breathed, sounding relieved.

"Well, you don't have to stress. I'll arrive a little early so you can go over everything I need to know for Amelie. Can you text me your address?" I held up my phone, waiting for her to give me her number. She did, and I could see the smile on her lips, a real one. A thankful one.

She glanced up at me then, her expression unreadable for a moment. "Thank you, Casey."

"No worries, Mer. You're one of the nicest people I've met here. I'd love to help." I flashed her one of her own trademark winks, and she grinned.

"Amelie can be a bit of a handful. Pretty sure Haldon's grandma spoils her while we're at school."

I laughed, "It'll be fine. Just… don't blame me if she's not in bed by the time you get home. Kids sense a weakness in me and like to take advantage of it. I'm a sucker for a cute face."

The next day, I woke up late. Last night was awful. Keith hadn't been drinking last night, but I sensed a familiar sort of hostility from him that I remembered from childhood. He'd asked about my day, so I gave him a watered-down version, keeping it to the basics about my classes, and then he grunted in response and turned on the TV. When I went to the fridge to see what I could make for dinner, I found it was pretty bare, yet the freezer was jammed full of frozen meals. So I threw one into the microwave for us to split before he left for his shift. We ate in silence in front of the television, watching some cop show I'd never heard of, and then he left for work without a word. I'd spent the rest of the night reviewing my notes, rewriting them, and finishing the smaller homework assignments. Then, I spent the remaining night hours aimlessly traveling down the social media rabbit hole before calling it around midnight. I woke up every half hour, sitting upright in bed as I gasped for air and struggled to calm myself. I always woke up feeling like I was in the middle of being hunted.

Several times, I would tug the curtain back to peer out the window. The sounds of sirens, the occasional rumble of an engine, or shouts down the street, disturbing the peace—all the sounds I had once been used to. But I kept thinking about what Meredith had said in Home Ec.

The real bad guys are outside of these walls, and they're trying to break in. What the hell did that mean? And she mentioned that was why Hunter and his gang were so dangerous. So what was their goal? If the Celtic Beasts and the Faceless were using them, then it was some serious shit. Was it drugs?

As for Vail, Lee, and Shaw, it would appear they were fighting on the other side, trying to protect the students from that bullshit. But then why did it matter what side I chose? Why did *I* matter at all?

Right now though, I was just scrambling to get ready. I

had put on a pair of black leggings, a casual canary yellow tank top, and a white cardigan. I left my hair down, finding it helped act as a curtain to hide behind. I kept reminding myself I needed to shop locally for some new things, but at the same time, I didn't really want to change who I was. On the other hand, I wasn't sure if I even *liked* who I was. I was basically a product of someone who adapted to a new environment and was now struggling in another. I was going to be seventeen at the end of November, and I had no idea who the hell I was, and with all this social drama, I was just as confused as ever.

I felt more anxious going to school today than I had yesterday. I stared at myself in the mirror, wondering what the hell I was going to do. Meredith seemed sure that something was coming, to stay close to her because the crew hadn't written me off yet, but her words had put me on edge.

At school, not too much had changed. Celeste was still casting me death glares, and whispers followed wherever I went. However, I could sense some sort of tension in the air. Despite the whispers from the Skank Squad, everyone else pretty much left me alone. Everyone else, however, was on edge and moved quickly, keeping their heads down. Any loud noises, like someone dropping their books, the slam of a classroom door, had kids throwing themselves back, making everyone wary and watchful.

What the hell was going on?

By the time lunch came around, I was tempted to call it a day and go home. I felt like I was walking on eggshells the entire morning. I hadn't seen Meredith all morning, despite her warning to stay close to her. Hard to do when the only class you shared together was in the afternoon.

I bought the same meal from yesterday and sat in the same spot off to the side. I had brought Othello with me again and sat on my own, pretending to read while I ate, when actually, I was observing everyone around me.

I could make out Hunter and his group on the opposite side of the room, close to the doors leading to the Atrium. Vendetta was near the back, along the walls with the prison barred windows. Meredith's blue head stood out amongst them all, and I thought I could see Shaw but no one else. Vail wasn't there. Neither was Lee. Or Meredith's man. I know she'd said to stay close, but I felt awkward about going over to that table when I wasn't a member.

The two crews, and those around them, were quiet, heads bowed over their lunches, casting suspicious glances at each other every so often. Occasionally, I'd peek up through my lashes and notice Shaw staring my way, not even bothering to look away when I caught him watching me several times.

The other students, meanwhile, the ones that belonged to other cliques, were chattering away, though some seemed anxious, as well. Something was happening... they, like me, just didn't know what.

I had almost finished picking at my food when the atmosphere shifted from quiet and ominous to a sudden explosion of activity.

Out in the hall, there came yelling and shouting and the sound of lockers slamming. At once, several security guards raced out of the cafeteria to break up what I could only assume was a small fight. Several other kids ran out, too, hoping to get a look at the feud, but I remained behind, not wanting to be a rubber-necker.

It was strange, though, I thought, because when the fight broke out in the hall, not one member of Vendetta moved an inch. No one watched, flinched, or left their seats when the shouting began, nor when it sounded like it had escalated a bit to a more physical altercation. Mrs. Reeves ran out after the security guards, and when she made it into the hall, I could hear her scolding what I assumed were two juniors for their "trivial squabble." Her words, not mine.

I wiped my hands off on my napkin and gathered my garbage together onto my tray, noticing that a crowd was forming near the doors leading out to the atrium where the adults had disappeared to. The sound of chairs scraping across the floor as students rose to their feet made the hairs on my neck stand on end.

I jumped in my seat when I saw Vail standing over the far table, his fist gripping Hunter's shirt. Their faces were close, both red with rage, both staring each other down with mutual loathing. Lee was standing at Vail's back, along with Meredith's guy, Haldon, forming a wall of muscle as they fought back members of the Jackals to keep them from saving their leader. At the cafeteria doors, other members of Vendetta and who I thought were simply random students were blocking the exit, some looking out the windows into the hall, some watching the rest of the room.

I stared in shock, unable to hear the words exchanged between the two guys, but at one point, Hunter's gaze flickered over to me. Vail gave him a rough shake then, bringing him back around, but Hunter was undeterred. He shoved Vail back, sending him into Lee and Haldon, and straightened up to his full height, almost reaching Lee's massive size. They stared each other down, their mouths moving as they quietly threatened each other, but I was still too far away to hear.

Meanwhile, members of the Jackals and Vendetta were flying across the room, clashing in the open space in the middle of the cafeteria. Fists were flying, and people were thrown into tables while chairs were kicked out of the way. Kids outside of the two gangs watched, picked sides, and shouted at the fighters, while some of the jocks were trying in vain to intervene. It was chaos as I shrank back against the wall, looking around for an escape route. At the doors, I could hear the shouting from teachers and security as they tried to break through, but the kids standing watch had formed a sort of crush, blocking any from entering. Seconds later, an alarm went off overhead, and a loud blaring echoed throughout the school, the Jackals flashing lights almost blinding me. Either the two groups were too far gone to be reasoned with to stop, or they couldn't hear over the blaring of the alarm system.

"Enough! Everyone, settle down!" Mrs. Reeves had returned and attempted to push her way through the line of kids barricading the entry of the Atrium, but there were too many blocking her way. I also heard security guards and other staff members trying to get the students to settle down, but it was like a riot in here.

I shifted along the wall, dodging students who had chosen to hide rather than stay and watch, preferring instead to stay out of the fight, and making my way towards the Emergency Exit near the far end of the room. Another group of Vendetta were standing there, like guards on duty, but they allowed some kids to leave, so I figured this was my best bet. I hitched my bag onto my shoulder and had to climb over several tables to safely get by the pandemonium in the middle of the room. But just as I was about ten feet from the doors, I saw a flash of blue in the mass of fighters.

Meredith!

I froze at the sight of her; teeth bared, and her face twisted in pure hate as she took on one of the Jackals' girls. She was fierce, relentless, as she ripped at the girl's hair and clawed at any part of her she could reach. The girl she'd been pummeling was on the floor on her back, her hands up to defend herself, while her legs were kicking wildly. But even when she landed a mark or two, it did nothing to halt Meredith, who was in full attack mode. As alarming as it was to see Meredith giggling, cute nickname calling Meredith being so ruthless, it was the sight of Celeste coming up behind her, a stool in her hands, that scared me the most. She raised her skinny arms, lifting them high over her head, and I realized she was about to bash it on the back of Meredith's skull.

I made a mad dash into the crowd, my focus entirely on Celeste. I jumped over the bodies of kids who were rolling on the ground, struggling with their own rivals as they pummeled each other and tried to gain the upper hand. I saw Meredith straighten, and her eyes caught mine, hers changing from fury to recognition and then bewilderment.

"Mer, look out!" I yelled, desperate to be heard over members of security who had finally broken through and were slowly separating kids pair by pair. The alarm was still ringing with a shrill, along with the shouting and screaming of the room, it was nearly deafening.

Meredith didn't hear me. If anything, she moved back a step closer to Celeste, who smiled like the psycho-bitch that she was as she swung, bringing her weapon down. I threw myself at her, right past Meredith, and barreled into Celeste's stomach, knocking her back. The stool fell to the floor beside us, missing its mark, and we both rolled. When I stopped, I was on my stomach and quickly pushed up onto my hands and knees, my eyes darting around as I searched for signs of a threat. Sure enough, Celeste was also quickly recovering from the fall, and she crawled forward, her coloured hair falling over her face so that her eyes, lasered on me, were staring through the strands. She reminded me of that girl from The Ring, the way she moved and glared at me with pure hatred.

I scrambled back several feet, occasionally getting struck by a flailing fist or other limbs, but I didn't look away from her as she attempted to stand.

"Casey!"

I heard my name, but I couldn't see who it was in all the chaos around me. I rolled over and pushed up off the ground, running back through the crowd, hoping to free myself so I could make a break to the kitchens again.

"*Casey!*" I heard it again, but I couldn't see shit. I ducked under an arm that swung dangerously close to my head and pushed past several pairs of fighters. I sidestepped out of the way from another two who flew back into the wall beneath the barred windows, and when I did, I felt someone's nails rake over my scalp before seizing a fistful of my hair. My head was roughly yanked back, my neck kinking painfully, and I found myself looking up into Celeste's panting, sweaty face.

"Fucking whore!" she practically spat the words out. "You've been nothing but a fucking pain in my ass! What is it that they all want? You got a magic pussy, slut?" It was then that I saw the stitches in her ears, and my hands flew up, seizing hold of them, and pulled. Celeste shrieked, pulling her head away, which only made it worse as the stitches were ripped open. She released me, crying in pain, and I stumbled sideways into the wall. I'd been about to make another break for it, when one of her cronies stepped in and grasped my arms from behind, lifting me up into the air. Celeste came at me, her lobes red and bloody, and picked up a discarded fork from the floor.

"I'm gonna make you bleed, bitch!" she snarled, lifting it up over my head. I struggled against her friend's hold, even attempting to reverse head-butt her, but she managed to dodge me at every time.

A huge figure came flying at us, slamming into Celeste, and made her shriek in a way that sounded like a pig squealing in pain. Hunter seized her by her throat and lifted her up off the ground while also slamming the hand that had been holding the fork, over and over again into the wall by her head. His grip was so tight, I could make out how his forearm was flexing, the tendons tightening beneath his skin.

"Staaaahp!" She choked out.

"Fucking drop it, cunt!" Hunter's lip was bleeding, one of his lip piercings was gone, and his dark brown hair was disheveled. He was breathing hard like he'd just fought like hell to get here.

"H-Hunterrrr..." Celeste coughed against his hold and kicked her legs as her face slowly started to turn purple. "L-let goooo... bitch... deserves... it!"

"You fucking touch her, and I'll give you to *him* to sell, do you understand?"

At his words, Celeste's eyes widened in fear, and her kicking stopped. Just as she dropped the fork, the girl that had been restraining me disappeared. I spun around to see her thrown face-first into the wall with a sickening crack, and she slid down into a heap on the floor. I stared in shock at the thin trail of blood that oozed from her, but I didn't have time to register any of it because the next thing I knew, the person who attacked her seized my hand and tore me away from the crowd. I hurried after them, having no choice but to follow as the grip on me was so tight I lost the feeling in my fingers.

Shaw was urgently pulling me along, guiding me around the crush toward the emergency exit. The lights were still flashing, but it was dying down as more members of the faculty broke in. In the distance, I could hear sirens blaring from outside. Around us, injured kids were either lying on the floor bleeding, while some sat along the walls, looking thoroughly beaten down. From the doors leading to the atrium, a flood of people were scattering, students and members of the gangs, all making a break for it.

"Come *on*!" Shaw hissed at me, and he let go of my hand

to jump over the counter. I followed suit, trailing him as he shoved open the doors into the back. We ran past the work tables, oven, and fridges until an emergency exit came into view near the back. Shaw ran right toward it, and I continued following, both of us running out into the cold, October air.

Chapter ten

Casey

SHAW and I kept running until we reached a vacant park. All the kids' swings were destroyed, with the seats ripped up or the chains tangled in knots so bad, no kid could untie them for use. The slide was covered in graffiti, and I could see used needles scattering the ground beneath the jungle gym. I wearily sagged against the trunk of a large maple, its branches bare and clawed as they loomed overhead. My breath was coming out in white clouds, and I shivered as a cold breeze ripped through me. My jacket was still in my locker at school, so all I had on was my cardigan for warmth

When I finally caught my breath, I looked up to see Shaw standing there, hands in his pockets, looking completely calm and casual, as if we hadn't just been running from a gang brawl. He was not even out of breath. He just stood there like a statue, his blue eyes observing me, but I couldn't tell what he was thinking. He just seemed... *bored*.

"What the hell was that back there?" I gasped finally, straightening up to look at him.

"Come on, we gotta put some distance between the school and us." He grabbed my hand, ignoring my question, and urged me to continue running. I was about to argue when the sound of sirens coming up the street, heading to the school, promptly shut me up. Enough kids had disappeared by the time Shaw and I had left, which meant either they'd been dragged into the office, or they'd made a run for it. Which meant the Jackals were probably roaming the streets with us. We needed to get somewhere safe. So I followed him, taking back roads and alleys until we were on my street, heading right to my townhouse.

"How the he-" I was about to ask him how the hell he knew where I lived when I remembered... *Lee*. He'd escorted me home just last week. Of course, he told the others where I lived.

Shaw stopped beside the steps to my front door and glanced down at me. As usual, he was hiding in an oversized, dark hoodie, his face shadowed and terrifying, yet beautiful all at once, and rasped, "Go in, get what you need to spend the night at Meredith's, and I'll bring you there."

"How did you know-"

"Just do it, Casey." He released me and moved around to stand at the corner of my house, semi-shielded by the garbage cans and green bags of trash piled there.

I hurried up the steps, the urgency in his tone scaring me a little. That, and the fact that I saw him basically smash some chick's head into a stone wall, had me questioning a lot about Shaw at the moment. I reached into my bag, which had been slung crossbody on me this entire time, and found my keys. Nervously, I unlocked the door's several locks and walked in as quietly as I could. I was home early, and I had no idea if Keith was up, and if he was, what sort of mood he'd be in.

Blissfully, when I stepped inside, he was passed out on the sofa, an empty bottle of God knows what on the floor close by. As softly as I could, I tip-toed up the stairs, as I did my best to avoid the creaky boards as much as possible. I grabbed my black duffle bag in my room and shoved some clothes, my school bag with my textbooks and stuff, my laptop and phone charger inside, zipped it up, and then grabbed a thicker, white fleece to wear over my cardigan. I'd been walking carefully down the stairs when I heard Keith's growly voice rumbling, "Where the hell are you going? And why are you not in school?"

I groaned and now thudded down the steps. Like this asshole really cared about my education. "There was a fight at school, and afternoon classes were cancelled," I added, the lie coming easily.

"Where the hell are you going?" Keith glared at me from the living room where he'd been stirring on the sofa.

"I'm babysitting tonight," I told him.

"For who?"

"A girl at school."

He made another snorting sound that sickened me and muttered, "Fucking sluts…"

At once, my anger reached its boiling point in seconds, and I couldn't hold back as I took a seat on the stairs so that I could get my shoes on. I may not have been best buddies with Meredith, but I hated the way he was painting her this way, when she'd been one of the few kind people I'd met here and liked. "At least she takes care of her kid. And who are you to cast judgement on anyone, anyway?" I glanced over at him, disgusted just at the sight of him. "At least she cares for her kid and looks after her even while she tries to finish high school. She could have dropped out, but she didn't. She wants to earn her diploma. Are you really going to stand there and insult her when she's working her ass off so she can have a better life?"

His face reddened, and he slammed his fists onto the coffee table and got to his feet. "Are you going to get knocked up now, too? Is that your plan, Casey?"

"Oh yes, that's what I want to do. Life goals, get preggers and sit at home all day watching daytime TV." I shook my head at the ridiculous statement and quickly finished tying my laces. "You fucking know *nothing* about me..." I muttered under my breath.

He shoved the coffee table aside, making it flip and sending several empty beer bottles crashing to the opposite wall, and stomped toward me. "What the fuck was that?" he screamed, spittle flying from his lip as he approached. I shrank back, shocked by the sudden fury in his pale eyes. "You *never* talk back to me. Ever!" He reached out as if to grab me, and I made a break for it, grabbing my bag and lunging for the door. I flung the door open and ran out just as he grabbed the back of my sweater. He yanked me and sent me flying back into the house, but he was so drunk he stumbled when he slammed the front door closed. I tripped when he threw me back and fell to the floor, but I quickly rolled to the side and ran for the back door, which sat to the side of the kitchen. I flung open those locks as he staggered after me, howling and swearing as he threatened me not to leave. I was seconds away from flinging the door open when I felt a hand wrap around the nape of my neck before viscously ripping me back. Keith threw me to the floor where I sprawled, but it only took a second before he was crouched over me, hand over my throat keeping me in place.

"You're a fucking liar, just like your mother..." he breathed, his breath reeking of booze. I gagged at the smell and squirmed, twisting my legs in an attempt to free myself. "Just another lying, cheating-"

"Mom met Matthew years after she left your sorry ass!" I shouted into his face. At my words, his hand flexed, squeezing around my windpipe, and raised his free hand high into the air, fist clenched, ready to strike.

But before he could...

Crash!

We were both shocked to see Shaw come running inside, taking in the scene before him. Guess Keith had forgotten his own rule... lock the door behind you. Upon seeing Shaw standing there, he started shouting, "Who the fuck are you? Get the fuck out of my house or I'll call the police!" His hold on me had relaxed, and I immediately tried to twist away, only to have him grip me even harder before slamming my head back into the floorboards.

It wasn't the crazed, drunken look in Keith's eyes that scared me.

It was Shaw's reaction to seeing us this way, with my father crouched over my body, his hold choking me slightly, with me clawing at his hands to free myself. That dead look he carried ever since I saw him again shifted, his chin dropping, and the shadows around his eyes were growing. He stood there, as still as death for several seconds, and then, something changed. He shifted, his eyes going wide, looking slightly crazed before he moved, coming at us so quickly, neither Keith nor I were prepared for it. One second, Shaw was standing in the doorway, and the next, he had thrown himself at Keith, both of them falling to the side and down the hall.

I gasped as I sat up, catching my breath, and got to my feet, turning to see Shaw holding my father in the exact same way I'd just been restrained. Both of Shaw's hands were wrapped around Keith's throat. His pale eyes were bulging, spittle covering his blubbery-looking lips. He reached up, trying in vain to strike at his attacker's face, but Shaw had pulled back just enough to stay out of reach. Shaw had a look of insanity, with the way his eyes widened and how his mouth twisted as his teeth clenched tightly together, his arms shaking as he squeezed so hard, my dad began to turn purple.

"Shaw, stop!" I rushed over and pulled at one of his arms, but he didn't budge. He didn't even acknowledge me. It was like he was lost in some dark spell, and no rhyme or reason could reach him. "Shaw!" I shouted in his face as I tried to pry his fingers free. To my relief, one hand did retract, but all he did was reach beneath his overly large hoodie and seized something strapped to his side. When he raised his hand high over his head, I saw the black Honshu Karambit blade clenched tight in his fist. As a kid, Shaw had expressed an interest in knives the summer before I left, and he always seemed to favour this terrifying, cruel-looking, curved blade.

"I *warned* you not to touch!" Shaw's raspy voice broke on every other word, and his blue eyes filled with tears as he held my father down. Keith's eyes had widened in fear at the sight of the weapon, and he was practically clawing at Shaw's chest, his face almost blue now. Shaw, however, was trembling from head to foot, tears now streaming down his face. I jumped up and grabbed his arm from behind, fighting him from committing a mistake he could never come back from. "*No* touching! Never fucking touch again!" Shaw was raving over and over as he fought to free his arm from me. "No choking!" He cried. "No stroking! Never again! *Never* again, you son of a bitch!"

"Shaw, snap out of it!" I shouted desperately, wrenching his arm. Fuck, he was insanely strong for someone who wasn't rippling with muscle.

"What did I tell you!" he screamed, his voice cracking.

Hearing him shout like this snapped me back to the cafeteria and to the mystery person who had been calling my name. It had been Shaw. Whispering, quiet Shaw. I came back to it and pulled at his fingers, trying to loosen the knife from his hold as he wailed. He released Keith's throat, only to reach up and seize a fistful of his greying reddish-brown hair. With a sharp thrust, he smashed Keith's head back into the floor.

"I told you that you could no longer do this!" Shaw sobbed, bashing his head back. "No more. I don't like it. I don't like it!" *Smash!* "Why did you do this to me?" *Smash!* "I'm your son!" *Smash!* "You were supposed to protect me!" He shook his arm, trying to free his hand. When he couldn't, he dragged it forward and me with it, shocking me at his strength. The tip of the blade touched my father's side, causing his body to flinch away sharply.

"SHAW!" I screamed.

Beneath me, his entire body trembled violently, head dropping. He still held the blade to Keith's side, still held him by his hair, but he was no longer raving. Beneath his bowed head, from under the hood, I could hear his ragged breathing, the small sniffles he made as he came out of one of the many memories that haunted him.

Carefully, I pulled the blade free and flung it aside. Slowly, I reached out and touched the side of his face, turning him toward me. He fought it, but I didn't let him hide away. I grasped both sides of his face, cupping it, and forced him to look at me. His eyes were down, avoiding my stare, but I saw the trail of tears on his cheeks, and with my thumbs, I gently wiped them away and whispered, "Shaw?" When he didn't move or look at me, I gave him a small, little shake. "Shaw! Look. At. Me!"

Gradually, his beautiful blue eyes looked up, straight into mine, and he trembled. I could see the pain left behind by his piece of shit father. I could see the scars in his mind and the ghostly memories that terrorized him. I offered him the smallest of smiles and said in a hushed tone, "I'm here now, okay?"

At my words, his face crumpled and his eyes closed. He shuddered violently and finally released Keith, letting him fall to the floor, and he reached up to hold me instead. He clung to me desperately, and his sobs were muffled as he buried his face into my collarbone. I shushed and embraced him tight as I told him over and over, "That monster can't touch you now. He's gone. He'll never touch you again. I promise."

We only held each other for about a minute before Keith stirred, coughing, choking, and spitting as he tried to roll on to his side. I straightened up and grasped Shaw's knife that I'd tossed aside and, after a brief pause, handed it to him. Shaw immediately took it back, sliding it into its sheath that was strapped beneath his sweater. Scooping up my discarded bag on the floor close to the back door, I turned, ready to leave this shithole.

Shaw, however, stood and his cold, distant, brooding self was back in full force. Good. That meant he was back in control again. He picked up my father's cell from the coffee table, dialed a number, then dropped the phone on the floor by my father's twitching form. Without a word, he strode over to me, seized me by my upper arm, and shoved open the back door, pulling me along with him into the cold, Autumn air.

We ran across the field behind my house to the parking lot on the other side, where a small mini-mall sat, and I sagged against a lamp post to catch my breath. My heart was racing, and my hands were shaking, but I was more worried about

Shaw at the moment. When I glanced over at him, though, he was staring off in the distance, his eyes glazed over, like he didn't really see anything.

"How far is Meredith's?" I asked, shivering as a blast of wind cut through me. Even with my fleece sweater on, I shivered.

"About twenty minutes," he mumbled, back to the same boy I'd seen drifting through the hallways at school. I pulled my phone out of my bag, conscious of the knife inside, and checked the time. It was close to three now, and I wasn't supposed to be at her place till later, but Shaw didn't seem concerned about that. Instead, he nodded to me, a brow raised in question, and I nodded, ready to keep moving. I pocketed my phone quickly, not wanting to attract thieves, pulled my hood up over my head, and started off with my hands in the pockets of my sweater as I hurried. We ended up walking down the main street with thrift stores, pawnshops, pool halls, and bars. Very few people were actually walking with it being this cold out, so we didn't have to fight foot traffic.

My mind was still reeling from what a turn today took. First with school and whatever the hell went on between Vail and Hunter, then Celeste's weird psycho moment that got interrupted and Hunter's cryptic message, Shaw attacking her friend, and then us running from the police and members of Jackal. The cherry on top was my drunk-ass sad excuse of a father who went off the deep end tonight. Though Shaw almost killed him, I'm not surprised that I felt zero remorse for what just happened back there with Keith. Him being my blood relative meant nothing to me. Not when Matthew proved to be a caring, amazing dad in the short time I had him.

I was more concerned about Shaw and his mental state.

Childhood memories came flooding back to me, of the

times that we were both alone playing or when we slept side by side during our sleepovers, holding hands and whispering secrets to each other while Lee and Vail slept.

And some of those secrets were dark. Stuff I didn't quite understand at six, but when I asked my mother about it, saying it was stuff I overheard kids gossiping about in the schoolyard, I couldn't look any of the guys in the eye for about a week when she told me. And then, to think his father subjected him to such acts, it made me sick. I could only imagine what it looked like when he stormed into my father's house and saw him crouched over my body, holding me down by my throat.

I nervously peered up at him, but his sole focus was on getting us to Meredith's and Haldon's safely. He tugged me along, pulling me in close when someone else went to pass us, separating me from the strangers with his own body.

When we were about halfway there, I could barely even feel my face, and my teeth were chattering so hard I couldn't hear the cars rushing past us. Up ahead, beside a small food mart, was a dollar store, and I tugged at his arm, urging him inside with me so I could warm up for a few minutes.

"What?" he asked, his blue eyes shifting around as they took in every shopper in the vicinity. Jeez, is he always... *on*?

"I'm freezing. And might as well grab some supplies for tonight, too." I picked up a wired basket and made my way up the aisle. With Shaw so close on my heels, he might as well have been my shadow. My nose and my fingers were stinging a bit from the blast of warm air circulating through the store, and I rubbed my hands, holding the basket in the crook of my arm, as I browsed up and down the aisles. I felt the handle tug against my elbow, and I glimpsed down to see Shaw pulling at the basket. I allowed him to take it, and he carried it around for me while I started picking out random toys and gifts to bring to

Amelie. I found a pack of bubbles, a glitter art set, and a mound of stickers and crayons. When I found a pair of black-framed fake glasses with a light-up pumpkin nose, seeing as Halloween was only days away, I turned them on and slid them into place on my face as I veered down the next aisle.

"Um..."

I turned and saw Shaw watching me carefully, his stony demeanor forever in place. I grinned up at him nervously.

"What do you think? Will I win any popularity contests with this look?" I raised my brows and held my hands out at my sides, smiling wide, knowing I looked like an idiot, but he'd already seen me, so I might as well own it.

He shook his head and reached for the glasses, tossing them into the basket of goodies I'd collected for Amelie. "If you don't, I'd be shocked as hell," he murmured.

I smirked and moved around him, heading down the food aisle, tossing some candies, a box of crackers, some noodle soup cups, and a jug of fruit juice, then led the way to the checkout.

"Your dad hit you like that a lot?" Shaw whispered.

I avoided his eyes, choosing to add some mints to the basket, too. "I've only been here a week and a half. In that time, he slapped me once before what he did today. When I was younger..." I stiffened, thinking back that far. Mom had gotten us out when I was about six, so my memories were vague. But I did recall nights where I'd woken up to the sounds of his drunken rages, the banging, and the cries of my mother. I remembered leaving my bed once or twice and had come upon him standing over her still form. "It wasn't directed at me." I glanced down at the basket he was still carrying for me and changed the subject. "Think Amelie will like this stuff?" I asked.

His eyes remained on me for a long time, and I shifted

uncomfortably until his stare moved away. "No doubt," he murmured.

I paid with cash, a large chunk still leftover from the savings I'd accumulated over the years from birthdays, Christmases, and allowances. Shaw took the plastic bag of goodies before I could pick it up and carried it outside for me. I walked out after him, and he took my hand and guided us up the street without another word. After only a minute or two of walking, I heard a vibration come from the front pocket of his sweater, and he pulled out his cell phone, checking the name before quickly answering, too fast for me to see whose name had come up.

"Yeah?" he rasped, his steps moving a little quicker. I half-jogged to keep up with him. "Of course she's with me... there was a... complication." The sideways look he gave me said it all. He was talking about fucking Keith. But whatever the person on the other end of the phone said, it pissed Shaw off enough that he spit out, "Do you really think I'd fucking let that happen?" His voice rose ever so slightly, and instinctively, I reached out for the hand that'd been carrying my dollar store purchases, and I stroked the back of it with my fingertips. He immediately calmed and slowed his gait, still seeming agitated with whoever was on the other line. "Whatever, we'll be there in five minutes." He hung up, thrusting his phone back into his pocket, then passed his bag to his other hand so he could snatch at mine. He held it tight, interlocking our fingers together.

Holding hands like this with Shaw, I felt myself choking on the emotional impact of it, which was threatening to knock me off my feet. It felt so familiar and so right, and yet, I still knew nothing of who he had become. All I did know was that very quickly, old feelings, old ties, already felt more important to me than my old kin, my father. It wasn't my father I comforted or was worried about back there... It was

Shaw. When his thumb tentatively began to glide up and down the top of my hand, I peered up to see him watching me, his sideways look apprehensive. But when I squeezed his hand in return, the tiniest flicker of a smile threatened to crack through his stony disposition for just the briefest of moments. But I knew I saw it.

"I'm proud of you for standing up to that bitch, Celeste," he told me as we waited for the light to change so we could cross the busy intersection.

I chuckled a little and rolled my eyes. "Don't know what her deal is, but I'm getting sick of it. I guess everyone has a limit, right? I just thought mine would have lasted longer…"

"Honestly, I think everyone in the school expected you to crumble after the first day," he said, leading the way across when the WALK light turned green.

I raised my brows, and he glanced at me, flashing me a beautiful, crooked smile. "Oh really? Were there bets or something?"

He shrugged. "Wouldn't you like to know?"

"Yes, cuz I would have wanted to make one of my own."

He bowed his head, hiding that tiny smile from me, as we turned into a small apartment complex. "You're still the same," he said softly, affection lacing every one of his words. He almost sounded relieved.

"You are, too. In some ways," I said, studying him, despite how he tried to hide his face from me. "But in other ways, you're different."

"How?" He asked curiously.

"I don't know… darker. Scarier…"

He said nothing but continued to stroke my hand with his thumb, which told me he wasn't offended by my statement. If Shaw were ever upset in the past, he'd withdraw from everyone. No one could touch him. He wouldn't allow it. Even me, on the rare occasion.

Meredith, Lee, and their roommate lived on the top floor of a four-story apartment building, which, on the outside, looked like it had seen better days. The brick walls were covered with graffiti art, the design and overall aesthetic were very seventies, and the parking lot was pitted with potholes. The inside was no better. The property owner either didn't give a shit about the people who lived here, or they couldn't afford the upkeep. The yellow wallpaper in the halls was peeling, and there were heavy water stains in the ceiling and, in some places, the water had managed to leak through completely, leaving holes that revealed the plumbing above. The floors were cream and olive green tiling that was cracked and uneven, and when we climbed the stairs, as there was no elevator, I could hear yelling from some units, TV's blaring in others, and smell booze and cigarettes from most.

When we got to the top floor, Shaw knocked on the dark wood-grained door on the end, and after a momentary pause, we could hear several locks snapping open as we waited. Meredith opened the door and greeted Shaw with a smile, not seeming at all surprised to see us together, and ushered us in. When she closed the door behind us and turned around, I saw an angry red mark on her left cheek, no doubt a souvenir from the massive fight in the cafeteria hours earlier.

The apartment was small and cozy. The living room was shared with the small kitchen. There was a hallway leading left and one leading right, and I could only assume those led to where their bedrooms were. Haldon was relaxing on their couch, an old grey one that was covered in pale pink and blue pillows and blankets, and on the floor, sitting between his outstretched legs, was the cutest little girl. Amelie was a blend of Haldon and Meredith, with paler skin but jet black hair and dark, brown eyes that matched her father's. Her face, however, reminded me strongly of Mer when she glanced up to smile at Shaw, her pudgy little cheeks dimpling.

"Amelie, this is Casey. She's going to be babysitting you tonight," Meredith said, gesturing to me as she took my fleece sweater and hung it on a coat tree. Amelie peered up, noticing me, a stranger, and her smile became shyer, more uncertain. I took the bag of goodies from Shaw and crouched down so I was at her level. "Do you like stickers?" I asked as Shaw and Haldon greeted each other in low murmurs. Meredith and the two guys moved over into the kitchen, speaking so low that I couldn't hear a thing. But I ignored them as I gave the little girl my whole attention.

At once, I could see I'd piqued her interest. Her eyes darted down to the bag with curiosity, and she craned her neck to try to see inside. I reached in and pulled out a sheet of unicorn and star stickers and showed them to her. At once, her face brightened up, and she reached for them. I handed them over and watched as her mouth ticked up into a smile.

"She's already had her supper," Meredith said, strolling back into the room. "She can stay up for another four hours before she has to go to bed," Meredith said the last few words like they were more of a warning to her little girl than a suggestion to me. She led me down the hallway to her and Haldon's room, where there was a big, queen-sized bed in one corner, and at the end of it, is a small little toddler-sized bed with princess sheets and a comforter. There was a nightlight beside it, and her little purple PJs were folded nicely on the pillow.

"She needs to brush her teeth before, and she can have two stories… *no more,* right Amelie?" Meredith brought me back into the living room, where Shaw had made himself comfortable on one end of the couch while Haldon was scrolling through his phone, texting wildly.

Amelie, however, was distracted by the stickers. I chuckled. "Don't worry about it. I'll take care of things. You just concentrate on your... uh, crew business?" I said with uncertainty, and glanced around the kitchen. "Is there an emergency contact, just in case? Is she allergic to anything?" I asked.

"Yes, I've got Haldon's grandmother's number written on the fridge. She lives in the apartment below us, so if anything happens or if you need someone, feel free to knock on her door. She knows you're here," Meredith said. "And Amelie hasn't shown any signs of allergies to anything," she added as she took a seat on the opposite end of the sofa from Shaw. "We just need to wait for the all-clear, and then we're off."

I knew better than to pry into their private club business, so I made myself comfortable on the floor in front of Shaw, sitting across from Amelie, and helped her peel off some of the stickers so she could paste them into her colouring book. Behind me, I had felt him shift, and slowly, one of his legs extended, moving forward until it rested alongside me, pressing into my side. I leaned into him, finding comfort in this familiar closeness, and ignored Meredith's inquisitive stare.

From down the hall, I heard a door snap shut, followed by the running of a shower. I raised a brow at her, and she just grinned. "That'd be the roomie. He usually works the graveyard shift at a warehouse on the south side." She hesitated a moment, chewing the corner of her lip, smiling when Amelie squealed over a rainbow sticker that seemed to be her favourite. "Just a heads up, he's kind of sensitive about his appearance, so I'm just giving you forewarning not to react when you see him."

"What do you mean?" I asked, alarmingly. Behind me,

Shaw shifted in his seat before I felt his hands reach around my middle to slide me back so that I was resting against the couch, sitting between his legs. I let him move me and settle in, feeling more comfortable having the sofa to relax against, but I was curious as to what the hell Meredith was talking about.

"He was attacked by some biker when he was a kid," she said softly, glancing at Amelie, but she was too distracted by her television show and the stickers to pay us any attention. "Had a bunch of surgeries. Hard palate, teeth, he's nearly blind in one of his eyes, and they had to completely recon- struct his nose."

I felt a numbness seeping into me at what she was saying. "He was a *kid*?" I asked, incredulously.

"Thirteen, yeah," she said, shaking her head, her face twisted in anger. "Fucking jumped walking home. But he's a great guy. Really nice, and he's awesome with Amelie. Helps us out a lot. Wants Haldon and I to finish high school." Haldon came over then, sitting on the arm of the couch at Mer's side, and wrapped an arm around her. She snuggled into his side and reached up to play with his long, dark hair. When Amelie burst into a fit of giggles at something that happened on her show, I saw Haldon's face light up at the sound. Despite their circumstances, being teenage parents, living in Harley of all places, they were obviously happy, and I felt a flicker of jealousy. What I wouldn't give to have that closeness with someone, to feel that love again.

The moment was broken when Haldon's phone buzzed. He checked it and was on his feet in an instant, moving over to the front door. I peered over my shoulder at Shaw, and sure enough, he was watching everything like a hawk, his eyes following his crew member. A minute later, someone pounded three times on the front door in quick succession. Haldon opened the door in a flash, and my mouth dropped to see Vail and Lee storm in. I didn't see any sign of them when Shaw and I had ran out of the cafeteria. I had no idea what had happened to them. As soon as the door was shut and bolted behind them, Vail greeted Haldon with a fist bump and a shoulder hug before turning to the rest of us.

When his hazel eyes spotted me sitting on the floor between Shaw's legs, he didn't seem the least bit surprised, though his lips had pressed tightly together, as if it bothered him in some way. Instead of saying anything to us, he just gave his brother a quick nod before turning to Meredith. "You okay?" he asked, passing by Amelie with a little pat on her head. The little girl didn't move an inch, evidently already comfortable and familiar with these guys.

"Please, this is nothing," Meredith scoffed, flipping her blue hair over her shoulder as she peered up at Shaw, coming off as confident as always. "That bitch just got one punch in. I got about fifty. But man, you should have seen *Casey*..."

I felt everyone's eyes move to me, and I shrank back between Shaw's legs, suddenly embarrassed.

"She saved my ass from that Jackal 'ho, Celeste. Casey tackled her like a linebacker! It was fucking brilliant! I didn't see what happened after cuz Mrs. Reeves grabbed me and pushed me out into the hall, but seeing Celeste's skeletal body flailing like a wacky-waving-inflatable-arm-tube-man was amazing." She peeked up at Vail, brows raised high. "They didn't keep you long?"

"No, not this time. But I'll be MIA from school this week."

"We can't have that!" Haldon said from the door, speaking for the first time. "What if the Jackals pull something while you're gone?"

"They won't. Hunter is suspended for the week, too," Vail said confidently.

"Vail," Shaw said suddenly, standing up over me, "I need to talk to you."

171

The tightness in his voice made me instantly wary as he stepped away, heading down the hall to Meredith's family's bedroom, with Vail hot on his heels. Before I could follow to intervene, as I had a sneaking suspicion he was going to fill him in on what happened with Keith, Lee sauntered over, slid his hands beneath my armpits, and lifted me up off the ground. I squealed in surprise at being lifted so easily, but he just sat in Shaw's vacated spot, settling me so that I was literally straddling his lap, and pulled me close so that my ear was pressed against his chest. His hands remained on my waist, and his voice rumbled against me as he asked, "You okay, Babe?"

"I'm fine," I muttered, feeling so on display to be sitting so intimately with him, but Meredith and Haldon were moving around, each grabbing a backpack and their black leather jackets.

Lee reached up with one hand and cupped my chin, urging me to lift my face so he could see me. He held me carefully as he turned my head to the side, his eyes catching the marks Keith left behind on my throat, and his dark brows pulled together as he glowered. I hadn't seen myself yet, but I was sure there would be some bruising forming there. It was still tender as hell. "What the fuck is this?" he snarled.

"Nothing, just-"

"It's *not* nothing, Casey. What the hell happened? Was this from someone in the cafeteria?"

"No, it's not that, I-"

Vail came storming out into the living room, his hazel eyes burning with rage as he stomped over to Lee and me. Wordlessly, he lifted me out of Lee's lap, and I grumbled, "What is it with you guys and manhandling me? My legs aren't broken! I can walk!"

But Vail ignored me as he lifted my chin to get a look at

my throat and growled. He peeked over his shoulder as Shaw joined us again and snapped. "How did-"

"Called an ambulance and we left," Shaw grunted, moving to the front door and leaned against the wall. "Don't know what else happened, but we should make a stop by later when it's quiet."

Vail nodded, releasing me, and Lee pulled me back down into his lap, arms wrapping around me again as he snuggled me close. "So you're cool watching things here tonight, man?"

"We're good here," Lee said, and nodded to Amelie. "What say you, kiddo? You down to hang out with Casey and me tonight?" I raised my brows, surprised, and glanced over at Meredith, who seemed utterly unfazed by this information. I thought I was babysitting on my own? Now it suddenly felt like I was the one being babysat.

Amelie leaned back, tilting her head so that she was peering at us nearly upside down, and grinned wide, nodding enthusiastically just as the door down the hall opened and someone else joined us.

When I looked at Meredith's roommate, peering over my shoulder from Lee's lap, I suddenly put together what she had said about his face and how sensitive he was about it. He had a long, crooked scar running up the middle of it, partially over his upper lip connecting to his nose and up over his left eye. His light brown hair was long, nearly to his shoulders, and it was still wet from his shower. He let it fall over his face, which was also covered in pitted scars aside from the surgical one, hiding himself.

Holy shit... I thought when I saw the damage that had been done to him. And he was just thirteen when it happened? My God... what kind of fucking psycho would do such a thing?

"Hi, I'm Casey." I went to get up, but Lee held on to my waist, keeping me where I was, which was awkward enough in front of the others but to be here meeting a complete stranger, I could feel my cheeks turning a little pink. So I held out my hand instead. He came over, a hint of what I thought was supposed to be a smile on his face, but it was warped due to his scars.

"Hi Casey, I'm Eli." He shook my hand with a firm grip, and as I grinned up at him, for just a moment, I thought I could see what he would have looked like if he hadn't been attacked, and he was actually very handsome. Eli's dark brown eyes scrunch up for just a moment when he got a better look at my face, and for a second, I wondered if I had a bruise elsewhere since his reaction was a bit off. He dropped my hand and stepped back slightly, looking a little perturbed. But when he peered into my eyes again, something like relief seemed to roll off him, and he let out a harsh breath. "Sorry, I-I'm tired, I think. Long night last night and another one tonight…" His voice trailed off, sounding uncertain.

"You working, Eli?" Amelie got to her feet and ran over to him, her arms outstretched. Eli scooped her up and gave the top of her head a little kiss.

"Sorry, Princess. No babysitting from me tonight."

She pouted a little before she threw her arms around his neck.

"What am I? Chopped liver?" Lee called out sarcastically.

But Amelie just held on to Eli while Vail, Shaw, and her parents talked in quick, low whispers for a minute before Meredith straightened and reached for her daughter. Amelie was passed over to her, and Eli plonked himself down on the lounger chair by the door, his hair falling over his face while he tied up his work boots.

"You be a good girl for Lee and Casey, alright? You do what they say." She gave her a little kiss on her nose, and Amelie giggled. She set her daughter down and headed over to the guys standing at the door, but Vail had moved away,

174

walking right up to Lee and me, standing so close I couldn't help but wish he'd stop being such a prick already.

"And *you* listen to Lee," he said, ruining any moment of weakness I'd felt for him. When I narrowed my eyes, Vail leaned down, his hands clasping my upper arms as he turned me to face him. "I mean it, Casey!" he snapped, giving me a little shake.

"Jeez, Vail! Chill! What the hell do you think I'm gonna do?" I shook him off me and climbed off Lee's lap.

"It's been a long time since you lived here, Casey," Vail said sharply, following me closely. When I turned away, he snatched my wrist and tugged me into the dark hallway, away from everyone else, and pressed me against the wall with his hips. "It's not like when we were kids, darling," he whispered, his face cold and lifeless. "The shit that's happened, that *could* happen... it's life and death. And I don't think you understand that."

"Give me some credit, Vail," I hissed at him, raising my chin a little in a challenge. "I don't have a death wish. I'm not gonna run out of here or let strangers into the apartment-"

Vail slammed his hand over my head, and I shut up, staring up at him wide-eyed, knowing he could see how much he scared me. He leaned close, so close that the tips of our noses brushed each other. "Goddamn it, Casey!" His lower lip trembled ever so slightly, and he licked it, his eyes staring deep into mine in a way that knocked the air from my lungs. "It's not the time for your smart-mouth. I'm fucking serious..." I felt the brush of his rough, calloused fingers as they stroked along my collarbone. His touch on my skin made my breath catch, and he heard it. Vail sagged a little, his stony demeanor falling just the tiniest fraction, and he lightly touched his forehead to mine, closing his eyes. "Why did you come back?" he whispered at last, his voice strained like he was in pain.

I deliberated, trying to remember how to breathe at that moment. Vail had always rocked my emotions and had always had this weird power over me. But when I was younger, I took it as a sign of his natural right as leader of our little group. Now? He seemed like he was battling some inner turmoil. Something was tormenting him. What, I didn't know, but the way he whispered those words made it feel like a knife was cutting into my heart.

"Mom…" I breathed.

Vail's eyes snapped open, and having him see me when I spoke was too much. I stared down at the floor to where his feet stood on either side of mine. "What happened?" he asked gently.

I sucked in a shaky breath between my teeth, memories of my mother now rushing back, haunting me. "She's gone, Vail."

His hand at the base of my throat paused, and then ever so slowly, he lowered it, sliding it down until it rested right over my heart. I tentatively peered up at him and saw the broken look in his eyes when he finally nodded and looked away, his gaze resting at a spot over my head. He understood precisely what I meant when I said she was gone. Here, in this place, *gone* meant just that. Nevermore. When he met my eyes again, his expression seemed less troubled. In fact, it had morphed completely, as though that battle in his mind had finally ended, and one side had won.

Hand still pressed to my heart, Vail leaned in, his lips brushing over mine, while his other hand cupped my cheek and murmured, "We're your family now." Without another word to me, he let go, striding away with a new purpose, his posture confident and ready. "Okay, guys. Let's get going. I want to be back here no later than three."

The others all nodded, having not heard our whispered conversation, and went to follow his orders. Eli was already gone, and Meredith and Haldon gave Amelie another kiss goodbye before they followed Vail out. I stepped back into the living room to see Shaw lingering, waiting. He watched me, his face as cold and expressionless as always, but something in his eyes was burning into my soul.

"Shaw?" I was still trembling from my interaction with Vail, but seeing Shaw looking so conflicted makes me nervous. Was he about to go off the deep end again?

Shaw, however, suddenly stormed toward me, the dark shadows under his eyes giving him an almost gaunt expression. But I was caught off guard when he embraced me tightly, holding my face in his hands, and crushed his mouth to mine. Shaw's lips had always been pouty and full, and when he kissed me, I could feel how soft they were. They moulded to mine, his hold fierce and intense. His lips moved against mine, and when the shock wore off after a few seconds, I kissed him back.

It didn't last long, but when he pulled back, still holding me, he was breathless, and I could see the tiniest fraction of light in his eyes that hadn't been there before. They were less strained, his cheeks slightly pinked, bringing colour into his face for once.

"Listen to Lee," he rasped, giving my forehead a soft, goodbye kiss, and turned, stalking out behind the others before closing the door securely behind himself.

Lee, who had been standing off to the side, slid the locks into place, looking the slightest bit miffed, while Amelie giggled. "Ewww... you kissed a boy!"

I quickly turned away before Lee could cast me a judgemental glare and reached into the plastic bag of goodies. "Hey Amelie, do you like bubbles?"

Chapter eleven

Casey

HOLY CRAP... if babysitting a two and a half-year-old didn't work as birth control, I didn't know what else would. By the time I got Amelie down and asleep, it'd been an hour past her bedtime. When the others left, she and I played with the bubbles while Lee busied himself in the kitchen, putting together the noodle cups and crackers for us to have. While he and I ate, Amelie busied herself with the stickers, choosing instead to put them all over her face, and then decided both Lee and I needed to be "decorated" too. For the better part of the night, he walked around with two unicorns on his cheeks and a rainbow on his forehead, while I was littered with an assortment of flowers, stars, and butterflies.

We settled her down a little by using the glitter pens I got for her, and I put my artistic skills to use when I showed her how to draw a house. That distraction only lasted about ten minutes before she took the pink and purple pens and smeared some on my cheeks, giggling wildly in the process.

She had eaten some of the candy, and that set her off into a crazy sugar rush. I spent a good half hour chasing her around, pretending she was a princess and I was a dragon trying to capture her and put her in my tower (which was the cushy armchair in the far corner). Lee came swooping in as her brave knight in shining armour and literally picked me up and threw me onto the couch, sitting on my legs to keep me from moving. Amelie, loving the game change, took the opportunity to jump on my stomach and giggle wildly as Lee tickled her.

We finished the night by brushing her teeth, getting her into her PJ's, and because she insisted I wear the fake glasses with the glowing pumpkin nose, I wore them while I read her *four* books, rather than the two her mother had insisted upon. But I mean, how could I not? She was too freaking cute and used that power against me with her big, puppy dog eyes. So I gave in, but luckily, near the end of the last book, when I peeked down at her, she was sprawled out on her pillow with her mouth partly open and her hair messily strewn over her face. I carefully brushed it off her face, tucked her into her little bed, then turned on the nightlight and tiptoed out of the room, leaving the door slightly ajar in case she called for me.

When I stepped back out into the living room where Lee was lying sprawled on the sofa, he took one look at me and chuckled before lifting his phone and taking a picture. I jumped back, shielding myself with my hand to prevent him from taking any more.

"Wha-?" I stopped, realizing that I hadn't removed any of the stickers, glitter, or glowing nose glasses. "Delete that photo."

"No," he grinned, still holding it aloft.

"Lee, c'mon," I grumbled, moving closer and throwing the glasses aside. I should have thought of getting a picture of him with his unicorn and rainbow stickers earlier, but he'd already removed them. "Last thing I need is blackmail material. Give it." I reached out with my other hand, wiggling my fingers at him.

Lee smirked and rested his hands behind his head, phone now hidden behind his dreads. "Make me." He gave me a flirty little wink before puckering his lips and blowing me a kiss.

"Funny. C'mon. Delete it, please." I let my hands drop, narrowing my eyes at him. I wasn't in the mood to walk into school tomorrow to find this had been printed out and stuck on the walls all over the building with some kinky bullcrap written on it. Lee once attached a bunch of star caps meant for toy guns and glued them under the seats of every toilet in school so that when the poor students or teachers sat down, well, you can imagine the freak out the faculty had over it. He wasn't caught for that one. Another time, he took a polaroid of Shaw in the middle of our Friday night sleepovers while he was in the middle of a dare, which was to act like a chicken until his next turn. The photo was blown up and pasted over every hanging portrait in the library at school after he had stolen a teacher's ID card and snuck into the lounge to use their copier. While the staff had questioned Shaw, he never sold out his friend, but later, Lee did get punched in the gut for it.

So my nerves were a little rattled at the idea of him having my photo looking like I got puked on by kids' craft supplies. "Lee, please..." I was standing beside him, hands now on my hips while he was lying stretched out like a lazy king on the sofa, taking up every bit of space with his bulk. His smirk was irritating the hell out of me, even though I was annoyed mostly with myself for finding him so freaking sexy at this moment. His arms were bulging with muscles, his dark charcoal t-shirt was stretching over his broad chest. I could actually see the lines of his stomach as though the shirt was too small for him. And God help me, but the way his dark eyes roamed over me, looking as though he enjoyed what he was seeing with the glitter, stickers, and all, had my heart hammering against my chest.

"I like that," he said, his playful smile still in place.

"Like what?"

"You saying, 'Lee, please'..." He bit his lip, and I rolled my eyes at him. "It's sexy as hell," he added, unfazed by my attitude.

"I was being polite, which you are not."

"I never said I *was* polite."

"No, but I'd appreciate you not screwing with me on this. I don't need to give anyone at school more ammo," I said softly.

At that, his smirk dropped, his expression morphing to one of clarity. "No one is going to fuck with you at school anymore, Casey," he said seriously.

I scoffed and went to sit down, but the bastard was so freaking huge, there was no space for me. "Move over, would you?"

"Only if you say, *Lee, please!*" He grinned.

"Oh, for the love of…" I turned, about to head to the easy chair, when his hand whipped out, wrapping around my wrist, and he tugged me down, so I was sitting on his thighs. "I can sit over there-"

"Just relax, babe. We used to cuddle all the time, remember?"

I did, but I wasn't going to get into that. Besides, things are different now. We were older, and with the flirtatious way he was interacting with me, I knew what he was doing. But I still wasn't sure where I stood with these guys. Vail had said, *we're your family now,* but I had no idea what that meant. And the others hadn't heard him, so whatever was on his mind, it wasn't knowledge to his crew. Lee, however, didn't seem to care one way or another. So when I remained silent, he gently tugged at my wrist, urging me closer.

"Okay, I'll delete the photo if you cuddle with me like we used to," he said, his expression utterly void of humour.

"Seriously?" I raised a brow skeptically at him, and he just nodded. "Fine. Delete the photo first so that I can see."

He brought his phone around, unlocked it, and opened his photo gallery. With me watching, he deliberately deleted the picture from his phone, and thank God he did because, on top of the ridiculous glasses, stickers, and glitter, I resembled a deer in headlights in the shot. But it was gone now, and I appreciated his honesty.

"Now, you need to fulfill your end of the bargain." Lee's lips curled up, and he patted his chest.

I wanted to roll my eyes again at his confident yet obvious flirtation, but instead, I laid on top of him as he spread his legs so I could rest between them. I angled my head to the side and rested it over his heart, facing the television, playing some tv show about superheroes. I felt his arms come up around me, holding me against himself in that old familiar way, except now, he was built like the Terminator. But it was still comfortable, lying this way with him. His warmth radiating from him like he was a furnace or something. His hold was gentle, and occasionally, I felt his fingers combing through my hair, an old habit now coming back to life.

❀

"How'd it go?" Lee's voice stirred me out of my slumber. I was awake, but I kept my eyes closed. I was too comfy right now. I was lying on my side with him spooning me from behind on the couch, our positions having shifted in sleep.

After all the chaos of yesterday and then babysitting, I was beat.

"Fucking shit... thought we had the schedule right, but someone must have tipped them off," Vail said.

"Maverick's informant?" Shaw rasped. *Maverick? Who the hell was Maverick?*

"We don't know that," Meredith's calm voice whispered, "We're lucky we all got out of there in one piece. Just wish I could have made it into the basement to confirm-"

"I know, Mer." *Haldon? I think.* "But I didn't want you sneaking down there alone."

"I can handle myself," she insisted, in true Meredith fashion.

"I know, *mon chaton*, but I would never forgive myself if we were wrong and it was one of the Beasts traps, or worse... the Faceless."

Meredith mumbled something but quieted down at her boyfriend's words. Finally, she said in a hushed voice. "How was babysitting?"

"It was great," Lee murmured back, keeping his voice low. "Amelie was a sweetheart, but holy God, I don't know how you two do this..."

Meredith chuckled as Haldon said, "I'm gonna go check on her real quick. You guys are free to sleep here tonight. I'll get out some blankets." And his light footsteps disappeared down the hall.

"Looks like my baby isn't the only one who got tired out," she added, sounding amused. "Casey looks wiped. I can see Amelie had her way with her." She chuckled a little, obviously noticing the stickers and glitter still on my cheeks.

I felt someone brush my hair away from my face, the fingers more slender than Lee's, and then a soft pair of lips touched my forehead. Shaw. He didn't say a word but remained close, his forehead resting to mine.

"Did you guys get her stuff?" Lee asked.

Huh?

"Shaw got me in. Found whatever I could of hers and shoved it in this hockey bag," Meredith said. "I'm gonna check on Amelie, then bring you guys some of Haldon's sweats to change into. You all okay sleeping out here?"

"We'll be fine," Vail said from somewhere close by. "Like old times..." His voice was gentle at those words, his tone completely different than it had been since I arrived back here. In the background, I could hear everyone quietly shuffling around, and I peeked through my lashes to see that they'd moved the coffee table aside and were laying out several quilts onto the floor as cushioning from the hard surface. Haldon appeared in a pair of sweats, his chest bare and what seemed like tribal markings tattooed over his chest and upper arms. He was carrying an armload of pillows and extra clothes for the guys to change into.

Behind me, Lee stirred, carefully moving me into his arms and lifting me before I felt the soft touch of the blankets beneath me. I rolled onto my side, cradling a pillow beneath my head, feeling so perfectly safe and... it was weird, as well as nostalgic. Vail was right. It was like old times.

I laid still, halfway between asleep and awake, my brain slowly trying to register what was happening.

"Who was that one guy?" Haldon asked suddenly, and for some reason, a chilly silence followed his question. "The biker that showed up with the Beasts? He wasn't wearing a cut like the others..."

"I don't fucking know," Vail murmured, sounding perturbed. *Who the hell were they talking about that even Vail seemed scared?* "Whoever he was, he didn't give a shit that we were just high school kids. Seeing him grab Bryce and..." Vail's voice grew tight, his stony demeanor faltering fast. "I actually felt bad for that fucker. I know he was Hunter's closest ally, but holy shit..."

A pair of footsteps came back into the room. "You guys talking about that scary-ass motherfucker who used the chainsaw on-"

"Yeah," Haldon quickly cut her off, sounding sick. "That guy..."

More silence followed until finally, Meredith spoke again, though she sounded severely shaken, "If Elias has guys like *that* working for him... even with Maverick and his guys backing us, what can *we* do?"

"Fucking survive, and fight like hell to save as many as we can," Vail sighed heavily, "I know it's dangerous as fuck. Hell, I don't blame anyone for backing out. Especially you guys... you both have a kid to think about. But, if the cops can't do anything or those fucking assholes in City Hall... then it's up to us to defend our own. Girls keep getting taken, and I'm sick of everyone turning their heads away just because they're from Harley. "

Everyone was quiet until Haldon murmured, "Let's all get some rest, yeah? I'm beat, and Amelie has been getting up early in the mornings. Thank fuck for Mamie..." I could hear his footsteps padding away down the hall.

"I agree. Rest up, guys, we'll talk tomorrow, alright?" Meredith said gently. "Tonight wasn't a failure. That fact that we tried is more than anyone else has done."

"Night, Mer," Lee said, and her footsteps disappeared down the hall.

As I laid there, I could feel the guys shifting around me for a few minutes, the sounds of material telling me that they were changing. As much as I wanted to have a look, I didn't want to be caught eavesdropping. So I laid as still as could be, breathing softly, hoping I was convincing enough.

"Shaw, I know you want to but..." Vail's voice trailed off a little, and it worried me how disturbed he sounded, "... but I *need* her tonight."

Shaw remained quiet for a few seconds before his gravelly whisper broke the silence, "Go ahead, brother."

I felt the blankets shift a little, and then a pair of arms were wrapping around me, rolling me over and pulling me in. Vail held me tight, turning my face into his neck so that he could bury his nose into my hair. He took a deep breath and released a long, shuddering sigh. His body was tense for a moment before he finally relaxed. I felt him cover us with a blanket, and I sensed the other two settling in around us.

For a long while, no one said anything. We just laid there, like we'd done so many times before, safe together once more.

"Vail," Shaw rasped.

"Yeah?" His voice was sleepy, relaxed, and for once, sounded content. I nestled in a little closer, feeling like I was home in his arms.

Shaw paused for a moment before whispering, "We're keeping her now, right?"

From behind us, I could hear Lee suck in a sharp breath, then stop, as though he was holding it as he waited with anticipation for an answer.

I felt Vail's lips in my hair, his nose lightly skimming along my temple, before he breathed, "Yes."

Chapter twelve

Casey

"OH MY GOD, LEE!" Meredith's voice whispered, but it woke me up anyway. "Did they sleep like that last night? Holy crap, they're so cute!"

"Keep it down, woman," Lee's insanely baritone voice murmured from the kitchen area. "Let them sleep! It was a rough night..."

There was a little bit of silence following this. I realized then that I had been curled up on the thick layer of blankets on the floor, and I was wholly enveloped in Vail's arms. My face was tucked beneath his jaw, and one of his hands was cupping the back of my head, the other wrapped around, holding me flush against the muscled planes of his body. At my back, I could feel Shaw huddled up against me, his forehead pressing into the space between my shoulder blades. I could tell by how soft both of their breathing was that they were passed out still, so I did my best to relax, keeping my eyes closed as I pretended to keep sleeping, listening in.

"Best if we all lay low today," Lee said softly. "I doubt anyone from Vendetta will show up at school. Same with the Jackals-"

"*Especially* the Jackals," Meredith interrupted him. "Bryce…"

"Yeah," Lee's voice choked up a bit at the mention of Bryce Fraser. I thought back to what I overheard last night. Something about a biker? And… and a chainsaw…

I felt the bile rising in my throat. *What the fuck happened last night? What were they doing?!*

As I shivered at the ominous suggestion of Bryce's fate, I instinctively clung to Vail, who released a little grunt in his sleep, but then only tossed a leg over both of mine before settling back into his slumber.

"So, what's going to happen to Casey now?" Meredith whispered. "If you give me the keys, I can drop her off at school after she wakes up and has some breakfast." It was then that I smelled coffee and maple syrup and… *oh lord help me, bacon!* My stomach involuntarily rumbled, but thankfully, not loud enough for the others to have heard.

"Casey won't be going to school today," Lee said firmly, like a decision had already been made.

"Won't that just draw attention to her?" Meredith said, her voice filled with warning. "She is still legally under her father's care-"

"That asshole won't be for long." He responded confidently.

"Oh?" I could hear the surprise in her voice. "When was this decision made? You guys haven't talked-"

"This was made a long time ago, before you even lived here, Mer."

A momentary silence followed before she spoke up again, "Childhood pacts don't mean anything, Lee."

"They do in Harley."

I heard the jingle of keys in the locks, the metal sliding as each one was turned before the door opened, and I listened to Haldon murmur, "Amelie is with Mamie for the morning, and I gotta get ready for work-"

"No, Baby!" Meredith sounds pained at the thought of him going out. "I thought you booked today off? We need to lay low, remember? That's why we're skipping school."

"We need the money, *mon chaton*." I heard a little smack of their lips. "And if I'm not in school today, might as well make some extra cash."

I could hear her grumbling at his logical reasoning, followed by him letting out a short, deep chuckle. "Gonna go get ready. Stay inside today. Enjoy a day off. You never get one."

"Neither do you." she reminded him.

"I'll be home tonight, okay? I'll grab some groceries, and we can have a family supper for once. Amelie will love it."

My heart wrenched for them as more and more of their situation became clear. I hadn't even considered how Meredith and Haldon supported their daughter or afforded this place. They must work after school and on weekends to make enough money.

"What are you guys up to today?" Haldon asked quietly as he moved around the kitchen.

"Bringing Casey home with us," Lee said, still sounding as confident and sure of himself as ever.

Home with them? What did that mean exactly? My mind was racing at the thought of living with these guys. But then again, did they all live with each other? Or with one of their parents? The only ones I remember being in the picture were Shaw's aunt and uncle, Lee's parents, and Vail's mother, who was a write-off.

Surprisingly, the thought of leaving Keith and living with one, two, or all three of them had me feeling completely...

calm. I felt a warmth spread throughout my body at the thought. After Vail's statement last night, *we're your family now*, how everything in him seemed to change with those words, I felt like I'd found three missing pieces of my soul again. All four of us, lying together on the blankets last night, just like we used to, it felt right. We were together again.

"What are you guys planning, Lee?" she asked after several minutes. "From how I understand it, Casey is biding her time until she can leave this place." She sounded suspicious as hell.

"We'll do what we have to in order to keep her safe," he said, as calm as ever.

Meredith sighed, sounding upset, "She won't like it-"

"Tough shit." Lee scoffed. "That's life. You just have to go with it and take what it throws at you." It's the first time I'd really heard him speak like this, and honestly, it caught me off guard. Lee was always so calm and collected, but he was speaking like a leader, someone who made the calls right now, and it hit me. I always thought Shaw was Vail's second, when in actuality, it was Lee. With Vail passed out here with me, Lee was speaking for him and the other two.

I peered through my eyes, but I couldn't see anything except for the curve of Vail's throat. One of Shaw's hands, which were resting on my thigh, twitched like he was slowly coming to.

"Not this, though," Meredith said softly. "She's not an object."

"No. But she's in Harley, and if she wants to survive, then she'll have to adjust and accept that that's the way shit gets done around here. It's how we've survived and it's kept us safe. So she's gonna have to fucking fall in line and do it fast."

"You can be a real asshole sometimes, Knight."

"The problem is, Mer, that with Hunter expressing an interest and with the disappearances, we need to make sure she's safe. Think about Heather..." His voice trailed off, and the room grew quiet for a moment. *Heather? Who was Heather?* "That was just the week before Casey got here. No one has talked about her. No one is asking where the fuck she is. Then there was Rachelle and Monica on the same fucking day, then-"

"I know, fuck..." Meredith whispered, her voice tight, as though she had been trying not to cry. "I know, Lee. Look, Hunter and the Jackals may very well be doing this as a sort of fucked up way of trying to get in good with Elias and the Faceless, but would he do that with Casey? He's treated her differently than Celeste and the others..."

"I have no fucking clue what that asshole wants with her, but I'm not gonna let him touch her *ever* again!" Lee snarled, and I knew he was thinking about that day in the classroom when they had to come in and save my ass. "We need to get her away from her dad first so that she's with one of us at all times. Anyone can come in and grab her, just like the others..." He sighed deeply, sounding weary and exhausted. "It's just a matter of which one of us is going to chance crossing the line to do it." When I heard this, I felt a tremor of fear running through my veins like ice.

What in the hell is he talking about? Who will cross a line? Hunter? Or them? Or is he talking about someone else? God, as this was running through my head, my feet were practically convulsing to freaking book it out of this apartment and out of town. I didn't want to get caught in the middle of two gangs. But if I ran away, what kind of crap would I abandon my three boys in? I was so freaked out and confused that I didn't realize Vail was stirring until his grip on me tightened as he stretched and yawned. *Crap...* I think. I kept the act going a little longer as he came to.

"Yo," Lee half-whispered to him from the kitchen table. "You up?"

Vail grunted a little, one of his hands sliding away, and I could feel him shifting a little beside me. He'd been quiet for a few seconds, and then I felt his arms wrap around me again, pulling me back to himself, and he buried his nose into my hair. *Holy shit...*

I listened to Lee chuckle, "Sleep okay?" His tone was teasing.

"Better than I ever have," Vail murmured back, keeping his voice low.

"Want some breakfast?" Meredith asked.

"Yeah, that'd be great, Mer." But he didn't move. I felt his lips as he kissed my temple, up along my forehead, and into my hair. When he ran his whiskered jaw along mine before nuzzling the curve of my neck, it took all of my self-control not to squirm against him.

"You going to join us at the table?" Haldon sounded like he was teasing him.

"Fuck off. Let me enjoy this for a few more minutes." His voice was low and semi-muffled from pressing into my skin. Behind me, I heard Shaw yawn and grumble a little as he started to come to.

"You're such a creep, Vail!" Meredith's disapproving tone had cut in then. "Get your greedy hands off of her and let her sleep! Amelie probably put her through the wringer last night. Look at her face!"

Vail pulled back slightly and chuckled. When I felt his fingers gently peeling the stickers away from my cheeks, I knew I couldn't keep up the charade any longer and opened my eyes slowly, like I was just waking up, and saw his face so close to mine. His lovely lips were pulled up at the corners in that cocky grin I remembered from childhood, and he said, "Good morning, Darling."

Even though I had been listening in for the past five minutes, feeling his lips coast kisses along my face and in my hair, the look he was giving me made me feel like I'd stepped back in time to that night he dared me to kiss him. I found myself speechless. He had the same smirk on his face, only now, I was feeling something, too.

From behind me, Shaw sat up and kissed my neck, just below my ear, before quietly whispering in his rough, broken voice, "Good morning, Casey."

I felt so on the spot, sensing everyone's eyes watching me, that I almost said, *fuck it*, and hid beneath the blankets. Except Lee chose that moment to rise up from the round table of four, carefully stepping over our legs, and scooped me up into his arms. He carried me over to the table and sat down, perching me upon his lap, and pulled an empty plate towards us as Meredith gave Haldon a little kiss before she flipped the bacon on the pan, the sound of it sizzling filling the kitchen.

"I can sit there-" I pointed at one of the empty chairs, but Lee only placed a hand over my stomach, keeping me where I was.

"Limited seating, babe," he said simply, as though that was the end of it. Shaw stumbled into the kitchen just as he pulled his sweater over his head, leaving the hood down. His blond hair was rumpled, sitting in messy disarray which he didn't care to fix. He just shuffled past Meredith to the coffee machine and poured two cups. I glanced over at Vail, who was now standing, stretching as he yawned, his stomach and chest muscles taught and defined.

Someone tapped my nose, and I peered over my shoulder at Lee, who was smirking at me for having caught me ogling our friend. I bit the inside of my cheek and looked away as Vail disappeared down the hall to the washroom, and Meredith placed a huge platter of eggs, bacon, and toast in the middle of the table. She sat on Haldon's lap, both of them sharing a plate, and when Shaw took one of the vacant chairs, he slid one of the cups of coffee he'd just poured toward me.

"Thank you," I said gratefully, taking it. Lee piled food onto the plate before us while Shaw just nibbled on some toast he'd covered in bacon. Meredith was feeding Haldon off a shared fork, both of them giving each other googly eyes. "So, what's the plan today?" I asked, pretending to be ignorant of what I'd eavesdropped in on earlier. "School in an hour?" I glanced at the clock over the stove, noting it was a quarter to eight.

I noted how Meredith's blue eyes flickered to Lee over my shoulder before looking away, minding her business by staying quiet.

"No, we won't be doing that." Lee scooped up a forkful of eggs and brought it up to my mouth.

"I can feed mys-" He stuffed the food into my mouth, nearly causing me to choke. I coughed, trying to keep my mouth closed so I didn't spew eggs everywhere. Shaw nudged the coffee cup back toward me again. I took a long sip and glared at Lee over my shoulder. "Don't *do* that!"

"Eat up. We have a lot to do today," he said, flashing me that playful smile of his, ignoring my indignation. I ignored him and took the fork from his hand, deciding it was safer and more practical just to feed myself.

"What exactly are we doing?" I questioned after I chewed and passed the fork back to Lee so he could have a bite, too.

"Moving you in with us, darling," Vail said, sauntering back into the room. His sweats were hanging low on his hips, showing off that beautiful V-line. He strolled over to the coffee pot and poured himself a cup before taking the last empty chair on my left and started piling food onto his plate.

"Newsflash," I told him, "I can't just move in with you guys. Keith is my guardian, and he won't approve of-"

"I'm gonna be real blunt here with you, Casey," Vail said,

not looking at me as he focused on his meal. "It's not safe for you with your dad."

"Well, no shit. Especially after what the fucker did yesterday." One of my hands flew up and rubbed at my throat. Surprisingly, I didn't feel too emotional about it. But then again, I figured if someone like Matthew had attacked me that way, it would have hurt me way more emotionally. I didn't feel any love for Keith. And knowing the past, how abusive he'd been to Mom, I honestly wasn't surprised.

Vail's eyes flick to my throat, his lips pressing together a little more tightly than necessary, before he turns toward me in his seat, holding my gaze. "Casey, why do you think your dad was so eager to take responsibility for you suddenly?"

I shrug. "Probably because of the government cheques he'd get?"

He scoffed, "Those *payments* are bullshit. They barely cover a week's worth of groceries for a family."

I glanced at Meredith, who nodded minutely in agreement without looking up from her seat on Haldon's lap.

"Okay, then why did he want guardianship?" I questioned, rolling my eyes. "Because he sure as hell didn't have a sudden epiphany to want to be a better father."

"It's your inheritance, Casey…"

"Wha-"

"He has access to all your money. He's in charge of managing it and can spend it on whatever he wants if he claims it's for your well-being. That means he can buy himself a new car and claim he needed to buy it with that money because he uses it to drive you around, get groceries, or whatever the fuck. Hell, he could even buy a bigger house and say it was because he wanted to give you a nicer, safer home. He could use *your* money to do it."

I feel an unsettling weight suddenly bloom in my chest. *What. The. Actual. FUCK?!*

"No, he's not-"

"I can guarantee that he paid social Services some sort of percentage so he could claim guardianship and get his hands on that money. I wouldn't put it past him."

I shake my head, feeling like I'm going to be sick. "He can't just take my money and-"

"He can, because he paid off those assholes who brought you to him. No system in their right mind would have allowed you to live with him again. He was locked up for beating on your mom, signing fake cheques, and shit. He's been a drunken mess since."

I could feel my face and fingers start to tingle and go cold. I felt slightly light-headed as I thought it over and realized how much sense it all makes. Of course, that's what happened. It also explained why Mr. Bryant was so pissed and confrontational with Jackie MacDonald, my social worker. He just couldn't prove it. And he wouldn't have access to my funds to find any evidence. "So, what do I do?" I asked softly.

"First, you're moving in with us." He nodded to Lee and glanced at Shaw. Did that mean that all three of them were living together? "Then we'll be paying a visit to your old man-"

"Vail, no!"

"Yes, Casey!" he shouted, cutting me off. I shrunk back where I'd been sitting, which only has me pressing into Lee's bulky, muscled chest. His arms came around me, hugging me to him like a protective shield, but he didn't stop Vail. "We get him to agree to sign over your inheritance to a court-ordered custodian who will properly monitor and can invest it for you. You're turning seventeen at the end of the month, which means you won't see this money for another fucking year. By then, Keith will have pissed it all away, and you'll be left with nothing!"

196

I sucked in a long breath, closing my eyes tight as I fought to control myself. Why must I tear up every time I feel angry? It was annoying as fuck. So I concentrated on my breathing, and when I calmed down, I slowly opened them again to see Vail was watching me closely.

"How are you going to get him to agree to this?"

He lounged back in his chair, his arm resting behind him on the backrest, and sipped his coffee, still observing me, like I might be making a run for it or something. "Don't worry about that. You'll stay home with Shaw and Lee, and I will go."

I almost wanted to ask what exactly Vail was going to do. He was just a teenager from a rundown neighborhood. Could he really persuade him to release the custodial owner-ship of my money? Keith was a selfish, selfish man. There was no way he was gonna say goodbye to it.

I guess my reservations were showing on my face because he smirked at me and bit into his toast. "Have a little faith in us, Darling."

I rolled my eyes at the stupid nickname he'd been using on me and took the fork offered to me by Lee. I couldn't help but wonder how Mom would feel about all of this. To think of Keith doing anything with the money left to me would have her rolling in her grave. My heart clenched at the thought, and I shook it away quickly. Every time I thought of my mother, it made me feel like I was drowning, and I couldn't break down in front of them. I'd play along. If it meant I could get out of that house with that man and be with the three people who made me feel the safest in the world, then I'd try anything.

It turned out all three boys did live together in a low-income townhouse complex called, The Village. The buildings were aged, with grey stucco on the outside, which appeared ever drearier in the cold, grey Autumn morning. All the buildings were faced inwards to a parking lot that circled what I assumed was a green space with a playground in the middle, but the grass was dead, everything covered in frost, and there were no signs that any flowers had bloomed in the beds for years.

Lee carried my bag as we walked two blocks down from Meredith's apartment, with Vail leading the way and Shaw watching our backs. It made me uneasy about walking down the street, seeing them acting so paranoid. Was this all necessary? What did I know? So I stayed between Lee and Vail, doing my best to keep up with his longer strides.

We stopped outside one of the townhouses, and Vail punched in a code, unlocking several key locks, and used a weird, black disc that he slowly slid across a weird pattern over the old, wooden panels until something clicked. Pushing open the door, he ushered the rest of us in before himself, casting a long, searching look around the parking lot and green space before he followed us back in and carefully did up all the locks again, which included two deadbolts, and set an alarm system with a little electric panel on the wall. Shaw kicked off his shoes and hurried up the steps to what I assumed was the main floor while Lee and I struggled in the foyer, which was extremely small and cramped.

The space was lovely, much bigger than I had anticipated for three boys in high school. The buildings were probably built in the late seventies or early eighties, judging by the wood panelling on the walls. The carpet had been replaced with something more modern and wasn't as comfy as the shag that it probably originally had come with. I hung up my coat in the cramped front closet, noting the folding doors on the opposite wall. I peeked between the crack and found an old washer and dryer inside.

Lee carried my bag up the steps, and I followed with Vail bringing up the rear. I was curious to see how their living situation was, how they managed, and I wanted to know how long they'd been living together.

The next floor had a living room and dining area in a shared space, with a tiny kitchen around the corner. The furniture was clearly second-hand, probably from the Goodwill down the street, but it looked cozy. There was a curved, emerald couch facing a wood-burning fireplace and a TV, complete with a gaming system because, you know, boys, along with two cushy-looking patchwork armchairs. The coffee table was a long, wicker piece covered in what looked like schoolwork or something. Shaw was scrambling to collect it together. In fact, even Lee had bypassed the dining area, which had a small round, light oak thing with four mismatched, patched-up chairs gathered round it, and disappeared around the corner to where I assumed the kitchen was. Seconds later, I could hear water running and the sound of china clattering. Dishes.

I hid a smirk when I realized they were cleaning up the place, like I'd judge them for being messy or something. I didn't care. Being here, knowing that this was where they lived and that they wanted me to live with them... for the first time since Mom died, I felt like I was home again.

Yeah, it was sparse. They had nothing around to catch dust, nothing of value on display, excluding the TV and game system, and only had the basics. The only other personal items I could see were a set of weights by the large bay window next to the dining table.

But I didn't care how simple it all was. All it did was remind me of the basement suite Mom and I had lived in, and how when we first moved, we had a mattress on the floor of the bedroom and used a cardboard box to eat our meals off of. Over the years, she added little pieces of which she got some fantastic deals on, once she had saved enough. But we were safe and together. That's what mattered.

And that's all that mattered now.

I turned away and started lugging my bag up the steps, which freaked me out as they were the cantilever kind. I could just picture Lee reaching through them one day when I'm coming down the steps just to scare the crap out of me. I'd have to be mindful of that every time I made a trip up or down.

I grunted, still tired even after that amazing breakfast Meredith made for all of us this morning, and struggled to lug my insanely heavy bag.

"Are you crazy?" Vail came rushing over, his brows pulled down over his eyes in disapproval. "You're going to pull something. Let me." He pulled the straps free from my hands and easily lifted them up, giving me a nod to lead the way up to the top floor. When I got there, however, I had no idea where to go. I saw multiple doors, one of which I'd been pretty sure was a linen closet, judging by how narrow it was, but the others were obviously a washroom and their bedrooms. Where the hell was I going to sleep?

Vail decided for me and carried my bag to the room at the end of the hall, and went in. I followed and found myself in a space much larger than I'd anticipated. The bed was sitting on one of those black box frames with drawers that lined the entire thing and was covered in a thick grey, white, yellow, and black comforter, which was balled up like it'd been kicked aside when the sleeper had risen. There was a long, black dresser, a closet hidden behind a grey and white striped curtain, a hamper, and a tiny black desk where a laptop sat and a few school books.

"Whose room is this?" I asked when he set my bag on the

floor by the dresser.

"Ours," he said without hesitation, turning to the bed to shake out the blanket.

"*Ours?*" I said incredulously, my face flushing a little. *Was he serious or just fucking with me?* The thought of sharing a room with Vail felt a little too... domestic.

"I have the biggest room in the house, so it makes sense, right?" He glanced at me, the corner of one side of his mouth curling up.

"Well, I guess..." I sat on the floor beside my hockey bag, ready to find some comfy stuff to put on. I'd been wearing the same clothes for over twenty-four hours now, and I needed a shower, too. I zipped open my bag, searching through it to see what Meredith grabbed. I was so grateful to see she thought of packing my toiletries, on top of my books. But she had also grabbed my stuffed lamb, the photo of Matthew, Mom, and me from Christmas that I had framed, and the mother-of-pearl jewelry box.

I held the photo in my hands, studying the faces in it. How different life had been less than a year ago. Two people that stared back at me in this picture were gone forever. Did they deserve what happened to them? No. I could think of a handful of others who earned such a painful, bloody end, but life just didn't fucking work that way.

A pale hand gently tugged the photo away. I gaped at Vail as he inspected the frozen memory for a second before setting it out on display on the dresser. He reached for my jewelry box and stuffed lamb, too, and carefully arranged them together, giving them a place. I saw how he gave the lamb, in particular, a little squeeze, and I knew he recognized it from our childhood. Since I was a baby, I had that thing with me and never slept without it until I was fourteen. After that, I had it out so I could see it each day. Bluebell, that's the name my Mom had given it, and I'd kept it, was something all the guys had teased me over during our sleepovers. But there was no teasing from Vail now.

Instead, he reached down and lifted me up by sliding his hands beneath my armpits. As self-conscious as I was to have him grab me there, I rose to my feet, following his lead, only to find him enveloping me in his arms. His chin rested on top of my head, and for a minute, and we said nothing. I sunk against him, taking the comfort he was offering, so grateful that I had him back.

"Rule number one," he said, not pulling away. "You don't go anywhere without one of us accompanying you."

"But-" I tried pulling back to see his face, but he wouldn't let me. He pressed my face to his chest, one of his hands reaching up to grab a fistful of my hair.

"No, Casey. This isn't a debate. This is law. You don't go anywhere without letting us know and without an escort."

I flinched at his words. I felt like an errant child. "And why is that?"

"Not now. Stay here, have a shower, rest up," he said, his grip relaxing a little. "Lee and I need to talk to your dad first. When we get back, we can fill you in on things."

"Okay… what's the next rule?"

"You do what we say. I overrule all, then Lee and Shaw. We need a system of hierarchy here to follow, or else people fuck up, and mistakes are made. And a mistake here can cost you your life."

"Are you serious?" I asked, laughing nervously. I mean, I knew shit was bad here; however, wasn't this a little over-the-top?

"Mark DeLuca," he said simply.

Mark… Hunter's childhood friend. I still didn't know what had happened to him, but I supposed that was something that would be elaborated on later tonight.

"Okay. So seniority rules. Gotcha."

I could hear a huff of air as he sharply exhaled through his nose, like he was trying not to laugh at my peppy attitude. Yeah, I had questions and doubts, but in the end, I trusted that these three knew what the hell they were doing. They lived here longer than I had. They were involved in stuff that I just didn't understand. I needed to fall in line if I wanted to survive.

"Lastly, keep the doors and windows locked at all times. Shaw can show you how to work the alarm system, but we need to be careful about always having it armed."

This rule didn't shock me. It was the same as Keith's. Speaking of Keith. "How do you guys know he's home? What if he's still in the hospital after what Shaw-"

"He returned home late last night, not long after we grabbed your stuff," he said confidently. Vail released me and turned to the dresser, where he had begun to clear several drawers for my stuff, squashing his things into the ones beneath the bed. I had taken that as a cue to start putting my own things away when he pulled out a pair of dark sweats and a hoodie, reminding me very much of Shaw's style. When he began stripping down in front of me, I purposefully kept my face turned away. It's been too damn long since Patrick and I had last hooked up, and seeing Vail's sculpted, adonis-like stomach... dirty thoughts of him entered my mind...

Him as he was crushing me against the wall as our tongue's danced together. Him as he was fisting my hair as he'd just done a minute ago, his body between my legs. I could just imagine what his body felt like, and I imagined running my fingers and my tongue over every inch...

Goddamn Vail and his beautiful stomach muscles, the cocky bastard... I just bet he knew he was hot shit, too, the way he was slowly getting changed behind me. It's like he knew I was avoiding looking at him. When I think of how Patrick looked, it just doesn't compare. Patrick, though a little beefier than the typical boys at the Academy from playing football, had nothing like the muscles that Lee and Vail were packing. I carefully folded up my things, discreetly shoving my undies and bras into the bottom drawer and quickly shutting it closed before I did something stupid like decide to let him see the silky pieces I had, just to find out what his reaction would be. But no. I needed to focus. Some serious shit was about to go down. All else could wait until later…

Later… like when we'd be sleeping side by side. *Ugh! Focus Casey!* I seriously needed to get a grip.

"So what are you going to say to convince Keith to give up his role as the trustee to my inheritance?" I asked, trying to keep my head in the game. "He's not gonna want to give that up, especially if he's doing what you're claiming-"

"He is. I guarantee it." His voice was muffled, most likely because he had been pulling the sweater over his head. "That department is as crooked as City Hall. You're not going to get justice from them. It needs to be resigned. I was betting if we brought this to the attention of the courts and they asked for receipts, Keith would be fucked."

I was doubtful of their plan. Was Keith really gonna be intimidated by two teenage boys and their threats to expose what they *think* he did? I don't know… I really am having a hard time believing it. But do I want to give up and go back to him? No, no, I fucking do not.

I think my silence only revealed how skeptical I was because Vail stepped up behind me then, placing both his hands on my shoulders. I tipped my head back, peering up at him upside down from where I was still sitting on the floor. He was fully dressed now, and had the smallest of smiles on his lips. "Have ye a little faith," he said the familiar line again. Before I could say a word, he leaned down until his lips were brushing over my forehead then to my temple. His fingers moved to cup my throat lightly, and he whispered, "Casey... I was serious when I said that we were your family now. We're not going to let you down. We'll always protect you, darling. And that includes saving you from your piece of shit father."

"Vail..." I whispered as his fingers stroked my skin, so lightly, it was like a feather was floating across my neck.

"I'm not letting you go this time," he breathed, his lips pressing a kiss just below my ear. "*We* won't let you go." He crouched down and turned me to face him, still lightly holding my throat. The pupils of his eyes were blown, almost inking out the hazel colour. He caressed my neck, stroking the marks Keith left behind as though these gentle minor strokes would make them all better. He stared at my mouth for a second before he leaned in and kissed me. While Shaw's was full of hunger, impulse, and wildness, Vail's kiss was ardent, full of passion, and assuredness. His tongue swept my mouth, demanding I return his kiss, and I did. Vail's kiss made me forget everything at the moment except for him and me, and I gladly fell into him.

When he finally pulled away, we were both breathless, both leaning into each other, as though we needed the other's support to stand. For a minute, neither of us spoke as we held on to each other, both comfortable with the silence between us. It was like we could *feel* what the other wanted, and it was reciprocated. "You know why I won't let you go?" he whispered at last.

My head was spinning from that kiss, so lost in the moment that I couldn't even remember my own name right at that second. I gave my head a little shake.

The hand on my throat moved up and cupped my cheek, his thumb lightly stroking it, and murmured, "Because my heart aches for you, my soul cries for you. I *need* you and you need me. I've loved you from the very first moment, Casey. That's never changed."

I was speechless, caught off guard by how beautiful and heart-wrenching his words were. Before I could even think of what to say back, he pulled away, giving the tip of my nose a small kiss before he strode over to the door as if nothing happened. "We'll be back in a couple of hours," he called over his shoulder, giving me a wink before departing.

I could hear the guys talking to each other briefly; their voices were unclear from where I was up the stairs. I was still feeling light-headed from Vail's kiss, his proclamation. I had eventually snapped out of it when the sounds of the locks on the front door opened and then slammed. I ran into the hall and peered down the steps only to hear the beeping of the alarm system, followed by the locks sliding back into place.

I was feeling so confused about everything as I tried to continue putting my stuff away.

I'd spent the night with Lee, flirting and being all domestic with Amelie, then again at breakfast as he held me close and fed me like I was his sweetheart. But then there was Shaw... Shaw, who needed me so badly, and a part of my soul needed him. His kiss last night... it was like a part of me had found itself in him and was uniting at last. But then... there was *Vail*, who was just... Vail. Vail, who said he *loved* me.

My head was whirling. Even though I had managed to fit most of my clothes in the dresser and found space for my books along the one shaded windowsill, overlooking out onto the porch that only Vail's (*our*) room had access to, I was feeling incredibly anxious and confused.

What was I doing? What was I going to do? I overheard them last night and this morning. Shaw's kiss, Lee's flirtations, and Vail's sudden change of heart; all told me one thing... they all wanted me here. But not only that, it was clear that they *all* wanted me. If I could sense all of this, then there was no way the guys were ignorant of each other's feelings, either. I wanted them... all three of them. Each one touched a part of my soul in different ways, and when one of the three were gone, I found myself aching for them. When I lived on The Hill, I missed all three, thought about all three, *missed* all three. How could I choose only one? I *needed* all three.

So how was this going to work?

I shook my head, unable to deal with this at the moment. I was too nervous about the idea of Lee and Vail walking into my father's home and making demands. What if he calls the cops or pulls a weapon on them?

I grabbed my toiletries and headed out into the hall, checking the linen closet for a towel. It's sparse, with only two extra, so I took one and walked into the bathroom. I spent about five percent of the time shampooing, shaving, and scrubbing myself down, and then the other ninety-five percent I stared at the yellow, tiled wall, feeling on edge.

A gentle knock on the door snapped me out of my contemplation, and I wiped the water out of my eyes as I stuck my head out from behind the shower curtain. "Yeah?"

I heard a muffled voice behind the door, and I knew it was Shaw. But I couldn't hear him over the shower, not with his raspy whisper. I'm done anyway, so I shut it off, wrapping the towel around my chest to hide my body, and opened the door. "What was that?" I asked.

Shaw's blue eyes widened a fraction at the sight of me in a towel, and very slowly, his gaze perused down my body, then slowly up again. His pale cheeks reddened ever so faintly, and he cleared his throat, suddenly looking incredibly bashful. I hadn't expected that.

"Um, I was... I wondered..." His voice trailed off, and the next thing I knew, there was a tent in his pants. But wow, holy shit, something I hadn't expected to see... Shaw Bishop was packing! I could tell he was uncomfortable by the way he hunched over ever so slightly and shifted his legs, as though trying to hide that extra limb between his legs, but it was too late. I didn't know whether to laugh or feel bad for him, as he seemed really embarrassed by it. I was about to let him know it was fine, but he just backed up and headed down the hall to the room on the other side of the linen closet, and quickly shut the door behind himself.

I chuckled a little to myself. *Still got it!* I couldn't help but think as I walked into Vail's (frick! Mine... Vail's, and *my* room. That's going to take some getting used to) to dry off and change.

By the time I'd slipped on a pair of pale pink sweats and a grey sweater, my hair was damp-dry, and I french-braided it so that it would stay out of my face as I rummaged through my bookbag, deciding to make sure I would be caught up on schoolwork since I was missing today. I searched for a pencil so I could make some notes on Othello, but my bag had become a dumping ground for loose papers and receipts. Rather than take the thirty seconds to clean it out, because I'm that lazy, I wandered over to Vail's desk to borrow one from there.

The surface was immaculately clean, with only his closed laptop sitting there, so I opened one of the side drawers only to find a well-used copy of *The Body*, a novella by Stephen King. The cover is worn, the spine cracked, and some of the pages have been bent, much to my chagrin. I hate it when people fold the pages of books. But I didn't know that Vail was ever a big reader, but evidently, this was his favourite. I carefully picked it up and flipped through the pages, wondering if I might like the story, too, when something slipped out and fluttered to the floor.

I furrowed my brow in confusion at the photograph he had stowed away. Bending down to pick it up, I turned it over to reveal the image, and gasped.

It's me.

My class photo from the beginning of the year that I had left in Harley, where I'm wearing that ugly maroon corduroy overall dress Mom had forced me to wear. Back then, I'd always worn my dark hair in a ponytail but had promised to let my mother style it by braiding it the night so that it fell in waves. I'd also vowed to smile with my teeth showing, and even though I was giving the tiniest of smiles, I kept my word. I'd been so embarrassed walking into school that way, dressed up like a girl rather than one of the boys. It was the first time I'd noticed the way they all looked at me. It had been… different. I could feel it. I may have only been two months shy of my eleventh birthday on class photo day, but I knew full well what was going through my three boys' minds. And I wasn't having it. I'd threatened them, and after that, I got nothing from them indicating they were interested in me that way. That was, until the night that druggie broke into our house during my Saturday night sleepover, and Vail had dared me to kiss him.

And he had my photo…

The room had been trashed, from both the intruder ransacking it as he searched for stuff to steal, and from Vail almost killing the guy. The frame had been found shattered, but no picture. I just figured it had been ripped up or something and thrown out. But no, here it was. Folded up a bit, aged… but he'd had it the whole time.

Because my heart aches for you, my soul cries for you. I need you and you need me. I've loved you from the very first moment, Casey. That's never changed.

Oh fuck, I thought as my heart practically swelled. I was in *so* much trouble.

"Casey?"

I slid the photo back into Vail's book, closing the drawer before turning at the sound of Shaw's voice. He was standing in the doorway, hard-on gone, and was looking incredibly uncertain.

"Hey, what's up?" I said, climbing up onto the bed, ignoring the fact that he'd caught me snooping. Shaw strolled slowly into the room, looking a little flushed but otherwise okay. His hood was off his head for once, and I could see how pale his blond hair was as it flopped over his brow and into his eyes. I could sense that he was a little embarrassed about earlier, so I acted as casually as I could, lounging on the bed, hands behind my head as I stretched out. Last night, sleeping on the floor wasn't as comfortable as I remember from when we would do it as kids, even with the layers of quilts beneath me. So lying out on a soft mattress with blankets and pillows is a Godsend.

"I just wanted to check on you," he said at last as he sank on the very edge of the other side of the bed. He'd been keeping a careful distance between us, and I have no idea why. But I didn't push him. One thing I've always known about Shaw was to allow him time to acclimate to things at his own pace. He never liked being forced to do something if he felt uncomfortable. Lucky for him, Vail had always proven to be a leader that was aware of our limits and was cautious about how we used to do things. I couldn't imagine him changing in that aspect.

"I'm doing okay," I said to him, playing along as I tried to figure out what he really wanted. "A little tired, though. Amelie is super cute, but holy crap. What an excellent method of birth control, eh? Go babysit a toddler," I laughed, "Thank fuck I have the implant." I observed him as he bowed his head, his fingers fiddling with a corner of the blanket. He didn't react. "How are *you*?" I ask.

"I'm…" His voice trails off, and for a moment, he looks legitimately confused.

"Shaw," I said gently and held a hand out to him. He

peeked over at me, his blue eyes revealing his vulnerability, and I couldn't help but think how he reminded me of a cornered animal, desperate for love and attention, however, he wasn't sure how to go about it. "Come here, please?" I knew better than to tell him what to do. I always gave him an option.

He inched a little closer, slowly reaching out to touch the tips of my fingers with his. He stroked the skin of my palm, up the length of my index, then forefinger, and finally, very lightly up and down my ring one, the touch so light it tickled a little.

"It's weird being back here," I said softly, continuing to watch his finger trail over mine again and again.

"In what way?" he murmured, staring at our hands on the tartan-style bedding.

"Just, seeing everything after being gone so long... seeing it all with new eyes," I confessed and carefully turned our hands over so his were splayed, and I could run my nails over his palm. He relaxed once I did, and I noticed that he was inching a little higher up on the bed. "Everything is harder, a little darker... I feel like as a kid, I'd been wandering around with a blindfold on and missed what things were actually like here."

"A lot's changed, too," he said, watching my hand as my nails were moving down to his wrist, then up to the tips of his fingers, and back down again. "It was always rough, but we'd grown up in it. We were used to it. Then, after you left, it got worse and worse... things *are* harder, darker... we've just been trying to survive while saving as many of our people as we can."

I stare at him, shocked by his little speech. It was probably the most he's ever said at one time. But I wasn't going to react. Instead, I lay back amongst the pillows again, continuing the trail over his skin. I could feel the bed shift as he moved closer until he was lying in the space next to me. He interlocks our fingers and holds my hand, his confidence back, and lies on his side, so he is facing me. I turned to face him, relaxing on Vail's ridiculously comfortable bed, and stared into the beautiful, haunting depth of Shaw's eyes.

"What was it like, living on The Hill?" he asked in his low, raspy voice.

"Safe. Comfortable," I said, my voice was flat as I thought about it. "Matthew was kind to me, sweet to my mother, and his home was big and beautiful, and in the summertime, he took us boating on his yacht. I won't lie... I was incredibly... privileged." I felt like an asshole saying that word, but it was the truth. "I became one of those people that we always used to make fun of."

"I don't believe that."

"You saw me on my first day back. I'd forgotten what it was like here." I rolled my eyes. "I mean, come on... pearl earrings? I was so bloody stupid." I sighed heavily.

"Were the kids there nice to you?"

I made a face, scrunching up my nose as the memories of my first few weeks came back. "I mean, it could have been worse, I suppose. I wasn't beat up or anything like that. More like name-calling, typical pranks, and stuff." His hand squeezed mine hard when I added, "I think I called you guys ten times each after school every day that first week." I remembered that, too. How confused I was, how abandoned and lonely I had felt. I quickly changed the subject. If I were going to confront anyone about that, it would be Vail, not Shaw. "But one girl, my friend Nylah, she eventually broke down my walls and became my best friend..." I felt my heart clench thinking about her. I hadn't talked to Nylah in days, and the last time I received a message from her, she was checking in on me, but I'd put off replying because I was trying to focus on surviving this place. If I answered her feeling like I had, she would have known something was wrong, and the last thing I wanted was to be a problem for her.

"Nylah... she was good to you?"

"The best. Her mom and dad are the sweetest people, and Nylah is just so... together. She's smart and pretty, and I know she'll go places." I sighed heavily, trying to hold it together. I missed her. I missed her badly. I missed how she would run after me to paint my nails or help with my makeup. I missed how she and I used to go to the park on weekends to play basketball together before grabbing brunch at The Station, the central shopping hub on the East-End. Or the way she'd literally pick me up and carry me around, laughing when I'd resist by playing possum and going dead weight on her.

"I missed you, Casey..." he whispers finally. When I look up into his eyes, I can see the ache there, the longing and grief he suffered in my absence. So why did he let me go?

But I didn't say anything about that now. Instead, I brought his hand up to my lips and kissed it. "I missed you, too. More than you know..."

Shaw reached forward then with his other hand and lightly touched my cheek, catching me off guard. I didn't even realize I had several tears running down my face until he pulled his hand away, the shine from the drops clear on his fingertips. Before I could laugh off my emotions, he brought the finger to his mouth and licked my tears away. My mouth fell at the sight. What the heck was he doing? It was a little strange, but then again, so was Shaw. He moved over then, coming so close that our bodies were completely flush together. For a long time, we laid in absolute silence, until at some point, we both fell asleep, not as we used to by holding hands... but now, by holding each other.

Chapter thirteen

Casey

"Come on, you lazy asses. Wake up!" I sat up and gasped in surprise at the rude awakening to find Vail rummaging in his dresser. Beside me, Shaw grumbled and rolled over while I rubbed my eyes, trying to come to. Why was it that napping in the middle of the day made me feel like I've slept for ten years straight? I woke up having no idea what day it was, time, where I was...

I looked up just as Vail stripped off his sweater to pull on a grey t-shirt, choosing to keep his dark sweats on. Again, I got a glimpse of his stomach and that glorious V. Because I was already out of it, I zoned out as I stared at him, mouth hanging open slightly as I drank up the glorious sight of his body.

"Casey!"

"What!" I jumped in surprise as Vail chuckled, and I realized he caught me staring at him like an idiot. Instead of saying anything else about it, he leaned over the bed, his fists planted on either side of my thighs, and gave me a long, lingering kiss. I melted against him, always finding it easy to get sucked into Vail's orbit. He pulled back to side-eye Shaw, who had fallen back asleep, and half-shouted, "Hey! Asswipe! Get up! I need you to grab the first aid supplies and bring them downstairs for Lee."

"What?" I instantly straightened, almost hitting him in the chin. "Why does Lee need first aid?"

"It's just for his knuckles. Don't worry about it," Vail gave me another kiss before straightening up to head back downstairs.

Shaw was up, too, and immediately headed into the washroom, digging under the sink of a giant tub filled with gauze, adhesive bandages, antiseptic ointments, tape, Q-tips, antibiotic treatments, elastic wraps, and more. He hurried down the stairs with me hot on his heels to find Lee sitting on the couch in the living room, his hands soaking in two silver mixing bowls of ice water.

"What did you do?" I practically screeched at the sight of him sitting there, his face screwed up in pain as he forced his hands to remain under the freezing water.

"It's fine," he hissed between clenched teeth as Shaw moved around the couch, reaching in for things from the bin.

"This is *not* fine!" I stood opposite him on the other side of the coffee table, my hands on my hips, and glared at him. "What the hell did you do? What happened? Who do I need to knock out?"

"Calm down, darling." Vail came back into the room from the kitchen, phone in hand, typing furiously away on it as he said, "We had a little run-in on our way back from your dad's."

"A run-in?" I narrowed my eyes, my thoughts immediately thinking of Hunter. "With who?"

"Who do you think?" Lee muttered, confirming my suspicions.

"Casey, this happens to us all the time," Vail said, finally setting his phone aside. "Why do you think we've stocked up on medical supplies?"

I stared between the three of them, thinking about the fact they were in some crew called Vendetta, and as far as I could tell, they didn't like the Jackals. I had my suspicions on what the hell it was exactly they got up to, but I wanted to hear the truth now. All the facts. But first...

I moved around and sat on Lee's other side, reaching over him for some hydrogen peroxide solution, bandages, and paper towel. When he finally pulled his hands free, sucking a sharp breath in between his teeth, I gasped at the sight of his knuckles. They were angry and red, the first layer of skin gone on a few, while others were bleeding a bit, like the middle ones. "What in the fuck happened?" I whispered as I took his hands and carefully dabbed at the spots. To his credit, he didn't flinch away, but I was betting it hurt like a bitch.

"Normally, I'd have my brass knuckles with me... but I wasn't anticipating needing them just by talking to your old man."

"Which, by the way, is all settled," Vail interjected, turning on a laptop that's sitting on the kitchen table.

"What... *how?*"

"Lucky for us, we work closely with some people who have the means to hack into people's accounts to look at their activity. Your dad *was* paying off Social Services. Gave them about thirty thousand dollars from the money you'll get from your mom's life insurance. Looks like he was planning something more with that money, too..." he added, going quiet as he typed away on the laptop. "It seems like *daddy* has a new hobby... he likes to gamble."

For fucks sake. Why did this not surprise me? But then I replayed what he said over again in my head. "Your... *friends*... they hacked into his computer?"

"They did," he said casually, like this was no big thing.

"Wh-when? How the hell did they do that?"

"Casey, we've been keeping tabs on you since we found out you moved back here," he said and cast a, *Duh,* sort of look.

I, however, raised my brows and accidentally pressed a little harder on Lee's knuckles than I had meant to, making him grunt a little from the sting. "Sorry! Sorry!" I said, fumbling a little as I took in this information. I grabbed the antiseptic and went about cleaning his wounds. "You fuckers were *spying* on me?" I asked, a little taken aback.

"Of course," Vail said easily, like it was a totally normal thing to do. "For example, why do you think Lee accompanied you home that one time?"

"Bunch of psychos..." I muttered under my breath, deciding it wasn't worth the battle. It was over now, and thanks to them, I was no longer living with that sad excuse for a dad. "Okay, so what's the deal, you guys?" I worked carefully on Lee's hands, hating the sight of him like this. But I was betting anything that the guys he fought against were way worse off, which gave me a satisfying sense of pleasure. "What exactly is it that you guys are doing here? Because obviously, Vendetta is more than just a high school crew that has cafeteria fights with childhood rivals."

Vail stopped what he was doing and strode over to the rest of us, taking a seat on the easy chair closest to me, and leaned forward, his elbows on his knees, and asked, "How much do you know about the Faceless?"

"The Faceless? You mean that mob, or gang, or whatever, in the city?" I instantly thought of Phillip Bryant and how stressed he was as of late with his job. Nylah's father worked tirelessly for years trying to end the corruption that the Faceless had created in City Hall. They run this city. Them and their biker goons, the Celtic Beasts.

He nodded. "You've seen the news articles, I'm sure. Even on The Hill," he smirked at that jab, and I chose to just roll my eyes at him.

"Yes, I wasn't *that* sheltered, fuck-face," I said to him, and his eyes sparkled at my insult, as though he found it more endearing than insulting.

"What did you read?"

"Stuff about bodies of rival bikers popping up around the border towns and drug dealers going missing, then turning up in the morgue. Fights between the Beasts and the street thugs, drugs, the usual bullshit you get with a group like them running the place..." My voice trailed off when I noticed how Vail was slowly shaking his head at me. "No?" I asked, arching a brow. Beside me, Lee shifted a little, and I quickly applied some ointment over the gashes before I started to carefully wrap his hands.

"Here's the deal, Casey." Vail watched as I tended to Lee. "Harley has always been the shit-pit of Ashland. When we were kids, we saw break-ins and addicts and learned what it was like to hear our neighbors beat the shit out of their spouses and their kids. Fuck, I mean... *we* all dealt with..." His voice trailed off, glancing at Shaw, who was still sitting on the other end of the couch. He sat motionless and silent this entire time, his eyes on me, and his expression void of any sort of emotion. "Things are different now. The Faceless, their leader, have been taking advantage of the fact that Ashland has neglected this community and the people for years."

"In what way?" I asked, as I finished bandaging Lee's knuckles, but I didn't move away from him. Instead, I lounged back into the couch, holding his injured hands in my lap as my thumbs stroked over the skin that was visible on the backs. Lee sank further in against me while Shaw shifted the tiniest bit on the other end, his focus still entirely on me.

Vail's eyes shadowed over, all signs of humour gone. "Girls have been disappearing," he said, finally.

"What?" I furrowed my brow, the conversation I'd overheard at Meredith's and Haldon's place now coming back to me.

"Girls have been disappearing in the community, most from Harley Institute. One girl vanished about a week before you arrived, Heather Mackie. Two others before her at the end of September. Then another girl at the beginning of the school year. Over the summer, it had amped up, with four other girls vanishing. At first, people around here thought some psychopath serial killer was on the loose, but then... everyone just shut up about it." Vail's nostrils flared slightly in anger, and I could feel the rage from the injustice rolling off of him. "Even before, girls from Harley Public are nowhere to be seen, but no one has done shit. No one asks any questions. Only the parents are begging for answers, and the police stonewall them. Why? Because they're in the Faceless' pockets... *Elias's.*"

Elias. They'd mentioned his name several times last night and this morning. "Elias is... he's the leader of The Faceless?"

Vail nodded, his stern demeanor unchanging. "If he's taking girls, there's no question in my mind that the fucker is trafficking them. Drugging them up and using them for his fucking benefit. And Ashland is doing *nothing* to stop him because the girls are from Harley. If he took someone from The Hill, it wouldn't go down as quietly. There'd be an uproar if the daughter of some hotshot lawyer or doctor, who went to a private school and lived a safe, perfect life, were taken. But here? No one gives a shit. But I do. *We* do." He nodded to the others, and Lee's hand cupped my knee.

I couldn't believe that this sort of thing was happening here and that the police were really doing nothing about it. But at the same time, what Vail was telling me made perfect sense. *Once a Harley Rat, always a Harley Rat...* People from here weren't seen as worthy, as important as the rest of the city. It was absolute bullshit.

"Did-" I stopped, taking a breath before I tentatively asked, "Did you guys know any of the girls?"

Lee nodded. "We did. Friends or girlfriends of our friends. All sweet and kind people. All easy prey for assholes like The Faceless and the Beasts." I could hear the venom in his voice. "That's when we formed Vendetta, about a year ago, when disappearances were thought to be runaways. It started out as the boyfriends and friends of those girls uniting as a front of protection to others. Whether they needed to be escorted home if they were at school late or were nervous about a guy that wouldn't leave them alone. Just a unit to protect our own, since the cops weren't doing shit."

My heart swelled thinking of my three boys turning into protectors of their classmates. At that moment, all I wanted was to just pull them all into me and hold them all close.

"And then Hunter started parading around Harley like he fucking owned the place," Vail practically growled. "Him and Bryce and the rest of them, calling themselves The Jackals, acting like they were untouchable. They began to talk themselves up, gloating that they hung out with the Celtic Beasts like we would admire them for it. Fucking idiots..." He shook his head, his fists balling up and clenching hard. *Jesus... what else have they seen?*

"That's when more shit started happening at school," Shaw said, speaking up for Vail while he calmed down. "Monica and Rachelle started hanging out with them, groupies, and then they were just fucking *gone*. And no one said shit. That's when we started suspecting that maybe Hunter wasn't just talk-"

"Wait, wait, hold up." I leaned around Lee to see Shaw better, and I was sure I resembled a deer in headlights with how big my eyes probably were, but this was just too much to take in. "You guys are saying that *Hunter*... Hunter, who we used to duke it out with as kids, is giving girls to Elias and the Faceless so that they can be trafficked?"

When no one said anything, that dreadful silence only confirmed it. I felt sick. If this was true, then what in the fuck happened to Hunter that made him stoop to such a level?

"Some people will do anything for a little taste of power, Casey," Lee said, seeing the confusion, the doubt on my face, "And Hunter is one of them. If you can't beat those in charge, then suck up and hope that you can prove yourself worthy enough to be included in their bullshit. Then you aren't a victim. And here, being a victim is a death sentence to most."

A sudden thought horrified me as I slowly digested this information. "Wait a minute... with all that shit with Hunter and me... you don't think..." I struggled to say the words, feeling like I really might be sick if I didn't get a grip soon. "Was he going to take me to The Faceless?"

"We don't know," Vail said quickly, and I turned to face him. Lee wrapped an arm around my shoulders, pulling me into his warmth, and I realized I had been shaking. "We weren't going to take that chance, Casey. There was no fucking way!"

Even though Hunter had been an enemy back when we were kids, there was still a sense of camaraderie with him and his group of friends. If an outsider had come into Harley and tried to mess with us, a kid from Public, or a cop, we all stuck together. Him betraying me that way, well, it struck a chord. I sucked in a long, slow breath, doing my best to keep calm as Vail continued.

"We wanted to find out where they were taking girls, but we're just a bunch of high school kids. What the fuck can we do against someone like Elias?" he said, running his hands through his hair. "It wasn't until Haldon joined up and used his connection with the Black Spades that we got the help we needed. His cousin, Taz, is a member, and he introduced us to Maverick."

"Who is Maverick?"

"He's the President of their MC, and he's been our biggest supporter in all of this. The Spades have been backing Vendetta and helping us find out information on the Beasts and The Faceless."

"But why would they help you guys?" I'm so confused right now.

"He's got his own issues. Lost his wife to drugs years ago. Her supplier?" Vail arched his brows at me. "I guess she was having a hard time adjusting to life in a trailer park with a biker husband. He'd hoped once they had a kid together, she'd adjust, but... well..." He sighed heavily as though exhausted. He'd always been sensitive towards addicts and alcoholics because of his dad. "He admitted that he went about it wrong, and after she died, he tried to force his own son into the club, afraid that he'd lose him, too. But he's gone now. Moved away or something. He doesn't talk about it..." My heart broke a little at that. "The Black Spades are the ones who have been hacking and looking into hotspots where the girls could be hidden. Problem is... The Celtic Beasts recognize most of them. That's where we've stepped in to help."

"Maverick was just cool with sending in a bunch of high school kids to find out if a major crime organization is trafficking girls?" I raised my eyebrows a little at that.

"The guys in his club had done a lot more riskier shit at

our age when they were pledging. I don't know if he knows any different. Their way of life is not like ours."

I was trying to wrap my head around all of it, but it was almost too much for me to handle. I rubbed my eyes, thinking about it over and over when it hit me. "Is all of this why you wanted me to leave?" I suddenly remembered what an asshole Vail had been when he saw I was back. "Because you thought if I stayed, I'd be taken?" The boys were quiet now, and though I looked at the other two, they avoided my eyes. Only Vail stared at me dead-on, so I leaned towards him, not letting him sidestep this one. "Tell me."

"We made a pact when you left, Casey…" he whispered, his eyes tightening in the corners. "That we would give you a chance to live your life away from us, away from Harley. We didn't want to drag you down when you had an opportunity to escape this place…"

"But I asked for you guys to-"

"We know. But we agreed that we would shut you out, let you be mad at us so that you would move on and accept your new, better life."

I wanted to slap him. But I also wanted to kiss him. I wanted to kiss all of them. When I peered between them all, I saw the way Lee's head was bowed, his jaw tight as though he had been holding in years of pain and loss. Shaw, well, he'd retreated into his hoodie, rocking slightly on the edge of the couch as he glared at the floor. I shifted my gaze back to Vail, whose eyes were shimmering with unshed tears. He wouldn't cry. He was too controlled for that now, but I could still see the pain on his face from what that decision had cost him.

"And now?" I asked softly.

He reached out slowly and opened a hand to me, giving me a choice to take it. Hesitating, I studied the open palm that he had extended to me, but after a few seconds, I took it. The moment I slid my hand into his, his fingers curled around mine, and he muttered, "Now, it'll be like it was supposed to."

It turned out, the only food in the house had been a loaf of bread, some noodle cups, and crackers. In terms of everything else, like cleaning supplies and basic kitchenware (save for a few paper plates that were used again and again judging by the stains and how crinkled they were), there was none. I still had access to my bank account, which had a considerable amount placed into it before Mom and Matthew passed. So tomorrow, I would stop by the dollar store and buy a bunch of stuff to make this place a little more... comfortable... and some food. I knew there was a local grocery nearby where I could grab some fresh fruit and veggies and other foods. I couldn't imagine how long the guys were living this way. When I asked about money, Vail said something about that not being an issue but didn't expand further than that.

In a way, it was like a blessing in disguise that I had come here. If I could help in any way, then that's what I'd do for my guys. So that was my plan, to make this place feel more like a home once I was done with my day at school. It was surprisingly comfortable being here with the guys. Though neither of them seemed bothered when one of them would stop what they were doing to kiss my head, or in Lee's case, pull a pouty lip, puppy-dog face on me, claiming he needed extra snuggles because he was injured. I laughed, rolling my eyes at him, but gladly laid on the couch with him, snuggling up as we had at Meredith's while Shaw played his video games on the other end.

It wasn't until late that night, when we were getting ready for bed, that there was a hint of jealousy between them. I changed into a pair of grey cotton sleep pants and a pale blue top, when Vail came into the room and stripped down to a pair of boxers while Shaw narrowed his eyes across the hall from the washroom.

"You got your time last night, ass!" Lee shouted from the other side of the wall he shared with Vail. I awkwardly stood by the dresser, brush in hand, in the middle of combing out the knots when this all happened. Vail stalked across the room, his hand brushing against my ass as he passed, and stuck his head out the door shouting back, "We agreed I would share my room since it's the biggest! It's her room now, so it just makes sense that she sleeps here!"

"You're such a dick!" Lee yelled back.

"Eat shit!"

"Blow me!"

Meanwhile, Shaw leaned against the bathroom counter, brushed his teeth, and cast Vail some serious stink-eye. I was tempted just to choose to sleep in his room because he was being such a baby about the whole thing. I caught Shaw's eye and raised my brows at him, to which he nodded. Quietly, we passed Lee's room where he and Vail were still shouting obscenities at each other and softly shut the door behind us. His room was definitely the smallest, but he'd arranged it comfortably so that his bed faced the door, and it was covered in pillows and blankets, like a nest, which totally made sense for him. It was like protection against the shadows, something to hold when the memories forced their way back into his mind. He didn't have a desk or anything personal. Just a dresser for his clothes, the top of it covered with piles of books, and an open closet, displaying his knife collection, all arranged on stands set up along the length of the wall.

The sight of his vast collection didn't bother me in the slightest. In fact, it only made me feel safer being here, as I knew Shaw could handle each and every one of them. He changed out of his hoodie, choosing to wear sweats and a t-shirt to bed. I clambered over the mass amounts of blankets and pillows and snuggled in while he shut the curtains and turned off the hurricane torchiere table lamp by his bed, where he then crawled in beside me.

However, before we could get truly settled, the door to his room swung open with a bang, and Vail stood there, glowering at the sight of us together.

"What?" I snapped at him, squinting from the hallway light that shone behind him. "Close the door, we're sleeping here!"

But Vail didn't say a word. All he did was storm into the room, scoop me up out of bed, and left, carrying me down the hall back to his.

"What the hell is up your ass?" I snapped at him, kicking my legs a little. "Put me down, you psycho!"

He entered his room, kicking the door shut behind himself, and practically threw me into the bed. I landed with a bounce and crawled to the other side, fully intending to skirt around him and go back to Shaw's when his fingers wrapped around my ankle, and he dragged me back to him.

"Let *go*, Vail!" I rolled onto my back and slapped his shoulder, but all he did was move me to the head of the bed, so I was resting on the pillows, then forced my legs open. He laid between them, leaned over to turn off the light, and rested his head on my chest over my heart, his arms wrapped around me tightly. I was so freaking tired I didn't bother physically trying to overpower him. I'd only lose. But I still muttered under my breath about him being an alpha-asshole.

"Shush, darling. I'm trying to sleep here." Was all he said in response and pressed a kiss to the hollow at the base of my throat before settling back down again. His weight wasn't uncomfortable or suffocating, despite how much bigger he was. It was oddly cozy, warm, and most of his weight was in his pelvis anyways, which was settled just below mine on the mattress. The sneaky bugger had to use his dead weight to keep me with him, knowing there was no possible way that I'd be able to leave now without him waking up.

"You know, Lee had a point," I goaded him. "Technically, you and I slept together last night, so tonight is someone else's turn."

His hand came up, his index and middle fingers pressing against my lips to silence me, and he muttered against my skin, "Shaw got to nap with you today. That means his turn is over. Lee kept you at his side all day pretending to be a whiny bitch because of a couple of bruised knuckles. That's *his* turn over. Now it's mine again."

"Are we seriously going to do it that way? All ring around the rosie, hot potato style?" My words were slightly muffled against his fingers, which were still pressed against my mouth.

"For now? Yes. But since I'm the leader of our tribe, I get the final say." He tapped my lips before sliding his arm back around me again, shifting a little to get comfortable. His stomach pressed against me, and for a moment, my girly bits seemed to stir a little. I couldn't help squeezing my thighs a little to relieve the ache, though his bulk prevented me from actually easing that itch. All I did was tighten my legs around the small of his waist, and then the feel of his hard muscles pressing into me only rubbed a little harder.

Fuck, not now. Or maybe...? No! He was being too much of a douche to just fall into that. He hasn't earned it yet, the bastard. I debated back and forth with myself, my pussy begging for attention, while my brain was telling her to calm the fuck down and just go to sleep. I couldn't just cave when he was being such a turd about his dominance in our group.

Ultimately, he decided for me when I heard his breathing

deepen and his hold slackened as he fell into a slumber. Well, I guess that settled that internal war for me. So I relaxed beneath him, my eyes adjusting to the darkness of the room. Outside, I could hear the wind blow, the cold arrival of Fall coming in with the promise of snow. In the distance, the sound of sirens grew louder before disappearing in the distance, and I felt my eyelids beginning to droop. Old sounds from the past lulled me to sleep, and soon, I'd passed out in Vail's arms, finally home.

Chapter fourteen

Casey

"I *HAVE* to go to school today, you guys!" I was literally standing in the living room, dressed for the day, my book bag slung over my shoulder, but was met by a wall of male testosterone. All three of them were standing and blocking the stairway leading to the front door.

"No, you're not," Vail said, as though the decision had already been made.

I stared at him in aghast, before gesturing wildly in his and Shaw's directions. "Well, what the fuck! Why are you two dressed and heading out then?" I asked.

When I woke up that morning, Vail and I had shifted in the night, though he still held me close to his body. I was lying on my side, face pressed into his chest, but found that Shaw had crept into bed with us in the middle of the night and was huddled at my back. Sleepily, I glanced over at the clock on the nightstand and saw I had about an hour before school started, so I crawled out of bed, leaving the two boys behind to sleep a little longer, so I could grab a shower. When I'd come out, Vail's bedroom was empty, his bed a tangle of blankets and sheets, and I could hear him and the other guys downstairs talking softly. Peering down, I could see they were dressed in jeans and long sleeve shirts, ready for the day, so I'd hurried to catch up to them. Now I was getting *this* bullshit.

"I've been suspended for the rest of the week, darling," Vail said, eyes on me like he thought I was gonna be suicidal and try to throw myself down the stairs just to get to school.

"So, where are you two going?" I asked, noticing that Lee was the only one still in his sleep sweats and a loose over-sized t-shirt, his feet bare.

"Gotta talk to Maverick, hun. So you stay here today," Vail said.

I started feeling a little panicky. "I *can't* miss another day of school, guys." I pulled out my phone to check the time, noticing that I also had a missed call from Nylah. *Shit!*

"You can, and you will. You can't be alone in that school without us there to protect you."

"Oh for…" I sagged my shoulders, my bag sliding off them to the floor with a thump. "First of all, Hunter isn't even gonna be there. Wasn't he suspended, too?"

"He was."

"See? And it's the middle of the day. They aren't gonna grab me at school in the middle of the day and hand me off in some sketchy deal with the Faceless. Not in front of every-body." I wanted to add that I highly doubted that Hunter was actually going to sell me off. I mean, yeah, he was a douchebag and all, but the more I thought about it, the less likely it was that he was setting me up. He had dozens of girls at his disposal. There was no reason to go out of his way for one that wasn't even interested. And then, there was him saving me from Celeste in the cafeteria. If he hadn't swooped in when he did, well, I would have had my eye gouged out with a fork by the bitch.

"It's not just him. It's the rest of the Jackals. And we're *not* arguing about this, Casey!" Vail snapped at me and stepped forward, snatching up my bag and tossing it over his shoulder. "These are the rules. Obey my command and *fall in*."

I sighed, remembering that I'd agreed to all of this. I guess I hadn't expected their rules to interfere with my education. But it was for my protection, so I'd go along with it. But I was still tempted to brat out to Vail. "Aye-aye, *Captain*." I narrowed my eyes at him, hands on my hips as we glared each other down. He wanted to go all domineering asshole on me; then he was going to get an attitude. If he'd just sat me down and talked to me like a normal person, I would have been fine rather than having this sprung on me at the last minute and spoken to like a soldier.

Vail watched me carefully for a minute until the smallest of smiles curled his lips, and I knew I was fucked. "Lee?"

"Yeah?" Lee moved forward, stopping just short behind him, his arms bulging as they crossed over his massive chest.

"She does anything against the rules, you have my permission to discipline her."

My mouth dropped at that, and I swear, if I could get away with it, I would have slapped him across the face. Instead, I flipped him off with both hands before I stomped over to the kitchen to get some food, which ended up just being some bread with peanut butter spread over it, as it was the only condiment I found.

"Later, sweet thing!" Vail called from the hallway.

"Frig off, ass!" I yelled back, stepping out to sit at the table in the dining area.

From down the stairs, I heard him laugh loudly and leave, with a silent Shaw behind them. When Lee came back up the stairs after locking up, he walked right over and leaned over the chair across from me, holding onto its back. "It's for your own-"

"Don't even finish that sentence," I warned him. "I'm not in the mood right now."

He stepped back, his bandaged hands raised. I guess he had put together that it was *not* the time to fuck with me, and then just sat on the couch to play some video games. We sat in silence while I finished eating. After I threw my dishes in the sink, I disappeared upstairs to brush my teeth and fume on my own. But Lee came up shortly after, interrupting me as I laid on Vail's bed, staring up at the ceiling and contemplating how I was gonna make Vail pay later.

"Still pouting, hey?" He winked at me, leaning against the wall of the doorway, and chuckled.

"I'm *not* pouting. I'm just... thinking."

"Pouting, babe. You're pouting. Like a little girl who hasn't gotten her way," he laughed, then strolled in, grinning wickedly at me.

"You're just gloating cuz Captain Asswipe gave you "disciplinary" rights." I used my fingers, indicating the bunny ears around the word. "Seriously, how obnoxious can you get?"

"Obnoxious. Why do you say that?" Lee asked, sitting on the edge of the bed.

I scooted up to the head of the bed and sat with my hands clasped in my lap as I faced him. "Telling you to discipline me. I mean, what is this? The Nineteen-Fifties?" I giggled. "Yeah, real funny joke, Vail."

However, Lee wasn't laughing. In fact, his expression didn't change at all. He was watching me with his dark eyes, the corner of his mouth lifted just in the slightest, as though he'd been the tiniest bit amused by my ranting.

"What?" I sneered, not liking his silence.

"He wasn't making a joke, Casey," he said, brows raised, now looking absolutely delighted at the shock that was without a doubt clear on my face. "If you fuck up here and don't do what we say, even me, then I get to punish you."

I crossed my arms over my chest and straightened up, hoping that I appeared as pissed as I felt. "Fuck off, no, you wouldn't."

Lee just chuckled. "Please, don't tempt me... I've been itching to get my hands on you."

"Lee!" My mouth dropped at his words. "What the hell?"

"Hey, just being honest here, babe." He winked at me before deciding to get all serious as he stretched out at the foot of the bed, his fingers gliding over my ankles. "Just be grateful he asked *me* to dish it out and not himself."

I scoffed, rolling my eyes at him, but I didn't pull away from his touch. It was nice, and then I remembered how he had fought last night to have a chance to have me with him. I was sort of glad I was getting a little one-on-one time with him. "Yeah, well, I think His Royal Highness wouldn't want to put in the energy to teach me a lesson."

Lee's smile disappeared completely, and he gripped my ankle hard, catching my attention. "He didn't ask me to punish you because he was too lazy to do it himself, Casey..." he said slowly, making sure I heard every word he uttered. "He asked me because he is protecting you from himself."

I gaped at him, a little taken aback by his words, and honestly, I wasn't sure how to take it. "What do you mean?" I asked finally, realizing that he wasn't trying to fuck with me.

"I'm sure you've noticed how others react to him and Shaw..." he said, like he was really trying to make his words sink in.

I thought about how Bryce reacted when Shaw had come on the scene that day in the classroom. He'd nervously shrunk back. As for Vail, the only thing I'd noticed was that people tended to give him a wide berth, but I figured that was just due to respect, with him being Vendetta's leader and all.

"Shaw... he scares people because when he goes off, he's like a loose cannon. You don't know what he'll do, but what's guaranteed is that you're going to suffer. He likes causing pain, and I'm sure you can understand why, given what he went through."

I understood that. Shaw had serious demons in his closet, and remembering how quickly he reacted to seeing my father attack me, I believed what Lee was saying. Shaw would try to cause an adversary as much pain as possible because for so long, the pain was always what *he* endured.

"Now me," he chuckled a little, though it fell flat with the seriousness of the topic at hand. "I tend to knock people out with one punch, thanks to my size. Going up against me, even if you lose, chances are you won't remember it." He released me to tenderly touch his bandaged knuckles as though he were checking to see if they still hurt. He didn't react, which was hopefully a good sign that he was on the mend. "Now *Vail...*" he said, his voice changing at the name. It deepened, his tone without a doubt serious when he said, "Vail won't punish you, because even though he would *never* intentionally hurt you... he will never put himself in a position even to risk it."

I felt all the hairs on my arms stand on end, and now I was wishing I'd chosen a sweater instead of a t-shirt to wear. *What the hell does that mean?*

"Vail is more fucked up than you realize, Casey," Lee said, and though his words were ugly, I could hear in his voice how much he respected him. "The violence would consume him. He'd get lost in it. If Shaw is coming for you, you know you're going to suffer; you're going to hurt. With Vail, if he is coming for you, you're going to fucking die."

I stared at him, feeling like I'd fallen into a vat of freezing cold water. I remembered the night of our last sleepover as kids, how Vail, at only eleven years old, nearly killed that guy who broke in. He was like a wild animal, lashing out at anyone that tried to pull him off.

Lee reached out, sliding one of his hands into mine, and squeezed, yet his face remained serious and somber. "His dad-"

"That was an accident," I said, coming to Vail's defense. "It was self-defence. He was protecting his mom-"

"Vail killed his dad, Casey. He knew what he was doing when he grabbed the kitchen mallet. He *wanted* to."

I couldn't believe that. He was just a kid. He'd just turned eleven a month before the incident in January. How could he be capable of it? I recalled how he was forced to go to therapy after, but he'd been cleared after only a few sessions. Once the shock of what he did wore off, his caseworker said he had made amazing progress, and he'd been released.

"He knew what he was doing," Lee repeated. "He knew what to do to get the social workers to back the fuck up. Vail killed his dad, Casey. And he's killed more than just him."

"What?" I gasped, my heart crashing in my chest, and I squeezed Lee's hand, needing the stability.

"Why do you think Vail is the leader of Vendetta?" Lee arched a brow at me. "He's the most controlled, the most dangerous person at Harley Institute. Hunter is just a fucking idiot, and he's fucking lucky that Vail hasn't lost himself around him."

"You honestly think Vail would hurt me?" I whispered, now terrified.

He shook his head and brushed one of his dreads out of his face. "I don't think he'd intentionally hurt you, Casey. He *loves* you. We all do. More than any fucking thing in our lives. And that's why if you don't follow orders, you'll be punished." He rose then, heading to the door. "I saw that little list of yours. Give me ten minutes, and we'll head out together, yeah?" He changed the subject so abruptly I'd been a little thrown off.

"So... I can't go to school, but I can go out shopping in Harley now?" I said, struggling to understand. I knew I was being a brat, but I couldn't help it. I didn't sign up for whatever the hell *this* was. If any of the guys tried to punish me, I'd make sure that as soon as it was over, I'd make them regret it with a swift kick in the balls. I just prayed to fuck that it wasn't Vail.

We were at the dollar store, filling up a little cart with food. I ended up actually grabbing a second one for things like extra bath towels, cleaning products, some plates and cups, kitchenware, bathroom supplies, and some things I'd need, as I had to use one of the guy's shampoo this morning and I just feel off. Lee raises a brow when I add things like candles and couch pillows, too.

"Geez, since when did you become Martha Stewart?" Lee asked when I added some pots and pans to his cart before moving on to throw in dishcloths and a toilet scrubber.

"Since I moved in with three teenage boys," I said, looking at a container of laundry detergent. "You guys have any of this?" I asked him.

"What is it?"

I immediately added it to the cart.

He just laughed, "You don't have to do this, babe." He chuckled as we moved on.

"Yes, I do," I said and pressed on, noticing a stack of drawing paper sketchbooks, and decided to grab several, as well as some drawing pencils, too. I missed doodling and sketching. I only did it while Meredith and I waited for whatever we were baking in Home Ec. to finish, which was why my notebook was almost full. I was hoping to get back into it.

"Casey, I-"

"Lee, just, please... let me do this. I *want* to." I peeked back at him, noticing that he appeared a little uncomfortable. I softened a bit and reached out, cupping the side of his face, loving how smooth it was. "You guys are everything to me. If I can help in any way, then I will. And doing this makes *me* feel better. So really, I'm being selfish."

He chuckled a little but leaned into my touch before pressing a soft kiss to my palm. He stared down at me in a way that made me feel like the most beautiful girl in the world, and not just some teenager in ripped boyfriend jeans and a t-shirt with her purple hair tossed up in a messy bun. When Lee looked at me this way, I could see the burn in his dark eyes. Every thought that crossed his mind at that moment was so clear to me.

"I really fucking missed you, Casey," he said, reaching out to slide his hand over my waist to the small of my back. He started pulling me in when I felt a vibration in my back pocket.

Wait, what?

I reached back and felt my phone buzzing away. Lee raised his brows in question as I pulled it out and checked the missed call. *Nylah.* Shit. I couldn't keep avoiding her. But how the hell was I going to explain everything that had been happening? I didn't want to lie to her, but this has gotten so insane, I knew she'd freak out and drive down here, and Nylah in Harley would stand out. She'd only put herself in danger. My phone buzzed again, a text coming through, and I knew she was probably bitching me out. I didn't blame her. I needed to explain some things, but I couldn't with Lee around.

I slid my phone back into my pocket. "Let's pay for this stuff," I told him and led the way to the cash. There was a small line up there, and the whole time we were waiting, I felt my phone going off. *Shit... I needed to do something.*

"Hey, I just remembered that we need containers to store this stuff in." I turned to walk away.

"I can grab some, Casey," he said, ever the gentleman.

"Naw, I saw some specific ones I like. Save our spot in line. Be right back!" I ran down an aisle and out of sight. The containers were at the opposite end of the store, but rather than heading there, I snuck outside when Lee wasn't looking and huddled off to the side, out of view of the store windows, and pulled out my phone. Sure enough, there were several angry text messages from my best friend, and the guilt was starting to choke me. I needed to say *something...* just not everything. Not now, at least. I pressed the call button and waited, but she picked up on the first ring.

"Casey!" She practically shouted through the other end.

"Ny, I'm so, so sorry that I haven't called. It's been crazy here-"

"My God, do you have any idea how worried I've been?" She cut me off, but I couldn't be mad at her. She had every right to be upset right now.

"I know, I'm sorry," I said again, but she wasn't having it.

"I've barely heard a word from you, and my last message goes unanswered?" she said, sounding incredibly hurt. *Ugh! It felt like a knife had stabbed me in the gut.* "At first, I was upset, but then I got so freaking scared because you're living in fucking Harley, and when I didn't hear back, I thought you'd been attacked or some shit! I was about ready to tell my dad to take me down there to make sure you were still alive!"

I had no doubt she would have done it, too. Thank fuck I called her back now.

"Casey, I've been freaking out!" I heard the break in her

voice, and I leaned against the brick wall of the building, feeling like shit.

"Ny, I can't say sorry enough cuz it won't change what I did. But please know that I am. You didn't deserve that. I just… I dunno. I guess I was worried about distracting you-"

"Distracting me?" she said incredulously. "What are you talking about?"

"You have basketball, the social committee, and school to think about. I want you to get into McGill and go places. If I'm texting you all the time telling you how I'm-" I stopped suddenly, not wanting her to think that I'd been struggling. "I didn't want you to worry about me."

"Well, that kinda backfired, girl." I could hear the Nylah sass coming in, which told me she was on her way out of her angry fit. In the background, I could hear her moving things around and I wanted to laugh. She's always been a little OCD with her space and would carefully line things like knick-knacks and books up so that everything in the room was perfectly spaced apart and presentable. If she weren't so into science, I would push her into interior design. "Do you really think I'd just forget about you now that you're there?" she asked. "Seriously." She paused to cough, the sound like a deep rattle in her chest. "I ought to come down there and kick your ass myself!"

"Are you sick?" I could hear her wheezing a little.

"Don't change the subject-"

"Good lord, get into bed now!" I snapped at her while she sniffled.

"I will, when you tell me what the heck is going on?" she said, coughing again. "I'll survive this flu bug, but I care more about my best friend. Honestly? I'm gonna blame you for making me sick. You made me so worried that I became ill. That's how it happened."

Dammit, she really knew how to tug at my heartstrings

and while also making me laugh all at the same time. "I…" I honestly didn't have anything to say. I knew she was right. But again, I didn't want her to sense that I'd been stressed to hell, worried about what was happening here in Harley and the girls who had disappeared, or thinking that I was in any danger. She'd send Mr. Bryant my way to collect me, and I refused to abandon my boys now. "I miss you," I told her, finally, unable to think of anything else to say. So I just ended up telling her the truth.

I heard her grow quiet on the other end, and I could just picture her twisting one of her honey brown curls around her long slender finger, wanting to be mad with me still so she could continue to vent, but it was rare that I expressed myself like this. "Damn you, Casey," she muttered at last, and I knew her brief moment of rage had finally fizzled out. "I miss you, too, you moody bitch." She sighed a little, and I could hear the rustling of blankets. I was relieved to hear that she was crawling back into bed, and sniggered a little when I remembered how she used to call me a Moody Millie when we first met because I had been so suspicious of her all the time.

"Well, I miss you more-" I was cut off suddenly when a large shadow blocked out the sun. Nervously, I peered up to see Lee standing over me, bags in hand, but the look on his face had me actually shaking where I stood. "Uh, Ny, I'll call you later, okay?"

"Well, wait! We just started-"

"I know but I'm at school and I'm late for next period," I lied quickly.

"Aw shit, yeah, I'm sorry. I was bored and didn't think about it being a school day…" As she went on, coughing a little more, I hadn't taken my gaze off of Lee, who kept standing over me like an angry bear. His size was actually scaring me now more than it ever had before.

"Okay, love you, girl. I'll call soon," I said quickly.

"Bye, love you!"

I hung up, shoved my phone back into my pocket, and stood there, twisting my fingers together, unsure of what to say. I mean, I was sure that my lying to him was what had him so livid with me, yet now I'm wondering if my leaving the store for just a minute without him knowing was a major no-no, too. I mean, Lee was just inside. And I *needed* to call my friend, which meant I needed privacy.

"Lee, I-"

"Don't, Casey." The way he said those two words had me involuntarily stepping back in surprise. I didn't think I'd ever seen Lee look at me this way, and I wasn't sure I liked it.

"I just needed to tell my friend-"

"I don't want to hear excuses. We're going home. *Now!*" He thrust one of the bags at me, still carrying the other four, and nodded at me to come along. We walked in uncomfortable silence the entire way back to the townhouse. When we got there, I raced up the steps, tossing the bags onto the coffee table, and then raced for it up the stairs, fully intending to lock myself in the washroom until he'd cooled down.

But when I was only two steps up, his hand reached from the space in between and grabbed my ankle. I fell forward, catching myself on the carpeted stairs as he came storming up. The moment he'd released my ankle, however, I had frantically started climbing the steps like a dog, on all fours, in an attempt to move faster. I hadn't done that since I was a kid, but I didn't care how it made me look. With a very pissed-off, muscled, giant Lee who was tearing after me, I'd do whatever I could to keep him away.

I made it to the top of the stairs and booked it down the hall to the washroom, just reaching the door when two massive hands grabbed the small of my waist, and I found myself lifted into the air.

"Lee!" I shouted, kicking my legs. "Put me down now!"

But he ignored me. Instead, he carried me into his room, kicking the door shut behind himself, and I could feel a sense of panic overwhelming me. Being locked in a room with an angry Lee? No thank you! I was flailing now, throwing my head back in an attempt to reverse headbutt him, but he held me out far enough that I was nowhere close to reaching him.

His room was dark, and the blackout curtains were drawn over his large window with his bed sitting right beneath it. His room was meticulously clean, his orange comforter over the navy sheets were made up and straight, while his shelves held piles of vintage records all arranged nicely in a row, and then his collection of brass knuckles shiny and lined up like trophies, ranged in colours from gunmetal, black, silver, to gold and brass. He had a desk stacked neatly with papers and notebooks for school, while his dresser had his record player sitting in the prime display spot in the middle. Suddenly Lee had angled me towards his bed, and I knew what he was about to do.

"Don't-" I started to say when he threw me, much like Vail had last night. I bounced and fell on my stomach, but I tried to crawl to the end of the bed to make a break for it. Lee simply slid an arm beneath my stomach and lifted my rear up, pulling me back towards him as he sat on the edge of the mattress, and arranged me so my stomach was lying across his thighs.

Oh, hell no! I thought, and I grabbed handfuls of his blankets to try to pull away, my legs flailing.

"You fucking ran off, Casey," Lee rumbled, his voice reminding me of thunder like he was Thor himself, and I fought harder. He grunted when I managed to kick his shin, and he brought a leg up over both of mine, securing them so they were flat behind me. "You *knew* you weren't supposed to leave the store. And you lied. What did Vail say I could do if you went against orders?"

"You never gave me the order!" I protested, reaching back to try to scratch him.

"I shouldn't have to tell you what should be common sense." He seized my wrists and bent them so they were angled up high on my back, pressing them down with one hand and making me completely immobile. "You need to behave and fall in."

"I am, I am!" I insisted, still trying to squirm free, but I felt like I had literally been caught in a vice. "I swear, I am. I just needed to call my friend back. Her dad is a cop! I couldn't risk them coming here!"

"You lied, Casey." Lee's free hand glided down my back, caressing the curve of my hip before he slid it beneath me. My eyes widened in alarm when I felt him flick the button of my jeans open, before sliding the zipper down. I squealed and struggled more, but with one hard tug, he pulled my pants down to just above my knees, where his thick, muscled thigh was restraining my legs. He then cupped one of my ass cheeks from over my panties, and I stiffened over his legs, sensing what he was about to do, and I was not having it.

"You better fucking not," I warned him. "I've never been spanked in my life, and I have no intention of-"

Smack!

I gasped as his hand suddenly swung down, slapping me right across my right cheek. I tried to get up, but the strain from the angle of my arms kept me flat. "Lee!" I screeched.

Smack!

I attempted to kick again, but he was relentless as he brought his huge hand down again, striking the other cheek.

"You could have been taken, Casey. Someone could have seen you there alone and taken you. We can't have anarchy or someone choosing to go rogue at the last minute. That could hurt the rest of us. So you need to fall in fucking line," He told me, his voice sounding like a deep purr.

"You son of a-"

Smack!

I squealed again, the sting from the slap like a shock to my body. "Fuuuuuu yewwwwwww!" I screamed into the blanket as the asshole just chuckled like he was enjoying it.

Smack!

Okay, *that* one hurt. I grunted, squeezing my eyes shut as he brought his palm down again, changing sides, moving his hand around to my upper thighs, then back up the curve of my bottom again. I'm embarrassed as hell to be having Lee do this to me, and angry tears were welling out the corner of my eyes. I was determined to fucking get him after this.

But just as I started plotting payback, he stopped. His hand was brushing over the area so lightly instead. It had been like a feather skimming across my skin. He blew on it, causing me to shiver. *What is he doing now?* I was so confused by the sudden change, the gentleness. Just as I thought he was done, he gave me another hard slap, only this time his fingers smacked closer to my actual pussy.

Okay... whoa! What the hell was that? I stilled beneath him from that one, the feel of him hitting that area had sent a small jolt through my system.

"You were a bad girl today, Casey," Lee murmured, now caressing my ass again before giving it a lighter, minor spank before he reached between my legs and *cupped* me there!

"Lee!" I gasped, shaking a little as his fingers stroked along my folds, flicking up to my clit, and down again.

Smack!

Okay, for some reason, that one felt different. A familiar feeling was returning, one I normally got when I'd fucked around with Patrick at parties. I was getting fucking turned on by this! Holy shit…

His hand came back to stroke along my lips, only this time, his thumb pressed down on my clit and began to circle it, slowly, the pressure changing every so often. I could feel my cheeks flush, and I bit my lip, holding back a moan at the feeling that was starting to stir in me. It had been a little over two months since I last had sex, and with Lee playing with me like this, well… let's just say my girly bits were hungry as fuck.

"Lee," I whispered, my voice hoarse from shouting, and also because, if he keeps doing what he's doing, I'm gonna lose it. He pulled the material of my panties aside, now touching my bare skin, and he glided his fingers between my folds and moaned.

"You're so fucking wet…" He stopped touching me, and when I peered over my shoulder at him, he was sucking on the two fingers he used to play with me. Holy hell, that was hot. He gave me another hard spank. "Now, are you going to be a good girl?"

Why the hell would I be good when this is what I get for being a brat? I had thought. I bit my lip, deliberating as he gave me another, harder slap.

"Casey?" He prodded as he rubbed a little faster over my wet pussy, making sure that he was squeezing and rubbing at my clit harder than before. "Are you gonna be good and follow orders?"

"Bite me," I moaned. Seconds later, I felt him shift and bend over my backside. When his teeth actually clamped down on my ass cheek, I practically shrieked and tried to pull away. "Lee!"

"Are you gonna be a good girl?" He asked me again and slapped my pussy. I quivered on his lap, trying to squeeze my thighs shut as he furiously stroked me, his fingers occasionally sliding completely in, curling, and dragging out.

"Why the fuck would I be when this is what happens when I'm bad?" I snapped at him, unable to stop my mouth from running off.

"You like this punishment, babe?" His lips were so close to my ear, his warm breath on my skin left goosebumps behind. His tongue licked up the side of my neck until his teeth nipped at my earlobe, at the same time that he suddenly focused all his attention on my clit. I could feel that pulse between my legs growing stronger, building up from his attention, and I gasped in his lap while clinging to the blankets for dear life. "Well?" he asked, pressing a little harder against me, and the tiniest little whine escaped me. "You like this?"

"Y-yes… yes…" I choked out, getting so close. Beneath me, I could feel his hard length pressing up into my stomach, and knowing he was just as turned on by this as I was, had me pressing back into his hand.

"If you're a good girl, then you'll be rewarded," he said and kissed along my neck. "How about that for a compromise?"

"Okay…" I gasped, squeezing my legs around his hand, like I wanted to trap it there.

"Casey?"

"Y-yeah?"

"You gonna be a good girl and come for me?"

I moaned again, "Fuck yes… almost…" I buried my face into his comforter, rolling my hips against his movements, feeling so close.

"That's it… come… ride it and let go…" he breathed in my ear, and I felt that building pulse suddenly snap, sending a wave of pleasure throughout my system. I cried into the blanket, my movements jerky and slowing as he slowly started to stop. "I'm not done with you." He pulled at my panties, the material snagging around my hips hard before ripping away, and then he roughly pulled my jeans off of me. Next thing I knew, he had pulled me up, so I was straddling his lap, face to face with him. Our lips were so close that I couldn't help but take the opportunity to lean in to bite his lower lip. I could feel the rumble in his chest as he groaned and yanked my shirt up while I attacked his clothes.

It had been too fucking long. I needed this badly.

I dragged his shirt off, revealing his smooth skin and bulging muscles. Seriously, Lee was like a Greek God of perfection. When I fumbled with his belt, he leaned in and ripped my lacy, blue bra off.

"You're fucking paying for that," I whispered against his neck, and I latched on, sucking hard while he took over, undoing his pants himself. I hung on, my legs wrapping around his waist when he stood to kick them off before sitting back down. I felt his thick, smooth length rub against my pussy as I moved closer to him, curling my hips so that I was rubbing myself against him.

I almost couldn't believe that Lee and I were doing this, that the boy who once carried me around piggyback, who held me down and tickled me till I almost peed my pants, and braided my hair as we watched movies together, was now holding me in his arms. The possessive way he was holding me against his large body was gentle yet authoritative all at once. He made me feel so small in his arms, and for once, I liked it. I had wanted him to take me, to overpower me, and to throw me around his fucking bed.

I spat in my hand and reached between us, holding his dark gaze as I encircled his thick dick and gently squeezed as I pumped it.

"You wanna fuck me, Lee?" I whispered against his lips. He shuddered beneath me, his hands on my hips squeezing hard, digging into my flesh, and I loved it. "You want to be the first one to fuck me? What would Vail say?" I said, baiting him. Sure enough, he let out a little growl at that, and I grinned against his mouth as I gave him teasing kisses and bites. "Vail wouldn't like that, would he? If he were here, he'd tell you to stop, is that right?" His hands gave me another squeeze, and I saw the fire burning in his eyes. I giggled and said softly, "He'd tell you to stop, and you would. Because unlike me, you follow orders like a good boy. Isn't that right?"

"You little brat..." His voice trailed off when I pumped him a bit harder, and he groaned, letting his head fall back as he thrusted up into my hand.

"That's right. I am." I grinned at the sight of him unfolding beneath me, and I lifted myself, lining him up with my entrance. "And you love it." Slowly, I sank down, easing my way around his cock. He was a lot thicker than Patrick was, so it felt tight, but I licked my lips as he filled me, the pressure only starting to reawaken the orgasm I'd just had minutes before I grinned. This was going to be fun. I sank lower, now releasing his length so I could hold onto his shoulders, my legs wrapped tight around his waist for support, until finally, our pelvises met with a bit of a smack.

"Holy shit, Casey..." he moaned, holding me there for a moment as though he was savouring the feeling before he encouraged me to move. I lifted my hips, dropping them back down again, moving slowly at first, and I kissed him. Lee's lips were soft, yet he took control; his rhythm matched perfectly with how I was riding him. "Move faster, baby," he moaned and urged me on, helping by lifting me up. So I did. I moved faster, causing him to lay back on the bed, holding me to him. I reached back, balancing my hands on his knees, and rocked my hips forward and back, earning another delicious moan from him. I gasped as I felt his dick moving against the spot inside me that started to make me stir again.

Lee reached up and pulled my hair tie free, tossing it aside as my lilac curls fell over my breasts and down my back. He brushed it away, one hand squeezing around my breast, while the other grabbed a fistful of my purple locks and yanked back, arching my head upwards to the ceiling. I gasped when he pinched my nipple hard, and I rocked faster over him, moving my hips back and forth, rubbing my clit over his pelvis. It felt so fucking good.

"Why are we being quiet?" Lee's deep baritone was husky, which only turned me on more. So I picked up the pace, riding him harder while he guided me, his hands moving my hips over himself. When he spanked my ass before rubbing his thumb over my clit, I let out a strangled sort of cry, feeling myself getting closer and closer. "That's right, baby... but I wanna hear you scream as I fuck you." He flipped us then but pulled me up, turning me so I was on my hands and knees. Grabbing the small of my waist, he pulled me back onto his length, hitting me deeper, and my breath caught in my throat at the feeling. Lee didn't go slow. He fucked me hard, hauling me back over his dick all fast and furious.

"Don't hold it in, baby," he hissed through gritted teeth as he pumped away. I wanted to squeeze my legs together again as that tingling pulse was building, but he wouldn't allow that. One of his hands slid around under my stomach and down to play with my clit, rubbing it hard while he was thrusting. My ass was stinging from all the spanking, and I thought I would be on the verge of crying if I didn't get that release again soon. "You feel so good on my cock." He gave me another hard spank before he shoved my face down into the mattress and fucked me so hard and fast I felt like I was gonna pass out. My pussy was throbbing, begging, and finally, I exploded, sending a shock wave over my body. I screamed as he continued to pound away, prolonging the feeling.

"Oh shit, I'm gonna..." He pulled out suddenly, and seconds later, I felt the wet warmth of his cum as it shot out onto my backside. We were both panting hard, both sweaty and spent, and I could barely move. I felt him massaging his cum all over my ass, like he was rubbing it in. I trembled beneath him, still rocking from my second orgasm, and then I thought, thank *fuck,* Mom had let me start birth control this year. This was stupid and reckless of me, but holy shit, I wouldn't have done it any other way.

"So..." I whispered when Lee collapsed beside me. "Think you're gonna get into trouble with the Boss Man?"

His head whipped my way, glared, and then gave me one last spank.

By the time the other two had come back, Lee and I already spent most of the morning fucking all over his bedroom. It wasn't until I remembered the groceries and stuff that I had to fight my way out of his grip and run downstairs to make sure nothing had gone bad. But the moment I finished putting away the last of the food and was about to move on to the other stuff, he threw me over his shoulder and carried me back upstairs. We were showering together, him pressing me up against the tiled wall, kissing me deeply when a loud shout from downstairs snapped us out of our little world.

"Where the fuck are you two? What's all this crap?" Vail's voice echoed up the stairs, and I realized he had found the bags of cleaning supplies, pillows, candles, and other little bits I'd purchased but had forgotten to put away.

"Oh shit!" I shut off the water and clambered out, grabbing one of the towels hanging off the door while Lee followed, though he was moving more leisurely than I was. I felt panicked. Despite knowing that he would never hurt me, Vail's potential jealous rage was still a terrifying prospect, but Lee seemed as calm as ever, grinning like a cocky bastard and walking with a bit of swagger to his step. "You can wipe that smug smile off your face any time now," I demanded, but instead of listening to me, he just wrapped a towel around his waist and reached around me, opening the door just as Vail appeared in the hall, and I froze.

His hazel eyes checked me over, standing there, dripping wet in just a towel, with Lee right behind me. There was no denying that we were just showering together, so I stood there, doing my best to look as chilled as Lee was, but inside, I thought my heart was gonna burst through my chest.

Vail looked to Lee, taking in his current state, then back at me. He moved towards Lee's room and peeked inside after smashing the door open. I bit my lip, knowing that he saw the blankets on the bed in disarray, the papers on his desk scattered on the floor. Even his record player had been moved over to make room for me as I sat up on the dresser while Lee went down on me, pleasuring me over and over again as he ate me out.

Slowly, Vail turned, and his glare locked on to Lee, fists clenching, and he muttered, "You son of a bitch..." He sounded half-furious and half-impressed, though he seemed more enraged than anything.

"What's happening?" Shaw's quiet voice floated up the stairs, and I just wanted to fall in a hole in the floor and die. I tore away from Lee and disappeared into Vail's room, hoping to get into a change of clothes before a fight broke out. I hadn't thought this through. Honestly, I had no idea what the hell I was feeling. I loved all my boys. I really did. My relationship with each one was different and unique. If they were going to tell me I had to choose, well, I'd prefer to be dressed for it.

But Vail chased after me, only to slam the door behind himself.

"Leave," I told him, opening the drawers and quickly grabbing a pair of sweats and a long sleeve shirt, forgoing a bra and underwear.

"So you guys screwed, huh?" he snapped, his cheeks all red.

"What do you think, Vail?" I answered without looking at him. "You told him to punish me if I didn't follow your stupid rules, remember?"

"Must have been a pretty big fucking rule to get that type of punishment, darling." His voice was tight, and I knew he was working hard to remain in control.

I whipped around to face him and threw the towel aside, standing before him completely naked, and I grabbed the black sweats I'd pulled from the drawer, righting them. His eyes were moving over my body as I did that, and I could see the greedy lust there. His breathing changed, going from fast and furious to a deeper, heavier sort. He slowly licked his lips, watching as I stepped into the legs and pulled them up to my waist, tying them off. "The rule wasn't specified. But I think Lee taught me a lesson." I arched a brow at him, picking up the heather blue shirt. "So noted. No leaving your guys' sight while we're out. Got it."

"You left his sight?" Vail said slowly, his tone shifting. He was pissed off before, but now, his demeanor changed all together as he stared me down like I just told him I was joining a nunnery.

"I was just making a phone call to my friend, Nylah. I stepped outside for like, five minutes. That's all," I said as I pulled the shirt on. When I got my arms through the sleeves and pulled it over my head, straightening it around my waist, Vail moved closer, barely half a foot away.

"You... went outside? Alone?" he asked slowly, his face morphing to one void of expression. His mask. *Oh shit.*

"It was just five minutes, Vail," I told him, softening my tone. *Don't be snarky with him, Casey. He's not like Lee.* "But I know now. I won't do that again. I promise."

He didn't say anything, nor did he move. He just stares at me, his mouth slightly open, and I hear how quickly his breathing is coming. It's like he was on the verge of losing it.

"Hey... hey!" I reached out, taking his hand, but it was limp in mine. I squeezed it, holding it before my chest. "I'm sorry. I swear, I didn't know that was a rule. I know it was stupid, I-"

"You could have been taken."

"It was just five minutes-"

"You could have been taken, Casey," he said, spitting out each word between his teeth. "Five minutes? That's more than enough time for a van to pull up, two guys to reach out and knab you, and throw you inside and drive away. And that would be it. Ten seconds, tops. That's all it takes for someone to disappear." He slowly brought a hand up, cupping one of my cheeks, and I realized he was shaking ever so slightly. "They could have taken you from me..." he whispered.

"I'm sorry..." I said again. I waited, wondering if he was going to say anything else about Lee and me, but he didn't. Instead, he just reached up with his thumb, running it along my lower lip before dragging it down slightly. Wordlessly, he let me go and picked up the towel from the floor, then ran it over my hair, towel drying it for me, his touch surprisingly gentle.

"Come downstairs and show us all what you got," he said at last, tossing it in the hamper in the corner. "Cuz I saw what looks like some weird girl shit, a brush as long as my goddamn arm, and I have no idea what to do with it..."

"You mean the new toilet brush? For cleaning, smartass?" I asked, so relieved to have normal Vail back.

"Whatever, I'm starving. You show me what you bought while I eat something." He turned and headed toward the door, but just as he opened it, he called over his shoulder before leaving, "And brace yourself, darling. Lee might have had his fun, but you're still standing. When I'm through with you, you won't be able to walk for days."

Chapter fifteen

Casey

THE REST of the day with the guys was… well, interesting.

Shaw didn't seem at all surprised or bothered at the news of Lee and me. In fact, he acted no differently than before. When I came downstairs and sat on the couch to unpack everything, he simply curled up behind me and wrapped his arms around my waist, eyes closed as I tried to pull the barcode stickers off in one piece. After finding the food I'd bought for everyone, Vail appeared, a bowl of Kraft Dinner in his hands. He sat on one of the lounge chairs while Lee took the other on the opposite side. It was so unbearably quiet that I turned on the TV just to have some background noise while I went through all the new things I bought.

Several times when I paused to glance up at the two sitting across from each other, I caught them glaring daggers each other's way… or rather, Vail was glaring while Lee was smirking. Ugh! He needed to cut that out. Shaw, meanwhile, was like a cat all curled up behind me, half asleep, his body completely relaxed.

"So, what happened?" I asked as I ripped the tag out of the throw pillows I'd purchased for the couch. "What did Maverick say?" Reaching behind, I carefully lifted Shaw's head and slid the pillow beneath it before turning back to check out the various candles I'd gotten.

Vail's head lazily dropped to the side to look at me, his brows raised as though surprised I'd spoken at all. "Are you sure you're fit to hear this? Your eardrums aren't still ringing from having your head pounded into the headboard, the wall, the shower tile?"

I narrowed my eyes on him, wishing that I had powers of telepathy so I could make the chair he was sitting in, toss him across the room, and say nothing. I waited, letting him decide if he thought it was a good idea to keep baiting me this way.

Make the smart choice, St. James... I thought as I glared him down.

The bastard looked away, his own scowl landing on Lee, as though he blamed him completely for what we did. "Maverick's informant came through. He says we can move in on La Maison Rouge next week."

As glad as I was that he moved on, I was confused by everything he just said.

"Is he sure this time?" Shaw growled from behind me, his grip around my waist tightening. "We almost got fucking killed last time when the Beasts showed up last second at their warehouse by St. Lawrence..."

"That was a last-minute change by O'Hare, apparently," Vail said, stretching his legs out before him. "According to Maverick's inside guy, the man is a paranoid fuck lately... with Elias taking out the Beasts Prez and VP and their family and shit, we think Sheik is feeling the pressure as the new leader of their MC."

"So can we guarantee that there won't be a last-minute change of plans?" Lee asked. "A heads up for the other night could have fucking helped."

Before answering, Vail gave Lee major side-eye, "I guess their inside man wasn't with them when this happened."

"What exactly happened last time?" I asked, trying to keep up.

Vail glanced at me, his scowl softening as he watched me arrange some candles on the coffee table before lighting them with the matches I'd also purchased. "Elias has private docks out in a border town by St. Lawrence. We suspected he trafficks girls out of the country that way, rather than dealing with border bullshit. We were scoping it out, hoping to catch them in the act or see one of our girls." Vail looked away from all of us, running his hand over his face before he rested his chin upon his knuckles. "Fucking Hunter and the Jackals were there, for whatever the fuck reason…"

"They're trying to climb up the power ladder." Shaw's voice was filled with disgust. "They want to get on Elias' good side. I can see Hunter volunteering his guys to act as extra security on runs like that. And that Faceless fucker wouldn't give a shit that they're just high school wannabe punks. He's using them."

"Does Hunter know this?" I asked, leaning back against Shaw's stomach.

"Probably," Vail said quietly. "But like us, he's trying to survive, too, right? He's just going about it a different way. Instead of hiding from the Faceless, hoping to sneak through the cracks without getting stepped on, he's met them head-on, hoping for a bit of that power if he proves himself enough."

I got what Vail was saying, though it didn't stop me from

hating Hunter's guts. His working alongside the Faceless immediately made him dirt in my eyes. "So we know for sure the Jackals are giving the Beasts' girls to bring to Elias and his guys?" I asked.

"No definitive proof of that, but that's what we suspect," Lee said, his dark eyes still on Vail. They're both silently watching each other now, as if having some silent conversation between them.

"So what exactly happened then at the docks?" I asked.

Vail didn't look away from Lee, his mask firmly in place as he stared his friend down. "Vendetta was there trying to get some proof of the trafficking, like Lee said, to see one of our girls there. When Hunter and his group of jackasses caught us, they notified the Faceless. We tried to get out the way we had broken into the area, but then the fucking Celtic Beasts showed up, blocking our exit."

"How many of you in Vendetta are there?" I asked curiously.

"Within the school?" Shaw mumbled. "About fifty. On the streets? Another fifty. Lots of local guys who are sick of the city not giving a shit about Harley. We stick together. It's the only way we can survive."

"How many of you were there that night?"

"Ten," Vail said. "There were about twenty of Hunter's guys moving through the area, searching for trespassers past the fence line. When the Beasts showed up, the Jackals had already gathered near the way in and out. That's when that psycho biker who was with them literally jumped off his bike, grabbed a chainsaw from one of the construction piles, and just attacked the closest kid within his reach…" He paused, and for a moment, the memory of it was still fresh in his mind. "He attacked Bryce Fraser. Started hacking and sawing away like he was nothing. The way he screamed…"

I wasn't supposed to know about Bryce yet, but I didn't

push or question it. To see something like that was seriously fucked, and the fact that Vail and Shaw were holding it together so well after it was absolutely mind-blowing. I was proud of their strength, but I also wanted them to know that showing me their vulnerability was more than okay. "So Bryce is…" I let the words hang there, and their silence only confirmed it.

"He's gone," Shaw said quietly. "Just like Mark DeLuca and so many others."

"What happened to Mark?"

"Drive-by," was all Lee said, he and Vail resuming their staring match.

I sighed shakily, my mind reeling from what they'd told me. But even though it felt like my head was gonna explode, I still had questions. "So what about La Maison Rouge? What does that mean when Maverick says you can move in?"

"La Maison Rouge is an exclusive "Gentleman's Club" run by the Faceless." I could hear the sarcasm in his voice when Vail said, *gentleman's club.* "If girls haven't been sold, then we suspect they are held in the basement and are being used for entertainment there. I've gone there twice with Meredith, hoping to recognize some of the girls, but nothing. We were going to go there last week, but we were told that the Beasts were going to be there that night, which was why we thought to go to the docks and scope it out instead."

"You and Meredith have gone *inside?*" I asked incredulously.

"She plays the part of my pet," he explained. "Just a way to be convincing when I treat a girl like shit. But Mer is a good sport about it, and we know it's an act. Built up a whole backstory for my character and everything. But after the docks, I think too many people saw me. I won't be able to go again." He broke his gaze with Lee to look over to Shaw, who was still curled around me. "We're gonna need a whole new persona and backstory built."

"I've already been working on one for Lee."

"Wait, for Lee?" I glanced around at them, confused.

"He's going to take my place on the next run into La Maison Rouge," Vail explained. "We've already talked about it." Seeing the panicked look on my face, he gentled his tone a bit. "He'll be okay, Casey. Shaw's great with online stuff and setting up fake accounts, profiles, and IDs. Lee will be all set."

"Why the hell do *any* of you have to go in there? Why not Maverick or one of his guys? An actual adult?" I was furious, pissed off that these guys were basically taking all the risks in this collaboration or whatever the fuck you wanted to call the business relationship Vendetta had with the Black Spades.

"The Faceless and Beasts know them all. They have a bad history with each other going back decades. They'd be instantly recognized." Even though I understood what Vail was saying, I still didn't like it. But as I thought about what he told me before, about the bikers being different in that most of these guys had grown up living a dangerous lifestyle and started their initiation at young ages to be accepted into their MC. They didn't know any different. So while I gathered why, that didn't mean I had to like it. "Anyways, gonna have the crew over in a couple of days to organize this run. This time, with it looking like a quiet night, Maverick feels confident about breaking into the basement to see if the girls are being held there. Lee, it'll be up to you and Meredith to watch and make sure the ones on the inside aren't aware of the break-in."

"How would they know that?"

"Faceless are guests in La Maison Rouge, too." Vail and Lee stared each other down for another long, silent minute before finally, Vail shrugged and relaxed in his seat. Lee did, too, looking relieved and his stiff posture eased back into his chair. I had no idea what just happened, but the tension between them was gone now. "I'm gonna be talking to Maverick tomorrow about backup. He feels like shit for what happened to us at St. Lawrence-"

"As he should," Shaw muttered.

"They've been there for us when we went to La Maison," he pointed out, casting Shaw a warning look. "He's got our backs. I trust him completely."

"Why do you trust him?"

"How do you think we afford this place?" he said, brows raised. "We help each other. That's what you do when you find an ally. You hold the fuck onto them and keep them going, so that you aren't left alone when the big bads come knocking on your door."

"You're sleeping *where* tonight?" Vail was leaning with his hands on the doorframe to the washroom, watching as I brushed my teeth. It was late, and he'd hovered around me for the remainder of the day as I cleaned up the place, put things away, and made supper for everyone, which was spaghetti and garlic toast. Now, at bedtime, I announced I was going to sleep in Shaw's room, and he wasn't taking it too well.

"I'm exhausted," I said after I rinsed out my mouth and started brushing out my hair. I knew that the moment I stepped foot in Vail's room, he'd either want to pick a fight or pounce on me. I was guessing the latter, but I'm not in the mood to find out. I could have said that I was going to sleep with Lee, but I knew that wouldn't go over well. Shaw was the safest bet and most likely to just let me rest. Shaw was standing to the side, brushing his own teeth, and had been ignoring Vail completely, unbothered by his leader's obvious animosity.

"Your room is *that* one!" Vail seethed, pointing at his master suite across the hall. "It's where you *should* be sleeping!"

"Well, tonight I'm having a sleepover with Shaw." I started plaiting my hair into two french braids. I was already in my pajamas, a pair of cotton sleep pants and tank top, having snuck up to change before Vail could corner me in his room. Lee, however, had already disappeared into his room, and I could hear him putting stuff away, cleaning it up from our sex-fest.

"Shaw got to snuggle with you all day," he said, like he'd been tallying points or something.

"So?"

"So, it's my turn now."

I almost laughed, but at the same time, it was so damn sweet that I also found this vulnerable side of Vail so endearing. I tied off my braids and turned to face him. He was still glowering, hanging onto the frame yet leaning forward like an angry predator ready to pounce. I reached up, cupping his face with my hands, and squished his cheeks so that his lips were smushed together. "Shaw needs me tonight. I'll give you all day tomorrow, okay?"

His hazel eyes flickered over my shoulder to Shaw for a moment before his shoulders relaxed, and I loosened my hands so that I cupped his face instead, my thumbs stroking the hollows beneath his cheekbones, skimming a little over his whisker. "I'm holding you to your promise, Cooper," he said, his voice dropping as he looked back to me.

I giggled and reached up to reach his mouth, and gave them a little kiss. "I wouldn't expect anything different from you, St. James," I whispered against his lips. His hands slid around my waist to my lower back before sliding down where he grabbed my ass in both hands, and I squealed, giving his shoulder a little slap.

"Brace yourself for tomorrow, darling," he murmured in my ear. "I'm giving you the day off." He leaned in and lightly bit on my bottom lip, pulling it a little before letting me go. He glanced over my shoulder again to Shaw, nodded, and stalked into his bedroom, shutting the door with a snap.

Shaw's room was much like it was last night, with his bed of pillows and blankets, his books, the display of weapons close by and at his disposal. As I passed his dresser, I glanced at a few of the titles, noticing he has a few Ann Rule true crime books, some Stephen King, and a book called, The Works of Oscar Wilde. I smiled a little at that, but followed him over to the bed, letting him have the side with the best view of the doorway, which was also closest to his knives. We climbed in together, and the moment I lay down and the light was out, I felt him reach for me. I went limp, letting Shaw move around me in a way that worked best for him, knowing how much he needed this.

He settled by throwing a leg over both of mine, his arms wrapped around my waist to hug me into his stomach, and buried his face into my hair. I hug him back, running my nails through his soft hair, earning a little groan from him, and trace pictures over his back. Beneath my touch, through the fabric of his shirt, I could feel the bumps from the scars left behind from his father, and I held him tighter.

Shaw melted into me, and I knew he felt safe. It was like how it was when we were kids... I was the only one who could hold him like this. If anyone else tried to touch or grab him, he'd fly into panic mode, cringing as though contact with another human being physically pained him. This was all he needed from me, and I was more than happy to be that safety net for him.

We drifted, lulled into sleep by distant sirens, that I now

found the sound to be more familiar. Comfortable. I could feel my eyes growing heavy from fatigue, and soon, I was dead to the world.

I could feel something smooth and soft gliding around my ankles, almost like a snake. If snakes bothered me, I would have been yelling at myself to wake up now, but they didn't. So I kept lying where I was cuz I was comfy as hell. When the snake tightened a little too hard, though, I tried to roll over, but then I realized it was *two* snakes, and the little bastards had suddenly yanked my legs apart. I tried to close them, but the hold was firm. I felt two more loops around my wrists, and soon they were spreading up over my head, too.

"What the fuck?" I muttered under my breath, squeezing my eyes tight before blearily opening them. Sunlight was streaming through the corner of the blinds, which were drawn, keeping the room dim, but I could still see clearly, and the first thing I realized was that I was no longer in Shaw's room. I was in Vail's. And the dirty bastard was literally tying me to his goddamn bed!

"Oh, you motherf-" I stopped myself, seething when I yanked on the white silk ties that were holding me down. I could swing them a little, but the harder I pulled, the tighter they became. And wouldn't you know, the cocky prick was standing at the foot of the bed, staring right at me, arms crossed, his expression only the slightest bit smug. I was naked, the door was shut, and I didn't hear the others. "What the hell are you doing, you psycho?" I yelled at him, furious that he was calling the shots. "You undressed me, you creep?"

"You pissed me off last night, Casey," he said casually, reaching down to check the tie on my right ankle. He'd looped them through the pulls to the drawers around the base of the bed, and all were completely secured. I know. I checked. "You were being a brat."

"And *you* were being a domineering dick!" I hated how he was still in a pair of light grey sweats while I had been completely nude. He *would* set that up. Power move. Typical, annoying Vail.

His lips twitched, fighting a smile as he straightened and moved a little closer to the edge of the bed where I was so embarrassingly on display for him. But I wouldn't let him see that being so exposed actually made me uncomfortable. I refused to give him the satisfaction. So I held his hazel eyes, hoping that I appeared like the enraged, dangerous creature that I thought I was, and not like a cute, pissy kitten. I knew it was the latter when he swung his hand and slapped my naked breast. Not hard, but enough that I let out a little yelp. "Oh, darling," he said, his lips spreading to reveal his white smile. "You haven't seen domineering yet, but you're about to."

"Are you certifiable?" I snapped at him. "Do you really think I'm going to let you fuck me after your temper tantrum last night and now this? Where are the others? Lee! Shaw!" I shouted, hoping that if they were still asleep, they'd wake up and come to my rescue.

"It's funny that you think I need your permission," he said, his hand sliding down the valley between my breasts and lightly stroking at the soft skin over my stomach.

"Yeah, you fucking do, or else it's rape, asshole."

"Casey." He shook his head, his laugh light and breathy, barely there. "You have wanted me between your legs since the beginning. We were just too young to understand." His hand skimmed along the curve of my hips, sliding down towards my center. "It's inevitable that we would end up here. We were always meant to end up together."

I honestly had no idea what to say. One minute, he was

being a cocky jackass, and the next, he was spouting truths that I couldn't even deny. Yes, we had both always gravitated towards each other. Something was always between us. But I hated that he was using that truth now to get his way. So I kept that in mind when I decided to up the ante and go mega-brat on his ass. "I always fantasized about fucking Lee and Shaw before I ever thought about doing it with you."

Vail's smile immediately fell from his face, and his eyes narrowed. Like a fool, I kept going.

"You think I won't be daydreaming about the others I've had? Oh Patrick," I pretend to swoon as I let my eyes roll up to the ceiling. "Patrick, that trick you did with your-"

Before I could even finish, Vail had thrown himself over me, like a furious animal, his jaw flexing tight, and all of his muscles were strained. One hand was on my throat, though he didn't squeeze; it was just pressing ever so slightly, like a warning. "Never, *ever,* mention another man's name in this room. Lee and Shaw, I don't give a fuck about, but anyone else? I'll leave you here, tied to the bed, find them, and castrate them, and make them fuck themselves with their own dick. You got it?"

I sucked in a sharp breath between my teeth and instinctively tried to close my legs and my arms to hide myself, but the ties only flexed around my limbs.

Vail leaned down, his body a hair's breadth away from mine. I could feel the heat rolling off of him, and his lips were featherlight on my jaw as he pressed little kisses up towards my temple. I felt the soft touch of them and the warmth of his breath on my ear as he whispered, "It was always me and you, Casey. And while I'll share you with my brothers, I will still have the final say, because our souls always belonged together. And that's why, when we finally get the fuck out of Harley, *I'm* going to be the one who marries you and gets dibs on the first baby."

I opened my mouth, even though I had no words, and he had pressed two fingers over my lips.

"No. Don't brat out now. I know it's something you love to do, especially with me, but not now. Because, darling, I'm telling you how it's going to be. There is no alternative, and the others know it."

"So I just have to go along with this?" I mumbled bitterly, while at the same time, Vail's words made my heart sing.

He smirked just the tiniest fraction and nodded. "'Fraid so. You're ours, yeah. I won't deny that. It's been that way since we became a foursome. We all only work when we're together. But I'm still in charge. Always have been, always will be. And I'm telling you now how it's going to be. Understand?"

My heart was frantically racing in my chest, and my stupid stomach was jumping around like there were butterflies in it. How the hell did a speech like that give me actual butterflies? It was so stupid, yet I couldn't help my body's response. I wanted to tell him *no*, because he was right. I did love challenging him. But at the same time, I knew it was a battle I wouldn't win, and honestly... not one I wanted to win. So all my dignity could muster at this moment was to allow me to let out a little huff. "Fine!"

Vail's grin was back, and he leaned in to whisper in my ear again, "Good. Now that that's out of the way... I've sent Lee and Shaw out to see Maverick because I wanted you to myself. So hold on to your ties, Darling. I'm gonna fuck the shit out of you today."

"Wear a condom, ass. I don't want to catch shit from you," I sneered at him, though inside, I felt a little thrill. Vail and I have always been this way. Butting heads, challenging each other.

"I'm fucking you bare..."

I jumped a little, eyes widening at his words. "Uh, no thank you. I don't want to catch-"

"Casey, do you really think I'd risk giving you an STI? Lee and I always were careful about wrapping it up. And I know you've had the shot. We're clear."

"I-"

"I want to feel you around me. I wanna feel your heat, your cream on my dick. I want to come in you every fucking time, because I want to know you're walking around with a part of me inside you."

Before I could argue any further, Vail slid down my body, pausing at my breasts to suck one nipple into his mouth. I felt his teeth grazing it as he suckled hard before letting it out with a 'pop', and moved on to the other. One hand snaked down my stomach, over my mound and started slowly sliding his finger along my folds. The other hand remained on my throat, as though I could move away. I closed my eyes at the feeling of him sucking, biting, and playing with my body, like he already knew how to turn me on.

"You cocky bastard..." I whispered, my voice cracking as he swiped his finger up to brush it over my clit.

He let out a moan, the vibration sending a pleasant chill through me, and I could actually *feel* my nipples hardening in response just as he dipped a finger inside of me.

"There you go," he whispered, letting go of my breast. "Open your pussy up for me." He flexed it in and out slowly at first, before his palm pressed onto my clit, and he began to start shifting his hand back and forth. As he moved faster, I could hear how wet I was as a second finger joined the other inside, both curling along my inner walls, making me clench tight around them. "Fucking God..." he moaned, moving it faster and faster, making sure to rub my clit at the same time.

"Holy shit, Vail..." I gasped, as I moved my hips to

enhance the feeling, that delicious building of energy that was going to make me crumble beneath him. But just as I was getting close, he stopped. "Vail, n-no! Keep going!" I begged, horrified when he completely pulled away. I knew he was turned on because that tent in his pants wasn't for fucking camping. I glared at him as he stepped back, leaning against the wall opposite, all casual and clearly, not in any hurry. Holding my gaze, he brought his fingers, the ones he had been using to fuck me with, up to his mouth and slowly licked them. I watched, oddly fascinated as he did, before sliding both past his lips to suck on them, closing his eyes as though what he was tasting was pure heaven.

"You are such a prick!" I snarled at him.

"Oh, Princess." He laughed when I struggled again to free myself, only to find it as fruitless as before. "You'll come when I want you to come."

"I am going to make you fucking regret this, St. James!" I flailed a bit, wishing that one of the ties on my wrists would break, but of course, they didn't.

He laughed again, coming closer, and dropped to his knees before my pussy, his hands pressing down on my inner thighs to keep them spread and up. "You're cute when you're pissed off," was all he said before he dived in and sucked on my clit, *hard!* The feeling had me lifting my hips up off the bed, to which he responded by pressing me back down with one hand, the other still holding my leg wide and up.

"Oh holy shit!" I gasped with a little cry. His tongue whirled around, flicking the tip at it, then latched on with his lips and sucked, running his teeth over it, before starting again. "Fu-uuuuck, Vail!" I writhed beneath him, my hands gripping the blankets beneath me as I desperately fought against my bonds. He teased me this way for a bit before giving harder, longer strokes, then moving up a little higher on my clit, and that made me absolutely cry out and shake. "Vail, I-I… I'm gonna come!"

And then the fucker stopped.

"No! No, don't do that… please, I-"

"Begging?" Vail slid his sweats off, freeing his beautiful curved dick, and started pumping it with his hand. "Fuck me, I love it. You wanna come, love? Beg me. Beg me to make you come."

I was so fucking wound up, so desperate for release, but I bit my lip and turned my head away. He was entirely undeterred as he stepped up and slapped at my pussy with his cock several times before he braced one fist on the mattress next to my backside and slowly began to push forward. I could feel him enter me, that upward curve of his cock running along my inner walls in a way that had my toes curling.

"Oh my God, yes…" He breathed when he completely fit himself inside me. Vail started to roll his hips, his head raised upwards, and eyes squeezed shut, as though he entered a plain of bliss that he'd always dreamed about. His thrusts had my body rocking on the bed, my breasts swaying with the motion, and slowly, I felt that pulse begin to rise again.

Vail draped himself over me, running a hand up the back of my neck, gripping a handful of my hair, while the other hooked under my knee and gripped my ass. He buried his face into my neck, pressing lazy kisses along the side while also nuzzling along my jaw. He began to pump a little harder, a little faster, our joining making a loud smack each time.

"It was always meant to be us, Casey," he told me, and kissed my throat again. His thrusts were so rough now that I was shifting up the bed, however the ties were the only things keeping me from sliding the whole way up.

"Vail…" I cried, squeezing my eyes shut.

"I know, I know… just one more… one more minute…"

he panted heavily, his muscles completely taught as he started to fuck me like a man crazed. He gripped me hard, slamming into me again and again, like he was hoping to leave a mark behind. He bit at my throat, sucking on it, and kissed me so deep that I felt light-headed. "Oh God, I love you so fucking much!" He reached down and began strumming on my clit, causing me to scream just as that orgasm he'd been denying me suddenly exploded. Wave after wave hit my body like a current, unstoppable, and Vail was relentless as he kept going until he gave one final thrust and, with a loud groan, came and collapsed on top of me, his head on my chest.

We both laid there, gasping and sweaty, and I could feel my legs twitch each time he shifted against me, though he hadn't pulled out yet.

"I love you, too," I told him.

"I know."

I wanted to smack him upside the back of his head, but I couldn't, so I just sniggered and rolled my eyes. "You're still hard," I said, noticing he still hadn't pulled out yet.

"Of course I am. I've been dreaming about claiming this pussy for years. I told you I sent the others out so I could have you to myself for the day, and I fucking meant it." He reached over for the silk wrapped around my left hand. "Now I'm gonna untie you, but then I wanna lie back and watch you bounce on my cock for the next fifteen minutes." He slid them free with a simple pull of the knot and gave me a long, lingering kiss. "I want to play out every fucking fantasy I've had of you at least two times over..."

"Okay, this is serious. I need everyone to sit down and shut it for ten minutes, okay?" Vail stood before us, while Lee, Shaw, and I all sat on the couch, and Meredith and Haldon were snuggled together in an armchair, but for some reason, she seemed nervous. Since this had been so out of character for her, it also put me on edge. I was about to go over and sit on her other side, but Lee kept me in my seat on his lap in one of the loungers. When I tried to get up again, he reached under my shirt to tickle my sides. I bit my lip, trying not to scream in a fit of laughter, and smacked his arm.

"Can you not?" Vail raised his brows, arms crossed over his chest, watching as Lee continued with his attack, intent on making me crack. If it had been three days ago, I was sure he would have stormed over here and snatched me out of his arms, but after spending all day literally fucking me everywhere he could in the house, I thoughthe may have made his point. He'd share me with his brothers because he loved them, and he knew I needed them as much as they needed me. But he had made it clear that it would be him and me officially on paper in the end.

And he kept his promise about me not being able to fucking walk right after. There were bruises between my thighs, hickeys on my throat, which Meredith was quick to point out with a giggle, and every time I sat down, I would wince in pain. So with Lee relentlessly tickling me right now, every time I squirmed, I felt that ache between my thighs.

"Enough, please..." Vail raised his eyes to the ceiling, as though begging a higher power for some patience. Lee stopped, pulling me in tight and nuzzling behind my neck. I gave him one last little slap and muttered, "Douche-canoe," to which he chuckled.

"Straight to it, then." Vail turned to Meredith and Haldon, getting ready to catch them up on everything, "Maverick's informant claims that the Beasts will definitely be out of the city Monday night. La Maison Rouge will be easier to infiltrate without a fucking MC patrolling the house or the area,"

Vail said, leaning back against the wall. All morning, Vail was on the phone with Maverick, and when he was done, he immediately reached out to Haldon and Meredith, the closest members of Vendetta, to bring them in to discuss the next "gameplan."

"This is a guarantee?" Haldon asked seriously, his black brows pulling close together. "At the docks, that crazy biker showed up with practically all the Beasts-"

"I know, I know..." Vail said gently as Haldon's French accent started to get a little thicker the more upset he was. He squeezed Meredith around her middle, hugging her close. She leaned in to him, one hand reaching up so that she was stroking one long lock of his beautiful shiny black hair over and over until the tension left him. "Look, the informant tried to give us a heads up, but we'd turned our phones off, yeah? We didn't want calls while we were scouting. Something went down at the clubhouse, and they were called out last minute."

"So?" Haldon pressed on, "Can we guarantee that won't happen at La Maison Rouge?"

"Maverick and what's left of the Spades will be there. Which brings me to the plan..."

I observed Meredith carefully, as that earlier anxiety seemed to have returned to her. She had released Haldon's hair, and her hands were back in her lap, fingers tightly clasped, her eyes on the floor as she listened to Vail.

"The shit thing is... I don't know how many of them saw me at the warehouse." Vail sounded pissed at this. "I'm sure Hunter recognized me there, and he would have told any of the Faceless who I was. My cover at La Maison Rouge is no good. Lee has agreed to go instead. This means I'll be on guard with Maverick and the Spades while Shaw works his magic getting into the basement. If we can prove the girls are being held there, we can go to the next phase and figure out how to save them and nail Elias for the shit he's done. Thank fuck we have the MC backing us." He ran his fingers through his hair, clearly stressed to shit. For the first time since I'd been back, Vail let his crew see the strain that holding leadership was having on him.

"And if we find nothing?" I asked quietly, worried about the alternative.

Vail grimaced. "Then we have to check out the docks again…"

"We've already searched there." Haldon was *not* happy hearing this. "Any time we've looked into the warehouses along his private quay, one of us has gotten hurt, or nearly caught. It's too dangerous. I can't go back there."

Vail didn't argue with him. He merely nodded and gawped at Meredith, brows raised, waiting.

Meredith released a long, shaky breath, avoiding his eyes. "I want to keep helping. You guys know I do. But I can't risk going back into La Maison Rouge." She gripped a handful of her hair, playing with it nervously, twisting the blue strands around her fingers. "I can't risk leaving Amelie without a mother," she said finally.

No one said anything for a minute, but Vail broke the silence first. "Mer… I will *never* ask you or Haldon to do something you don't want to do. It's okay. We'll work around this, alright?"

"I know it's last minute, but-"

"No, it's fine. Alright?"

"I still want to help-"

"And you will." Vail's voice was gentle, but firm, as he cut her off. "You *can* help, but not where you feel uncomfortable. What was one of the top rules I made clear when joining Vendetta? I won't make you guys do something you aren't cool with… but you need to tell me ahead of time, so it doesn't jeopardize anyone else. So, it's okay, Mer. I'm glad you said something now."

Meredith buried her face in her hands, head bowed over her knees and shivered. I couldn't tell if she was crying or not as Haldon stroked small circles across her back. When she raised her head, there were small, wet trails on her cheeks, and she got to her feet, marching right over to Vail, where she threw her arms around his neck and hugged him tightly. "Thank you… thank you…"

"It's okay. We have you guys' backs, alright? That includes Amelie."

He hugged her back for a minute before she finally let go and offered him a shaky smile before returning to Haldon, who looked equally relieved. "So… who will be going in with Lee?" she asked, and the moment she did, I already had an answer.

"Me, obviously," I said easily.

Beneath me, Lee tensed ever so slightly, and Vail's gaze darkened a little as he slowly focused on me, as if I'd gone nuts. But it was Shaw whose reaction was the most explosive. He sat up, throwing his hood back as he leaned forward in his chair, glaring hard at me beneath his mop of hair.

"I appreciate that, Casey… but what these men do is seriously fucked up-" Meredith started to say when she had been cut off again, only this time, by Shaw.

"You aren't fucking going in there," he said, as though this was final.

"Of course, I am. You guys need someone you trust to go with Lee. And I can assume that since Meredith *was* originally going in, you need a girl, yes? Well, hello!" I waved at them all, as though I'd been invisible this entire time and was only now making an entrance. "I know I've been away for some time, but I'm not a fragile little snowflake. Meredith, you can coach me on what to do, and I'll be with Lee. I-"

"You *aren't* going in there I said," Shaw interrupted me, his voice deep, the raspy whisper more evident than ever.

I raised my brows to Vail, needing him to make the call. Because no matter what I said, I felt like Shaw wouldn't be able to hear it.

Vail stared at me for a few seconds, and I could see the struggle on his face. On the one hand, being someone in love, I knew he'd rather lock me up in a cage in his closet than let me go into that place. But on the other hand, being the leader of our group, he was looking at the bigger picture, which was that it *did* make more sense to send me this late in the game. There were other girls in Vendetta, very few, but I knew that the boys trusted me more than anyone.

Finally, he gave the slightest, subtlest nod, and Shaw absolutely freaked out. He lurched to his feet, the angry, strangled sort of yell tearing from his throat as he grabbed one of the new candles I'd bought the other day and threw it. The glass shattered when it struck, gouging a hole in the wall.

"Shaw…" Vail reached out to him, but Shaw viscously pulled away from him.

"Don't touch me!" He screamed. "Nobody fucking touch me!" He ripped at his hair, like he was trying to tear it from his skull again. "She can't go in there, she can't. I don't want her to. Tell her no, Vail. Tell her she can't go in…"

"We trust her more than anyone," Lee said gently, but I could hear the strain in his voice. He was putting on a calm front, hoping to reassure his brother. "I'll be with her, and we'll have the Spades-"

"I don't want her anywhere close to those fuckers!" Shaw's voice had torn from his scream, his blue eyes sparkling as he struggled to hold back tears. "Too dangerous. Too close. Too close…" he chanted over and over again, crouching where he stood as if he was going to be sick.

I slid off Lee's lap and tentatively reached out to him, taking slow, careful steps and whispering, "Shaw…"

He snapped up, eyes wide and crazed as he stared down at me, shaking, like he'd completely lost his mind. "No… no, Casey!" He snatched the front of my shirt and stomped away, dragging me with him. I struggled to keep up, stumbling over the stairs as he began to climb. Behind us, I heard the others shouting and protesting, and I could see Lee storming after us.

"Don't!" I held up my hand to him as Shaw got a better grip and yanked me up after him. "Let me calm him down."

The others watched, their expressions a mixture of trepidation, concern, and a little fear. Especially from Meredith, who Haldon was trying to persuade to follow him downstairs to the front door. I caught my footing, scrambling to keep up with Shaw. When we reached the landing, he immediately headed for his room and thrust me inside. I flew in, luckily catching myself so I didn't fall, and he slammed the door shut.

"Shaw, it's the only way that makes sense-"

"No!" He came right up to me, holding my face tight in his hands. The only light in the room was coming from his little lamp on the side table, and with the beautiful myriad of colours from the porcelain shade, casting a warm, orangey-pink hue over his skin. "Casey, I can't let you go in there. If something happened… if you got hurt… if I lost you…" He attempted to finish the sentence, and in the end, he didn't bother. He simply crushed his mouth to mine and kissed me as though he feared it would be the last time.

Shaw's full lips were soft, yet the kiss was aggressive. I felt like he was on the attack, but I knew if I fought back against him while his mind was in this state, it wouldn't help. He would spiral farther down… down… lost in the haunting memories that plague his mind.

"Casey… I need you…" he whispered, backing me up to his bed laden with pillows and blankets.

I knew precisely what he meant. With Shaw, I always did. We'd been able to connect without words since we were kids. And honestly, I needed him, too. I could feel this rising impulse coming to life, and all I wanted was to be closer to him, to feel as connected to him as I did the others.

His jaw clenched, his eyes strained as he pushed back on some inner turmoil, desperately trying to focus on me. I knew he wanted to speak by the way his lower lip quivered, but that demon in his head was holding him back. So I slowly reached up, brushing my fingers down the length of his jaw, first on one side, then the other. He trembled hard beneath my touch, fighting like hell to be with me here. I brought my fingertip up, keeping my touch featherlight, and ran it along his lower lip, then over the upper. I lightly ran them up with both thumbs, gliding them over the dark lines beneath his eyes before smoothing them over his closed eyelids.

Shaw released a hard, shaky breath, like he was torn between pain and pleasure from this, but he remained where he was, letting me trace his face over and over again. He was so hauntingly beautiful with his pale skin, the depth of his blue eyes, and his full, pouty lips. If he'd lived another life, he could have been in high fashion magazines. Even the shadows beneath his eyes were such a distinctive aspect that only added to his face's sharp, captivating features.

"Casey, I haven't been with anyone since…" His voice trailed off, breaking apart, but he didn't need to finish, because I already knew. His hands were trembling on my lower back, but he finally opened his eyes to gaze down at me, and whispered, "You're the only one I ever wanted."

I ran my thumb over his lip again. "What can I do to make it easier for you?" I asked, not moving from my spot.

He brought his lips down, kissing the crown of my head, and murmured, "Just... let me call the shots, okay?"

I could do that. I was able to brat out, fight back, take over in terms of power in bed, and do all I wanted with the other two. However, with Shaw, it would be different. As much as Vail loved to dominate, or Lee with his thrill of throwing me around like a rag doll, Shaw *needed* the control.

So I nodded against him, and let him take the lead.

He gently pushed me down so I was sitting at the edge of the bed, staring up at him with wide eyes, watching for the emotions on his face that told me all I needed to know of what he was thinking. Slowly, he reached out, caressing my cheek a moment, before sliding his hand down the side of my throat to then run along my collarbone. His fingers shifted beneath the collar of my shirt, moving it aside as he began to undress me. I helped by lifting my arms so he could pull it off me. As soon as he did, he took off his hoodie, standing before me shirtless in his jeans. He was slender, yet toned, which was also how I knew that he was going to be deceptively strong. His skin was pale, his blond hair always mussed about his head from having a hood pulled over it, but I wouldn't have him any other way.

Shaw sank to his knees on the bed, grabbed my face tight, and kissed me. But the kiss wasn't like the ones before, where they were demanding, unyielding, and assertive. This one was tender, delicate, and the way his lips moved against mine, had me sinking deeper into him. I reached down to undo his jeans, but holy fuck, he was as hard as a rock, pressing up against the zipper, and I was trying not to hurt him as I worked to get them off.

He stopped a moment to help, reaching down and adjusting his massive girth before managing to zip them down and slide them and his boxer briefs off. For a moment, I was actually scared because Shaw was so fucking big, it was actually quite intimidating. But I was also feeling relieved as hell that I had been with Lee and Vail first, since Shaw would have destroyed me for them. It was official. I was officially going to need a wheelchair to get around tomorrow. I had no idea based on just how truly big he was, only that I was positive it would be closer to rivaling a ruler.

And he was as hard as a rock.

Shaw didn't stop, though. He started to move a little faster, his movements a little more reckless and agitated as he tried to figure out my bra, before quickly losing his patience and merely ripping it off. I didn't scold him like I would have the others, but waited to see what he needed. He pushed me back, and I slid up the bed so that I was near the head amongst the pile of pillows he kept there. He crawled up my legs, tugging at my sweats, which he yanked off and threw over his shoulder.

His eyes wandered over my naked body, and slowly, he ran his hands up my thighs, caressing the skin along the way. He bowed over my body, kissing the bruises on my thighs. He moved his lips up to my stomach, pressing kiss after kiss, making me feel worshipped. I ran my fingers through his hair, watching as he gradually moved up to my breasts, where he almost tentatively stroked the curve of one, before following the trail with his tongue, latching onto my nipple. I gasped as he suckled even harder than Vail had, his arms squeezing around my waist, running over my body. As he did, he began to rub between my folds, moving up and down, creating a friction that soon had me pressing back against his massive length.

When Shaw lifted his head to kiss me, I made the mistake of hungrily reaching between us to stroke his rolling pin of a cock, and he froze. I stopped when his kisses suddenly disappeared, and I opened my eyes to see him trembling over me, his own eyes tightly squeezed shut.

"It's me," I told him again and again. "It's Casey... it's just me. It's just us."

"Casey..." he whispered.

"Yes."

Slowly, he started moving again, sliding into my wetness, and shuddered when I reached up to press a little kiss to his throat.

"Casey," he breathed, as though reminding himself that it was me here and no one else.

"That's right. It's just us two." I kissed the other side of his neck, and wrapped my arms around him, the bumpy feel of the scars on his back beneath my hands, and waited for him to signal what he needed. "You're in control, Shaw. You." I had told him, "You're always safe with me."

He shifted a little over me, before I felt him start to push through my folds again. Slowly, inch by inch, he worked his way in, and I had to hold back the small whimpers of pain I made as he pushed and stretched me. His body was shaking, and he kept peppering kisses all over my face until finally, he finally buried himself within me completely. I bit my lip to keep from crying out, because right now, I didn't give a shit about the pain. I just needed to feel this with Shaw, that connection that we'd always had needed to come full circle.

Shaw didn't move, but held himself up over my body, shaking slightly, his breaths coming out in small little pants. When I started to move my hands again, stroking along his back, he pulled back just the slightest so he could grasp my wrists and press them down into the pillows on either side of my head. It was then that he started to move.

Holding me beneath him, Shaw began with smaller, uncertain thrusts, much to my relief. I was already sore as hell, but slowly, I started to adjust to him. His eyes were squeezed shut, like he was focusing hard, concentrating, and I could only imagine the inner turmoil he'd been struggling with. With my arms pinned, I strained to reach up so I could press a kiss to his lips, and when I did, he melted against me. Though he was still holding me down, he let his body relax, the pumping motion now picking up pace. Eventually, he released my wrists to wrap his arms around me, and we embraced each other tightly as he kept going.

Our kisses were sweet, our embrace was a safety net for each other, and I felt my heart swell at this moment with him. "I love you, Shaw..." I whispered before I peppered little kisses along his sharp jaw.

At my words, he buried his face into my neck, and his hips smacked against mine again and again. I squeezed around him, both of us holding on to the other so tight, it felt like we were trying to get lost in the other. "I love you... I love you..." I told him repeatedly.

He moaned, the vibration from deep in his chest rumbling against me, and with several more hard thrusts, he stilled, grinding into me as deep as he could. I winced a little but took him, because now, feeling him inside me this way, it was like we'd sealed our bond permanently. We were both panting hard as we laid there, with him still between my legs, both of us still clinging on as though worried some dark force would come and pry us apart. When Shaw finally lifted himself up on one forearm, he was actually smiling down at me, a certain light shining from his eyes that I hadn't seen before. Holding my chin, he leaned in, our lips brushing over the others, and softly murmured, "I love you, too, Casey. Always have."

Chapter sixteen

Casey

God, I was so nervous. Tonight was our scouting mission to La Maison Rouge, and I was having a hard time keeping still. All morning during class, I fidgeted, played all day with my pencil, and tapped my heel repeatedly on my chair leg. By the time lunch came around, I was so on edge that when Lee went to grab my tray of food, I noted that he held a white milk rather than chocolate. Winking at me from the seat he took at my side, he slid the tray my way and took a long sip of his soda. On my left, Vail was quietly talking with Haldon, who was sitting on his other side. While across from us, Shaw, who was barely eating anything and was repeatedly scanning the room, was watchful of every person that walked in and out. More often than not, he looked to the Jackals table, wary of Hunter.

With Vail being back in school, that meant Hunter's suspension was over, too. And all day, he'd been watching us all with narrowed eyes, occasionally casting me looks of pure loathing. I had been wondering what he'd heard from last week? Gossip spread like wildfire in this school, and by now, I was thinking most of the student body was aware of my situation with the boys. It was all I heard when I walked into the building this morning, followed by the catcalls, mostly from girls, calling me a whore, groupie, and gangbanger.

"Babe, chill." Lee slid a hand up my back and massaged the nape of my neck.

"I'm just a little nervous," I murmured, knowing that honesty was always the best way to go. They could all read me like a book, so there was no point in denying that my nerves were getting the better of me.

"Oh yeah? I couldn't tell. I honestly thought you were practicing playing the drums." He chuckled, and I rolled my eyes at him. "It'll be fine, Casey. Just do what we say, don't draw attention to yourself, and if Shaw can work his magic, then we'll know for sure about the missing girls tonight. Once we have proof, the Spades will figure out how to move forward."

"I still think that Nylah's dad-"

"I know, but keep in mind, he's just one man. That's not enough to make a difference. Most of the force is corrupt, so we have to be careful about who we turn to."

I knew what he was saying, and I hated it. Even with that smaller MC helping us, It still wasn't enough to take on the Beasts and the Faceless.

Down the table, I could see Meredith worrying her bottom lip with her teeth. She was hardly eating, choosing instead to play with her food and not saying a word to anyone. I knew she felt terrible for stepping down, but I couldn't blame her. She had a little girl, and with Haldon being so involved in this case, what if something happened to both of them, and it left Amelie parentless? It made more sense that I went in her stead. I just wished she didn't look so guilty about it.

Shaw reacted suddenly, lurching up from the table, his hand flying beneath his hoodie, and his sparkling blue eyes were locked on to the cafeteria entrance. There was a small commotion from the double doors leading in, and the rest of us twisted in our seats, ready to spring into action, but all I could see were a couple I didn't recognize.

They stood together, clearly *together*, and the first thing I thought was that, *damn, they'd make some hot babies one day.* The guy had golden blond hair and the greenest eyes I'd ever seen. Even from here, they stood out. The girl reminded me a lot of Nylah, only that she was blonde, pale, and with cinnamon coloured eyes. The second thing I deduced was that they did *not* belong here. The guy was wearing the type of jeans you'd see boys on The Hill flaunting. However, his expensive clothing clashed with the hardcore ink that appeared to be covering his body, just judging by the way it snaked from under the collar of his shirt, down his arms all the way to his fingers. The girl seemed too innocent. Nice, but not someone who had been through the kind of shit kids in Harley have had to endure. Lastly, they were searching for someone, based on how they were scanning the room carefully.

The boy suddenly walked forward, his hand reaching back to hold his girl's as he led the way in, scrutinizing every person he met with a look full of cocky judgment. I could tell he was a prick right away.

Beside me, Vail tensed up, and Shaw, who was leaning over the table, one hand still under his shirt, no doubt holding onto the handle of his knife, was waiting for any sign that he needed to strike. Lee reached out and pulled me into his lap, twisting his body sideways so that I'm partially concealed. What does he think is going to happen? That a fight might break out? As I peered over his shoulder, I suddenly got the sense that it just might be a possibility. This couple, the guy, in particular, was asking for trouble just waltzing in here like he owned the place.

"I'm looking for Vail St. James?" The guy had stopped in front of the jock table, addressing Peter, who sat near the end closest to him. He's smart, because if anyone in this school would know who the "go-to" people were, it was the football team.

Peter glanced our way, but instead of answering, said, "Who the fuck are you?"

Instead of answering, the new guy just looked toward our table, having caught Peter's slip, and headed directly in our direction.

"Stupid motherfucker…" Vail muttered under his breath, obviously pissed off that Peter had given us away. Though it was unintentional, we didn't know who this guy was. "No one rise. No one looks away from him for a second. If he makes any movement to grab anything other than his girl, we take him around the back of the school, keep it quiet, and dispose of him quickly."

Then, the quiet tension in the room abruptly ended and blew the fuck up instead.

As the couple passed the Jackals on their way to us, I saw Hunter reaching out to grab the girl's ass, which caused her to jump a little and cast what I thought was meant to be a look of disgust, but she just reminded me of an angry bunny. Her halting so suddenly, jerked on the hand of the guy she was clearly with, who looked around, his head whipping back and forth between her and Hunter.

"What did he do?" he asked his girl. He sounded composed, yet I sensed some sort of silky, underlying danger coating every molecule of that calm.

"Nothing," she answered much too quickly.

Oh my god, this girl was the worst liar in the world. Her eyes went wide, her expression of disgust quickly morphing to one that made her look panicked.

"Did he touch you?" he asked, that same eerie facade still in place.

"Aren't we here to talk to-"

"Did you fucking touch her?" He looked at Hunter, turning away so I couldn't see his face. Hunter, however, I could see as plain as day, and the douche just grinned up at this strange boy, lazily lounging back in his chair.

"Your bitch is full of it. Why would I waste my time on that truffle when I'm rolling in hot pussy here?" He reached over and gave Celeste's leg a rub, his hand sliding up the inside of her thigh to stroke her over her jeans. She smirked, satisfied with his attention, and sneered at the new girl.

The blond guy tossed his head back, laughing like a psycho for a moment, before he suddenly shoved Hunter aside, reared back, and punched Celeste right in her face. She went flying, her chair tipping over backwards, but he wasn't done yet. In a flash, he spun to where Hunter was gathering himself and kicked the leg of the chair so that it flipped. Hunter fell to the floor, and this guy stepped on his throat while his girl screamed at him to stop.

"Intervene," Vail said the moment the Jackals rose, his mask in place. Immediately, all the members of Vendetta were on their feet and raced towards the chaos. I ran, grabbing the girlfriend, who was still shouting at everyone to stop, and pulled her aside and out of harm's way. I could hear Celeste wailing from where she sat on the floor, the blood spouting from her broken nose visible from here. The jocks got up and blocked the doorway, preventing teachers and security from storming in here. Vendetta pushed back Hunter's group to keep them away from the newcomer, who still stood there with his heel pressing into his throat.

The new guy nodded to Celeste and said loudly, "Not so hot now, huh?"

Hunter gasped and flailed, clawing up this crazies leg as he fought to free himself, and managed to slide out from beneath the heel on his throat. But as he rose, Vail suddenly stepped forward, blocking the new guy from Hunter, and spoke in a calm, assured sort of way. "Look, it's our first day back. Whatever this freak wants, it's nothing to do with you. Count your losses and move the fuck on. I promise everyone will forget about it, yeah?"

Hunter's face was red, a vein bulging in his neck as he glared at the blond who was standing like a cocky, confident ass behind Vail, and nodded to his men. Jackals and Vendetta separated, and Celeste's skank squad helped her to her feet, guiding her through the crowd to get to the washrooms. Teachers and security broke in, and Vail turned to the shit disturber. "Who the fuck are you, and what do you want?"

"I might just be the man of your dreams if you can help me out," The cocky prick responded, not sounding at all perturbed by the chaos he'd brought upon us. The girl I was holding onto facepalmed and repeatedly apologized for whatever the guy was about to say.

The guy came over and slid his arms around the leggy blonde at my side. His green eyes were looking straight at me before he said with more sincerity than I expected, "Thank you," and turned back to Vail. "I'm Logan Hudson, from Florida, and if you're Vail St. James, then apparently, you're the guy to talk to about getting something done around here."

He was being vague on purpose, I could tell, and as the chaos of the room began to settle, Vail nodded to several members of his crew before saying, "I am, and it's better that we don't talk here. C'mon." He turned, heading towards the security exit, leading the group away. Logan Hudson and his girl followed, with Haldon and Meredith accompanying them. I didn't think I'd need to be included in whatever business they had going, but Lee came over and took my hand, squeezing it as he followed, tugging me behind him.

Turns out, Logan Hudson came with a whole group of people. Along with his girlfriend, there was another chick with her leg in a cast, and a guy that looked like he was suffering from some sort of virus, judging by how pale he appeared. It was agreed upon that we would meet up at our townhouse, as it was the most secure place. For some reason, Vail seemed curious about this guy and their situation. Though he was suspicious, after having Shaw look into their backgrounds to confirm they were who they said they were, there weren't any suspicious ties from what we could figure out. However, he had decided it would be safer to bring them to our townhouse. As Logan climbed into the minivan's driver's seat, the other two were lying out on the backseats. He was muttering something about missing *Betty*, whoever the hell *that* girl was. I thought this leggy blonde was his chick?

I climbed into Haldon's beater car, having no choice but to sit sprawled across Vail, Lee, and Shaw's laps in the back while they hung on to me. Knowing that my mother was killed in a car accident, drunk driver or not, along with sitting like this without a seatbelt, had my anxiety hitting new levels.

"Why are we helping them again?" Lee asked aloud as we weaved along the roads, the minivan on our tail.

"We aren't. We're hearing them out," Vail said, his demeanor cool and collected as always. Meredith glanced back from the front seat; one of her dark brows arched like she was confused by this whole situation. I guess it wasn't often that outsiders came into Harley asking for help, let alone someone dressed in preppy, designer clothes. What kind of a psycho walks into a school like Harley, flaunting his wealth and birth status, punches out a girl, and attacks a kid he didn't even know was surrounded by his friends, with no backup, and just demanded to speak with the leader of Vendetta? Something was off with that guy, that's for sure.

"Why the hell are we doing that?" Meredith asked. "I mean, no disrespect, Vail, but that guy and his friends... they're from the states, they're clearly on the run, and trying to hide from someone... what if they attract them here? We're basically inviting trouble to come after us, and we have enough problems at the moment."

"I hear you guys," Vail said, his eyes staring out the window as we took some of the backroads to get to our townhouse. "But I think for someone to have the balls to do what he did, they must be pretty desperate, too. Nothing looks bad in their background, right?" he added, staring at Shaw, who reluctantly nodded. "And where else can we talk in peace? Not Midnight's where we would be risking Amelie. Or at the second house Daniel runs." *Daniel?* "Despite the fact this kid is clearly privileged, he's coming to *us*. If we were that desperate to travel as far as they did, wouldn't you at least hope that they'd hear you out?"

The others had gone quiet as we pulled into the parking lot of our complex. I glanced back at the minivan to see it pulling into the visitor parking, and from here, I could see that small girl in the crutches smacking that blond guy on the back of the head. Guess she couldn't stand his cocky attitude, either.

"Okay, Lee, security. Haldon, I need you looking out. If they've attracted anyone here, I want a heads up before they move in. Shaw..." Vail finally looked away from the window and turned to Shaw, who was squashed in the middle between him and Lee, whose lap I was currently sitting on. Shaw peered sideways at Vail, saying nothing, and the two simply stared at each other in silence for several seconds before nodding, as though they'd just had some telepathic conversation between them.

The four from the van were venturing over, the blond guy supporting his friend who looked like he was on his deathbed. Seriously, what the fuck happened to that guy?

"Let's go." Vail opened his door and climbed out but didn't move towards our home. None of them did. They remained in the parking lot, watching as the newcomers slowly approached. The girl on crutches slipped slightly on the ground, but the blonde girl quickly caught her, only to be brushed off the next second, the injured one muttering, "I can *do* it!" She seemed like a bit of a spitfire.

"Lee will need to do a weapons search before we let you in, you understand?" Vail said when they stopped several feet away. When the blond guy, Logan, glanced toward his injured buddy, who nodded his approval. He conceded, carefully leaning him against Haldon's car for support before spreading his arms out to his side, waiting. Huh, so the zombie guy was in charge here. Wasn't expecting that.

Lee moved forward, and we observed nervously as he checked the guy, taking his time searching along his legs for concealed weapons, even going as far as to step on the ends of his feet, and toeing the sides, as if a blade or something could be concealed in his shoes. When he scuffed the guy's designer leather kicks, I noticed that his green eyes tightened in the corners, as though that seriously pained him to see this happen.

Lee moved on to the sick guy, who he quickly and carefully checked out, before clearing his throat, looking uncomfortable as he glanced at the girls. "Look, guys, I can put it together that these are your women, but I need to search them. Do I have your permission?"

I could tell immediately that the blond psycho didn't like that... *at all.* Even their leader seemed a little put off by that question, but with a warning look to his friend, he stiffly nodded to me, "She can do it."

"I can speak for myself!" The brunette in the crutches snapped, glaring at her guy.

"Shut up, Mouse..." he muttered.

I could tell that the idea of me being the one to search for them was more reassuring, and honestly, I didn't want to give the one called Logan an excuse to try to hurt Lee. I stepped forward as he whispered in my ear, "The cast."

I was careful as I did it, asking for the girl's permission before I checked their bra areas. This was as uncomfortable for them as it was for me, so I tried to be as quick, but thorough, as I could be.

"I need to check your cast," I told her apologetically.

"What are you going to-" their leader started to say when she cut him off.

"It's fine! Do what you gotta do so we can get inside. It's fucking freezing out here!" She was shivering as she stood there, and I figured that if they were from Florida, they most likely had never experienced a Canadian Autumn or Winter, depending on how long they were staying. I placed a hand on one side of her cast and knocked on the side of the other. I didn't feel movement or a rattle, and I decided she'd had enough. I finished with the blonde and gave Vail a nod of approval.

"Okay, inside. Lee, can you help get that guy in?" He nodded to their leader, who seemed like he needed to lie down. Lee moved forward to support his other side while his friend assisted on the other.

It was cramped as hell in the entryway, but we managed

to shimmy upstairs and arrange the newcomers on the sofa, their leader lying across them with his head in the one he called *Mouse*'s lap. Haldon stood close to the bay window, lingering in the background, watching outside as he listened in. Meredith sat close to him at the dining table, her wide, blue eyes locked on our American guests, and waited.

I stood alongside Vail and Lee opposite the couch, leaning back against the wall, while Shaw armed the house and came up, moving to sit in one of the armchairs, his shadowed face almost completely hidden beneath his hood. His hands were in the pockets of his hoodie, and I knew that he was holding onto his knife.

"So," Vail spoke first, his eyes on the leader, "Who are you, how did you hear of us, and why did you come here?

The guy raked his brown hair out of his eyes and sat up on his elbow, facing Vail so he could speak to him directly. "My name is Micha Kessler, from Ashen Springs, Florida, and we're looking for a safehouse. Came into town and asked around. Apparently, if you want to disappear, Harley is the place to do it in Ashland. And if anyone is going to help someone here, Vendetta are the ones to speak with. Your crew defends its people. We were hoping to receive the same courtesy."

"And why would you expect that? Who the fuck would someone like you be running from?" None of us missed the fact that this Micha Kessler was also wearing high-end clothes and spoke with an air of authority you didn't just discover as a teenager. You had to be born into it or trained. It was similar to how Vail behaved, except he learned his way through abuse and a will to survive.

"Riley," His hand rested on the leg of the spitfire brunette beneath him, "has a hit out on her."

Okay, *this* I was not expecting. I glanced at the girl,

wondering how the hell someone like her would end up in this situation.

"Her uncle is the president of the Lost Souls MC, Miami, Florida. Their rival club is being run by his brother, who killed his wife and baby. We were all attacked in front of the clubhouse in a shootout and made a run for it as soon as we could get out of the hospital."

Huh, that explained why this guy looked like he was on death's door and the cast on his girl's leg. He must have been shot. I was also concerned about the fact that some dude who had no problem killing his brother's kid and wife was looking for Micha's girl, the little spitfire sitting on my couch. I peered sideways at the boys, wondering if they were as nervous as I felt, when I noticed that this entire time, Shaw and the one called Logan were in the middle of a staring contest. It wasn't threatening, more like... a weird curiosity and understanding were being communicated through their eyes to each other. It was really weird.

"So how the hell did you guys get involved in this shit, then?" Vail asked Micha. "If you're just some guy from Ashen Springs?" I knew he was downplaying Micha's position. He obviously knew there was more to this, but he was giving him a chance to be honest with us.

"Let's just say that, because of who I am, my hometown is *mine*." Vail looked between him and the girl named Riley, and his expression softened. Riley was absentmindedly running her nails up and down Micha's arm while he spoke, and he leaned further into her, their bodies moving with each other in tandem. I could sense the love and protection they both felt for each other.

"So why are that psycho and his girl here?" Lee asked suddenly, narrowing his eyes at Logan. Clearly, he didn't think much of him.

Micha sighed as though he'd been dreading having to

explain his friend to us but finally said, "Cuz that guy is a paranoid fucker." To which the blonde girl simply nodded, like this was just an accepted fact between them all.

"If you're so powerful, why can't you just hide yourselves?" Vail asked, ignoring Logan, who seemed unfazed by his friend's description of him.

"Given who I am, any connections I have or use can easily be traced. I'm out of options, but I won't be separated from her," he said vehemently.

"I told you I'd be fine on my own-" Riley started to say, but Micha quickly cut her off.

"Shut up, Mouse."

I could feel Vail's eyes on me, and in my peripheral, I saw him smirking as he glimpsed my way. I knew he was comparing my attitude with this girl, but I'd like to think I was a little more amiable than she was.

Logan piped up then, exclaiming, "Your big bad crime spree was painting shit on walls back home. You would NOT be okay on your own, even with your fork." And his girl simply nodded again.

Haldon muttered from the window, and I bit my inner cheek to keep from laughing.

"What the fuck language was that?" Logan swiveled around in his seat to eye Haldon. "It was sexy as hell!"

"Why do you think he managed to knock me up on our first date?" Meredith rolled her eyes, but grinned up at her man.

Logan slowly looked around, eyeing his girl's stomach as if considering something along the lines of Meredith's statement, to which she finally spoke but said just one word, "No."

I had noticed that every time this guy opened his mouth, Lee leaned his head back, looking up at the ceiling as though he'd been praying for serenity, all while cracking his knuckles like he was refraining from punching this guy out.

This time, I'm not the only one who noticed because Riley called over to him, "Don't worry, I feel exactly the same way."

Vail looked between the four who were crammed together on the chesterfield, analyzing each one carefully, before finally settling his eyes on the psycho. "You're really gonna have to try harder to blend in here if you wanna stay under the radar, dude."

Riley leaned over Micha's head, which had fallen back into her lap, and snapped, "I *told* you so!"

"I'm already driving a minivan! What more do you want from me?" Logan was absolutely flabbergasted to be singled out this way. But I got it.

Riley? She'd have no problem blending in. I could tell by her attitude, the way she carried herself, and that she'd seen some shit. She would blend in easily. Micha seemed like a pretty level-headed guy, so I thought he'd definitely adapt to survive, but mostly, to keep *her* safe. Then there was the blonde girl that I was more concerned about. She was just so damn pretty that I worried for her. Vail was really going to have to be clear on what was happening in Harley if they were gonna keep themselves out of trouble, away from the eyes of the Beasts and the Faceless. Logan, however... this guy, despite his scary tats and confidence, was clearly being fed from a golden spoon and had been living in luxury for most, if not all, of his life. He was very comfortable with his lifestyle. Giving it up to scrounge like the rest of us was going to be an adjustment, I could tell. I tried to hide a smile at the thought of this guy trying to "blend in." I learned after my leather satchel got nicked from me on day two. I had a feeling he'd be putting up a fight, which wouldn't help their cause if they needed to be hiding.

Vail peered over at Lee and nodded his head. Some serious Jedi communication passed between them before Lee

ASHES

stepped forward, crossing his arms over his broad chest while ignoring Logan's outburst to talk to the others. I fought another urge to laugh. This blond guy from Ashen Springs was clearly grating on his nerves. "The basement suite we use as a safe house should be empty. I'll call the landlord that lives on the top floor and confirm so you guys can move in tomorrow. The good news is that there's a market down the street that you can-"

"A basement suite?" Logan stared incredulously up at Lee like he'd grown an extra head. "What in the fuck is that?"

His girl raised her eyes to the ceiling, reminiscent of Lee at that moment, as she looked to be praying to a higher power, while Riley muttered, "Pretty boy..."

"Does this mean...?" Micha looks to Vail, hope evident in his eyes.

Vail nodded. "You can stay here tonight. You two, take Shaw's room. Matthew McConaughey and his girl can have Lee's." At this, Lee tensed up, and I heard an unmistakable groan coming from deep in his chest at the thought of Logan sleeping in his bed. Neither he nor Shaw asked where they'd be sleeping, though. They just went along with it, not objecting to the orders.

"I think," Meredith pulled out her cell, typing furiously away on it, "that since you guys are officially staying, we need to pick you up some new gear."

"Gear-"

Before Logan could say anything else that might have earned him a punch in the face from Lee, I quickly cut in, "Clothes. There's a Goodwill down the street you can get some stuff at."

The girl with Logan stood, looking excited at the prospect of shopping. "I'll go. I need to stretch my legs a bit..." she added, doing a little stretch that had her guy watching her backside a little too openly given present company.

"Haldon and I will go with you." Meredith nodded to her guy. "You should call Mamie and let her know that Eli will be taking Amelie tonight," she added, showing him her phone screen. I guess that was who she was talking to at the mention of a change of plans. There was no way Vail would just leave these four alone in his house while we did our mission tonight. I felt horrible taking her away from her daughter, but at least she wouldn't be inside La Maison Rouge.

"Shelby Grace," the blonde said to Meredith, clearly eager to get out and about.

"Meredith Nadeau." Meredith smiled at her, her blue eyes taking in everything about Miss Shelby Grace, looking at her the same way she looked at me on my first day back in Harley.

"I'm coming, too." Logan got to his feet, clearly not liking the idea of his girl going out on the streets without him.

"No way, not dressed like that you're not." Meredith arched a brow and slowly skimmed Logan up and down, but she wasn't checking him out. She was clearly noting the expensive labels on his clothes and, no doubt, was also worried that his smart mouth would get him into trouble.

"Midnight is very capable, I promise you," Vail said, aware of Logan's reluctance.

"Midnight?" He looked Haldon up and down in wonder, clearly fascinated with him, while Haldon stared blankly back with his black eyes. "Do you have a giant penis, too? Is that why you look grumpy?" Riley reached over with one of her crutches and jabbed him hard in his back, before Shelby took his face in her hands and planted a long, deep kiss on him. I coughed a little and turned away just as the little spit-fire reached over, as she snuck his wallet out of his back pocket before looking at Lee and motioning him over. I ran up the stairs and grabbed some painkillers from under the sink in the bathroom. Micha looked worse for wear, and I was sure Riley had been hurting more than she was letting on.

"WHAT HAVE YOU DONE?!" Logan hollered from downstairs.

"They'll track them, you idiot!" Riley sniped back.

"That was a Black card, little sister," *Little sister? They didn't look related at all,* "I can buy a house with that thing…"

"You mean *could* have," Lee chuckled as I came back down. Sure enough, there were several pieces of cut-up plastic on the coffee table, along with a pair of scissors she must have asked Lee to fetch for her.

"We have plenty of cash to last us," she said to him, not looking at all perturbed that she just cut up something that could have paid for several hundred thousand dollars worth of stuff.

Logan was gawping at her like she'd lost her mind while Shelby, Meredith, and Haldon got their coats and shoes on to go out.

"Don't take long," Vail called after them. "One hour."

Haldon nodded, saying nothing as usual, as he escorted the girls outside.

"I'm ordering some Swiss Chalet for supper." Lee sat at the dining table beside Vail, who had taken a seat and was working away furiously on the laptop he'd left there this morning. Shaw wordlessly turned on the TV and set up some shooter game I didn't know, and held out an extra controller to Logan, who was still gaping at the shredded pieces of credit cards, which he had been cradling in his hands. But he accepted Shaw's offer, and they both sat quietly, leaning back against the couch on the floor as they played each other, without saying a word. It was weird how they were together, but I didn't question it. It was kind of nice to see Shaw being so okay with another person, even if it was this guy, who was a walking contradiction with his badass tattoos, yet mourned the loss of his plastic.

I walked over to Riley. "Thought you guys might need some of this," I said, shaking the bottle of painkillers at her.

"Thanks." She softened a little, taking the bottle while I got them some water. I was kind of glad to be having this distraction from thinking about tonight. School just wasn't cutting it. When I came back out, Riley had gotten Micha to remove his shirt, and his pants had been pulled down enough to reveal his thighs and show off the extent of his injuries. He had five bullet wounds, two in his right side, one in his left shoulder and mid-thigh, and one that looked like it missed his heart by no more than an inch or two. Each area was stitched up, angry and red, surrounded by severe purple and yellow bruising. These were *very* new. Less than a week old, I'd say.

"Uhhh," I stared at the glasses of water in my hands and the bottle of painkiller I'd handed to Riley and muttered, "We're gonna need some more stuff."

I gathered together a large mixing bowl of water, soap, a washcloth, polysporin, and clean bandages from our expansive first aid kit upstairs and then sat on the floor on the other side of Shaw. I spent my time watching Riley as she tended to Micha, occasionally muttering under her breath to him to stop fidgeting, and turning my focus to the television, not really seeing what was happening on the screen.

"May I ask you something?" I said as Riley washed the healing wound over his chest. He winced the slightest bit but bore it well, his eyes locked onto the game that the other two were playing.

"Go for it," she said, glancing up to see me watching her.

"What exactly happened down in Florida?" For a

moment, everyone grew quiet, and I quickly added, "If you can't or don't want to say, you don't have to. Sorry…"

"You Canadians really *are* so damn polite," Logan said under his breath as he blew up what looked like some sort of chemical factory on-screen. I saw Shaw's guy die instantly on his side of the TV, and his shoulders tensed ever so slightly, a sign that he was displeased.

"It's alright," Micha hissed between clenched teeth when Riley carefully dabbed some polysporin along the stitches. "We do owe you guys an explanation." From the dining room, Lee and Vail, who had been whispering with each other, grew quiet, listening in.

"Her uncle is the president of the Lost Souls MC, and there's a war brewing between them and the Reapers in Miami, who are run by his brother, that asshole who killed his nephew and brother's wife that I'd told you about earlier. We…" he nodded to Riley. "We were outside the Lost Souls clubhouse when they did a drive-by, and you can see how that turned out." He flinched ever so slightly when she moved on to clean the wound on his arm.

"This idiot threw himself over me."

"Shouldn't that be seen as something heroic and romantic?" Lee asked, raising a brow at her name-calling for the man who saved her life.

All she did in response was look over the back of the couch at him, finger raised in a warning, and said, "Don't start with me."

"It's not worth it, dude," Logan piped up. "Just let it go."

I snickered a little at that, and that was when my eyes fell on her cast, looking over the few pieces of artwork that had been scribbled on there already. I angled my head a little to the side to get a better look, impressed by the perfect Minnie Mouse covering a large portion of it. There were a few lilies and what seemed like a half-finished tree near the top. "Did you do these?" I asked.

"Had a lot of time to pass on the plane and drive here from Ottawa," she said.

"You took a *plane* here?" Vail snapped incredulously. "The first thing they'd do is check travel records!" For a moment, I thought he was about to throw these guys out of here.

"There are benefits to owning your own airline. Ever heard of Hudson Avionics?"

"No," he replied simply.

Logan shrugged, "Well, if you ever need to fly anywhere, let me know."

"I'll keep that in mind…" Vail muttered, looking back to his screen.

"I like to draw, too." I ignored the guys back and forth and refocused on Riley. I picked up my bag by the stairs and brought it over, pulling out my notebook to show her. She stopped what she was doing to Micha and looked in my notebook, pausing on the dragon sketch I did my first week in Harley.

"I love this," she said, her blue eyes taking in the tear sliding off its nose. She pointed at the scales. "The use of shading and light are perfect… and that sparkle in its tear makes it look so life-like."

"Thank you." I could feel my cheeks pinken a little at her compliment. "I love your lilies. Impressive considering what you had to work with," I said, gesturing at her cast.

"I've worked on tougher surfaces. Brick walls don't make for good texture."

"You're a graffiti artist?" I raised my brows, smiling, putting together Logan's earlier comment.

"Yeah, she caused a real ruckus at our school that one time," Micha added in, listening in on our conversation.

"Naomi deserved it, the fucking bitch!" Riley snapped at

him in defense.

"Sounds like every school has a "Naomi" in it. Celeste Wood just so happens to be mine. I swear, no matter what country you're from, you're going to have that one bitch in school that runs the show, and everyone just lets them."

"Maybe so." Riley makes a face. "But did Celeste fuck your uncle?"

I raise my brows at her. "Your uncle, the Lost Souls MC Prez?"

"That's the one!" Though her tone was playful, I knew she was pissed as all hell.

"What's your problem? Both Micha and I fucked her, too!" Logan said.

My mouth dropped at this information, considering how both guys were here with their current girlfriends, and Logan just felt the need to divulge this information to a group of strangers he just met? This guy really had a screw loose. From the dining table, Lee scraped his chair back and stomped off into the kitchen, as though he couldn't stand to be around this guy for another second.

"I love these flowers," Riley said, ignoring the guys and pointing to the hellebore I'd drawn around the dragon.

"Thanks," I bit the inside of my cheek, feeling like my chest was slowly compressing, "They were my mom's favourite."

Riley's gaze sharply cut to me, and I knew she could see the involuntary change. "Where is your mom?" she asked, obviously having put together that I didn't live with her.

I cleared my throat, my voice catching for a second. "She... died. Drunk driver..." I looked away, playing with a loose thread on my navy blue long sleeve; my fidgeting would increase as my discomfort rose. From beside me, Shaw let Logan kill his guy so that he could reach over and wrap his hand around my ankle, his thumb stroking the bare skin there. I ran my nails over the back of his hoodie. I wanted to wrap my arms around him and rest my head on his shoulder, but not here. I was not as big into PDA as Logan seemed to be.

"My mom was killed by a drunk driver, too," Riley said softly.

I looked her way to find her watching me, her face pained. "Did they catch the guy?"

She reached into her pocket and pulled out a small round gold and blue disc. Inscribed on the surface was a gold triangle with a *1 Month* in the center. She held it up so I could see it better and said, "This was hers, but the more I think about it, the more I doubt her sobriety." Her lips tightened, and her jaw clenched as she spat out the words. "Sometimes, the best lies are the ones we tell ourselves." *Holy shit...* I didn't know what to say.

We all sat in silence for a minute, and as we did, I watched Riley. Her rage was bubbling at the surface, and though I was pissed that someone's negligence killed my parents, I knew that I'd be furious and disappointed if my mother had been the perpetrator. "In life, people make good decisions and bad decisions. Even good people can make a mistake."

"Sometimes, they're not good people at all," Micha spat out, his own displeasure evident on his face. Riley gave him a look I couldn't decipher, but something passed between them briefly. There was more to that statement than what it seemed.

Logan raised his hand, not taking his eyes from the screen, and said, "My mom's awesome."

"But your dad was a piece of shit," Micha throws back at him.

Logan had gone quiet for a second or two, before nodding and saying, "Touche!"

From in front of me, Shaw muttered under his breath, his

304

words so quiet I almost didn't hear him when he said, "My dad was a piece of shit, too." Somehow, Logan heard, and his green eyes immediately looked over to Shaw, all humour gone from his face, and just gave him the slightest nod. The tension I felt under my fingers in Shaw's shoulders relaxed a little at that small acknowledgment, and they went back to their game.

By the time our order from Swiss Chalet arrived, Haldon had returned with the girls, who were each laden with shopping bags from the Goodwill. It looked as though Meredith had found a new best friend in Shelby as they chatted away about… well, I didn't even know, they were talking so fast.

"Holy shit, that smells good." Logan was attempting to peer into the paper bags of food that Lee was trying to get into the kitchen.

"Do you *mind?*" Lee sneered at him, looking like he wanted to elbow his face to get him away. "Get the fuck out of my way so we can actually eat!"

"All I've had today was some shitty coffee and a donut from a store owned by some guy called Tim. I'm fucking starving!" He snatched one of the bags from Lee's arms and ran ahead of him, unpacking it all directly onto the dining table to speed up the process. Lee muttered something under his breath and went into the kitchen, setting the bags down while I took out some plates and cups. We rarely splurged on food like this, but it was a one-time thing and the quickest way to feed everyone before we had to run out later.

By the time we'd all settled, Riley and Micha were together on the couch, talking quietly to each other while the rest of us ate at the small round dining table. With so few seating options, Meredith sat on Haldon's lap. I'm perched on Lee's, one arm wrapped under my chest to help keep my balance as we ate. Occasionally, I leaned back against his chest and closed my eyes, just enjoying the moment. Sure, we were sitting with a group of strangers, yet I felt an odd kinship with them. I felt like I was sitting with family. It's… nice.

Vail sat across from us, while Logan had Shelby sitting on his knee, but unlike Lee, who was carefully trying to keep me from falling, Logan was half bent over his plate, shoveling chicken and fries into his mouth like he hadn't eaten in days. Shelby, to her credit, came across just as hungry and didn't seem to notice, but held herself with more dignity than her guy.

Beside me, Haldon held up a forkful of rotisserie chicken to Meredith and murmured in her ear, "Mange, mon chaton. J'ai bien l'intention de te faire l'amour ce soir."

"You are one smooth motherfucker," Logan said, his eyes watching Haldon with obvious admiration, chewing around a large mouthful of food.

"You could be smooth, too." Shelby rolled her eyes. "If you didn't shovel all the food in your face before anyone else got some."

"All I'm saying is, I'm not into dudes, but I would let that guy in my ass," Logan said, around another mouthful. From the couch, I heard both Riley and Micha groan while at the table. Vail, very slowly raised his eyes, staring at Logan with a look of absolute incredulity etched upon his features, his expressionless mask wholly gone.

"Crazy ass motherfucker…" Lee muttered, staring at Logan like the guy had grown another head.

Haldon, however, was watching with that same blank expression in his dark eyes, his thoughts utterly unreadable as he watched the blond across from him shovel food into his mouth. "Better to remain silent and be thought a fool than to speak and remove all doubt," he said finally, his accent still clear in each word he spoke.

"Agreed," Logan nodded, stopping for a moment to drink some Pepsi.

"Why are you still talking?" Lee asked him.

"Well, why *aren't* you talking?"

Lee turned slightly in his seat, swiveling me with him, to glare Logan down, his face screwed up, his every thought clear in his expression, and that was exuding, *Are you fucking stupid?*

Riley muttered from the couch, "Yeah, I give him that look all the time, too."

Shelby twisted in his lap. "Hey, baby, try this sauce. It's amazing." She took a french fry and dipped it in the chalet sauce before holding it out in front of Logan's mouth. Eyes locked onto hers, he took it, his tongue snaking over her fingers, and I tried not to cringe. This guy was a little much. Funny, but I wouldn't be able to be stuck around him day in and day out. Hat's off to Shelby.

"So." Vail watched Logan for another second, as though trying to figure him out before deciding it wasn't worth it, and then spoke up, calling over to the couch. "How did you guys find us?"

Micha was looking much better than he did an hour ago. There was some colour in his face now, and he looked to be less… grumpy? That had been the best word I could use to describe him. Grumpy and intense. But now that he and Riley were snuggled up on the couch, eating, and having some space of their own, he seemed to be in a better mood. "One of the Lost Soul Bikers, Beast, told us about an ex Spade, or Black Spade, from Ashland who showed up in Florida, looking for help from Riley's Uncle. Beast explained that because Ashland has a heavy MC presence, it'd be safer to come here to hide, cuz no other MC in their right mind would come into their territory." He shifted a little, wincing slightly as he got comfortable again. "When we arrived, we basically drove around until we spotted a biker with a Spade on the back of their jacket, and he told us about you and Vendetta."

I felt Lee tense beneath me, and I rubbed his knee, reassuring him. The thought of our only allies giving us away to a bunch of strangers was definitely concerning.

"Why would a random biker help you guys?" Vail said smoothly, his demeanor as calm as ever, but the mask was back in place, and I could tell he was fighting to keep his cool.

"It was fucking weird," Logan said. "I feel like we just somehow said the magic word and, open sesame, the gates just swung open for us. Lucky break."

"What'd you say?" Vail asked, slowly chewing on some fries, not looking up from his plate.

"Just said we were friends with Chase Mathers and needed help…" Micha shrugged. "Hoped that they might know of him because of the Spade that came to us."

"Mathers?" Vail stopped chewing, and Lee, Shaw, Haldon and Meredith and I, all looked at each other. *Maverick!*

"Yeah?" The others noticed our exchange, and Micha was watching Vail with interest. "Why?"

But he shook his head in response. "Thought you said, *Matthews*, my bad."

To Micha's credit, he didn't press us, though I'm sure he knew Vail was lying.

"Whatever you do, do *not* approach a biker wearing a jacket with a blue dragon on the back," Lee said, sliding my soda closer to me so I didn't have to reach, pressing a kiss to the back of my head. "Only trust a Spade. If any of them ask questions, you're guests of Vendetta, that clear?"

"Crystal," Logan said around a mouthful of fries.

Chapter Seventeen

Casey

"Remember, Chickadee," Meredith said as she applied yet another layer of powder to the hollows of my cheekbones, "Subservient. Eyes down. Obedient. You need to act like his servant, holding his drink, having it ready when he's thirsty, kneeling beside him on the floor when he sits-"

"Excuse me, *what*?" Riley interrupted, her head snapping up from the page she'd been scribbling on, her pencil sliding to the side. "What is it with guys and making us kneel at their feet?" she muttered bitterly. She'd been perched at the head of Vails bed while I sat on the end, with Shelby and Meredith attacking me with makeup brushes, eyeshadows, and hairspray.

Though we hadn't divulged much of what we were doing tonight regarding our mission, when Shelby heard that Meredith was planning on dolling me up, she eagerly volunteered to help. Logan carried Riley up so she could hang out with us, with her clutching one of the extra sketchbooks I'd had lying around and gave her, along with some pencils, while muttering something about needing a break from the testosterone downstairs. As they primped me up for tonight, Meredith coached me on what I needed to do to blend in. Lee would be there as my "master," and though I cringed at the word, I trusted him implicitly. Vail would be waiting outside with Maverick, who I was going to officially meet tonight, and a few of the Black Spades, who were also ready in case we got into any trouble. Lee and I were to draw attention from the owners in the lounge so Shaw could break into the basement and see if the missing girls were actually being kept there.

"Wish we could have found something a little sluttier," Meredith said after she finished applying a pale pink to my lips and moved over to one of the bags from Goodwill they'd returned with. She peeked inside, curled her lip in distaste, and said, "Or some more money to afford something a little nicer."

"It'll most likely be low lighting in there," I reminded her as Shelby circled around me, curling my hair with an iron. "So they won't notice labels, and they're men... what do they know about fashion... uh, excluding your guys, of course," I added, thinking about the clothes that Micha and Logan had arrived in. Guaranteed their jeans alone were worth several hundred dollars.

"Still, the two dresses I have at home would be perfect, but I can't make a run back there now. Plus..." She glanced at me and smirked, "You're kinda shrimpy."

"I resent that." I rolled my eyes at her as Shelby carefully ran her nails through my curls to loosen them up a bit. "I'm not shrimpy. I'm a delicate little butterfly."

"Hopefully, the guys in that club will believe that, cuz no one in this room is gonna buy that bullshit. I saw what you did to Celeste's stitches..." She smirked.

"What'd you do?" Riley asked, looking up again from her sketch.

"Well, a few days before, I'd ripped her earrings out, the bitch was going to shove a fork in my face, so I ripped out the stitches."

Shelby finished curling my hair and backed away, setting the iron down to grab some bobby pins, but I noticed how one of her hands had touched her own ear, as though she were imagining what it would feel like to be in Celeste's shoes, and shivered.

"Trust me, she deserved it," I said when she returned, pulling sections of my hair back.

"A fork in the face?" she muttered, glancing at Riley for whatever reason. "I'd say that earns a stitch-rip."

"She's the one your crazy-ass boyfriend punched out today," Meredith added nonchalantly as she pulled out a black and silver-looking cocktail dress from the bag.

"Wait, what?!" Riley's head snapped up again, her mouth dropping in surprise, and looking at Shelby. "What part of being covert does your boyfriend not understand?"

"I know, I'm sorry!" she moaned. "Some guy grabbed my butt when we came in. Logan might've… overreacted a bit."

"He *punched* a girl?"

"To be fair, Celeste needed a punch in the face," I said as Shelby arranged my hair so that a layer was pinned back off my face, the lilac curls loose and falling down my back. "All set. I have no idea what kind of undercover mission you guys are about to go on tonight, but either way, Casey is gonna look hot as hell while she does it."

"C'mon, you!" Meredith nodded at me as she handed me the clothes. "Get changed. The others will be arriving soon."

I hurried into the bathroom as Shelby and Mer congratulated each other on a job well done. After closing the door behind myself, I could finally see what they'd done to me... and my mouth dropped.

I really did look over the top. My eyes were extra smoked out, with long, curling lashes added to the outer corners to make them stand out even more. All that bronzer Meredith applied to my cheeks made me look older somehow, and the pink she chose didn't clash with my hair like the first choice had. I quickly changed out of my clothes from the day and slipped on the black dress. It was a spaghetti strap, and the triangular cups over my boobs were so tight that they made my boobs swell together, creating ample cleavage. The material fanned out around my ass, down to a couple of inches above the knees, with silver slivers running up and down the black, gauzy material. She'd also given me a pair of black heels and some fishnet stockings that were more uncomfortable than I thought they'd be. They squeezed around my toes, and I feared that by the end of the night, I'd have diamond-shaped markings all over my legs. Shaking my hair out down my back, I stepped out to find Vail's bedroom empty.

The last thing I wanted was to walk down there by myself. Even after adapting to life on The Hill, I'd never dressed this girly. The thought of the guys seeing me this way had my stomach jumping up and down, and my heart was racing a little. I was starting to feel more nervous at the prospect of everyone seeing me this way rather than walking into La Maison Rouge, pretending to be a whore.

"Casey! Get your cute ass down here!" Meredith hollered up the stairs.

I took a deep breath and headed down, ambling carefully down the steps in my heels to avoid breaking an ankle. I kept my eyes down as I walked, hoping that I'd be able to slink by without anyone noticing, however the moment I emerged, I could hear a small breath catch from the lounger chair by the couch. I looked up to see Shaw staring at me from beneath his black hoodie, mouth slightly open, blue eyes wide as they took me in. Slowly, I looked to Lee, dressed in a dapper looking grey suit with a white button-up shirt underneath, undone at the neck. His eyes were smoldering as he slowly looked me up and down, making me feel like he was undressing me with his gaze. Then I looked to Vail, who appeared quite unmoved by me altogether. He was checking his phone, texting someone before glancing my way.

His hazel eyes flicked over me like he was checking to make sure I looked the part, and he just nodded as he turned away. "Good. C'mon. They're waiting." He tossed a grey teddy faux fur coat at me and slipped on a thick, black fleece sweater, carefully covering his hair in a black toque. Shaw was dressed similarly, in dark clothing, his hood pulled up over his head. They look like robbers more than anything.

I will admit I was a little hurt by his dismissal. It stung. But Vail was in "business mode" while Shaw looked nervous as hell as he watched me, like he was just itching to throw me over his shoulder and lock me in his bedroom. If we got caught tonight, we might end up being in another dangerous situation like they were in last time. I involuntarily shivered as I thought about that biker who killed Bryce with the saw. The way they described him... he sounded like a lunatic.

"Should we say good luck?" Logan asked from where he was sitting on the couch, Shelby cradled in his lap. On the other end, Micha and Riley were snuggled up beneath a blanket. I hid my smile as I tried not to laugh, but, the moment the sun went down and the temperature dropped, our Florida houseguests all began shivering. Even Logan, who sneered at first at the sweats and hoodies that the girls had bought for him from the Goodwill, changed into the comfier, thicker clothes to stay warm.

"I'd say that'd be *fitting*." Lee smiled at him, and I just knew he was thoroughly enjoying how Logan was cringing from having to wear second-hand clothes.

"Good luck, guys," Micha said from where he was lying.

"I get to keep Shaw's gaming system if shit goes down," Logan added, earning a smack on the back of his head from Shelby.

"Ignore him," she said, then covered his mouth with her hand to prevent him from saying anything further.

"We got things here, Boss," Meredith called over from the dining room table where she and Haldon were sitting close together, working on some homework.

Vail didn't respond, but I caught the subtle nod to Haldon, who returned it, the motion so minuscule that I almost missed it. He and Meredith had a lot on their plate watching these four. There was likely a group of Vendetta members hanging out close by in case backup was needed while we were gone. He tipped his head to the three of us and headed downstairs. I stayed close to Lee, my earlier anxiety and nerves about tonight rushing back to me. Lee wrapped his arm around me, sensing my unease. I was so glad that at least he'd be there with me.

"They're here. Let's go," Vail said, checking his phone. He looked through the peephole first before stepping outside, looking around the dark parking lot as though worried that we were being watched. But after a minute, he gave us the all-clear, and we followed. Waiting in the parking lot were two charcoal grey SUVs, and one of the rear doors was opened. Vail climbed in first, and Lee made sure I was right behind him before following. Shaw, however, got in the front passenger seat, and we were off.

I found myself squashed between Lee and Vail, who reached over and buckled me in like I was a toddler, but I didn't fight it. Vail showing any sort of concern for my safety was reassuring, especially with what I was going to do tonight. Once we started moving, I could finally take in the other men in the vehicle.

The SUV had been modified inside so that the two rows of rear seats faced each other, and when I took in the two men sitting across from us, I knew immediately that these were members of the Black Spades. One of the guys was big and beefy, with lighter, brown hair hanging down his back and a long beard to match. The coolest thing about him was probably the claws tattooed over the backs of his fingers, like a bear. He was probably in his mid to late twenties, and though he looked like a terrifying biker, he smiled kindly, and the guys acknowledged him with a fist bump. But the man to his left had my full attention.

He wasn't as big or brawny, but something about him demanded attention and immediate respect. His golden, tousled hair was streaked with grey, telling his age which I took to be his mid to late forties. Even the whisker on his chin was full of greys. But he had a handsome face, even though his forehead was marred with a massive pink scar that trailed down the left side of his eye. This was a new one, probably in the last few weeks or so.

"Casey, this is Maverick Mathers, President of the Black Spades, MC. Maverick, meet Casey Cooper," Lee said, introducing us.

"Casey." Maverick nodded to me, his voice as gravelly as Shaw's, though much deeper. "Nice to meet you, honey. We appreciate you helping us out here." His eyes roved around my face, studying my features, and his brows pulled together ever so slightly. "Cooper, you said?" he confirmed to Vail, who simply nodded.

"Thanks for coming with us this time," Vail said, lounging back in his seat. Every so often, he peered out the window or looked behind us, searching for a set of headlights that could be on our tail, but the road was dark and empty as we took a backroad leading south to the edge of the West End of town.

"I hate sending you guys in there," Maverick said, glowering at the thought. "Should be us putting ourselves at risk... but Elias's guys know our faces. I didn't realize he had the Beasts there at the docks that night. We got fucked over," he said bitterly, the fist resting on his knee clenching hard.

"Luckily none of our own got hurt, cuz the random biker they had with them who wasn't wearing a Beast's cut, killed one of Elias's own men..." Shaw muttered from the front seat.

"One of his own...?"

"A Jackal," Vail explained, "from the high school."

Maverick looked sharply at him, his eyes narrowed. "The biker wasn't wearing a cut?"

"He *was*... a vest over a t-shirt... but he had no emblem on it from what I could see. Just a rocker."

"Did it say, *Nomad*?"

"Can't say I got that close to him," Vail snapped. "Not while he was busy sawing away at a screaming high school kid..."

"Bryce knew what he was getting into when he and Hunter had the Jackals suck up to the Faceless," Shaw called from the front seat. "Aligning with them means you're gonna die young. They just got cocky..."

"I don't think Bryce deserved what he got," Lee said, sounding a little sick. "I doubt he expected Elias's own men to turn on him."

"That biker is not Elias's," Maverick said, sighing heavily as he sat back in his seat, looking overly troubled. It actually worried me. Who was this guy that had everyone so unsettled? "He's a nomad for hire. He's Jeremy."

"How do you know?" Vail asked him. "And who is Jeremy?"

"I know because only Jeremy is fucking crazy enough to walk into a gunfight with a chainsaw and attack the first person he sees with it. The fact that the kid was on the same side as him and he cut into him, not worrying at all about repercussions, on top of the actual act itself… well, that gives me my answer." He ran his hands over his face, rubbing his eyes as though exhausted. "I'd hoped he wouldn't turn up here, but I heard whispers that he was in town. This is the first official sighting."

"*Who* is he?" Vail asked, his mask slipping ever so slightly. I could see the rage burning in his eyes. What Jeremy did, even though it was to a Jackal, was fucked.

"Like, I said, he's a lone biker for hire and takes on jobs for insanely high payoffs, so the only ones who could afford him and would even *want* to are higher-up mob bosses or crime organizations. Hence, Elias is bringing him in. Jeremy…" Maverick trailed off, lost in thought for a moment as he chewed on his bottom lip. "Jeremy just kind of showed up out of nowhere. No one knows anything about him. Where he's from, relation, or even his fucking last name. It started with a talk between the MCs, people who have heard about a Nomad Biker who traveled across the country, rumours about him being a sociopath, or a psychopath or some shit. I can't remember the difference."

"Have you ever met him?" I asked, feeling the hairs on my arms rising.

Maverick shakes his head. "Haven't met him, no. But he's the reason I suddenly found myself President instead of VP in recent months," he spat out, his jaw clenched tight.

Oh, shit, I shuddered and leaned into Lee's side, feeling safer when Lee's arms were wrapped around me.

"Anyways, enough about that fucker. Tonight is just another night in the club, which means no Beasts. My informant said they had Church tonight."

"Church?" My brow furrows, and I half-laughed.

"It's what we call club meetings, honey." He smiled at me, as though he found my ignorance about MC life endearing.

"So why not just call it a meeting?" I asked, scrunching my face up.

The others all laughed at me, like what I had said was a great joke or something. But they moved on, not bothering to answer. "Lee, you've seen Vail do this with Meredith enough times." Maverick handed him a shiny, oval, onyx pin, which Lee would stick onto his lapel. "Flaunt the money." The big burly guy handed Lee a wad of cash, and when I said wad, I mean… like, hundreds upon hundreds of dollars. My mouth drops as Lee splits it into smaller folds, tucking them away in various pockets of his suit. "Confidence," Maverick added, "Don't take no shit. You're lucky you're a big guy, so you can pass for someone older, and most likely, the others in there won't fuck with you. But *you*, honey." He looked at me next. "I trust Meredith filled you in?"

I nodded, my hands twisting in my lap as we turned down a long, vacant road, pulling over to the side to where trees surrounded us. They leered overhead, bare branches shaking in the cold wind. There was no moon tonight, and the only light came from the glow of the dashboard as the drivers of both SUVs turned off their headlights.

"It's okay to let them see you're afraid," Maverick said, his eyes moving to my hands and back to my face again. "For all they know, Lee's taken you against your will, and you've been forced into your situation by him. Be meek. Be skittish. It'll be more convincing."

I nodded, sucking in a deep breath and holding it before exhaling.

"We'll message, GREEN, if we've finished and it's all clear for you to go. RED, if you need to get the fuck out of there. We'll be standing by and watching through that camera." He nodded to the lapel pin. He turned in his seat to look at Shaw. "You good if Animal covers you?"

Shaw twisted around in his seat to eye the massive guy sitting directly behind him. The two locked eyes for a few seconds before he gave a subtle nod. "As long as he isn't breathing down my neck while I break in. He stands out," he said, slouching in his seat. Honestly, I felt better knowing that there was a biker watching his back, and I breathed a little sigh of relief.

"Vail and I will be staking out in the woods keeping a lookout and watching the camera feed," Maverick said and turned to point at the SUV that was leading the way. "The others will be on standby in case we need backup. Any questions?"

"Let's fucking do this," Lee said, clapping his hands together.

Maverick opened the passenger door and climbed out with the big guy called Animal, and they headed for the first SUV. Shaw got out next, not saying a word as he looked back once to cast me a pained sort of expression. I'm about to tell him to be careful, to please be safe, that... I love him... but he closes the door before I could, and follows the two Spades.

"Casey..."

I turn in my seat to face Vail. He doesn't hesitate, but instead holds my face in his hands and leans in, crushing his lips to mine. He kisses me hungrily, his tongue snaking past my teeth to roll over my own, and I feel lightheaded. I held onto him, kissing him back just as deeply, not realizing until this moment exactly how much I needed this from him. When he stops, he only pulls back the tiniest fraction, the tips of our noses brushing against each other. "Be safe. Both of you. Stay close to each other. I want my family home with me tonight, you got that?"

"Yes," I breathed.

"We'll be fine, brother. As long as we can keep attention off of Shaw so he can get in and confirm our suspicions, then we can get the fuck out of there and hopefully move on to phase two."

"Yeah…" Vail slipped a little; his voice strained ever so slightly as he slowly, reluctantly, released me. "Okay. Let's fucking get this over with." His hazel eyes roved over me, and for a moment, he seemed like he wanted to say something, yet after a moment's pause, he shook his head and climbed out, closing the door behind himself before trudging on after Shaw. Overhead, tiny flakes of snow were beginning to fall, giving the otherwise ominous-looking roadway a more ethereal appearance. It felt out of place, the beautiful falling, fluffy flakes, given where we were and what we were trying to find out.

"Okay, let's do this," Lee said, and the Spade driving the SUV shifted into drive, turning the headlights back on, and pulled away from the curb. We passed the others, who stayed behind, readying for their roles in this insane plan.

"I'll be in here the whole time," the biker said, moving down the road before turning off onto another more desolate one. "So if you message the group chat, I'll get it, too, and I'll storm in there and get you kids out." He passed back what looked like an ID, which Lee took.

"Thanks, Taz." Lee pocketed the ID and pulled me close to his side, holding my head over his heart. I could hear his heart pumping loudly in his chest. Despite his cool outer appearance, Lee was as nervous as I was. From my angle, I saw the reflection of our driver, Taz, in the rearview mirror, and I held back a surprised gasp. He was probably around our age, if not older by two or three years, and the poor guy had thick, heavy scarring up his cheeks towards his ears, as though someone roughly sliced into his face a little before forcing his jaw open. His dark, shoulder-length hair was combed back into a ponytail at the nape of his neck, and his nearly black eyes are focused on the road. He reminded me of Haldon, and I realized he must be Metis, if not actually Indigenous.

But his scars! Who the fuck would do such a thing? I quickly looked away from Taz, unable to bear thinking about what pain he went through to earn such a horrible fate.

"Two minutes," he said from the front seat as we finally pulled off into a private drive. The area was fenced off by a high chain-link fence, complete with barbed wire wrapping around the top. There were security cameras, but the guys knew about them already. I kept telling myself that the others knew what they were doing. They knew how to get past the fence line and use the woods as cover. They'd be safe. Lee and I, however... we were marching right into the lion's den.

Taz drove us up the curved drive, the trees looming overhead, cutting off the night sky until finally, there was a break ahead, and we emerged from the treeline to a large, elaborate Georgian-style brick house. It was two stories, with four white framed windows looking out the front and a black door beneath a grand, white stone archway with an ugly statue of a gargoyle leering overhead. A large grey fountain stood empty in the middle of the drive, which circled around it, dead vines covering the entire thing, all the way up to the cherub that was perched at the top of its elaborate stonework. Red uplighting lined the house, giving it a rather forbidding appearance. Two men in black standing out front looked like they were almost as big as Animal, and though they stood stock still, their eyes watched our SUV approach. Before we could pull up, one stepped forward, hand extended to stop us, to which Taz complied.

Lee lowered his window, pulling out the ID and two one

hundred dollar bills, holding them aloft as the security came over to check him out.

"Mr. Chopard," The guard said, reading the name on the fake-out loud, "This says you're from British Columbia... you in town on business?" The security guard said, looking at the ID.

"My *father* is in town for business. Thought I'd... *explore* what Ashland has to offer?" Lee gave the guy a smile that would make me shudder if I didn't know him. It reeked of skeeze and a cockiness that I knew Lee didn't embody. He was always sweet and confident. But I knew he was playing a part right now, so I pushed it all aside.

"And this is?" The guy eyed me next, his gaze roaming over my fishnet-covered legs with interest.

"My pet." Lee slid his hand up my thigh, getting dangerously close to my center, his hand partially moving beneath the material of my coat.

"Is she for sharing?" The guy asked, and Lee's hand tightened on me for a fraction of a second before he quickly composed himself.

"She's just for me, if you know what I mean?"

"Got it." He handed back his ID, then pulled out a black marker and held his hand out to me.

What the fuck? I thought, not having been told about this part. What was he doing?

Lee sighed, as though impatient with me and seized my wrist, thrusting it forward so that the guy could draw a star on the back of my hand, then he stood back so we could drive forward.

"Just playing the part, okay?" he whispered as we undid our seatbelts. "I might be a little rough, but I love you more than anyone in the world, and I would never actually hurt you, babe," he said, catching my chin in his fingers and forcing my attention to him. "Do you trust me?"

I stared into Lee's dark eyes, breathless from hearing the words, *I love you,* over and over again in my head. I tried to say it back, as I was feeling the same sense of safety wash over me, but instead, I breathed, "Absolutely, I do."

"Good. Now forgive me for how I'm going to treat you…" I could see the distress on his face when he released me and opened the door, stepping out into the cold air. I followed, a little unsteady on these insane, black heels. It was still snowing, but the flakes had gotten bigger, and the eerie stillness in the lot, with the woods, gave me a sense of foreboding. I didn't feel right about this.

But before I could voice my reservations, Lee grabbed my arm and pulled me forward towards the stone steps leading up to that somber black door. I slipped a little on the steps, but he just laughed with the security guards at my fumble and grunted at me.

"Pick yourself up!" he snapped. "Don't fucking embarrass me in there!"

"Yes, Sir," I said meekly, bowing my head to him. I hated it. I fucking hated it, but we were just playing a part, I reminded myself. A member of security let him in, and I continued following. The inside entry was about the size of the bedroom I shared with Vail. The walls were made of dark wooden panelling with intricate carvings along the baseboards and along the top where it joined to the ceiling, which was made of copper tile. There was a plushy, red cushioned couch, fancy fern plants in black marble vases, and the dark wooden floorboards were shiny, my heels clicking off of them as we walked in. There was more security around, and they checked us in after looking at only Lee's ID. They didn't even bother asking for mine, for my name, or anything for that matter. They glanced at the star drawn on the back of my hand and looked away, nodding respectfully to Lee as he handed them hundred-dollar bills as tips.

"Bienvenu dans La Maison Rouge," One said, nodding towards the double doors leading into the mansion. Behind them, I heard the bass of the music pounding away, and though Meredith had briefed me on the layout of the place, I didn't know how I'd feel going back there.

When the double doors opened, I truly understood that descriptions could never have really prepared me for what we walked into.

The room descended down by two steps, into a seating area, with rich, plush red upholstered couches and chairs, like the one out front. There were mini-stages around the room, where girls danced seductively, some dancing with the poles, others simply using them to hold themselves up as they slowly worked their bodies to the music, looking like they were either exhausted or drugged up to hell. The song playing overhead was one I recognized by The Kills, U.R.A. Fever... and the feel of it with the scene sent a chill through my blood.

There were men in suits, maybe ten in total, of various ages, scattered about the space. Some had girls dancing on them as they drank from crystal glasses or smoked cigars. Others were talking with other men; their heads bowed close together as they leaned over a table lit with a single candle-light in a crystal vase. When I peered closer, I saw girls beneath the table, their feet sticking out from the other side, and I instantly felt sick.

Our entrance caught the others' attention, but servers ambled forward to guide us to a table and offer Lee a drink, all while carefully ignoring me. Lee sat in one of the richly upholstered chairs, crossing his ankle over a knee. I couldn't help but admire him at this moment, wearing that grey suit, the red, blue, pink, and purple lighting of the room bouncing off his beautiful, flawless skin, illuminating it, while adding shadows beneath his sharp cheekbones... he was beautiful.

But the moment was shattered in seconds when he snapped his fingers to me, and pointed at the floor by his feet, his face cold and expressionless.

It's an act. It's an act, I told myself again and again as I sank to my knees at his side, hands resting on my thighs and head bowed. Lee placed a large hand alongside my head and guided me in, so my cheek was pressed against his thigh. I rested there, knowing that he was reassuring me we were safe despite this power move.

The dancers switched off, and five other girls were coming out from a black door near the back of the room, barely visible behind a set of what appeared to be like a barred cage. Three of them were supported by a member of security, looking dazed and confused as they were escorted to one of the stages to dance. Some of the businessmen gestured to one or two, and if the girls were one of the lucid ones, they sauntered over in their leather booty shorts, bra tops, and incredibly high hooker heels, and danced for them, some had gotten right in their laps to grind into their hard-ons.

The server came back to Lee, placing his drink on a shiny, black coaster, and winked at him, which instantly pissed me off.

Back off bitch, I thought when she leaned over, much more than necessary to show off her bulging cleavage to him. Lee took the drink but turned away, watching one of the girls on the far stage, one that seemed like she was lost, with no idea where she was or what she should be doing. Our server let us be, but as she passed a table of men in suits, I automatically reached out and clung to Lee's leg.

"What is it?" he murmured, pretending to take a sip of the amber liquid in his crystal glass.

"Those guys are watching us... the table at our ten o'clock." I stared back down to the floor as he scanned the place, holding himself with a regal sort of air that didn't come off forced.

"One has called security over, and they're looking our way. Most likely asking who I am. Just keep calm, baby. I got you." He pretended to act interested in one of the better dancers, slowly swirling his drink in his hand.

"Did they ever talk to Vail when he and Meredith did this?" I asked, just loud enough so that he could hear me over the music.

"Only the first time, but they mostly just left him alone after. He'd pay for some dances, gambled a little on some of the machines in the next room. He would spend a couple hundred here on the nights he was scouting. He was a good client."

I tried to quash my jealousy at the idea of Vail getting a lapdance from one of these girls. I had no reason to be. If we were right about all of this, then these girls were victims themselves.

"They're coming over, Casey. Just keep your head down, alright?" he said, his fingers stroking my hair. To an outsider, it would seem like he was patting his dog, but I knew Lee, and I understood he was just trying to put me at ease. But my heart was hammering against my chest, and my palms were clammy as hell. *Who are these men?*

"Did Vail ever find out who they were?" I whispered.

"Vail never met these ones. I don't recognize them from the cam footage. The others were just rich businessmen looking for an exclusive night out." Lee gave my head the tiniest little tap, alerting me to be quiet, and I quickly bowed my head.

"You're Nathaniel Chopard," I heard the smooth, sickenly silky voice of our new companion say from over my head, "Heir to your father's Investment firm?"

Thank fuck that Shaw was great with computers. The alias

they'd created for Lee seemed to have fooled them. I inhaled the tiniest sigh of relief.

"I am… and you are?" Lee didn't move from his seat, his dark eyes moving up and down the man who had approached him.

"I'm the owner of this establishment," the man said, and I felt my blood turn to ice. "Elias Cartier." Lee shifted a little, I assumed to shake his hand, while I tried not to be sick. "I wanted to personally welcome you here and perhaps share a drink together?"

Though I could feel Lee's leg tense a little beneath my cheek, he knew better than to refuse. "By all means," he said, gesturing to the empty seat, a chesterfield, on his other side, farthest from me. I peeked up through my lashes as Elias Cartier walked around the table and sat, angling himself to face Lee, and I finally could put a face to the monster of Ashland.

Elias was stocky, but probably only around six feet. The suit he was wearing screamed of money, with a silk tie and pocket square, beautiful stitchwork, and a pair of shiny, black shoes to match. His hair was honey brown, short on the sides while longer on top, and combed back off his face. In this lighting, I *think* his eyes were a mossy green, but it was hard to tell. Clean-shaven, richly dressed, he looked like just another rich asshole. But, there was something about him that made me want to run away. Elias's smile was fake. It was forced upon his lips like it had been carved out of stone, and the way his eyes scanned over Lee, taking in everything about him like he was sizing him up rather than sitting here to welcome him, sent alarm bells off in my head. There was zero warmth there.

The music changed to something slower, with a jazzy sort of feel, and despite how beautiful it was, given our predicament, it only seemed to heighten the severity of the situation. Lord Huron's haunting words singing, When the Night is Over, only made me wish we were anywhere but here.

"How did you hear about my club?" Elias asked him as a girl hurried over, drink ready and in hand, to give to him. He took it, his eyes never leaving Lee for a second.

"Through friends of my father's. It's been a dull day, following him around meeting to meeting, with stiff old men, ready to drop dead any second..." Lee brought his glass to his lips, the sound of the ice cubes clinking together. "I was more interested in *other* ventures. Luckily, one of the sons was a regular here and told me about it."

"And who would that be?" Elias asked. As innocent as those words were, I knew better. He was testing us. Feeling us out.

"Cash Wittaker," Lee was poised, not hesitating in anything he said. I wanted to applaud him for holding it together.

"Ah yes, Cash..." Elias chuckled a little. "He does enjoy what we have to offer here," He gazed over at one of the girls dancing, one of the ones who appeared inebriated, and nodded his head to her. She clambered down from the stage, and a member of security escorted her over. "Heather is one of Cash's favourites."

Heather... Heather! She was one of the girls who went missing the week before I'd arrived here! I'd heard her name whispered here and there in the halls. Involuntarily, I looked up to see the young teenage girl walking like a zombie. Her eyes shown to be almost dead in this light, her face bland and heavily made up with layer upon layer of makeup. She'd been forced into a skimpy outfit of pink silk, her hair curled and pulled back into a ponytail. Her eyes moved to me, but it was like there was no one home in her head. She was just... going through the motions.

"Heather, why don't you give Nathaniel here a lapdance?" Elias said, gesturing to Lee, and we both tensed.

Oh shit... oh shit, no! Would she recognize him?

"I'm good for now," Lee said, turning his face away, looking disinterested, but I knew he was trying to hide himself from Heather. If she recognized him from school... would she blow our cover?

"Nonsense. She was a dancer before she came to my employ. She has a wild wiggle, don't you, sweetheart? So please, it's on me. Enjoy yourself." Elias gave her ass a sharp slap, and I saw how she flinched, recoiling from his touch.

"I have my own girl-"

"Bruce," Elias snapped, and immediately, a pair of hands reached beneath my upper arms and hauled me to my feet.

"Wait just a minute-" Lee started to stand, but Heather was forced down onto his lap, where she began to grind against him.

"I said, enjoy her." Elias's voice dropped dangerously, and I heard the threat behind his words. He wasn't fooled. He wasn't buying us. *Fuck! Fuck, Lee, send a code a RED, 911, something!* But as I was dragged away from him, Heather's thighs clamped together over his, preventing him from reaching his phone.

It's okay, they have the camera... the camera on his pin! They'll see...

I was so busy watching Lee, trying to figure out how to get him out of this, that I didn't even see where they were taking me until I found myself propped before Elias, standing there like a deer in headlights.

"Come, girl. Have a seat while your master enjoys something new." He reached out, grasping my hips, and pulled me in, forcing me to straddle his lap so that my face was inches from his. I couldn't stop myself from shaking when I found myself face to face with Elias, the man I'd heard countless horror stories about, the real-life boogeyman. "You're trembling like a leaf... calm yourself, girl," he said before grasping my chin. "I just want to look at you."

So I sat absolutely still, frozen, as Elias's cold gaze roved over my face, turning it this way and that. I had no idea what he was searching for, and he gave no hints as to what he was thinking. He just stared until finally, he turned me back to face him dead-on, his gaze boring into mine. Any hint of a smile disappeared, his nostrils flaring ever so slightly, and the corners of his eyes tightening, like he saw something he did *not* like. The hostility scared the shit out of me, but as quickly as it came, it was gone, and that fake-ass grin was back in place as he released my chin to take a sip of his drink, but he didn't let me leave.

"What's your name, love?" he asked casually.

"Rita," Lee called from his seat, throwing a random name out there. I glanced over at him to see that Heather was still rolling her hips, imitating the act of lovemaking without actually touching him. As far as I could see, she was too doped up to really know what was going on.

"Rita... what a coincidence. Keegan?" Elias called over to one of his men, who stepped up immediately. I looked around and realized then that we were surrounded by his security, like a wall of muscle blocking us out from everyone else in the club. Keegan looked like a mean motherfucker, with buzzed blond hair, pale eyes, and a scar over his bottom lip. "Isn't your little pet also called Rita?"

The one called Keegan grinned sickeningly and nodded. "She is. She's a fun little toy." His voice was deep and scratchy, and it made my stomach churn.

Elias chuckled. "Not a common name around here, Nathaniel. So I'm going to assume that it's a fake for your slave, hm? Now, will you be honest with me and tell me what her *real* name is?"

"Never bothered to learn it," Lee said, shifting a little beneath Heather, and I knew he was trying to reach his cell.

"Strange." Elias put down his drink and slid a hand to my lower back, gripping a handful of the dress, "to not learn anything about your plaything... you'd think you would want to be aware of her background, where she comes from, who her parents are..." His eyes flickered back to mine and remained there, glaring at me like I somehow personally offended him. "After all, you need to protect yourself from those who might be looking for her."

Red, Lee! Red! I looked away from Elias to Lee, whose hand was in his pocket, as he gently pushed Heather back a bit.

"No, no, love. Look at *me*." Elias pressed two fingers to my jaw, forcing me back to him. He was glowering, but in his eyes, I saw triumph. The slow smile curling his lips was real, but it wasn't kind. It was sick and terrifying, like a wolf who had caught something it'd been sniffing out for so long. "Be a good girl and tell me your name."

"Ashton."

He clicked his tongue, never taking his eyes away from mine as he shook his head. "No, no. No, lying to me." The hand that was gripping my dress painfully dug into my skin like he was clawing at me. "No lies. I hate it when people lie to me. It makes me go a little crazy... a little less... *controlled*. I get mad. I get so fucking enraged that sometimes, not even these men can stop me when I lose it... " he said, referring to his large, scary guard. "I like to break things when I do, *pretty* things," he spat the words between clenched teeth, and I could feel him shaking beneath me as the hand holding my jaw tapped my cheek.

Holy fuck, I think I'm going to pass out. I was so fucking scared I had no idea what to do. My mind was blank, my face felt numb, and all I wanted to do was run. Just fucking run!

"Your name, *Sweetness*." He smirked.

"Casey," I whispered, not knowing what else to do.

He nodded, but still didn't let me go. Instead, his hand released the back of my dress, sliding to the front of my body. I cringed when he ran his fingers over the curve of my breast, stroking the bare skin of my cleavage, before trailing the tips down my arm, which made my hair stand on end. He grabbed my wrist so tight I cried out a little. "Surname?"

"That's enough!" Lee snarled and grasped Heather's upper arms, not hard, but enough to get her to stop what she was doing. His eyes were burning as he glared at us, his chest heaving slightly as he fought back his rage. "That one is mine, and I didn't give you permission to-"

"I don't need your fucking permission," Elias seethed, not even bothering to look his way. His security moved in, the circle around us even tighter than before. I started to panic as I tried to tug my arm free from his grip, but he didn't let go. "Do you really think you could sneak in here and fuck with me?" Elias went on. "That I can't tell the difference between Harley Rats and the rest of them?" He leaned in as if to smell me, but curled his lip in disgust. "You're all the same. But the real question is... why are you here?"

Finally, he glanced at Lee, where then his expression shifted from disgust to fury. "Did you think you could save some of them?" Poor Heather on Lee's lap appeared to be coming to. She was shaking, crying a little, and now was clinging to Lee like he was her lifeline. "Did you think you could walk into *my* club, and try to pass yourself off as anything other than West-End trash? You both reek of it." I attempted to pull myself free, but his other hand whipped up, clasping a handful of my hair tight in his grasp as he practically snarled, "Come in and what? I'm listening, kid. What was your master plan? I'm trying to see your angle. Coming here alone? No backup?" he tsked, and shook his head. "Now,

I am asking for *one* thing from you, and one thing only…" He looked back at me, his lower lip quivering slightly in his rage. "What. Is. Your. Surname?"

"C-Cooper… it's Cooper."

He narrowed his eyes, as if he didn't believe me. Pulling me so close, that our noses were just inches from each other, he murmured, "Who are your parents?"

"M-my mom died about a month ago. Car crash. Her name was Liza."

"Your father," he said quickly, not giving a shit about my mother.

"Keith… Keith Cooper."

His eyes twitched slightly, and that pent-up fury burning in his eyes continued to simmer. "Keith Cooper?" He peered over at one of his men, who pulled out a tablet and began tapping the screen furiously. No one dared say a word as we waited, until the guy looked up and shook his head. The grip on my wrist loosened, and Elias sat back in his seat and laughed. He laughed and laughed, the sound like nails on a chalkboard to me. He sounded fucking insane. When he finally stopped, he seemed positively gleeful, like something amazing had just happened to him, and if Elias was happy, then the rest of us were fucked.

"Bruce, take this one into the basement with Heather," he said, releasing me at last as he shoved me to the floor. I fell on my back as Lee shouted, rising to his feet after moving Heather aside and out of harm's way.

"Stop it! Stop!" Lee shouted as Elias's men circled in. I looked up from where I was lying on the floor to see the bastard himself lounging back on the chesterfield, sipping his drink, his eyes on me like I was some sort of trophy. I fought against the men reaching for me, using my nails, kicking, and sliding backward towards Lee, who was standing before Heather, fists raised, daring anyone to come near him.

"Enough of this bullshit. Dispose of him, get the girls downstairs." Elias sounded bored now.

I watched as one of his men drew a gun out from beneath his suit, and I heard a ringing in my ears over the club's music. I was about to throw myself at him, when there was a sudden commotion from the foyer. Behind the double doors, I could hear shouting, screaming, and gunfire. Everyone stopped to look just as the doors blasted open. The beast that was Animal was entering the room with a goddamn pump-action rifle. He raised it, pointing at the one standing with the pistol, slid the forestock forward and back, and pulled the trigger.

The shot was louder than I expected, with more pop to it, and Elias's man crumpled to the floor while the others surrounded their boss, shielding him from the attack. More guns were drawn, but Lee moved, stepping to the closest guy, sliding a set of brass knuckles onto his fingers, and punched the guy directly in his throat. The guy choked, falling back, as spittle and blood spewed from his mouth. More men entered, and I saw Maverick and Taz drawing arms amongst them, and then they all started shooting. The girls all threw themselves to the floor for cover while I crawled to Heather, hoping to reach her and get her out of harm's way, when I felt a hand clasp my ankle and pull me back. I rolled, knowing that whoever had me wouldn't be able to maintain the hold as the quick movement would twist their wrist. I heard a grunt from behind me over all the chaos, and I peered over my shoulder quickly to see who it was.

Elias held his arm, huddled behind a knocked-over table, using it as a shield. Good. I flipped him off when he glared daggers at me, and I scrambled towards my group.

Not today, asshole. All around me, men were dropping. Glasses and lights exploded overhead, showering me in broken shards and sparks.

"Casey!"

Lee snagged the back of my dress and hauled me to my feet. He had Heather under his other arm, and we swiftly moved along the wall towards the Black Spades, while Elias and his men backed away to get some cover.

"Go, go!" Maverick shouted to us, reaching out to grab Lee's shoulder. He pushed us behind him, using his body as a barrier of protection while his men continued to shoot, giving us a chance to escape. The foyer had three bodies lying on the floor, one of them being the security guy that drew the star on the back of my hand. But we just stepped over them, running out the door.

The honking of a car horn alerted us to the two SUVs parked about twenty feet away. I could see Vail behind the wheel of one, motioning us over. We ran towards it, my ankles twisting a little from my stupid heels, which I ended up kicking off. I ignored the cuts into the bottom of my feet as I ran. The back passenger side door flew open, and Shaw was there, arms open, ready to grab me. I threw myself at him, and he pulled me in, followed closely by Lee, Heather, and Maverick. The door slammed shut, and Vail pushed on the gas, our tires peeling for a second on the cold, slippery ground before we lurched forward, taking off down the drive. The second one, with the rest of the Spades in it, followed close behind. I was sitting on Shaw's lap, my arms clasped tightly around his neck as I clung to him, gasping with each breath I took. I couldn't stop shaking.

"Hold on!" Vail shouted and pressed harder on the gas. We flew down the drive and burst through the chain-link gate, knocking it completely off and sending it flying into the street. I squeezed my eyes shut as we turned, speeding up the street before taking one of the backroads out of there.

"Is everyone okay? None of you kids hurt?" Maverick

shouted, reaching for us as though wanting to check for injuries.

"She's going to need medical attention," Lee panted, still holding Heather up.

"I'll take her. We'll make sure she gets what she needs." She was passed to Maverick, who carefully buckled her into the seat beside him, and checked her arms, noting the needle tracks and bruising there. He glanced over at me. "How about you, honey? You okay?"

"I-I'm fine," I said, my teeth chattering together. Shaw held me tight, his hand rubbing my back to try to calm me, but I was so freaked out and shocked by what just went down that I couldn't think straight. Am I fine? Compared to Heather, I've never been better. But holy shit... what the fuck happened back there?

Chapter eighteen

Shaw: Eleven Years Old

"You-you're what?"

"We're moving to The Hill," Casey said, her eyes on her lap. She spoke so softly I could barely hear her, and even though she repeated herself, I still couldn't believe I was hearing her right.

"You're leaving Harley," Vail said, his voice flat as he watched her closely. Vail, Lee, and I were sitting on the grass in her backyard, facing her as she sat across from us, looking like her world was ending.

It felt like *my* fucking world was ending. I didn't want to believe this. It couldn't be true. I could feel that familiar numb tingle flowing through me, rising up from my chest to my face, out to the tips of my fingers. I hunched over where I sat, trying to focus on my breathing. If I kept breathing, then that meant I was alive. And if I was alive, then that meant *he* didn't win. *He* didn't get to me. Wish I'd pulled a Vail and just killed the fucker when I had the chance.

Vail had come home to find his dad beating on his mother in the kitchen with a rolling pin. Don't know why, it was just what he did. Vail grabbed the mallet she'd been using to flatten the dough, walked up behind him, and swung. He told me his dad hadn't fallen, that he only had stumbled away from his mother, which was what he wanted. As soon as he left her alone, Vail went to work, smashing his dad's face and head with the mallet, again and again, his mother screaming at him to stop. It was deemed self-defense, and while Vail went through a psychological evaluation after, he was seen as a hero child, protecting his mother from the abusive asshole she had been trapped with. Little did they know that Vail had been waiting for an opportunity to do that to his old man for a while.

Then there was me... the little chickenshit... the one who had trembled in his father's presence, who just laid there like a fucking frozen statue, trying not to cry out in fear at night when the door opened, and the bed shifted when he'd climb in behind me. I was weak. I was pathetic. It was because of my father that I couldn't allow people to touch me. It made me sick. To physically be touched by someone actually hurt, and I cringed away every time.

Only Casey...

She's the only one who didn't scare me. She's the one who I trusted with every fibre of my soul, whose touch was nothing but warm and good.

And now, she was telling me that she was leaving.

"When?" Lee asked, his playful smile completely gone. I could hear it in their voices. They were as devastated as I was.

"November first," she mumbles, picking at the dead grass.

I could hear the rushing of my heart in my ears, and I dropped my head, clutching at my hair as I tried not to scream. I could feel a few strands rip free from my skull, but

I didn't fucking care. I didn't want anything but her, and she was leaving.

"We'll stay in touch, right?" she whispered, and I could hear the break in her voice. No, Casey never cried. If she did, I wouldn't be able to take it.

"Of course," Vail said, sounding as strong as he always did. "We'll call all the time."

"And you guys will visit me at my new house?" she asked, the hope evident in her voice.

"Any time you want us." I could practically hear the smile I was sure had been plastered across his face. The Hill? Yeah fucking right... the rich snobs of Ashland would have heart attacks if the three of us appeared in their community.

"I can come visit, too," she said, sounding more like herself. "For our Saturday night sleepovers."

"Sure, we can have them at my place," Lee offered, knowing full well that the last people who would be fit to have the four of us over were my aunt and uncle and Vail's mother. My aunt was a gambling addict and was always gone, hanging out at the casino on the North-End of town. Meanwhile, my actual blood relative, my uncle, was a hardass and lacked any sort of nurturing instincts. I had to fend for myself in their shithole of a house. I scrounged for food when I knew they'd done the shopping, grabbing what I could from the pantry to hide beneath my floorboards to save for when they both went on benders or disappeared for too long. I needed to know I had that reserve. And Vail's mom? She was a fucking ghost. He might as well be living in that bungalow on his own for all she did to support him.

"That sounds great," Casey said, her fingers playing with a dead flower from her mother's garden, a hellebore. "Yeah, it'll be like it always was." I heard the fake optimism in her voice like she'd been trying to convince herself and not us. "We'll still talk and hang out. I mean, it'll be hard during the week being at a new school, but at least I can call you guys and give you new names to add to our list of people to kick the shit out of." Her little laugh faltered and broke. When my gaze sharply cut to hers, I saw how even though she was smiling, her brows were pulled tight, and her eyes were glassy with unshed tears. "And yeah, I'll be lonely without you three at recess, but I'll just… I dunno… make up some new games we can play when we get together on weekends, right? Right?" Her voice cracked on the last word, and I couldn't fucking take it anymore.

I reacted without thinking, my body taking over like it started doing in the later years before my father was finally put behind bars for all the hell and pain he had put me through. My mind checked out, going along for the ride, while my whole system went into fight or flight mode.

And right now? It was flight mode.

I didn't remember running. I didn't remember hearing anyone calling my name or the feel of the branches of trees as they whipped across my cheeks, cutting the skin while I raced through the grey, dead forest, my feet hard and heavy on the ground that was littered with fallen leaves and twigs.

"Shaw!"

I shook my head, not stopping. If I stopped, then I'd have to face what was happening… that the only good fucking thing in my life, my brothers, Casey, our little family… was being torn apart. My *heart* was being torn apart. I could feel it pounding in my chest, but it hurt. It always fucking hurt. Except for those nights when I had Casey at my side with Vail and Lee close by. Those were the only times I felt safe and loved.

Not anymore… a voice whispered to me.

"Nooooo!" I screamed, my voice ripping out of my throat. Something in my arms whimpered, and I blinked hard, trying to focus. Since when was I carrying something? I looked down to see Casey crushed to my front, my arms wrapped around her so tight, she was practically forced into a little ball at my chest. "No," I rasped, stopping to collapse on the carpet of crinkly, dead leaves, and loosened my grip. "No, Casey, I'm sorry!" I croaked. She stirred in my arms, looking up at me with her beautiful, dark, doe-like eyes, and slowly, she reached up and placed a cold hand on my cheek and wiped a tear away. Huh, I didn't realize I was crying.

But I was.

I was fucking sobbing, heaving gut-wrenching wails, which felt like they were bursting out of me, having been held back for so long, like a dam that was breaking. I wouldn't cry in front of my father when he raped me or beat me down, my back a myriad of spider-webbing scars, evidence of his handiwork. I didn't cry when they finally took me away from him and my sad excuse of a mother. And I sure as fuck didn't cry when my new "home" proved to be as neglectful and unloving as the first. It was because I always had *them*. My real family. And it was falling apart.

I desperately clung to her, sobbing into her dark hair. "Casey… no-oooo…" I moaned, feeling like I was going to be sick. "Please no… don't leave me here. Don't…"

"Shaw," she whispered, her hands coming up to stroke my back. She never asked me about the scars she felt beneath my shirt. She wasn't like other people, who looked at them with pity and disgust. Other kids were grossed out by the marks my father's belt had left behind, a forever reminder of a taste of the pain he put me through. But Casey, she touched them lovingly, never flinching away, and never looked at me like I was something vile. In her eyes, I was *worthy*. And she was leaving me.

"Casey, please…" I choked out past my sobs as the sounds of approaching footsteps crunched over the leaves and twigs, signalling Vail and Lee's arrival.

"It'll be okay, Shaw. I'll call you, alright? I promise," she said as the other two sat on the forest floor close beside us. "We'll see each other all the time. It will be as it always was."

But that wasn't true. How could it be? She would be on the opposite side of the city in Snob-Central. They would have her every day, and I knew those pricks there wouldn't appreciate the gift they were given. Not like me, or Vail or Lee.

Vail shifted a little, and when I met his eyes over Casey's head, I saw the way his eyes were shining as he held back his own tears, but I didn't like the look on his face. It was too… controlled. And the way Lee was shaking, his head bowed over his lap, I knew that they had been talking in our absence. I wasn't going to like this.

"Right, guys?" Casey whispered, pulling back a bit to see them. As soon as she did, they both plastered fake smiles onto their faces, just as we heard Liza call her name in the distance, demanding she returns home for supper. As much as I appreciated Liza and everything she did for me, I hated her at this moment.

"Obviously," Vail rolled his eyes, his cocky, strong attitude back in place. "You think we'd let you move to a mansion and *not* have us over? We're gonna wreak hell on those rich bastards."

Lee nodded, though he wasn't hiding his feelings as well as Vail, in my opinion, "I can't wait for them to see us show up on your doorstep. Might cut you down on popularity points with the brat pack," he added, using a word we called the kids of the insanely wealthy on The Hill.

"Casey Suzanne Cooper!" her mother shouted into the woods from the edge of her property. "I know you all are playing in there! Get in for supper now!"

Casey looked up at me, cradling my face in her hands, and

wiped several more tears away with her thumbs. "See, Shaw? It'll be okay. I promise. We'll still be together."

I didn't trust myself to speak, especially when I noticed Vail watching me carefully, as though warning me not to fight her. So I just nodded, dropping my head, feeling like a part of my soul was pulling away as she rose to stand. I held her hand until the last possible second when her fingertips left mine, and she waved to us as she started back to her house. "I'll see you guys tomorrow, okay? We can challenge Hunter and his goons to a softball game and totally kick their asses!" She smirked, thinking of the last time we played them, before turning and running away.

"So, what's the deal?" I muttered, not looking at Vail when she eventually vanished from sight. I could sense it. He was going to say something that was going to ultimately piss me the fuck off. If I looked at his face while he said it, I wouldn't be able to stop myself from punching him right in his nose.

"Shaw, Casey has an opportunity to have a better life-"

"I know that!" I spit. She was going to live in the East End. She'll be out of Harley, free... and from what I've heard about her mom's new boyfriend, he honestly sounded too good to be true.

"If we keep bringing her back here to spend time with us... what do you think is gonna happen?"

No... he was really going to do this. I vehemently shook my head, clawing at the ground over and over again, my nails leaving gouges in the dirt.

"She won't ever leave," Lee said, his voice oddly flat, quite unlike his usual M.O. The traitor. He was going along with this.

"I love her," I rasped, my throat hurting from all the crying and screaming I'd done.

"I know you do," Vail murmured gently, and I felt his hand lightly touch my shoe, as though testing me to see if it was okay. I was okay with them touching me... *sometimes*. It just wasn't the same as when she did it. Though I flinched a little now, I remained where I was, eyes squeezed shut and fingers digging deeper into the earth. "We all love her," he said softly.

That I knew.

We all loved her. We all needed her in our own way. But we also needed each other. That was why we never fought about it. Sure, we liked to flaunt it when she gave one of us special attention, showing off to the other guys, but at the end of the day, we were a unit. And they were my brothers. We only worked well when we were together, and now, the most essential piece of our foursome was leaving, and they were letting it happen.

"If she calls, don't pick up," Vail said, his voice cracking ever so slightly. "If she writes, throw out the letter. If she tries to visit, we're busy." He was speaking as it'd already been decided.

"She *wants* us," I groaned, wishing the pain in my chest would stop. "She wants to be with us, I know it. Why do this?"

"Because we're all she knows," Vail sounded a little stronger now. "Once she adjusts to her new life and sees what opportunities and security she has there, she might want it more. Who are we to keep her in this shithole with us? That's not love."

Yeah, yeah, the whole, if you love something, you let it go, spiel. I fucking hate that saying. It's bullshit. If you love something, you hold onto it for dear life. There was too much bad shit in this world. That was why when you found something good, you kept it close, cared for it, and loved it with everything you had.

"I don't know if I can," Lee murmured finally. My head whipped up, feeling a bubble of hope. If Lee was on my side, we could overrule Vail. Why did we have to do what he said, anyway?

"It's gonna be hard," Vail agreed with him but shook his head. "But think about what is best for *her*. Not what *we* want."

Fuck him... seriously, fuck him. As much as I hated this, as much as it made me feel like I would never be happy again, he was right. What *was* best for Casey? We all talked about escaping Harley, but it had always been *together*. Not apart.

"What if..." I wiped my eyes one last time, vowing never to cry again if I could help it. Fuck this feeling. "What if she *does* come back?"

"Why the fuck would she come back to Harley?" Vail scoffed. He was lounging in the leaves, leaning on one elbow, while his legs were stretched out before him, crossed at the ankles. I could swear, this bastard was too good at turning off his emotions. Yet when he loses it, he was the scariest motherfucker I'd ever seen. He would change, becoming a monster, but the one that protected. I would never be afraid of him hurting any of us, even though he has one murder under his belt. He moved on from it as nothing had happened.

"She *could* possibly," Lee agreed with me, also watching Vail. "I don't know why she would, but maybe if her mom and Matthew separate, or if her new school bullies her to the point where Liza lets her come back here, where she's comfortable-"

"Liza wouldn't do that," Vail said thoughtfully. "She wouldn't send Casey to attend school here just cuz the rich kids might give her a hard time. Besides, she's tough as shit. They won't be able to break her down." He sounded proud as he spoke of Casey, and I got it. We were *all* proud of how she always handled herself. Tough with assholes, sweet with us... *most* of the time.

"Whatever, fuck the reason, then," Lee pressed on, staring Vail down as he leaned toward him, almost like he was challenging him. I observed, curious to see how this would play out. "I want to make some things clear… we'll play along and leave her alone, as hard as it will be, I agree with you. She needs to take advantage of this opportunity. *But…*" he added, holding up a finger, "She comes back to Harley, comes back into our lives, then we get to hold on. No more pushing her away. I wouldn't be able to handle that."

"Me neither," I added, watching Vail, daring him to disagree with us.

Vail went quiet for a minute, staring off through the trees as though lost in thought before he finally nodded. "Fine. If she comes back, but *only* for a real reason… not cuz she's pulling one of her brat-moments, and being stubborn and angry with us for ignoring her…" he sighed heavily, and I felt a spark of hope flicker in my chest when he nodded again. "Then we can keep her."

Chapter nineteen

Casey

OUR CARS SPLIT UP, the Spades going in one direction, while ours moved into downtown Ashland before circling the north end of the city where Vail could pull into a junkyard, up alongside a beater car. We climbed out of the SUV, leaving Heather in Maverick's care as he climbed into the front seat. He rolled down his window, locking eyes with Vail. "Fucking watch out, okay?" His eyes flickered to me before he added, "He was a little too interested in Casey for my liking."

I could feel everyone's eyes on me, and I shrank further into Shaw's arms. My hands were still shaking, my heart racing from what had happened. I couldn't believe we made it out of there in one piece.

"You guys keep an eye out," Maverick added as Lee opened the door to the run-down car, fished a key from under the seat, and started it, turning the heat on. "Elias will send the Jackals after her." He peered over his shoulder at the girl buckled in the back. "I'll make sure she gets the help she needs."

"Thanks, Maverick," Vail sighed heavily, running his hands through his bronze hair over and over again like he was stressed to hell. I didn't blame him. It came too fucking close tonight.

"You guys need the Spades, just message me, okay?" Maverick said. "Not gonna leave you kids alone to deal with this shit." He glances at me again before quickly looking away. "Things have just gotten a little more complicated..." The window slid up, and Maverick pulled away, disappearing out of the junkyard, heading south.

Not saying a word to each other, we all climbed into the beater car, Shaw and I snuggled close in the back, and Vail got in the passenger side while Lee drove us home. It was late, and from the black sky, flakes continued to fall, drifting down around us, coating the trees, buildings, and dead ground in a light blanket of white, beautifying everything. A sharp contrast to what we just went through.

By the time we parked in the parking lot of our townhome, I felt like I was about to pass the fuck out. My head was drooping on Shaw's chest, and I could barely keep my eyes open. The only reason I hadn't fallen completely asleep was that the heater in this car wasn't the best, and the cold air was biting at my skin. Shaw took off his jacket a while ago and tried to cover me as best he could with it, seeing as all I had on was this skimpy dress and no shoes, but all I wanted was to curl up in Vail's bed with my boys around me.

We parked in the empty spot beside Haldon's little car, and Lee carried me inside so I didn't have to step on the snow-covered ground. Meredith greeted us immediately, panic written all over her face. "I got the texts! Holy shit... I can't believe you all made it out okay!" She grabbed me, pulling me free from Lee's arms and hugging me tight, whispering over and over again, "I'm so sorry. So, so sorry! It should have been me there."

"Don't be ridiculous," I said, my voice cracking slightly. "What if something had happened to you? What about Amelie?"

Meredith's grip on me tightened before she finally nodded and let me go. She wiped away tears running down her face as Haldon appeared at the top of the stairs, his lips pressed tightly together and arms crossed over his puffed-out chest. He looked like he was holding back the urge to punch a hole in the wall. We wearily trudged up the steps and found the main living space empty, save for a movie that was paused on the TV screen that Mer and Haldon must have been watching.

"The Americans went to bed not too long ago," Haldon said, "And no unusual activity. Heard back from all three posts and nothing from the Jackals. Whatever happened with you all tonight, I don't think Elias has contacted them... yet."

Vail nodded, looking even more exhausted than any of us. I couldn't say I blamed him. He was our leader. He had to make all the decisions concerning everyone's welfare. And I also thought that seeing Heather like that rocked him a bit. "Are you two sure you don't wanna crash here tonight?" He asked the couple as they started to pull on their coats. "It's fucking late."

"Thanks, but we gotta relieve poor Eli," Meredith said, zipping up her coat. "And I want to be with Amelie the moment I open my eyes in the morning." She was off, like she was feeling extremely rattled by what went down tonight. That could easily have been her, but I was fucking glad it wasn't. If something had happened to her, then Amelie would be motherless, and Haldon would lose the love of his life.

"Message me when you're in, and the doors are locked,"

Vail told them, "Fucking watch out for any signs of being followed, and for any Jackals or Beasts. We need to lie low. I don't know what the hell Elias is gonna do now. We need to stay safe."

Haldon simply nodded and held out a hand to Meredith, pulling her in close under his arm before Shaw escorted them out, arming the place once they left.

The four of us headed upstairs, all squashing into the washroom to clean up. Lee jumped into the shower with me, carefully soaping me down and helping me wash my hair. I was still fucking shaking.

Goddammit! Get it together, Casey! I snapped at myself, wishing I could be stronger in this moment. Lee, despite the situation we had found ourselves in, was completely calm and cool. His movements were methodical, and his focus was entirely on helping me. As I washed the makeup off my face, I could hear Shaw and Vail moving around, washing up by the sink, murmuring to each other, their voices too quiet to be heard over the shower.

Finally, Lee shut off the water and gently toweled me off, stopping every few seconds to kiss my shoulder, my damp head, or my lips. "You're okay, baby," he murmured to me, carefully toweling me off. "I got you." He slid the curtain back, but the washroom was empty. However, it looked like one of the others had gotten our sleepwear for us, because my pajamas were sitting on the counter next to a pair of grey sweats for Lee. By the time I changed into my sleep pants and tank top, my damp hair braided down my back, and Lee had dried off and changed, we quietly slipped into Vail's room.

Vail had pulled his mattress off the box frame and it seemed like they also made a second section out of extra blankets and comforters beside it, so we could all lie together. I was so grateful for this, because what I needed most right now was feeling all my guys were here with me at that moment. One bullet, one misstep, and we could have lost one of us forever. We all fell into bed together, pulling up the blankets to cover us as we snuggled in. I had Vail on one side, Lee on the other, and Shaw was curled up between my legs, his head using my stomach as a pillow. Outside, the wind started to blow, and I could just picture the snowflakes as they whirled about in mini cyclones. Knowing that it was storming out there while I was snuggled up with the three most important people in my life in bed, safe and loved, had me smiling a little to myself, my eyes closed, and the feeling of sleep not far away…

"Fuck, that's it, Cherry Pie… rake your nails under my balls!"

What in the actual fuck?! My eyes snapped open as the sounds from the next room penetrated the thin walls. I could hear moaning, a small creak from Lee's bed, and then after about half a minute of this, the sound of Shelby gasping and gagging.

"Take me down your throat, baby. Fuck I love the sound of you choking on my dick…"

Beside me, Lee let out a small, agonized groan and I had to smother my mouth with both my hands. I knew that Logan had been rubbing him the wrong way since he got here, and hearing this going on in *his* bedroom must be pure torture.

The sounds changed, the creaking of the bed picking up as Logan and Shelby started fucking each other. The deep grunting from him, and her high-pitched cries were too loud and obnoxious to ignore. I held back a fit of giggles when Lee bemoaned, "That's *my* fucking bed! I could have gone my whole life hoping beyond hope that they hadn't screwed in it, but hearing it happen? No, fuck no!" He took one of the pillows and crushed it around his face, like he was hoping suffocation would solve all his problems.

That was when I heard Micha from down the hall. "Shut the FUCK up!" Well, at least Shaw's bed seemed to be safe from being fucked on tonight. But Micha's indignant shouting only seemed to encourage Logan, because the creaking of the bed escalated to the headboard now banging against the wall that was shared with Shaw's room.

"How much should I bet that if I left my knives in there, they'd all be on the floor now?" Shaw muttered into my stomach, and I choked on my laughter, realizing that the head of Lee's bed lined up perfectly with his closet.

"That's right, take me. Take all of me, my pretty little slut," Logan panted heavily, his pace picking up. Shelby's squeals heightened, and I couldn't help but think that Vail and Logan might be matched for stamina. I peeked over at Vail, who looked like he had passed the hell out beside me, not giving a shit about anything that was going on right now. The only sign that he was awake was that one of his hands was resting over my head, his fingers lightly stroking the slightly damp strands of my hair.

Lee, meanwhile, was losing his mind, cursing under his breath, and rolling around beside me, trying to find a position using the pillow and the mattress that would best suppress the noise through the wall.

I couldn't help but feel a wave of wickedness come over me at that moment; listening to Logan fucking the shit out of his girl in the next room was sort of turning me on. Between my legs, Shaw was still holding onto me, but with a free hand, I reached over, lightly running my nails over Lee's bare stomach. He stilled, laying on his back, the pillow still over his face, as I ran my fingertips down his waist, moving up and down that delicious V of his.

He didn't stop me as I slid my hand over his sweats,

stroking at his dick. It was semi-hard, but I'd change that. Slowly, I started gently massaging the bulge, concentrating on his reaction, his breathing. Sure enough, it changed, and he shifted his hips a little so I could reach him more comfortably. Logan and Shelby didn't sound even remotely close to being done in the next room, and I listened to their grunting and panting, using it to spur me on. I felt Lee's cock twitch as it started to harden, coming to life at my touch. When I peeked over at him again, in the dimness of the room, I saw he had removed the pillow, and his eyes were on me, shining in the low, orange light coming in from the streetlamp outside. I licked my lips as I reached back to slide my hand beneath the hemline, stroking the bare skin of his hips before I reached for his thick length. I quickly pulled out to lick my hand a little, reached in again, and slowly started pumping him.

Meanwhile, Shaw's head had lifted, resting his chin on my belly as he watched what Lee and I were doing with interest. Vail, however, was still lightly stroking my hair, apparently unaware of what I was doing. For a minute, I thought Shaw was just going to watch, but then I felt his lips on my bare skin, having pushed my tank top up a bit. His soft, pillowy lips moved around my belly button before moving down to my hips, and then I felt his tongue trail down, moving towards my center, and I trembled a little beneath him at that featherlight touch.

His fingers curled under the waistline of my cotton pants, and he shimmied them down, with me lifting myself a little making it easier. He got them all the way off, leaving me bare before him, all while I continued to stroke Lee, squeezing him, circling my finger over the tip, moving the damp precum that had gathered there around.

Shaw moved down the mattress, his sparkling deep blue eyes holding mine before he buried his face between my thighs, his tongue lightly flicking at my clit before he started to suck. I sighed, letting my head flop back and I started to pump Lee a little harder now. Behind me, Vail shifted, and I knew he was finally clued in to what was happening. On the other side of the wall, it sounded as though Logan had moved Shelby around, because the banging of the headboard stopped, but it was clear they were still fucking.

"Seriously, shut the fuck up, Hudson!" Micha shouted angrily.

"How about *you* shut up! I'm trying to sleep!" Riley snapped back. I giggled, despite the building tension Shaw was creating between my legs. I could imagine that poor Micha Kessler was suffering from major blue balls since his injury. Well, either way, I was not stopping because he wasn't getting any at the moment.

From behind, one of Vail's hands slid over my tank top, curling around my left breast before he leaned over me, kissing up the length of my throat. A little sigh escaped my lips when his teeth nipped below my ear before his mouth crushed over mine, his tongue demanding entry. I kissed him back, my hips thrusting up into Shaw as his hands spread my legs wider, sucking, licking, and biting at me, all while Lee moaned at my side, my hand still working him nice and slow.

"No, no, Cherry Pie... you get down on your knees..." Logan's voice was muted a little through the walls, but it was still clear enough. Next thing I heard, was the hard smack-smack as he clearly started fucking her from behind on the floor.

Vail was holding my face in one hand, the other reaching over to my right breast, sliding my top down to free it, and then pinching my nipple hard. I gasped into his mouth as he kept kissing me, and below, Shaw inserted a finger inside of me, curling it along as he thrust it in and out while he attacked my clit with a sudden surge of energy. I know Lee wants things to escalate by the way he was moving his hips into my hand, but I just needed Shaw to finish what he started. I hungrily kissed Vail back, loving the feel of his tongue on mine as he kissed me like a man starved.

My legs began to quiver, and my knees involuntarily tried to squeeze shut, but Shaw's hands pressed down on them, flattening them to the mattress, before going back to eating me out in an almost frenzied passion. With each groan, he emitted vibrations against my clit and I gasped as that addictive rising pulse quickened. I'm so fucking close!

"No, no, not yet." Logan's voice floated through the wall. "You don't get to come yet. Not until I say..."

The familiar phrase pushed me over the edge and I cried out as my orgasm exploded. I fought to lift my hips, desperate to squeeze my legs together, to pull the feeling into me, but Shaw wouldn't let go. He kept going, while Vail sucked on my throat, squeezing and pinching my nipples.

"Fuck... enough of this..." Lee grunted finally. He reached over while I trembled from my orgasm, but he didn't give me a moment to recover. Sitting up, his back against the box frame of Vail's bed, he slid me down over his dick, thrusting up with a loud smack, and I moaned as it only made the orgasm Shaw had just given me pulse again. Holding me over him, Lee began to thrust up into me so fast, I squeezed my eyes shut, his pelvis smacking hard into mine with each sharp push of his hips.

"Oh... my... God!" I cried out as he moved so hard and fast, I felt like I was experiencing one never-ending orgasm. I held onto his shoulders, head falling backwards towards the ceiling. But it wasn't long until Vail reached over and turned me to look at him so he could continue kissing me while his brother wildly fucked me. I had no idea where Shaw was, but at the moment, I couldn't think of anything else other than the feeling of Lee's thick cock inside of me, and Vail's tongue that was rolling over mine. It felt as though my orgasm never fully stopped, but when Vail reached down to furiously stroke my clit, I cried out, pulling away from his mouth as I felt myself coming again.

"Does everyone need to fuck tonight?" Micha yelled, but I ignored him. I wasn't gonna shut up for anyone.

Beneath me, Lee slammed me down several more times before he stilled inside of me, bathing my inner walls with his cum. I clenched around him, feeling the tears breaking free from the corners of my eyes as the rushing euphoria overwhelmed me. "Lee?" I whispered to him.

"Yes, gorgeous?" he panted, pressing several kisses along my collarbone.

"I love you, too."

Lee froze for just a second before reaching up to kiss me hungrily. I held his face, getting lost in his intoxicating kiss, the feel of his cock still buried inside of me. It felt so primal and beautiful to be with him at this moment that I didn't want it to end. Only...

Now, it was Vail's turn.

When I broke the kiss to catch my breath, Vail lifted me off of Lee's lap and sat next to him, lining me up over his long, curved cock, before he slowly slid me down, fully sheathing himself.

"Vail, I-I don't think I can-"

"You can, and you will. Now fuck me, darling." He held onto my waist and started rocking me over him, slowly at first, and I whimpered as my clit was practically throbbing at this point. "You're gonna come on my dick," he breathed, moving me back and forth over his lap, "You're gonna squeeze around me. Your hot, wet cunt begging for me to cream in you." His lips brushed against mine. "Isn't that right? My girl wants my cum in her?"

I bit my lip, the feeling in my legs coming back as Vail

moved me on him. I wrapped my arms around his neck, bracing my knees on the ground, and started to take over the movement. I stared deep into his hazel depths, my hips moving faster, the sound of our bodies sliding together just turning me on again. Vail grinned as I took over, his arms wrapping around me, holding me close as I fucked him, our eyes refusing to leave each other's.

"I fucking love you," he whispered against my lips, his tongue snaking out to glide over the bottom one before he sucked on it. "I seriously fucking love you more than anything. You're fucking it for me..." He kissed me hard and braced his hands under my ass before he stood and walked over to the wall, smashing me against it. He held me up by crushing his hips into mine, holding me there, and he felt so deep that I felt my eyes roll back into my head. "No matter what, I'm not close enough to you. I'm not deep enough. If I could have it my way, I'd never leave your delicious pussy." He gave the smallest of thrusts, pressing me back against the wall, and my toes curled. "When this bullshit is all over, and we've escaped this shithole together, I'm going to fuck you all hours of the day." He ran his tongue up my throat, his lips brushing against my ear. "I'm gonna buy a sex swing, strap you up in it, and fuck you for days... and it will still not be enough."

He started to move, holding me up easily by my ass, thrusts harder and deeper each time, and his breathing began to pick up.

"Vail..." I whispered, feeling like I was drunk on his words.

"Yes, darling?"

"Don't make promises you can't keep."

At that, he loses it and fucks me like an animal against the wall. He was grunting and sucking on my neck, my tits, even my lips, just any part of me he could reach.

"I'm gonna come," he panted after what felt like an age since we started.

"Fucking do it," I goaded him, linking my ankles behind his back.

He pounded into me several more times before he stilled, groaning loudly, and I felt the warmth of his cum fill me. He sagged, and I dropped my legs as he slowly pulled out, lowering me to the ground. But I was shaking so hard, my legs could barely support me. He turned us back to the mattress where Lee was sprawled out, looking utterly relaxed and on the verge of sleep if it wasn't for Vail and me. Logan and Shelby were quiet from the next room, but I had no idea when they stopped.

Shaw was lying at the end of the mattress, his feet lined up with Lee's, and he was watching as Vail supported me, guiding me over. Shaw was completely naked, his utterly massive cock erect and ready, but he didn't look as savage as the other guys did. His expression was soft, unsmiling, but I could see the warmth in his eyes. He reached for me, arms open, and I reached for him, too. Vail carefully passed me to him, and I collapsed on the mattress at his side, while Vail moved over to sleep next to Lee.

But Shaw and I just laid there, on our sides, staring into each other's eyes. One of his arms was wrapped around me, the other resting over my heart, feeling it pounding beneath his palm.

"I'm okay if you're too tired," he whispered.

Hell no, I thought, and my hand inched down between us. I watched his reaction, trying to decipher his feelings to see if this was okay, and to my relief, he didn't flinch or pull away. He let me run my fingers over his insanely huge dick, and I said quietly, "I need you tonight. I need to feel all three of you to know we made it out. We're together, and that's all that matters to me."

Shaw rolled me onto my back, settling himself between my legs. He was careful with his movements, as he pressed his forehead to mine and started to slide his huge girth between my folds. Eyes on me the entire time, he slowly pushed in, and I gasped at how full I felt, the pressure of it. It was probably a good thing Shaw went last, because he would have destroyed me before the other two even got a chance.

But unlike the other two, he went slow. He was not fucking me, he was making love to me. When he kissed me, his lips were soft and a little tentative, but I allowed him to lead. With Shaw, I always had to let him lead. He needed to feel like he was the one in control, and so I held him, returned his gentle kisses, and sighed at each gentle thrust and roll of his hips.

"I'll never let that fucker touch you again," He swore to me, and I knew he was talking about Elias. "If he does, if he tries, I'll fucking *end* him. I'll gladly go to jail for murder. I don't fucking care."

"Shaw-"

"No!" He snapped a little and I stopped. He rolled his hips in a way that had his pelvis rubbing over my clit with each pass, and I eagerly accepted his tender kisses. "Kill... them... all..." he grunted, shifting a little and bringing one of my legs up over his shoulder. "Fucking kill any motherfucker that touches you or tries to take you away..." He closed his eyes and let his head fall back as he got up on his knees, moving a little faster now. My breasts jiggled each time he smacked against me, and at the sight, he reached down, squeezing my left tit with a hand while turning his head to press a lazy kiss to my ankle. At this angle, he was hitting a little too deep with that giant cock of his and I whimpered each time he rocked into me. But I wouldn't stop him. This, what I'd done with all three of them tonight, was as much for them as it was for me. And right now, Shaw needed this.

Suddenly, his eyes snapped open, his expression becoming hungry. He shifted my leg, curling it back behind his hip, and leaned over me again. His thrusting quickened a little, that fucking amazing roll of his hips hitting me just right every time, and I squeezed around him, feeling like I was going to die if I had one more orgasm, but at the same time, I needed it.

"Come in me, Shaw," I begged him. "I want to feel you there, too." I focused on Shaw, my eyes filling with tears as he moved a little faster, his jaw clenched tight, his expression a mixture of pain and pleasure that I knew would probably always haunt him when it came to lovemaking. "Look at *me*, Shaw. You're with me, okay?" I told him fiercely.

He held my gaze, the tortured expression dissipating as he focused, and after another minute, we both came together, holding each other tight as we got lost in each other's eyes. He leaned down and kissed me again before resting his forehead on mine. I felt his dick twitch inside me, but he refused to pull away just yet, so I embraced him close, keeping him there.

From the next room, I heard Logan shout, "Holy shit, they outfucked us? C'mon, Cherry Pie, we're getting showed up-"

"Fuck off, I'm tired!" Shelby whined.

I could hear Lee let out a disgusted grumble from the other side of the bed while Vail's soft breathing told me that he was passed out. From beneath Shaw, I relaxed, my fingers running over his scarred back, keeping him to me. We fell asleep that way, embracing each other, still linked, while from the next room, I heard a squeaking of the mattress, signalling that Logan had gotten his way.

"For the love of... can everybody stop fucking each other so I can get to sleep?" Micha shouted from down the hall.

"How about *you* shut the fuck up?" Riley snapped. "Some of us were sleeping just fine!"

I smiled, exhausted beyond belief, ready to be curled up with my men, safe in our little world. And I did, as I found myself lulled into dreamland to the sound of Logan and Shelby moaning as they picked up where we left off.

If Logan didn't stop whining, I was actually worried that Lee was going to punch him out. When we arrived at the safe-house, which was only a couple of blocks away, it reminded me of the old basement my mother and I had once lived in. It was a little duplex, the top floor belonging to members of Vendetta, a group of students from our school who had escaped a horrible home life, and were living together in this space. They had prepared the suite for our American guests so that by the time we had arrived, the two mattresses in the one bedroom had fresh bedding on them, and the heat and lights were on.

I'd helped them unload their van of their new clothes, some groceries we'd grabbed on the way over (thanks to the leftover money Maverick had given Lee last night), and helped Shelby put things away while the guys assisted Logan in getting Micha and Riley inside in one piece. The entire morning, Logan complained about how cold it was, that his dick was going to freeze and fall off if it didn't stop snowing soon. Riley muttered threats to him under her breath, although she and Micha did spend breakfast shivering under a blanket on the chesterfield. Shelby, however, was totally entranced by the blanket of white that covered everything, and ate her cereal by the window beside the dining table.

Despite last night's sexcapades, no one mentioned anything about hearing each other this morning, until Logan saw Vail and said, "Hey! It's the jackhammer!"

I didn't bother telling him that, in fact, it hadn't just been

Vail and me. I felt like that information would just make his head explode. But Vail took advantage of his assumption of us being together by being incredibly handsy all morning, insisting that I sit on his knee at breakfast while he sat back in the lounger next to the couch so he could talk to Micha.

Now that we had them in the safehouse, and Micha was settled on the old brown and orange couch which was most definitely still alive from the eighties, Vail was standing next to him, giving him instructions and knowledge of the area. At the same time, Logan protested at the notion of living in the sort of place he would bury someone and not live in, while Riley had claimed it was better than the apartment she grew up in.

"Do *not* let your girls out on their own-" Vail was saying, which caught Riley's attention from the opposite end of the couch.

"What was that?" she snapped angrily. "What is it with you men and your chauvinistic-"

"*Because*," Vail narrowed his eyes at her, "There are MC grabbing girls. We rescued one of them last night from a trafficking ring."

Riley stopped talking at once and immediately sank back into the couch.

"I'm sorry to snap at you, but this is something we've been trying to figure out for months, and last night, we finally found one." He turned back to Micha. "So if you have to go out anywhere, it'll probably have to be Logan and Riley."

"What?" Riley furrowed her brow. "I can't go anywhere with this thing on my leg!"

"You blend in better with the people here," Lee said, bringing in the last of their stuff. "You're a little spitfire, and you can take care of yourself. And *that* guy shouldn't be allowed out alone since he was probably going to end up getting himself thrown into a dumpster. Your boyfriend is too sick. And the blonde..." He nodded his head down the hall where Shelby and Logan had disappeared to with their clothes. "She stands out. No offense meant, but with your injury, you can't exactly dance on tables or be used to fuck a guy silly, which is what they're looking for."

At that, Micha looked to Riley and shook his head at her, his dark brows pulled down over his eyes as though sensing she'd challenge this somehow. I fully expected her to speak up, but this time, she didn't. Instead, she slumped back and muttered something that sounded like, "Logan is definitely going to end up getting thrown into a dumpster..."

"Use these while you're here." Vail produced two burner cells he'd asked one of the members of Vendetta to pick up for us this morning. "The only numbers programmed in are each other, so you guys can call when you're out, a contact for Daniel and the other Vendetta members who live above you, and mine. We're lying low for the next little bit here because of what happened last night with the Faceless-"

"Wait, *what?*" Logan re-entered, wearing three pairs of sweats and two hoodies, looking absolutely miserable. "Who the fuck is Faceless? Who's this fucking guy? Now we have to worry about some deformed motherfucker? I told you we should have gone to the island!"

Micha chose to ignore him, and instead of replying, he tossed one of the phones to him, which Logan effortlessly caught.

"It's a goddamn flip phone! Look! There are actual buttons on this thing! It's like a goddamn pager!" He flipped the screen open and closed it again and again, completely fascinated. "I feel like we've time traveled or some shit."

Shelby appeared and reached around him, snatching the phone out of his hand.

"Hey!"

"No, you don't get this anymore. It's my phone now. You lost the right when you bitched about it."

The rest of us gathered near the steps leading up to the shared foyer between the upper and basement suites, watching as Micha reached out to Vail, hand held out, they shook, and said, "Thank you for everything. Just know that once things settle, when I can return the favour, I will."

Chapter twenty

Casey: Two Weeks Later

THESE PAST TWO weeks have been intense. We'd been hiding out, and I'd been homebound, except for the few times we went over to the safehouse to check in on the four Americans. It was always at night, under cover of darkness, that I was allowed to leave. The guys would blanket me up, hiding me (and Lee) in the back of the beater car, before hurrying inside and descending into the basement suite. I brought cards and a few board games along that I'd asked the guys to pick up for me from the dollar store and goodwill, and gave them to our guests to help pass the time.

Logan was absolutely miserable here, and I knew he was waiting for any opportunity to return to Florida. He shuffled around in the basement, wearing layers upon layers of clothes. Micha was starting to look better, but Riley and Shelby were dealing with everything the best. Shelby kept the place neat and clean and looked after Micha whenever Riley and Logan had to make a trip out.

But now, we were back, helping them pack up the place and their things. Micha had gotten in touch with his father and the all-clear had been given for them to return to Florida.

"If you need help, contact me on this number," Micha said, programming one into Vail's cell.

"Hopefully, we won't have to." Vail took the phone back and handed Micha two of the leftover hundred-dollar bills that Maverick had given us the night we were at La Maison Rouge. "For gas and food for your journey back."

Micha pressed his lips together, glancing around the shabby space that he'd called his home for the last two weeks while he recovered. I thought he would say something, but instead, he just nodded, looking like he didn't have words.

Since Riley was still in a cast, Shelby and I helped her up the steps and bundled her up into the back of the minivan. Meanwhile, Logan was throwing stuff into the back, muttering something about how glad he was he was gonna get out of here without his dick freezing off.

We said our final goodbyes, with Lee and I hidden beneath hoods and layers, doing our best to stay covert, and waved them off. The van pulled away, disappearing up the street, heading northwest out of Ashland towards Ottawa.

Now, we were home again, and Vail and I were going at it, yelling each other down.

"That bitch, Ms. McCuntFace, keeps calling and leaving me messages. Do you want her to show up here?" I stormed after him as he tried to evade me in our townhouse and finally cornered him by the fireplace in the living room. "She keeps saying that if I miss another day of school, she'll send me back to fucking Keith! Then what will I do?"

"If she does, she'll be lucky if I let her walk away…"

"Don't!" I seethed at him, frustrated. "You're not immune

to the system as much as you try to be. As corrupt as that bitch is, my meeting with a new caseworker isn't set till December. So she's still in charge of my case until then." I opened my phone and checked the last message from her. "She's been made aware of my two-week absence. Since I have a file with Social Services, I can't get away with missing so much. I need to return to school to get her off my back so I don't get forced back to Keith's. If I'm sent there, I'm more exposed to-"

"We'll do fucking homeschooling then!" he shouted back at me, moving out of his corner and getting right up in my face. His cheeks were red, a vein in his neck bulging, and I knew I'd pushed him too far. "You are *not* stepping back into that school and you're sure as hell not going back to that piece of shit! We're lucky that the Jackals don't know where we live, but being in that school gives them an opening. I won't take that chance! Not with fucking Elias-"

"Vendetta hasn't even seen the Jackals in a week," I reminded him. "They've been MIA. So if we go into Harley Institute tomorrow, who are we hiding from?" The Jackals had been mysteriously silent, and from what we'd heard from Maverick, the Beasts had also been laying low, too. Their informant confirmed that the Faceless haven't been giving them any sort of instruction or orders at all, so they'd been quietly hiding out in their clubhouse in a border town outside of Ashland. Both direct threats weren't around.

Vail raked his fingers through his hair repeatedly, making it stand on end, and sighed heavily. I could sense Lee and Shaw in the background, watching and listening, yet waiting for his final say. After an agonizing minute, he finally straightened and glared down at me. "Fine. We go back tomorrow... but I swear to fucking God, you don't go anywhere in that school without one of us or a member of

Vendetta escorting you." He sidestepped me and headed upstairs, his phone out already texting the others to let them know the change in plans.

I sank into the couch next to Lee and wrapped my arms around his waist, nestling into him while Shaw turned on his gaming system. Upstairs, we could hear the rumble of Vail's voice as he barked out his orders to the others. If we stuck together when we were out in public, we'd be fine. The girls that were taken were done on the sly, quietly, and out of sight. Everywhere I went, people surrounded me. I had no worries about going back. I wish we didn't have to, but if we wanted to get the hell out of Harley, we had to graduate.

"Haldon will escort you from English to P.E., and then Shaw will walk with you to lunch with us. Then I'll-"

"I know, Vail, I know," I cut him off as he started the spiel again for the hundredth time. We were standing outside of Harley Institute, my bulky black winter coat swamping my figure, and the hood pulled up to hide my face. I'd even dyed my lilac hair back to my natural shade of brown last night at his request, as an extra precaution. The purple stood out. This way, it was just another safety measure I agreed to upon returning to school. I was wearing a pair of torn bootcut jeans and a simple fitted pale pink t-shirt and sneakers. It was a sharp contrast to what I wore when I'd initially arrived at this place.

We walked through security with no issues, but the tension in the air was stifling. As we walked down the halls, the four of us moving in tandem, we kept our eyes open for members of the Jackals, but there were none that I recognized. However, the boys knew them all, and as more time passed and no sign of one appeared, I could sense Lee and Shaw relax slightly. Vail remained on high alert, watching anyone moving our way, and nodding to any secret Vendetta member we passed.

All three of my guys followed me up to English on the second floor, but Hunter didn't show up. Haldon, however, strolled in and moved over to where my desk was, taking the seat beside me. When the girl who normally sat there came in and saw him in her seat, she didn't even put up a fight. She just crossed the room and took his old spot.

"Go to your classes, it'll be fine," I told them when Mr. Kennard walked in, as jovial as always. He looked a little surprised to see Vail, Lee, and Shaw standing in his classroom but didn't do anything other than gesture at the clock, indicating they needed to get going.

"You both okay?" Vail asked, directing his question to Haldon.

"We'll be fine," Haldon reaffirmed. "I won't let anything happen."

The boys all leaned in, each kissing me goodbye one after the other, and I heard the collective gasp by some of the students. They'd heard about our group relationship for sure, but seeing us openly advertise it, only confirmed the rumours.

"Slut," one of the girls, who I recognized as part of Celeste's groupies, muttered from the front of the room.

At once, Shaw flew into a rage, running to the front of the room while reaching beneath his hoodie.

"Shaw, no!" I shouted just as Lee tore after him. Before Shaw could withdraw his knife, Lee grabbed him and hauled him back. Shaw lurched, fighting to break free, his face twisted in pain at being touched. Overhead, the bell rang to start the first class of the day, drowning out the screams from some of the girls, while most of the other students scrambled to get out of the way.

Mr. Kennard moved forward, hands held out, and raised his voice to be heard over Shaw's frenzied cries, "Mr. Bishop... Mr. Bishop!" He clapped his hands hard, snapping Shaw out of his trance. Mr. Kennard didn't touch him, but stood several feet away, hands held out to show he was unarmed, not a threat, and spoke gently to him, "Everything is fine. It's okay. Please calm yourself and let your friends take you to the washroom to steady yourself. Don't make a mistake you cannot come back from."

Shaw stared at him, cringing back as the man talked to him. Shaw was comfortable with very few men in his life, Maverick being one of the few I'd seen, but despite Mr. Kennard's pacifying tone, I could tell it bothered him to have had this man addressing him point-blank like that.

I jumped to my feet and moved forward, positioning myself before him and grasping his face in my hands. "Shaw, Shaw!" I forced him to look at me. At once, he stopped his lip quivering as he started to blink away the enraged fog he'd temporarily gotten caught up in. "It's fine, okay? It's alright." He squeezed his eyes shut before he sagged a little in Lee's arms.

"You good, man?" Lee asked him softly, turning him away from the gaping eyes of the other students.

"Yeah, I just... I just got a little..."

"It's okay. You don't have to explain to us." Lee gave me one last concerned look before he started to walk Shaw away. "C'mon, brother. Let's get some water or something. We're good. Alright? We're good." Shaw looked back at me one last time as Vail followed, nodding respectively to Mr. Kennard before he walked out, closing the door to the classroom shut behind himself.

"Okay, everyone… calm down, please! Let's settle down," Mr. Kennard said, all calm and bright, which helped ease the nerves of the students. "I want you to get out your homework assignments from the weekend. Mr. Dumas? Would you please collect them for me? Thank you. Miss Cooper," he called out to me. I moved over to his desk while the other students got their assignments out. "Miss Cooper, you have missed quite a few classes," he said, concerned.

"I know, I'm sorry." This is precisely what I was worried about. I'd missed two week's worth of work. "I was really, *really* sick…" Even to me, that excuse sounded fake and lame.

But to Mr. Kennard's credit, he didn't call me out on it. "I see." He pushed his glasses up his nose. "You had been doing so well before your unfortunate… illness. I want to see you pass this course. I can give you some work to do for extra credit-"

"Yes, please!" I said, accidentally cutting him off. "I mean, sorry to interrupt, but yes. I'll take the extra work. I know I can catch up."

He smiled warmly and nodded, reaching for the papers that Daniel Dumas collected for him. "I know you can, too. So please see me after school, and we'll quickly put together a plan for you."

"Yes, sir. Thank you!" I reminded myself not to blow this chance he was giving me. The last thing I wanted was to have to take my twelfth year over. As soon as spring would come, the boys and I *would be* graduating, and then we were getting the fuck out.

I went back to my desk, feeling relieved that English wouldn't be a problem. It was Math 30 that I was worried about, as Mr. Fortin hated my guts since that very first day when Vail carried me out and has since continued being a major douche by calling me out in class every day for answers even when I hadn't raised my hand. When I got them wrong (which was most of the time), he liked to make some remark about how the fancy private school I went to wasn't worth the money. I seriously hate that guy.

Class settled down, and Mr. Kennard started instructing us about our English 30 diploma examinations. We went over how we were to interpret literary text and break down the sentences to determine what the writer was saying. I dutifully took notes, noticing that beside me, Haldon was taking this as seriously as I was, his notebook covered in elegant handwriting as he copied everything Mr. Kennard was scribbling on the board.

Class was about halfway over when the phone on Mr. Kennard's desk rang with a shrill

"Quiet please," he told us as soon as several girls started chattering, taking advantage of his distraction to quickly catch up. I took a moment myself, stretching my fingers, my hand cramping from taking so many notes, when I heard him call, "Miss Cooper? You're wanted in the office."

I furrowed my brow. "In the office?"

Mr. Kennard still had the phone to his ear, and he looked as confused as I felt as he listened to whoever was on the other end. "Can it not wait until after class? Miss Cooper has a lot to catch up on from her absence-" He stopped abruptly, cut off by the person on the other end, but he did not look pleased. Sighing heavily, he hung and nodded to me. "I'm sorry, Miss Cooper. But Ms. Hoffman insists that it is of utmost importance." He rolled his eyes, and now I understood why he was so put off. If I had to talk to that miserable receptionist each day, I'd probably feel the same. "Principal Weiser will meet you in his office."

I gathered up my belongings, figuring that if this "important matter" was gonna be time-consuming, I might not be making it back to class.

"I'm going with her," Haldon said, getting his things together, too.

"No, Haldon, don't," I said, guilt now stewing away in my stomach. "Stay and take notes for both of us. I don't want you to miss out on-"

"Daniel will share his notes with us. You aren't going alone," he said in that matter-of-fact way. Mr. Kennard didn't even argue with him as we both left the room. We walked down the hall to the stairwell, but I still felt shitty for making him have to miss class just to walk me to the office.

"I'm so sorry," I told him, my cheeks red. "This is so stupid..."

"It is not." He didn't sound at all bothered, but it still wasn't making me feel any better. "Vendetta sticks together, yes? We are family." His French was incredibly pronounced in that sentence, making it sound all the more beautiful, and they filled me with warmth. He was right. It didn't matter where you came from. It was who you chose to surround yourself with, the people who had your back no matter what, who were your real family.

We reached the top of the steps, about to head down, when a loud shout echoed up the winding stairwell.

"Excuse me, but what do you think you are doing?" A loud voice, one I knew was Principal Weiser's from the deep masculine baritone. No one else in school sounded like that, and I remembered it from the day Vendetta and the Jackals had that fight in the cafeteria. Haldon and I both stopped in our tracks, listening for a second when...

BOOM!

I fell backwards, the building shaking and the breath of hot air coming up the steps. I swear, it felt like my eyebrows were singed off. Beside me, Haldon crumpled but quickly sat up, his black eyes fixed on the top of the stairs.

"What the hell is happen-" I cried, but was cut off.

BOOM!

From another part of the school, another loud explosion rattled the building. The overhead lights flickered and at once, the fire alarms went off, followed by the sprinkler system. All down the hall, classroom doors opened, and in a panic, wave after wave of students came running, terrified, desperate to escape.

I felt Haldon's hands pull me up to my feet before the stampede of kids could trample me. I could hear teachers shouting, demanding that everyone remain calm and file out as we had practiced, when...

BOOM!

A third explosion, this time coming from above, rattled the building, and several ceiling panels fell onto the students who were running beneath them. Haldon held me close, his long hair stuck to his forehead, cheeks, and neck as he looked one way and then the other, trying to determine which way was the safest. We wouldn't be heading down that stairwell, not after hearing what Principal Weiser had said before the first one went off. Someone was there. Someone was waiting...

"Viens avec moi. Vite!" he shouted over the blare of the alarms, and he dragged me up the west hallway, fighting against the crowd. I followed, holding onto his hand tightly, bracing myself for another explosion when a different sound echoed down the halls... screams. Kids were screaming.

"Merde..." Haldon swore and pulled me aside as students scattered, running any which way now. From down the hall, I saw Mr. Kennard and two other teachers ushering students away from the stairs, trying to calm them all while I saw the panic evident on their faces.

The screaming escalated, and smoke started billowing down the halls and through the open gaps in the ceiling. A fresh wave of students came tearing down from the third floor, only to be stopped at the sight of the flames blocking them from this stairwell.

"The west stairs!" Haldon shouted out suddenly. "Run to the west stairs!"

He was right. There had been three explosions, one here near the front of the school, one that sounded as though it came from the back, and the last one from the roof. That meant there were two possible exits... the cafeteria, and the basement, which had an emergency exit leading to the back buildings, and two storage trailers that lined up with the outdoor basketball court.

Mr. Kennard had heard him and started instructing kids to head further up the west hall, pausing every few seconds to look back over his shoulder. Haldon took my hand and pulled me along as we joined the crowd.

"Back, get back!" Someone was screaming from up ahead. "Let her go! Stop!"

I tried to see what the hell was going on, but my stupid five-foot-five wasn't helping, even when I tried to get up on my tiptoes.

"Fucking let her go now, asshole!"

I spun to see Daniel Dumas, the member of Vendetta who sat in English with us, and ran the safehouse for us, glaring over the crowd, absolute fury etched upon his face.

"Right fucking now!" Daniel shouted to be heard over the alarms and screaming.

I couldn't hear a response, but at his words, Haldon stopped me and spun us around. We pulled back, moving away from the west end just as Daniel pushed his way forward, desperate to reach whomever he was yelling at.

We cut down a hallway that ran through the middle of the school, a shortcut for kids having to reach a class on the opposite side. The smoke was building, getting thicker and heavier and I ran hunched over, coughing as I tried not to breathe any of it in.

Behind us, the screaming escalated, and I could hear the teachers shouting, but their words were cut out from the chaos. The noise was deafening, my heart racing, and I clung to Haldon, praying that we were all going to get out of this alive.

"Hey you!" Mr. Kennard's voice boomed. "Release those girls right-" But before he could finish, there was a loud popping sound, and I whipped my head around to see, beyond the figures of confused and terrified students running, the body of Mr. Kennard crumpled to the ground as blood pooled from his body.

"Haldon!" I screamed, tugging on his hand. "Oh my god! They have guns! Haldon, Haldon, we-" But he ignored me, only stopping at the corner that would join us to the east hall, and peered around the corner only to mutter, "Putain de merde!"

I craned my neck to peer around him and my mouth dropped at what I saw.

Guys in black masks shaped with pointed Doberman-looking ears, a long narrow nose, and bushy, brows pulled down over the slits for the eyes, were roaming the halls. Some had actual fucking rifles in their hands and others were holding onto girls. What in the *hell* were they...

And it hit me.

They were taking girls? This was all a ruse... they were herding kids and... I thought about what Mr. Kennard and Daniel had yelled, and it clicked what they were doing. I wanted nothing more than to go back and tackle them down.

But what was even more terrifying were the figures moving amongst them, taller, bigger men who were clearly older judging by their size compared to ones in the dog-like masks; however they were wearing black veiled ones, hiding their faces. *The Faceless...*

We spun back behind the corner before they could see us, squashed up against the wall. In one direction was smoke, someone with a gun, and in the other, more smoke, men in masks, and more guns. We were fucking trapped. Haldon grabbed me, shoving me behind himself, using his body as a shield when the creepy, faceless mask peered around the corner, followed by two more and two dog-like ones. Now that I was closer, I could get a better look at the detailing. They were like hoods, but the black veils that completely covered their faces, ended below their necks, the edges torn. Through the black covering, you could see the hint of an outline of a face, but it was so faint it looked more like a gaunt, pale, sightless skull staring out at you.

Haldon whipped around the other way just as two more dog masked men, and two Faceless, entered the hall, officially sealing us off. He backed me up, so we were more centered, but he kept me crushed between himself and the wall.

I kept looking in one direction, then the other, trying to judge who was closer, but they kept it pretty equal, their bodies blocking any hope of bypassing them.

"Hand her over, Cadot," One of the dog-masked wearing men shouted down the hall. But holy shit... I *knew* that voice. And with the size of the guy... *Hunter? Fucking Hunter? The dog masks were the Jackals!*

In response, Haldon simply looked away from him, shifting a little to hide me as best he could from the others.

Fuck, fuck, fuck, fuck...

From the other side, two Faceless raised their guns, one a glock, and the other, some sort of rifle. I clutched to the back of Haldon's t-shirt, my eyes welling with tears as I desperately tried to think of a way out of this.

"Midnight!" Hunter yelled, sounding much closer than before. "I said, hand her over."

"Dégage!" Haldon snapped back, his lips curled as he spat at him. "Tu es un tas de merde!"

I wrapped my arms around Haldon's middle, plastering my body to his. If they even *tried* to hurt him, they'd be inevitably hurting me, and I was the one they wanted, apparently. I peered around Haldon to see Hunter, whose amber eyes, which were just visible through the slits of the mask, immediately flicked to me, and his voice gentled just the slightest, "Casey... step away from him-"

"Do not talk to 'er!" Haldon snarled at him, his French becoming more and more pronounced the more he talked. "Where are you taking the others?"

"Do you want him to get hurt?" Hunter asked me, ignoring him completely. "Because that's what's going to happen if you don't step away from him right now."

Overhead, the orange lights from the alarms were flashing, the sprinklers were still running, and in the distance, I heard the sound of sirens. Surely the police and firefighters would get here in time and save us?

But...

I was sure these assholes would have a plan in place. And sure enough, the sirens didn't sound like they were getting any closer. The smoke was still building and Haldon shifted us down a bit so that we were crouched underneath the worst of it. This was going to end one of two ways...

One. They would swarm us and kill Haldon for not complying and take me. *Or*, I could hope that Hunter was being straight with me, that some part of him was still honourable, and they would leave Haldon if I just went with them. I could imagine Meredith, searching the school until she found him. And if he were dead, that would absolutely destroy her. I could almost see her throwing herself over his lifeless body. And what of their little girl?

"Haldon..." I whispered.

He shook his head, his soaking black hair still sticking to his neck as he remained solid before me. I tugged on his wet t-shirt, shivering from my own soaking clothes, and leaned close so he could hear me.

"Meredith..."

I felt him shake at the name, his whole body starting to tremble. He gasped, like he was in pain, but shook his head, like he was trying to ignore me.

"Amelie." I squeezed my arms around him, hugging him tight as he let out a small choking sound. "Meredith and Amelie."

"C'mon, Midnight," Hunter said, moving a little closer. "Don't be stupid. Just hand this one over, and then you can go back home to your girls." His voice was low, as if he was only trying to be heard by us and not the others who have cornered us in.

I made the decision for him.

I pushed him forward and jumped sideways where Hunter caught me and hauled me back, my feet dangling in the air. Haldon scrambled to get up, turning to glare daggers our way. I didn't fight Hunter, not until I knew that they'd stay true to their word and leave him alone. Hunter's arm was wrapped tight over my chest, easily holding me close, but I was already planning my own attack for when the fucker got us a safe distance away.

"Smart move," Hunter murmured in my ear, the long nose of the mask brushing against my temple. He moved back with the Jackals and the Faceless... that is, except for that one larger man holding the glock.

"Wait," I said breathlessly, watching in horror as he raised the gun at Haldon's back. "WAIT!"

A shot went off, and I watched, screaming, as Haldon fell forward and slammed onto the floor.

"What the fuck? I said we would leave him!" Hunter shouted at the guy.

"I don't take orders from teenage punks." The voice beneath the mask was eerily familiar. It'd been a deep, scratchy tone sparking a memory, and I suddenly remembered the man who had a pet, one of Elias's men... Keegan. I could picture his smug fucking face beneath that mask, the scar over his lip and his pale eyes. Right now, all I could think about was breaking free from Hunter's arms so I could add a few more scars to his fucking face.

"You son of a fucking bitch!" I screamed so loud that I felt like my vocal cords were tearing apart. "You fucking piece of shit!" I kicked and desperately tried to free myself from Hunter, but the bastard just turned and dragged me away, back toward the west hallway. "Haldon! Haldon!" I cried, squirming to try to get a glimpse of him, to see if he was moving at all.

To my intense relief, I did see him move; left behind by the Faceless and Jackals, he pushed himself up onto his knees, his hand holding a bloodied spot over his upper chest. He was watching them drag me away, but miraculously, he still tried to push himself up off the floor, attempting to follow.

I saw him collapse on the floor, but he'd been still breathing, and then my vision of him was cut off as I was carried around the corner.

"The deal is off, asshole!" I shouted and swung my arms up, letting my body go absolutely limp. As I'd hoped, Hunter lost his grip and dropped me. Instantly, I spun on my ass and swung up, nailing him right in the dick. The fucker went down, and I pushed myself up and ran back down the west hall, heading to the stairwell of the first explosion, just as the others looked back to see I had taken their guy out. I heard them shouting and the sounds of their heavy boots as they raced after me. I passed Mr. Kennard's body and the shortcut hallway where Haldon was still lying, but I kept going, drawing them away from the other students. They were yelling at each other, calling for the others to return, that I was making a run for it, just as I slid on the soaking wet floor to the stairs.

Water was streaming down them like a waterfall from the sprinklers. There was still smoke, and I wondered what the hell was burning, but I didn't stop. I sat on the bannister and slid, carefully holding on so I wouldn't go flying backwards to my death. When I reached the landing, I jumped down and followed the turn to the next set of stairs just as the rest of the Faceless and Jackals reached the top. This time, I attempted to run down the steps, but when I made it halfway, my wet sneakers slipped in the water and I fell. I felt my body float, like it was in suspended animation until my back smacked against one of the steps, and I rolled. I felt every sharp edge and hard concrete tile hit my body until I reached the bottom with a smack.

I lie there, stunned, my face lying sideways in about an inch of water. I blinked, trying to see, but all I thought was I'd temporarily lost my vision. All I could make out was lights popping, like fireworks. For a moment, I thought I was actually okay, and I blinked a little harder and rolled over on my back. That was when the urge to throw up slammed into my stomach and I gagged, and every part of my body started to scream in pain.

From the stairs, I heard the others come storming down, and I knew the moment they'd found me by their excited shouts. I felt someone reach down and grasp a handful of my shirt, pulling me up. I opened my eyes again, able to see a little clearer, but I was staring into that faceless mask.

Instead of saying anything, all he did was hold up a finger and slowly wave it back and forth in front of my face, like I was a naughty child. It was then that Hunter finally caught up, his mask pushed up to the top of his head, looking furious that I managed to get the better of him, and stormed over, snatching me from the creep wagging his finger at me.

"C'mon, let's move out before-"

A strangled shout rang down the hallway, fast approaching footsteps echoing in my head like a stampede. Though I was still disoriented, I shakily looked over just as I saw Shaw literally jump into the air, his curved karambit knife in hand, and tackle one of the masked fuckers. He swung, the blade easily tearing through the veil hiding his face, and though the guy started to scream, it was quickly cut off with a sickening gurgle when he managed to slice it deep in his throat.

From behind him, Lee and Vail appeared, surrounded by other members of Vendetta, and they dived in. Lee headed straight to the biggest masked guy, and I saw the shine of a pair of gold knuckles on his fisted hands. With one swing, he managed to get the guy right in his face, sending him flying back into a locker with a loud crash. And then there was Vail, who strolled over, his hazel eyes shadowed and dark, and I knew he was seconds away from losing all control. He swung a bat in one hand, the flow of it beautiful as he spun it round and round like he was about to play a game of ball... until I spotted the nails he'd hammered through the end.

The one Faceless member, Keegan, was shouting at his guys to kill them, raising his glock to shoot Lee, who had his back turned as he pummeled the guy he'd just sent flying. Vail calmly stepped in, lifting the bat up in both hands, and swung, bringing it sideways into Keegan's wrist. He screamed as the nails sank in, and he tried to pull away. He fell to his knees, his arm suspended by the crude weapon of

Vail's, who, in turn, casually lowered the bat to the ground and stepped on Keegan's hand, ripping it free again.

"You fucking little prick! Oh my God! Fuck! Fuck!" Keegan screamed, his hand dangling from his shattered wrist.

Vail, however, didn't react at all to him. Instead, he lifted the bat again, admiring the blood and bit of flesh dangling from the screws and nails, before he grinned down at the screaming man and swung once more. This time, he connected it with the side of his neck. Keegan's screaming gurgled, yet the man still tried to push the bat away. Vail helped, ripping it free before he struck him in the chest. He fell back onto the floor as Shaw appeared, blood spatter decorating his pale face, and he looked around wildly while Vail brought the bat down onto the mask, crushing him right in the faceless black shroud. Lee grabbed one of the Jackals, a bigger guy, and actually lifted him, holding him up in the air before he threw him like a goddamn rag doll into a trash can halfway up the hall. Shaw turned to a member of the Faceless, his mask having gotten lost in the scuffle, and slashed his blade, managing to slice into one side of the man's face. A stream of blood flew out, hitting Shaw in the face, but he was completely undeterred. His blue eyes were focused, deranged, and I knew all that was going through his mind was to protect his own.

"Vail!" I screamed as Hunter made a break for it with the leftover Jackals, dragging me with them. Vail whipped around, his breathing hard and heavy, and started to follow, when one of the remaining Faceless blocked his path, rifle in hand, raised and ready. "NOOOOO! Vail!" I yelled as we rounded the corner, heading away from the smoke and flames blocking the school's main entrance. We descended the stairs that lead into the basement, Hunter now absolutely crushing me to himself, my arms pinned at my sides by his.

From above, I heard the blast of the gun, and I screamed in horror.

No one followed us.

The Jackals took me down the dark hall, past the gymnasium and weight rooms, locker rooms, to the very back of the school. I was still disoriented from the fall, hurting, and I felt like I was going to throw up.

"Hunter," I moaned, "How could you? How…" My voice trailed off as another wave of nausea washed over me.

"It's all about survival, Casey," he muttered as he ran, panting heavily.

"Not like this… not like this…" I went limp, too dizzy, and in too much pain to keep fighting. I was exhausted. I kept thinking of Haldon, of Shaw fighting like a wild animal, of Lee and his insane strength, and Vail… Vail and his crazy side, something I hadn't witnessed since we were kids. And the Faceless pointing that gun at him, followed by the loud bang of the shot as it went off.

The guys burst through the emergency exit double doors, with Hunter carrying me up the steps to the back of the school. We were between the two storage units, and the ground was covered in snow that had been darkened with ash as it fell from the burning school. Parked off to the side, I saw several black vans waiting for us. In the distance, the sirens were still blaring, but there was no sign of any police cars or fire trucks.

"Looks like the blockade worked," One of them said as they made a break for the vans. "Put her in the middle one with the rest."

"No," Hunter said point-blank and moved us to the last one, the door sliding open by a man wearing the same cloaked, faceless veil. The back had no seating, but they all climbed in, Hunter resting on the floor, his legs outstretched, and me sitting between them, holding me so my head was resting against his chest. I was gasping for air, feeling like I was on the verge of breaking down. I could feel his heart pounding away as the door slid shut, immersing us in semi-darkness, and he threw the mask to the floor beside us. The engine roared to life, and I couldn't hold on any longer. I closed my eyes and fell into darkness.

Chapter twenty-one

Casey

I CAME TO SLOWLY, my head aching, body shivering, and when I opened my eyes, I could barely make out my surroundings in the dim light. Around me, I could hear whimpering, someone coughing, and hushed whispers. I wasn't alone. I rubbed my eyes, trying to snap out of it when my memories came flooding back to me, piece by piece.

Class in the morning, leaving with Haldon, the explosions one after another after another... the panic, students running and crying, the teachers trying desperately to remain calm and guide everyone out... Mr. Kennard, Hunter, the Faceless, Haldon, Shaw, Lee, and Vail...

I sat up so fast that someone nearby cried out in surprise.

I was in a cell, much like a prison cell. The walls and floor were concrete, but one wall was barred, shared by another cell, and another next to that. The other barred wall looked into an open space where a couch, a round, wooden table, and chairs sat. The only lighting came from industrial-looking lamps set up on side tables on either end of the rich brown leather chesterfield. There were none in the cells.

I shared mine with four other girls, while there were about ten more in total in the next two. I groaned as a sharp headache hit me, probably from my fall down the stairs. It felt like a nail was being driven into my skull. I breathed deeply, letting my head fall between my legs as I tried to wrap my head around my situation. This was bad, really-fucking bad. I was pretty convinced as to where we were and who was holding us here, but I just had no idea how I could possibly get out of this and save an additional fourteen girls.

Peering around at the others, I thought I recognized quite a few from Harley Institute, most likely taken today during the fire. The others, however, I had no idea. I wondered if any of them were the missing girls the guys had mentioned before I arrived? Rachelle? Monica? There were more than I thought were missing.

"Casey?"

I spun around to see a small figure huddled in the back corner of my cell. She was wearing a pair of dark leggings, a pretty mustard yellow blouse, and gold earrings. Even in the dim light, I could make out smudges of ash on her dark cheek, and her braids were gathered into a neat bun near the top of her head. She was one of the girls I recognized from school, and when I studied her face, I realized she was Rebecca Thompson, the head of the Social Committee and top of our class. She was usually pretty quiet, but everyone in school knew who she was, because she had posters every-where, begging students to support her ideas to help our school.

"Rebecca?" I crawled over to her, and she lunged at me, wrapping her arms around my neck, and started sobbing. I sat beside her in that back corner, holding her as she cried onto my shoulder. There was something about being around others who were scared and panicked that always gave me a sense of calm and control. Whenever Nylah was having a meltdown over all the homework she had to do (because I swear, she signed up for the hardest AP classes), or when she was worried about an upcoming game, she came to me and I'd always talk her down. It was how I could be there for her, and now, I'll be there for these girls.

I'd never spoken to Rebecca, but that didn't matter at this moment as we embraced each other for comfort.

"Wh-what do y-you think they're going to do with us?" she stammered through her quiet sobs.

Honestly? I knew exactly what they were going to do with us, but I didn't think she could handle that truth. So I just shrugged and muttered, "I don't know, but we should all try to stick together as best we-"

A loud, echoing clang echoed down the black hall that led out of the open space. At once, the girls in the other cells shrank into the back corners, huddled together, some crying harder than ever. The girls with me just looked up with curiosity and confusion, however judging by the reactions of the others, I had a feeling that whoever was walking down that hallway wasn't here to save us.

The other three sharing this prison with Rebecca and I all scuttled over, squeezing into our corner as the sounds of multiple footsteps came closer and closer until finally, several figures stepped out of the dark and into the free space. And the son of a bitch leading them, was Elias Cartier. He was dressed in a dark grey suit, his tie a silk navy and cream, and his shoes shiny and black. His honey-brown hair was neatly combed back off his face, and a five o'clock shadow covered his chin. His mossy green eyes scanned the girls in each cell, his expression holding none of the interest as he walked purposefully by, right to the end, where the other four and I were cowering together.

He halted before the bars separating us from him, and I'd never been so happy to be caged in my life. I'd buried my face into Rebecca's neck, praying to God that he wasn't looking for me, and let my now brown hair fall like a drape to conceal me further.

"Which one is she?" he snapped. I listened as another set of footsteps approached the bars.

"That one, with the dark brown hair in the back." Hunter's voice. I seethe silently, wishing I could fucking claw at his face!

"Why the fuck is she in with the others? Separate them!"

I could hear the metallic sound of keys, before the heavy clunk of a lock, and the squeaky swing of the door. The girls around me all started to sob, and we held onto each other, as though this would stop anything. Several of Elias's men, sans masks, ripped the other girls away from me. Two of them screamed, while Rebecca started sobbing even harder as they dragged them out, only to throw them into the next cell. I stayed where I was in my corner, watching as the door locked me in again. Elias looked at his phone, almost like he was more agitated and bored by the proceedings as the girls moved. He really didn't give a shit about any of them.

"He's here?" he asked one of his security guards, glancing up from his phone.

"Being escorted down now."

"Good." Elias's lips twisted into a smile that would make the Devil tremble. Seeing the sick satisfaction on his face almost had me heaving up my breakfast. "Keep the others away until I'm done with him. I've been waiting years for this…"

I sat there, my head resting against the cold concrete wall as even more footsteps echoed down the hall.

"Go," Elias muttered, moving to stand in front of my cage.

"But... you said-" Hunter glanced at me, his expression dropping, and he looked confused.

"Did I fucking stutter?" Elias's head whipped up, and Hunter stepped back.

"N-no, sorry. I just thought... you said I..." He looked at me again before mumbling, "You said I could keep her if I-"

"Plans changed." Elias slid his phone into the pocket lining of his expensive suit jacket. "Get used to disappointment, kid. Now get the fuck out. You can have some of the other pussy later."

This was a huge blow, apparently. Hunter's fists clenched tight and I could tell he was seething, but he knew better than to say anything arguing against it. Honestly? I couldn't blame him. He was one person surrounded by four of Elias's men, and staring into the deceptive handsome face of a demon in disguise. He had no choice other than to just nod before casting me one last, hopeless, yearning glance, before he entered the pitch-black hall. The others came closer, and soon, more men entered the room, but I didn't bother looking up. What's the point? It was just more of his men, all catering to this selfish piece of shit's needs. I dropped my gaze to the floor, letting my forehead rest against the wall, my hair falling over my shoulder to hide behind.

"Ah, Sheik." Elias sounded positively gleeful, his voice making every hair on my arm stand on end. "So glad you and your boys could make it."

"What do you want?" The newcomer's voice was deep, like the rumble of an engine, and he was brash with Elias, like he really didn't give a shit what he wanted to tell him. *Huh, weird... that's a first.* I figured everyone here either respected him or at least feared his power enough that there was some major ass-kissing going on, but this was new.

I peeked through my hair and realized he was a biker. He was wearing a black cut, the shoulder patch revealing a blue dragon, amongst other patches. He had "Pres" patched over the left chest pocket, but this guy looked more like someone who was wholly and utterly defeated, not someone who was revelling in their position.

He stood there, looking exhausted, shoulders slumped and, his messy dark hair had tons of grey peppering through it. Even the whisker on his chin was almost all grey. But his face was handsome, even with the deepening crow's feet at the corners of his dark eyes.

Why does he look so familiar?

"Mind yourself!" Elias snapped at him. At once, the biker, Sheik or whatever his name was, grimaced and nodded, his head slightly bowed.

"We weren't expecting a call from you, is all," He managed to spit out between his teeth, and I had the impression that speaking to this man with any sort of courtesy was actually a physical challenge for him. His fists flexed, relaxed, and flexed again. I could practically feel the stress and hate rolling off of this man. Holy shit... was Elias going to sell me to this crazy motherfucker?

"This is more personal. Come." He gestured for Sheik to move closer into the room. I noticed that as he moved, reluctantly, I might add, he avoided looking at any of the girls. "A few weeks ago, I came across something rather... intriguing..." Elias's voice was dripping with over-exaggerated joy. It was like he was playing a part of a scene he'd rehearsed in his mind again and again. "You and the Beasts have been loyal, for certain, these past few years. However, it has come at a price, no?"

Sheik stood beside my cell, but didn't even bother looking in at me. He was staring at the floor, a sense of unwilling obedience permeating from his being. But Elias was waiting for him to respond. The suited devil stared at him, the tiniest, cruelest looking smile carved into his face as he stood before the biker, watching him as though he was enjoying how this man struggled with his feelings. Elias was perfectly aware that this man disliked him, hell, probably that he hated him. But he loved that this guy was stuck working beneath him.

"Yes, it has," Sheik said, at last, his voice barely a whisper.

"You lost a lot, didn't you?"

Again, a grimace, before he grunted, "Yes."

"And you've done very well taking over leadership since your president was unfortunately removed. He was disappointing, I'll admit. I'd rather liked Bull at first, but he was a coward… a *Fils de pute*." He actually spit on the floor at the biker's feet.

Even though it was ill-lit, I could see how his cheeks reddened at the insult to the previous president of the Beasts. I had no idea why Elias ended him, but I could imagine it wasn't something the actual club supported.

"But, despite your allegiance, I sense a…" He deeply inhaled and sighed hard, as though he was lost in thought. "Rising hostility from you and your men?"

"We have done all that you've asked of us-"

"Reluctantly."

"We've never failed a mission-"

"Yet."

"I will not be held accountable now for any possible future mistakes!" Sheik snapped his head up, glaring into Elias's smug face, pure loathing clear in his expression.

"You see, Sheik, that is what concerns me. *Future mistakes.* That isn't something I accept from those who work for me. *Mistakes* are not an option, and your apparent disapproval of all that I do concerns me."

Sheik said nothing to this. There was no denying it. If I could sense it after five minutes of hearing them talk in here, then I was sure Elias had noticed for some time.

"So I need to remind you of who the fuck you are dealing

with!" Elias's smile disappeared, his eyes burning in the low light, and his hand whipped out, grasping a handful of the biker's hair at the back of his head, before twisting him around to slam his face between the bars of my prison. I cried out as the man grunted and struggled against the hold, his cheeks red and eyes shining as he tried to push back.

"Look at the girl, Sheik," Elias growled behind him, his tone filled with dark anticipation. "Look at her. *Now!*"

I sat absolutely still, staring up at the biker as he slowly raised his dark eyes to me. Even with his face crushed between the bars, I could still discern the features of this man, and I couldn't help but think again of how familiar he looked.

I watched as the rage, the pain on his face, and his struggle against his hold paused, as though he'd been suddenly frozen in place. Then, it melted away, his eyes, which had been squinting and narrowed, now widened in shock, his mouth falling open. Elias must have relaxed his hold on the back of his head, because the biker was able to pull back the slightest bit, so he was not overly smothered by the metal bars. His hands came up and they gripped the cold, metal cylinders separating us.

"You see it, then?" Elias confirmed.

But Sheik said nothing, only stared and stared, and I awkwardly shrank back again, completely confused as to what was happening.

"How?" he rumbled in response, his deep voice cracking slightly on the word.

"A byproduct of a one-nightstand with a woman named Liza?" Elias sneered, as his face appeared around the biker's shoulder.

Wait... what the fuck did he just say?

"Liza..." Sheik murmured, his face still one of disbelief.

"How old are you, Miss Cooper?" Elias asked me, and I

involuntarily flinched when his eyes moved to me. "Seventeen?"

"On the twenty-fourth," I said, my voice hoarse.

Elias beamed, the sadistic smile not fooling me. Nothing good could come from a man who smiled like that. "One got away from me, James..." he murmured, his voice dropping to a low whisper. "You know how displeased I was to find out what he had done. I like to play, and Shay denied me that." Sheik, James, whatever his name was, gripped the bars tight, his knuckles turning white, and I could hear how quick his breathing was coming. His eyes shined even more, and I knew he was struggling to hold back tears. Elias leaned in, his mouth close to his ear, and whispered, "Well, it looks like I will get to play, after all."

"Please," Sheik moaned like he was in pain. "Please, don't..."

"Begging? Not something I ever pictured you doing." Elias shoved his head forward one last time before releasing him and stepping away, but the biker remained at the bars, watching me like his heart was absolutely shattering.

I stared back at him, my own tears now sliding down my face as it all clicked into place. My lip quivered, and my breath came out in small, little gasps as I stared up at my father... my *real* father.

"I always get what I want," Elias said casually, pulling a silk handkerchief from his pocket and wiping his hands on it, as though ridding himself of any trace of the man he'd just grabbed. "Everything comes at a price. You knew that when that idiot Bull or Shawn or whatever the fuck his name was, came to me in the first place, begging for my help to back your pathetic MC so he could fuck over the Spades. I delivered on my end. So you must continue to honour the deal he made."

"But... her... please." Sheik was still begging, tears now

spilling out of his eyes as he continued to hold onto the bars, like they were the only thing keeping him from falling to his knees. "Please leave her-"

"Sacrifices have to be made, do they not?" Elias threw his handkerchief aside, as though it was ruined now. "Your son knew that. Now you have to face up to it, too." He glanced over his shoulder at the biker, all amusement gone, and boredom now taking over. He was through. "I'll be shipping out the girls tonight. And that one," He nodded to me, "Will pay for your son's 'sacrifice'." He turned to his men, "Send the rest of the Beasts down here. I don't fucking trust them for a second."

And he headed straight down the dark hall, his men following in his wake, leaving me, the girls, and my father alone.

"What is your name?" he asked, addressing me in a much gentler tone than when he'd spoken to Elias.

"Casey," I whispered. "Casey Cooper."

He closed his eyes for a moment, as though struggling to remember, before he finally muttered, "Keith?"

"Yes."

He nodded, pressing his lips together tight as though refraining from saying anything about the man who I had grown up believing was my real dad. But looking at James, searching his face, I could make out the features I'd just mistaken as my mother's, only because I'd looked nothing like Keith Cooper. I found that James's dark eyes and mine were the same, while Mom had a lighter brown. The dark bits of his hair that hadn't turned grey yet, were the same shade as my natural colour. While Mom's had warmer undertones, ours was cold. But there was more...

While yes, I definitely had Mom's nose and chin, James' lips and mine had that same defined cupid's bow, however

Mom's had been more rounded, and the same higher cheekbones.

"Where is Liza? How did they... how are you..." He kept stuttering over his sentences, and I could understand why. He wanted to know how I got here of all fucking places, caged with other girls.

"Mom," I whispered, choking for a moment on the word, "She-she died over a month ago. Killed by a drunk driver..."

James squeezed his eyes shut tight, letting his forehead fall forward against the bars as he took in this information.

"How did you two... I mean, when did you..." I guess the stammering was catching, because now I couldn't get the words out.

"She would come into my club whenever she and Keith fought. I always let her stay with me for a few days till he cooled off." He didn't move from where his head rested, his eyes still shut. "But then she just stopped coming. Looked into it, but she'd married the guy. So I moved on, met another woman, and married her." He sighed heavily and shook his head slightly from side to side. "I liked Liza a lot. But I knew I was nothing more than a backup. When I heard she got married, I let it go. Never knew she had-" He stopped and looked at me, clenching his jaw, the hands on the bars flexing again and again. "Have you... have you had a good life? You happy?" he asked.

I thought about that. Had I been happy? Did I consider myself one of the lucky ones who had no qualms over their life choices and past mistakes? When I grew up in Harley, it didn't matter that Mom and I lived in a basement. The moment we left Keith, I hardly ever remembered being unhappy. I had my mother, my friends, and that was enough. When we left for The Hill, I had Nylah, Mom, and Matthew. I got a chance to have it all. Though that life was ripped away, I had my boys back, Vail, Lee, and Shaw. And every moment I was with them, whenever Lee picked me up and tossed me around like I was a doll, pinning me down, he reminded me that it was okay to be silly and not to take life so seriously all the time. When Shaw snuggled into me, trusting me with every part of his soul, that was something special. To be someone's one sure thing. Whenever Vail looked at me, whether he was happy, pissed off, serious, or wearing that expressionless mask of his, I could always feel how he burned for me. I was his whole world. As for me? I loved them. I loved all three of them so completely with all my heart. They were the only ones who made me feel so absolutely loved, cherished, and complete.

"Yes," I told him, feeling the truth behind every word I said. "I'm very happy."

For some reason, this made his knees buckle, and he slowly slid down the bars, his serious expression crumpling as he broke out into quiet sobbing. He covered his face in his hands, gasping hard and shaking, muttering, "Thank fuck... thank you, God. Thank you..." After a minute, he looked up and, with one hand, reached through the bars, his eyes red from tears, his brows raised as if in question, and he beckoned me to him. I hesitated for only a second, but for some reason, though this man was a stranger and a Beast, I crawled over to him. His arm snaked around behind my back, and he pulled me in, hugging me awkwardly because of the barrier between us, but enough that I could feel every ounce of the emotion behind it. I reached through, feeling the soft leather of his jacket, and returned the hug as best I could, and sank against him, smelling a hint of tobacco and leather, the mix actually comforting. I let my head rest into the space between the bars, and James did the same, our foreheads barely touching each other.

I didn't know how much time passed before we heard a door slam, and numerous boots upon the hard floor echoed down the hall. I fearfully tried to pull back, thinking it was Elias and his men again, but James was undeterred, holding me in place as he peered over his shoulder, his position enabling him to see better who was coming.

"Storm," he rumbled.

When the newcomers arrived, it was only more bikers, the members of the Celtic Beasts, due to their cuts. The one leading the way was terrifying looking. His hair was black, styled into a mohawk, with multiple piercings covering his ears, and lips. His eyes were as dark as Haldon's, and I could see the tattoos peeking out from beneath the collar of his shirt, snaking up his neck and over the backs of his hands. Surprisingly, the girls didn't cower away from him, nor the others who walked in. Some even pulled water bottles out from the inside of their coats and passed them through the cells to the girls, who eagerly took them.

"What did Elias say?" James asked, still hugging me.

"Something about us waiting out down here?" The one he addressed as Storm said, his dark eyes flickering over the girls that had shared my cell with me before we were separated. "Mentioned Jeremy. He was calling him in to help him with a special project. No idea what the fuck he needs that crazy motherfucker for..." He stomped over to the leather couch and snatched a grey throw off the back and bitterly shoved it through the bars to the girls beside me, and they huddled beneath it.

"Jeremy..." There was a tremor of fear in his voice at the name, and I remembered Maverick, what he'd said about the insane lone biker, the one who had sawed Bryce Fraser apart, who worked for hire.

He was coming here? Oh God, no...

"He say anything about the girls?" James asked.

"They're being shipped out tonight." Storm sounded more and more disgusted as he spoke of Elias's plan. He came up behind James and glanced at me briefly before doing a double-take, his face somehow managing to pale despite how white he already was. "Who…"

"Gavin, meet Casey Cooper. Casey, this is Gavin, my second. Or you can call him by his road name, Storm." James was staring at the floor, his brows furrowed like he was deep in thought.

"Casey Cooper?" For some reason Storm, or rather, Gavin's expression changed from one of shock to curiosity and familiarity. He peered at me closely and mouthed a word at me behind James' back… *Ven-de-tta?*

What? He knew Vendetta? I balked at him, glad that James wasn't looking at either of us.

Black. Spades. He mouthed.

I gave him a tiny nod, and he straightened, turning away, moving over to the other bikers, talking softly amongst each other. *What the hell is going on?*

"In a couple of hours, the girls will disappear… and you'll pay for the mistake I made so many years ago…" James mumbled to himself. He wasn't speaking to me, more like to himself. I stared at him, wondering what the hell he meant? I heard them reference his son, Shay, several times. Which meant…

"Shay," I whispered.

James' gaze snapped up to mine, and I saw the hurt and pain there at the name.

"What-what did he do?" I asked, almost too afraid to ask the question.

James sucked in a deep breath through his nose and held it, like he was bracing himself, before he finally said, "He was my son. And he's the first one who gave Elias what was basically a big, *Fuck you.*"

I caught that he'd said that Shay *was* his son. That explained so much about how Elias threw him in James' face and the emotional response that brought about for him. It also meant I once had a big brother, one I would never get a chance to know.

"If I could, I would, too," I said.

James flinched at that, reaching through to pull me close again. "No. You don't get to do that. This time, it's *my* turn." He glanced over to where the other Beasts were watching us closely, and I noticed how most of them were also inspecting me closely, most wearing expressions of similar shock on their faces. I was guessing Shay and I must have looked quite a bit alike. After looking into Keith's face and not seeing any part of myself there, to look into James' and see pieces of myself, to hear about a brother I never knew of, and to think I shared so much with him, actually filled me with warmth.

"Storm?" James called to him.

"Yeah, Sheik?" Gavin stepped forward, arms crossed over his chest.

"We're getting these girls the fuck out of here. *Fuck* this bullshit! It's made me sick for years, and I can't fucking take it anymore."

One biker with curly brown hair and brownish-gray eyes raised his brows in surprise. He had a scar that ran from the edge of his left brow down part of his cheek, yet he still managed a smile despite the old injury. "Yeah? We finally going to give Elias the big, *fuck you?*"

"That's right." One corner of James' mouth curled up in the smallest hint of a smile, and I sensed the tense, defeated atmosphere shift to one of hope. Even the girls were listening in rapt attention. "We need to figure out how the fuck we're gonna get these girls out of here." He glanced back at me and reached up, his rough, calloused fingers gently touching my cheeks. "All of them."

Gavin actually grinned, the sight only making him look

more menacing than before, but he almost laughed in relief. "Thank you, God! I've been fucking waiting for this."

"Yeah, kid?" James chuckled half-heartedly. "You been waiting for me to find my balls, eh?"

He shrugged, "I knew you would, eventually."

"What do you have in mind, then?"

Gavin smirked and reached into his pocket, pulling out a burner cell, just like the one Vail gave Micha, and flipped it open. "I just so happen to have a friend who might be able to arrange something. Just keep in mind, when he and his crew get here, you all gotta put your shit aside and fucking man up if any of us are gonna get out of this alive, yeah?"

None hesitate. The Beasts all murmured in agreement, and Gavin pressed a button on the phone to make a call.

"I swear to fuck, if Jeremy beats them here…"

"He won't. They know this area of the docks well, and I let them know what sort of security we saw set up in the area," Gavin reassured James for the hundredth time. While they paced and bickered, I heard them addressing the scar-faced guy as Silver, or Aron, as he was breaking into the cells to get the girls out. He'd already gotten the first one open and was working away on the second while I watched from behind bars. Every so often, James came over and reached through the openings, pulling me close in some semblance of a hug.

"Got it!" Aron stepped back, swinging the door open, and the girls all hurried out, clinging to each other and shaking. The other Beasts approached them carefully, talking to them softly as they instructed them on the plan. Gavin had been on his phone, going back and forth with his "friend" on the game plan.

"Apparently, one of their guys has a boat. He used it to sneak across the St. Lawrence into the states in the past before they went clean. We'll get the girls over there until the Faceless are dealt with, and then bring them back up when Elias's head is thrown into the river." I liked his optimism, but it seemed too easy, and my nerves were practically fried.

Just as Aron stooped to work on the lock for my cell, there was a loud crash that rang down the hall. Everyone in the room froze, staring as voices from shouting men echoed down the space, the thundering of boots so loud that each one sent a chill through my body. The other girls cried out and ran, hiding behind the chesterfield, obviously nervous that we were about to get caught red-handed.

But when I saw a familiar face emerging from the dark, I breathed a sigh of relief and almost started laughing and crying at the same time.

Maverick entered, his grey cut with the black burning spade on the back and shoulders as clear as the blue dragons on the Beasts. He and James locked eyes, and for a brief moment, the hope we'd all felt temporarily abated as they grimaced at each other.

"This is your friend?" James asked, gruffly. "A Spade?"

"He's no different than the one you had me bring Mina to…" Gavin snapped at him.

At that, James immediately shut up and changed his tune, though he remained a little stiff as he nodded to the blond biker. "Mathers."

"O'Hare." He returned the nod before looking around at the group, his men now entering. I recognized Taz and Animal at once, by the distinctive scars and sheer size. But when three beautiful faces followed them in, I cried out and lunged for the barrier, reaching for them.

One by one, Vail, Lee, and Shaw rushed over, all reaching for me through the partition. I was crying hysterically, only now realizing I'd been pushing the thought of that gunshot I'd heard at the school having possibly hurt one of them. But they were fine! They were here, and they didn't look hurt or anything. I was so fucking grateful that I broke down completely as they all fired questions at me, all at the same time. Their voices mixed together as just noise in my ears, and I didn't hear a single fucking thing.

"Wait, wait!" I said, after pulling myself together. "You guys are okay? None of you are hurt? How about the others? How's Haldon? What about Meredith? Did anyone else get hurt?"

Lee reached through and seized a handful of my shirt, pulling me close. His warm smile was exactly what I needed to see right now. "Haldon will be okay. He'll have a sexy-ass scar, though." I laughed breathlessly—more relief. I'm starting to feel light-headed from it. "Meredith is fine. She's with him at the hospital right now. They tried to take her, but holy shit, that was a mistake. I think she severed four fingers off his right hand?"

"Three," Shaw confirmed, his blue eyes shimmering in the low light. He was probably pressing the hardest against the bars, desperate to get to me, and I was burning with the same need. I just wanted to feel all their arms around me with nothing blocking us. He seemed absolutely panicked, his face pinched and gaunt, like he'd been in hell for the past few hours. I reached for him, too, running my fingers up through his hair at the back of his head while he rested his head between the bars.

"Three," Lee grinned. I swore that nothing put this guy off. Well, except for Logan. "Then she went head to head with Celeste, who was helping the Jackals grab the girls. It's because of her that Rebecca was grabbed," he added darkly, his smile vanishing as quickly as it came.

Fucking Celeste! God, I wish I would get a chance to have a go at her.

"Meredith gouged one of her eyes out with a pen. Then took off her boot and used the heel as a way to hack into her."

"She's… Celeste is…?"

"No, not dead. But she's gonna carry a lot of fucking scars on her face from this." Lee didn't sound at all sympathetic, and I felt the same way. Celeste made a lot of bad choices and never learned anything from the repercussions. She was gladly putting other girls' lives in jeopardy, all because of her desire to be the top of the school, the queen standing at Hunter's side. Speaking of…

"How the hell did you guys get in here? The Jackals are around, and it sounded like Elias had security-"

"We snuck in the old way," Vail spoke at last, and I looked up at him, wishing that I could just wrap my arms around his neck and hold him so fucking tight that no one could pry us apart. Vail pulled me flush against the barrier, our noses just brushing over each other. "The Spades got in on their friend's boat. It'll come up to the docks as soon as we're ready to make a break for it."

I still had my doubts, but they all seemed so calm and sure of this plan, that I didn't question it.

"I can't believe you guys are here…" I whispered to them.

"Like we wouldn't come for you," Vail said softly, his fingers sliding into the belt loops of my jeans. I blinked away the tears that were welling up, not wanting to cry now, especially while we were still in danger. Yet, I was so grateful that they were here, that they came for me, that a few tears managed to free themselves from the corners of my eyes.

That was when the door to the cell clicked, and Aron swung it open. Before I could move an inch, Lee stepped in and lifted me up off the ground into a crushing hug.

"Don't fucking hog her!" Shaw snarled, pulling on my shirt.

"Give me one minute," Lee sighed, and I sank into him, my giant teddy bear.

Across the room, I could hear James and Maverick speaking softly to each other, and I only managed to catch snippets of their conversation as I clung to Lee.

"Heard from them?... When?... I know you can't say where, but... she what? A boy?... Really? And it's his for sure?... Fuck me..." James' voice had been breaking a little and when I peeked over Lee's shoulder at him, I saw him raking his hands through his hair, a wide grin breaking out upon his face, and several tears were falling from his eyes. Whatever Maverick just told him, it looked like it was the best news he had ever heard in his life. James pulled Maverick in, hugging him tightly, and muttered again and again, "Thank you. Thank you..."

"Guys, we gotta go *now!*" Animal was saying, phone pressed to his ear. "Something's going on topside. Mathers, call in the boat."

Maverick and James broke apart, and the Beasts and Spades ushered the girls together, assigned one or, in some instances, like with Animal, two. My three boys stuck by me, crowding me close, as we moved to the group.

"Remember, move fast and keep quiet. If we see someone, let *us* take care of it. No screaming. You got that? *Not a sound!*" Taz said, keeping Rebecca close to his side. "When we get to the docks and get you on our friend's boat, go right below. Listen to your partner. If we tell you to lie on the ground, you lie on the fucking ground. If we say to jump in the water, well, if you can't swim, hold on to someone who can. Alright?"

The girls all nodded, some biting into their fists to keep

quiet, but we all understood the severity of the situation. This was our only chance.

Taz led the way down the hall, our group moving after him, and Maverick and James brought up the rear with Gavin. I was surprised to find that, at the end, there was a metal grate set of stairs leading up. The thought of being trapped beneath the earth, that if I screamed and screamed, no one could possibly hear me, had my anxiety bubbling to the surface, but I grabbed Vail's arm, using him to focus on instead. He led our foursome up after the others, who gathered at a single metal door, with Taz peering out the small, foggy square glass window at his face. Beyond, I could tell it was night by the pitch-blacksky, which should help aid our escape. We waited, and waited, for what I wasn't sure, but I could only assume it was their friend with our transportation. He'd need to be sneaky to reach the docks without the Faceless noticing.

Behind us, James' phone buzzed in his pocket, and because we were all too afraid to even breathe loudly, the sound was clear as it angrily droned on and on.

Cursing under his breath, he pulled it out and held the screen up, the light from the screen illuminating his face. The moment he saw the caller, he paled and whispered, "Elias…"

"You have to answer it," Maverick said to him.

James gritted his teeth, and I knew the last person he ever wanted to talk to was that asshole, but we couldn't have the prick sending someone down there to see why he was being ignored. He answered and pressed the speaker so that we could hear. "Yeah?" he grunted.

"O'Hare." Elias's voice on the other end made me cringe, instinctively moving closer to Vail, who in turn, wrapped his arms around me to pull me in closer.

"What now?" James asked, frustrated. He was barely holding it together.

"I want to know what you're doing."

"What the fuck do you think I'm doing?" he snapped furiously. "I'm sitting here with a kid I never knew I fucking had-" The boys all looking to me, stunned. "-only to find out you're gonna put her through what you had planned for my son. All so you can break me because *he* outsmarted you, and your pride can't fucking take it. Well, congratulations, you fucking did it!"

When the soft, silky chuckle filled the space, it made me feel like he was right here with us, and I didn't like it. I wanted out. I needed out of here!

The laughter abruptly stopped, followed by a deathly silence on the other end, before Elias's voice dipped several octaves and seethed, "What are you doing?"

Maverick looked up at the rest of us, and he looked afraid. More than that. He appeared absolutely horrified. All around me, the girls started to shift where they stood, some whispering to each other in fear or confusion.

"Sheik," Elias called out again. "Again, I ask. What are you *doing?*"

"He knows." Maverick mouthed and gestured for Taz to check the door again. *We need to get the fuck out of here!* My heart was hammering and I was so terrified that I had actually been concerned I'd pass out in the middle of trying to escape.

"Ah, yes, thank you..." Elias's voice addressed someone else on the other end before he spoke to James one last time. "Someone special has arrived, and I'll be releasing them soon. Run, run as fast as you can, little beast. Your time of rule has come to an end, for you and all your friends." The line cut out.

James looked up at the others and shouted, "Run!"

At the door, Taz threw his body against it, sending it flying open, grabbing Rebecca's hand, and sprinted out into the night. Everyone followed, and despite how scared I knew we were all feeling, not one of the girls screamed. I raced up after Vail, slipping on the steps only once before we broke free into the middle of a wide concrete quay running along the wooden docks.

I peered around, noting the warehouses lined up facing the river, and the space surrounded by a chain-link fence with barbed wire looping the tops. The docks stretched along the riverbank, and there were numerous small shipping vessels lined up on the St. Lawrence, their transporter boats docked for supplies.

Vail tugged on my hand, taking off to the right after Taz and the others, and I followed, with Lee and Shaw close behind. I peeked back to see Maverick practically on our heels, with James and Gavin following.

BOOM!

The ground shook so violently that the water rippled and sloshed, the air around us burned as if on fire, the vibration had my knees buckling, and we all fell. I hit the pavement as a rush of hot air burned at my back, and instinctively covered my head with my arms. Several girls screamed, and before I could gather myself, another explosion went off.

BOOM!

This one burned hotter, the rush of heat flowing over us had more force, and debris falling everywhere... bits of wood, metal, and dirt sprayed through the air, and ahead of me, I heard someone scream. I looked up and saw Rebecca curled up on the ground, a jagged piece of metal sticking out of the side of her stomach.

Holy... fucking... shit!

"Get up, kids! Get up!" Maverick shouted, recovering first. He rolled towards us, grabbing Shaw and Lee by the backs of their shirts, and pulled them up off the ground while James moved to help Vail and me.

"Where are we running to?" I cried, desperately looking around for the others. Some of the girls got up, but others remained where they were lying. One girl, who had been held in the furthest cell from me, had a sizable chunk of concrete gouged into the back of her head, and she was motionless. Two others had larger pieces of piping going right through their backs into the earth, and another had been entirely cutin half by a piece of sheet metal that had impaled her across the chest. I gagged hard, while one girl actually heaved onto the ground. One of the Spades was gone, too... a burning piece of what looked like a wooden beam crushing him completely.

"The fence line! Stay by the river but get to the fence line!" Maverick shouted, pushing the boys forward. James gave Vail a small shove but kept me directly in front of him, urging us to keep moving. "We'll cut through it and meet with Scotty. Where's Taz?"

Taz was trying to help Rebecca, holding her hands aloft to keep her from pulling the offending intrusion out while yelling, "You'll bleed to death, girl! Wait until we're on the boat, and I can get a better look at it! Once we're across the river, we'll be getting medical attention, so-"

A shot rang out, and at once, the bikers pushed the girls down. James hauled me to the ground with him, using his body as a shield.

"Fucking Jeremy!" Maverick hissed from where he was doing his best to protect both Shaw and Lee. "Exploding slugs..." He started to shimmy to the side, towards the fourth warehouse, urging us all to follow. As we did, I turned back and saw that two of the warehouses furthest from us had wholly gone up in flames, and were slowly making their way in our direction. I saw the black silhouettes of the Faceless. Amongst them, an absolute beast of a man, one to rival both Animal and Lee, was shooting a 12ga shotgun at any barrier he came across, as though hoping to find us hiding behind one. I couldn't make out the details of his face, not with the bright flames burning behind him, but I knew that this was the biker everyone had been talking about.

"We need to slow them down so the girls can get out," Maverick panted, pressing against the corrugated metal wall. The survivors had gathered behind several barrel drums, and we listened to his plan, as death moved slowly in our direction. He looked to Vail, "If something happens to Taz, you and your boys need to head south along the embankment. Look for a white and blue Viking '68 convertible yacht." At this, Shaw pulled out his phone and started typing. "Ask for Scotty. Tell him you're Vendetta and Maverick sent you. If he asks where the fuck we all are…" At this, he glanced at James, who nodded back at him, as though they both understood something we were all missing. "Tell him there was a Joker in the Deck."

I raised my brows, confused. *What the hell does that mean?*

I was about to ask when, in the distance, there was another loud blast from the shotgun, followed by a skin-crawling, insane laugh that rang out across the shoreline and docks. I wouldn't be surprised if they heard it across the St. Lawrence into the States. When I looked back, Shaw was showing everyone a photo of what boat we were looking for, but I was watching the bikers. I didn't like the looks on their faces… a sort of grim, tense yet determined expression on each and every one.

"James?" I asked, reaching for him.

He peered over at me, reaching up to hold my face in his palms and staring into my face. He was eerily calm, and it was unsettling as hell, given that what looked like fifty men armed with guns, and a psychopathic murderer, were closing in about a hundred feet away. James pulled me in for a hug and murmured, "I'm sorry I wasn't there for you, Baby Girl."

I didn't know what else to do other than hug him back. When I did, I felt him pressing a kiss to the top of my head, and he said, "You keep being happy, alright?"

Someone tugged at the back of my shirt. "We gotta go." *Lee.*

James released me, pushing me to the guys, and turned to his men, reaching inside his leather jacket and withdrew two sleek black handguns. All around us, the Spades and other Beasts were taking out their weapons.

"No, Taz. You help them get the girls out," Maverick said when Taz started to hand Rebecca off to someone.

"I'm not leaving you guys behind!" Taz looked absolutely pissed at this, his heavily scarred mouth contorted in a pained expression.

"I need a Spade to go with them in case Scotty doesn't show. They need someone to get them away. I need you to do this, alright?" Maverick paused as Jeremy let off another shot, and we all heard something shatter apart. The worst part was how much closer it was. Too fucking close. We have to go *now!* "Once the girls are in safe hands, you take Casey and Vendetta to Florida…"

"Florida?"

"Look for Chase."

"Chase M-"

"Yes, him. Now fucking go. We'll hold them off!"

We all shuffled down the wall, but the further away we got from where the bikers were gathered behind the drums, the more we opened ourselves up to exposure. The flames grew brighter, turning the sky an almost darker, burnt orange as the fires reflected off the clouds and the water below.

We were so close to the corner of the building where we could hopefully hide. The men were closing in, and just as one appeared in the distance, breaking the vantage point concealing us, the Celtic Beasts and the Black Spades threw themselves out from behind their hiding spots, and started firing shots off in unison. The Faceless scattered, ducking behind construction equipment, stacked pallets, small cranes, or dry docked boats. When they did, Taz made a break for the fence, carrying Rebecca in his arms. I ran with the girls, with Vail, Lee, and Shaw bringing up the rear. I turned back to see several bikers had already fallen, but when we reached the fence and Taz began to yank, ripping and tugging at the bottom of the chainlink, I looked back just as I saw one of the Faceless get several shots off, knocking Maverick down.

Vail saw it, too, and I heard a choking sort of groan breaking past his lips. He took a step back, like he was about to run over there, but somehow managed to remain with us. I could see the agony and struggle written all over his face, his hands shaking as he watched Maverick crawl to the side behind a pile of junk, using it for cover. I reached out and gripped one of Vail's trembling hands, and we watched, feeling utterly helpless as we could do nothing but watch.

James ran over, managing to reach him unscathed. He looked as helpless as we felt watching as he scanned over the wounds on the Spade before he bowed his head over him, talking softly. Maverick's lips moved for just a few seconds, his body twitching, hands shaking, before he gave a small shake and stilled... gone.

Tears were falling down my face and Vail was visibly shaken. Never have I wished for swift vengeance in my life. Behind us, one by one, the girls were struggling to crawl beneath the small gap under the wiring and the dirt. There were eleven of us left now, and Rebecca was seriously injured. Taz half dragged her under while another girl helped move her legs.

"Hurry up! Hurry up!" Shaw hissed, looking back at the firefight. All I could hear were shots firing off in rapid succession. "Okay, Casey, you next." He shoved me down to my knees, and I did my best to crawl as fast as I could. The ground was cold, the metal slicing my back as I slid beneath. On the other side, the ground was covered with grass and dirt, an expanse of trees surrounding the area.

"There's a boat!" One of the girls called out, pointing to the water. I reached down, now helping to pull Shaw through, but quickly glanced over to see a power yacht approaching, its spotlight moving slowly along the shore.

"Scotty!" Taz waved his arms at him. "Here, bud! Here!" He hoisted Rebecca up and hurried down to the shore, the other girls following, but I waited for my boys as Lee now struggled to fit. I clung to the chainlink as Shaw and Vail helped get Lee through, and watched in horror at the scene unfolding behind us.

The fire has spread, burning away the third warehouse, and now each member of the Spades and Beasts were indiscernible to the other. They were just shadowed, dark outlines against the flames, and one by one, they all fell down, just dark, crumpled shapes on the ground. One after another, after another. I didn't know where James was, where he ran to. I couldn't tell if one was Animal or Gavin, or Aron. They were just moving shadows that dropped from the bright blast from the guns of the Faceless.

Vail crawled under next, as Taz helped the girls wade nearly chest high into the water to reach the boat, while the captain lowered a silver ladder off the stern into the water for them to climb. I glanced back to the carnage and noticed at least two shadows were hidden behind pallets far out on the dock, but the Faceless were moving in, led by one huge figure I knew to be Jeremy.

"Come on, we have to go!" Vail grabbed my hand and pulled me along behind him as he ran down the embankment to the water.

"What about those two?" I pointed back over my shoulder, desperate to save the last of them.

Lee looked, but shook his head. "It's too fucking late. Jeremy is heading right for them."

"But-"

"Casey!" Vail snapped. "It'd be suicide for us to go back! We can't! Now, fucking run!" He hauled me along, and we all jumped into the freezing cold water. I coughed and spat as some got into my mouth, nevertheless kicking as hard as I could, swimming and determined to make it. Taz climbed up as Vail reached the ladder, but reached back for my hand, pulling me to the ladder to go up first. I didn't argue and climbed, coughing and breathless and reaching down to help Shaw up next. He was shivering hard, his wet blond hair a mop upon his head. Vail made Lee board next, and I heard Taz talking to Scotty, both men noticeably shaken.

"So that's fucking it, then?" Scotty looked like he was about to go into shock.

"Not it. We still have a job to do," Taz nodded to the steps leading down below deck, where I could hear the girls crying and talking amongst themselves.

"Right. Right! Fucking right. Let's go. We got everyone on?" He glanced back at us just as Vail climbed up, pulling the ladder with him, nodding.

"No one else," he confirmed, shaking his hair out of his eyes.

Scotty climbed up to where I could only assume the helm or command center of the boat was, and the engine rumbled, coming to life. "Hang on!" he called down, and the four of us sank down onto the cushy seats, clinging to each other as we shivered in the cold night air. The boat lurched forward, gliding across the water, and I couldn't help but look back one last time.

The fourth warehouse had now caught fire, and as the

414

four of them burned, embers and ashes floated up into the air. It looked like hell, and the sound of gunfire had stopped. The devil had won, but somehow, we had made it out together. I nestled into my boys, trying not to think of the sacrifices that had been made to save us. My heart was ripping apart, thinking of James and Maverick. Of the others who so selflessly stayed behind. We were all gasping for air, all clinging to each other, and I was reeling... how was it that we made it out alive, together, while so many were gone?

"Thank fuck, I had the number memorized." Vail got to his feet, shaking from head to toe, and headed over to Taz.

"What?" I asked, but he ignored me. He spoke softly to Taz, who disappeared momentarily below deck, and came back up with a cell phone. Vail returned to us, pulling me onto his lap, and rested his chin on my head. "What?" I asked again as he punched in a number.

"I'm going to ask someone to return a favour."

Chapter twenty two

Casey

"WHEN DID Taz say they'd be here?" Lee asked impatiently, staring out one of the front windows of the cabin. He'd been sitting there for the last half hour now, waiting.

"Should be any time now," Vail answered. He was lounging in a chair in the kitchenette area, and then glanced at his phone, double-checking the time. In the background, Shaw was pacing back and forth, obviously nervous about these two strangers who were coming by to 'have a word with us'. So Taz said. We were told we had nothing to worry about, that Riley's uncle was a good guy and his friend was trustworthy. I trusted Taz, so I wouldn't question him.

It was the middle of December, and it was still hot as hell. In Florida, in the wintertime, the temperature was sitting at a stifling 27 degrees Celsius. I had several fans on and had been running around the place, straightening throw pillows, blankets, and putting dishes away. We'd been staying here in

Logan's family's cabin for the past two weeks. Micha had said that Ashen Springs was the safest place we could hide out in, and Logan had selflessly volunteered this little hunter's cabin in the bluffs for our use.

As they were both away at the University, Riley and Shelby were the ones who came by to check on us, though Shelby came a lot more than she needed to. She was super sweet, bringing us groceries and coming by for brief visits.

However, the last time they were here, I distinctly heard Riley mutter under her breath to her friend, "My God, you have to give them some space!" Shelby still continued to come by. I had no qualms with it. Living with three boys, as much as I loved them, I missed Nylah, and Shelby was like a pale, blonde version of her.

It was torture not being allowed to message my friend, but we didn't want any possible trace to link us here. I knew she'd be panicking, but I had to wait until it was safe. As well, I was worried as hell about her. She had been sick the last we talked, and my suspicions that she'd been downplaying being followed were still there. If it was the same guy each time, alone, what if it was Jeremy? The thought of Jeremy stalking my friend made me a nervous wreck, but Vail had no intention of returning to Ashland while Elias was running things there. Without the Beasts or the Spades to challenge him, the place was quickly becoming a hellhole. Knowing that Elias had some sick fantasy about hurting me for whatever my brother did to one-up him, had me going along with that plan. No way in hell was I going anywhere near that guy if I could help it.

Living with the boys those past two weeks had been a dream despite the move and the isolation from our old life. We moved in, and Logan gave us a black card to use. I asked Riley where a good second-hand store was, and she eagerly took me to one of her old haunts so I could grab some things for us all, seeing as we had left everything behind. Other than that, we only used the card for food, in spite of Logan laughing at our worries of sending him a hefty bill. In Ashen Springs, we could walk around freely, for shopping or sight-seeing, or even visit the ocean, which I loved. Micha said we had the Order of Ravens and Wolves protection (*whatever the heck that was*), so we didn't have to fear anything as long as we stayed within the city. Any activities we did were basically walking along the beach on the days it wasn't rainy and windy, or just wandering through the town, exploring.

Five days ago, however, Vail surprised me with an expense when I came home to find he'd ordered that sex swing he'd mentioned, and I'd basically spent three days being fucked silly in it.

I knew Logan had checked the purchase history on the card because a day later, Vail got a text that just said, "Nice!" with a winky emoji.

"There they are," Lee said suddenly. I hurried to his side, watching as a car appeared from the road winding up the side of the cliff and stopping before the cabin. It was pouring rain right now, so the figures that climbed out were slightly distorted, but I could see *three*, not two, running to the front door.

"Three," Lee called to the others. Vail nodded, remaining where he was in his seat, while Shaw moved in behind him, backing him up. Here, it was too hot for him to hide beneath his hoodie, but I knew that his short pockets had holes so his hands could reach through and grab the blades of his knives if need be.

"Let's just relax," Vail said softly, sensing Shaw's anxiety levels spiking. "Taz sent them. We know they're good."

Lee opened the door just as the three men came up the steps and ran inside.

"Holy fucking shit balls!" One with golden blond hair bent over, shaking it out. "I swear I'll never get used to the weather here. I miss snow."

"You'd rather snow than a little rain?" The tallest of the three shook out his messy brown hair before slipping a beanie on over the top, and looking around at us. He was probably in his mid-thirties, with a ton of tattoos and a five o'clock shadow on his chin. He looked like a badass biker.

"You see, here's the problem with the rain here," The blond said and straightened. The moment he did, my mouth dropped and I stared in shock, feeling like I was looking at a ghost. "Yeah, in Canada, we get some snow. It's kinda cold and shit, but down here when it gets a little windy, it blows cars and shit down the street."

This guy was the spitting image of Maverick, except his eyes were an insane glacier colour of blue. Beneath the collar of his t-shirt, I saw the start of a spider web tattoo, and both arms were covered. Besides the obvious similarities between him and our friend, I felt like I'd seen him before, yet couldn't place exactly where. He noticed me staring and flashed a mischievous smile before raising his left hand, wiggling his fingers as he showed off the gold band on the fourth one.

"N-no, sorry! I didn't mean…" I peered around to Lee, who moved closer to me and I could see that he noticed the similarities as well. "I'm sorry, you look like a friend of ours…"

"I'm guessing Maverick?" The older guy asked us, his voice carrying a similar rasp to Shaw's, except his was deeper.

"Yeah… Maverick."

At that, I saw the blond's face fall, his lips pressed tight together, and he looked sharply at his companion as though worried about his reaction.

"Yeah," the older guy grunted, "I noticed it, too." He looked around at the four of us, but his dark eyes settled on Vail, who hadn't moved from his spot at the kitchen table. "I take it you're in charge here?"

"I am. And all I know about you is that you're Riley's uncle and president of the Lost Souls MC in Florida?" Vail said, his voice as smooth and calm as always.

"That's me. Chase Mathers." He grunted and pulled a chair out opposite Vail, flipping it around so he could sit on it while resting his arms over the back. I noticed how he moved a little stiffly, and remembered what Riley had told us about his recent fight with that asshole brother of his.

"Mathers?" Lee moved closer, and I stayed with him. When I peeked over to the blond, I realized he was watching me a little more closely now. His eyes narrowed as if he was studying me. It freaked me out because it was the exact same way James, Elias, Gavin, Maverick, and all the others had looked at me, like I was the shadow of my lost brother. I wondered if he knew him, too?

"Yep. Maverick was my old man's brother."

I stared back to the third figure, who had remained mysteriously silent this whole time. He'd moved to the side, standing in the corner while leaning against the wall, choosing to stay back while the rest of us gathered close. He was probably only a couple of years younger than Keenan, and despite his casual dress, like the jean jacket he was sporting, something about him just had me on edge. It was like I could feel his aura, and it screamed, *Danger.* He ran a hand through his damp blond hair, and his grey eyes snapped to me, which had me instantly turning away. It was as if Jeremy was suddenly in the room with us.

"I'm Keenan Mathers." The friendlier blond took one of the vacant chairs, lounging back in it while kicking his legs out before himself, groaning when they cracked. "Mother-fucking knees are going already... goddamn garage..."

"Keenan Mathers?" Vail pressed, watching as the guy stretched, before relaxing in his seat. He had been moving like his cousin had, like he was recovering from a serious fight.

"Maverick was my dad," he said, his blue eyes suddenly tense around the edges. He bit the inner corner of his bottom lip and nodded to Chase, like he didn't want to speak anymore.

"Is that why you're here?" Vail asked, glancing at the figure in the corner before turning back to Chase. "To find out what happened? I thought Taz told you-"

"He did. He filled us in on his account of things. Was curious to hear what you kids saw, though..."

It was no secret that the Celtic Beasts and the Black Spades were wiped out in Ashland. What happened there, with the fight at the docks and the attack at the school, made international news. But what really fucking pissed me off about it, was that the blame was being put on the MCs, all arranged by Elias, of course. How much control did that prick have? News reports talked about the Beasts and Spades running a human trafficking and drug ring for years, but after an altercation and with what happened at Harley Insti-tute, they split, and at a standoff between the two at the docks, they killed each other.

But we knew the truth.

We knew that they were our saviours who sacrificed themselves to save us from the real monster. As soon as the girls were put into a safehouse that Maverick had arranged, Taz, Scotty, my boys, and I all rushed down to Florida. Micha was good on his word, and my boys and I were under his protection while Taz and Scotty filled the Lost Souls in on what actually happened. I wasn't sure what else we could say that they didn't already know?

"I don't know what else we can tell you," Vail said slowly. "Only that, we *know* it was one of the Faceless who killed Maverick. The Spades and the Beasts saved us. There was no fucking way we would have gotten out if not for..." He trailed off, his voice catching in his throat. He had been a rock this whole time, and I didn't recall him shedding a tear over what happened. But now, looking at his face, I could see the grief and anguish there. His foot was bouncing on its sole in rapid succession, and his hands were clasped together tight on the table's surface.

Moving around the others, I came up behind him, wrapping my arms tight around his chest as I rested my chin on his shoulder. One of his hands slid up to grasp my wrist, holding onto me while I kept him steady. Next to us, I could *feel* Keenan's eyes boring into me, but I ignored him, concentrating only on Vail.

Outside, the wind was whistling around our little cabin, and the rain pattered against the windows, breaking the silence.

"Listen, Keenan hasn't been back to Ashland in a little over three years, excluding a one-day trip on the outskirts of the city with his girl a couple of months back," Chase said, getting to the point. "And Taz and Scotty weren't able to move around through Ashland, being Spades and all."

Shaw had moved a little closer to the table, having remained as silent and as still as that guy in the corner. Now, however, he seemed to feel comfortable enough to take the last empty chair while Lee shifted in behind us all. I always felt safer, reassured when we stood together as a unit.

"We want information on the city. I wanna know about all the areas and how they work, who holds power where... I want to know about the Faceless, the docks, and about that piece of shit who's behind it all."

"Elias Cartier," Vail said, pulling me around to sit in his lap. I did, melting into him while his arms hugged me around my waist.

"Honestly, there's not a lot. Maverick said his past is unknown, that he literally showed up one day out of the blue for hire. Whoever pays the highest dollar, he works with. He doesn't have an allegiance to anyone. It's all about who has the deeper pockets. Unfortunately, in Ashland, that would fall to Elias." Any time Vail mentioned Maverick, I felt him tense. I got it. He respected the hell out of that man. He spent more time talking to him than any members of Vendetta. Maverick had given him money to pay the bills and buy food. And the biggest gift of all, he'd gotten us out.

But whenever he said 'Elias', nearly everyone in the room would cringe, like they were refraining from breaking something just at the mention of the name. Everyone, that is, except for Shaw, and the man in the corner, who both seemed to be studying each other curiously. Vail noticed because then, he finally addressed the creep. "Do I even want to know what the deal is with that guy?"

Keenan shook his head, laughing like what Vail asked reminded him of some hilarious inside joke. "You're better off not knowing anything."

But to my surprise, the jean jacket wearing blond spoke, his voice flat, "All I want is for you to tell me everything you know about the one they call Jeremy."

Vail raised his brows in surprise, and I knew he was just as curious as I was about this guy and his interest in the lone biker. "I've only seen Jeremy in action twice."

"That's enough for me," the man murmured.

Vail stared at him for a minute, catching the eerie void in his eyes before nodding. "Okay, I can do that." He glanced back at Chase, his anxiety gone and replaced with a sort of excited hope when he asked, "So… does this mean you and your guys are going to do something about Ashland?"

Chase leaned forward just the slightest bit, his dark eyes charged, and rumbled, "What do you think?"

Epilogue

Casey: Christmas Day

"SHIT! SHIT, IT'S FUCKING COLD!" Lee yelled as he ran from the water. I was laughing my ass off, watching as he bravely accomplished his dare from Vail, which was to completely dunk himself in the ocean. We were the only ones on the beach, as most families were inside today celebrating the twenty-fifth of December as a family. Well, so were we... just in our own way. Shaw, Vail, Lee, and I ventured out after breakfast and found a secluded spot on the coast near our cabin, and we huddled together on a blanket I'd set out over the sand. For Floridians, it was a cold twenty-five degrees Celcuis, but for us, this was t-shirt weather. It still didn't make the water any warmer, though.

Lee ran back to the blanket, his skin covered in goose-bumps. I got up, grabbing a towel to give to him, so he could dry off, earning a kiss as a thank you before we took our seats again. Shaw was snuggled into my side, his head in my lap as I combed my fingers through his hair. Thanks to the heat, he was slowly getting used to not hiding beneath a hoodie, but still preferred to be directly at my side when in public. I could see how uncomfortable he was at not having something to hide behind as we walked down the streets together, but I gladly took his hand, and together, with Vail and Lee, we took on those demons day by day.

Lee sank onto the blanket and, much to my disappointment, pulled his shirt back on, hiding his beautiful god-like perfection. With a wide, wicked grin, he turned his dark gaze to Shaw. "Your turn."

I could feel him cringe before he let out a long moan. Lee loved giving Shaw the most ridiculous dares, as though hoping it would get him to come out of his shell. Though he never showed it, I think Shaw liked performing the stupid shit that Lee had him do. It was rare that he did something that was silly, a little out of his comfort zone, but safely.

"What is it?" Shaw snapped, not moving his head from my lap.

Lee smirked at him and rubbed his hands together as though what he had planned was something so incredibly diabolical the anticipation would be worth the wait as he paused.

"Oh God," Shaw muttered, now sounding a little panicked. "What is it? What?"

"I dare you…" Lee said slowly, twisting the knife as he paused, the suspension building, making Shaw only more nervous as he waited. Even Vail was watching, curious but quiet, as we waited. In fact, Vail had been quiet most of the morning, which had me reaching over every so often to squeeze his hand, reassuringly, wondering what could be bothering him. "I dare you… to act like a chicken until your next turn."

I burst out laughing, the sound echoing against the cliff-side where we'd settled, ringing down the beach. Shaw peered up at me, the corners of his lips lifting in the tiniest of smiles, and it was the most beautiful thing I'd seen today. Well, that and Lee's glorious body.

We all watched as he slowly sat up on his knees, casting Lee a death glare, though that little smile never went away, and folded in his hands to his sides, elbows sticking out, and muttered, "Cluck cluck…"

Lee fell forward on the blanket, laughing like a maniac, while Vail and I both threw our heads back, cackling as Shaw even bobbed his head forward and back a little.

"Oh my God… yes!" Lee crowed triumphantly, fist-pumping as he rolled to his back, looking up at the sky. "Yes! Shit, wish I'd thought of this one before."

Shaw rolled his eyes, still bobbing his head slightly before he turned to Vail. "You ready? Cluck."

Vail's smile slowly broke out upon his face, and I knew he was enjoying seeing Shaw making a fool of himself. But to his credit, he didn't give him a hard time, and simply nodded.

"Cluck. Spank the person to your left… hard." His grin widened even more. "Cluck."

At that, Lee instantly stopped laughing and scowled while Vail tossed his head back, losing it. I giggled at the appalled look on Lee's face. "You son-of-a…"

"Ass in the air, Knight. This is gonna sting." Vail began rolling his right shoulder, like he was preparing for a good workout.

"This is for your dare, isn't it?" Lee grumbled as he complied, resting forward on his forearms, butt up, and head down towards the sand, his face hidden behind his dreads.

"Cluck, cluck, motherfucker." Shaw grinned, his elbows moving back and forth a little as though he was flapping his wings.

Vail actually got to his feet, moving a few steps back, stretching his arm out, and whirling it like a windmill. I stuffed my fists to my mouth, trying to hold back a giggle fit as I watched poor Lee brace himself. Vail even did two practice ones, bringing his hand in close but making no contact.

"For the love of all that is holy!" Lee shouted, "Get it fucking over with alread-"

Vail struck before Lee could finish, with Vail bringing his hand up high before swinging it down with a resounding smack, right on target. Lee actually grunted from the impact and remained where he was for several seconds, as though he was summoning any remnants of his pride he had left, before glaring up at Shaw, who watched him with the smallest of smug smiles.

"That dare was bullshit." Lee sat up as Vail took his seat again. "We shouldn't have dares that impact other players."

"Hey, hey," I laughed, "Don't be a sourpuss just cuz you... got your ass handed to you." I keeled over, my head brushing against Vail's leg, as I collapsed into uncontrollable giggles. I could hear the others chuckle as I remained where I was on my back, the sky above me a beautiful blue, speckled with fluffy white clouds. I hadn't smiled or laughed this much since... well, I couldn't remember. These past few weeks with the boys have been a dream, one I never wanted to wake up from.

Vail's face suddenly obstructed my view, leaning over me upside down, his mask in place, and I immediately sobered up.

"Cooper..." he said slowly.

"St. James." I arched a brow at him, trying to maintain a cool facade as I awaited my dare.

Instead of speaking, he reached down, his fingertips running along my cheek and he leaned in, his kiss so featherlight it was barely there. "I dare you..." He moved his lips over to my chin, pressing the smallest of kisses there, before moving to my nose, another kiss, "to marry me."

I stiffened beneath him, eyes widened, his words repeating over and over in my head. "Uh, what?"

Vail pulled back, and I quickly sat up, turning to face him while the other two watched. I stared into the depths of Vail's hazel eyes, searching for a sign that he was bullshitting me. His mask fell, and the almost timid, humbled look in how he'd been holding himself up, and all the apprehension that was written all over his face, shot straight to my heart. Vail vulnerable. It was such a bizarre yet tender thing to behold.

He shifted so that he was on one knee, looking down at me as he reached into his pocket and pulled out a ring. It was a pearl, with little flower petals adorning the band... like Mom's hellebore. "Marry me," he whispered.

"What are you... how did... *huh?*" I couldn't get a coherent sentence out to save my life.

"Bastard!" Lee said, but he was grinning like a maniac. "So you get the first kiss *and* you call dibs on marital rights?"

"Of course." Vail's moment of uncertainty dropped for a mere second as he looked at Lee, that familiar cocky smirk coming back. "I'm the leader. It's my right."

"Yeah, yeah, whatever." Lee rolled his eyes and winked at me.

"What about us, you dipshit?" Shaw had wholly dropped the chicken act, and though he was calling Vail out, I could sense the feeling of hope in his words. "You not gonna share?" he nodded to me, but he was smiling, too, like he already knew what the answer was.

"We're a family, period," Vail said, turning back to me, reaching for my left hand to hold the ring up to my fourth finger. "So no matter what, we're together. *All* of us." He met my gaze again, and that assuredness dropped away to one of trepidation. I stared at the ring he was holding and glanced around at the others before looking back at him. All of them. All their faces. My love for them all was overwhelming at this moment. I felt like I was floating. For some reason, the first words out of my mouth were, "We're only seventeen…"

"And I'll be eighteen in January. Come November twenty-fourth next year, I'm marrying you as soon as the courthouse opens that day. I love you, Casey. *We* love you. No matter what, we'll all be together, because we've all always belonged together. But I want it official." My breath hitched, and I could feel the tears slipping free as they slowly slid down my cheeks onto the blanket below. The corner of Vail's mouth lifted ever so slightly, and he leaned in, pressing his forehead to mine. "So, darling? What do you say? Do you accept the dare?"

I swallowed hard as I gathered myself together, more tears falling as I lost myself in his gaze, feeling so fucking happy, I didn't want to say anything that could ruin the moment. So I just whispered one word, "Yes."

Vail smiled like he'd never had before. It was radiant and beautiful and so unbelievably happy that I couldn't help but match it as he slid the ring onto my finger. Wordlessly, he wrapped his arms around me, holding me flush against his body, and I buried my face into his neck. Around us, the other two crawled over, and soon, I felt both their arms wrapping around us.

The future was still uncertain. Where would we be? Would we ever be safe from Elias and the Faceless? Would we ever return to Ashland? Would we even want to? What about school? Careers? It was all part of a broken web, but one thing was absolute… we would be together, as we were always meant to be.

The End

AFTERWORD

Thank you for reading the third book of the Bleeding Hearts Series! This was my first time writing an RH, and I truly did not want to do it a disservice with my inexperience. I hope I was able to give RH fans what they love about the trope. I have so much respect for the RH Queens who write these books. I also hope that I gave readers who are not used to reading the reverse harem romances something to love. Vail, Lee, and Shaw are all huge pieces of my heart, and honestly... it would be cruel to ask anyone to choose between them.

I also hope that you were able to find a connection to Casey. Her life was one upheaval after another, and to call her cold I think would be unfair. She is strictly in survival mode, trying to navigate and understand an old world that has since changed over the years. She was tough when she needed to be, questioned when she disagreed, and fell in line when she *fully* understood the seriousness of the situation. Any behaviour of hers that was seen as "defiant" simply comes from inexperience, age, and ignorance... something I think we are all guilty of from time to time. We are all imperfect, and Casey is no exception. And that's something we should embrace, not hide. The word "flaw" has such a negative connotation to it, but really, I see it as little ticks in people that truly individualize them and make them unique. And THAT, is beautiful.

There were old characters and new ones in Ashes, and my favourite new one is definitely Haldon (a.k.a. Midnight). He and Meredith together were so much fun to write and their relationship was so charming and sweet that the moments I had with their characters were actually the easiest for me to write. I felt like I'd known them both for years, but Haldon in particular, is a top favourite for me.

Again, thank you so much for daring to pick up another book by me. I hope to wrap up The Bleeding Hearts Series with the next book, book four.

To all my readers and supporters, thank you. From the bottom of my heart. All the messages, words of encouragement, reviews, and love that you have given has meant so much to me. I count myself so lucky to have such kind, amazing people reading my work. I hope I can bring you many more tales for years to come.

ACKNOWLEDGMENTS

Firstly, a HUGE thank you to Alexis and Veronica.

You two have been so amazingly supportive and your love of this world and its characters has been truly touching and humbling. You're both so sweet it gives me a toothache. A piece of this story belongs to the two of you. Thank you for your blood, tears, sweat, and dedication. I wish you both nothing but blessings.

I also want to thank some very special ladies: Tara Hodel, Billie Blue, Brooklyn Cross, Vivian Murdoch, Alyssa Lynn, and Drethi Anis. You girls are my rock! I'm so thankful to have such amazing, smart, funny, beautiful, and creative talent in my corner, cheering me on. I swear, I cry, I laugh so hard whenever I talk to you all. Thank you for being awesome-sauce.

To my editor, Angie. You are so genuinely kind and talented, my friend. I'm so happy you took the leap. I'm proud of you, and my apologies for all the "tense" moments ;)

For every death and heartache this book may cause, Gloria Thomas must be held accountable for my actions, as she gave me permission to do so.

ABOUT THE AUTHOR

Follow Dylan Page to keep up with all the fun and upcoming releases! Stalk her at...

Facebook, The Vault - A Dylan Page Reader Group: https://www.facebook.com/groups/693217751309879

Linktree: https://linktr.ee/AuthorDylanPage

Goodreads: https://www.goodreads.com/author/show/20841201.Dylan_Page

Amazon: https://www.amazon.ca/kindle-dbs/entity/author/B08P92QWMC?ref_=dbs_p_ebk_r00_abau_000000

Instagram: https://www.instagram.com/authordylanpage/

TikTok: https://www.tiktok.com/@authordylanpage?lang=en

Printed in Great Britain
by Amazon